KING'S WRATH

NINA LEVINE

Editing by Becky Johnson, Hot Tree Editing

Cover Design ©2018 by Romantic Book Affair Designs

Cover photography Wander Aguiar

Cover model Jacob Rodney Hogue

Dear Reader,

Thank you for taking this journey with me. For letting King into your heart. He's my most complex character to date and whether you love him or are just interested to see where his story goes, you will at least have a greater understanding of him by the end of this book.

King has been in my head since 2014. I thought I knew him well. It turns out I'd barely scratched the surface of this beautiful man. You may think beautiful is an odd word to describe King, but I see him as beautiful in so many ways.

This story really brings home how much the people in our lives influence our story. How they shape us, bend us, help define us, and how they help us to be either better or worse versions of ourselves.

May you always choose those people who make you love yourself better when you're with them.

I hope you love King as much as I do.

Nina x

Our love wasn't like everyone else's.

There wasn't a first date or flowers and gifts.

We didn't have a song or cute nicknames for each other.

There were no calls during the day to check in with me, no coming home to cook me dinner, and no foot massages at the end of a long day.

That wasn't how he loved.

But love me he did.

Madly, deeply, passionately, completely.

King loved with everything he had.

He just loved a little differently to most.

PART I

THE EARLY YEARS

1

Zachary King
Thirty Years Ago
Aged 9

Her screams called me.

They woke me in the night. It had been months since the last time, so I'd expected them for weeks. Dad had been getting angrier every day, and I knew that meant screams would come soon. Either from me or from them. I didn't know which type Dad preferred more.

I left my bed and crept down the hallway. It was a bad idea. I'd never done it before, but I wanted to know what was happening to make those girls scream and cry so bad.

If Mum or Dad caught me, I knew I'd be in for it. Dad would probably burn more cigarettes into my skin, or break my arm again, but I was getting good at zoning out when he did that. I'd found a way to ignore the pain. I'd found the voices in my head to talk to while he hurt me. They never let me down.

A loud scream came from the room at the bottom of the stairs—the room I wasn't ever allowed in. I froze. My head felt really warm. Full. Like hot, thick liquid filled it. And my heart beat fast and hard. I worried that it might get too big for my chest. I wasn't sure if that could happen, but it really felt like it could.

When the screams stopped, I carefully stepped onto the first step of the staircase. I made sure to be very quiet. I even held my breath. That wasn't hard to do. Being scared often made me do that. I could hold my breath for longer than anyone I knew.

I'd almost made it to the bottom when another scream sounded. My father spoke then, causing me to freeze again. "You think you're leaving here, bitch? No one fucking leaves here. I'm going to choke the fucking life out of you while I fuck you."

My arms and legs turned to jelly, and my whole body felt hot. I knew what fucking was. My school friends talked about sex. Mikey had even shown me one of his dad's videos. But somehow I knew this wasn't what we talked about at school. Something in the way my dad said that she wasn't leaving here made me think this was very bad. It was the same way he spoke to me when he hurt me.

"Lois!" my father barked. "Pass me that fucking knife."

The sounds of my mother doing as he'd said came through the wall in between us.

And then the screams came again.

I heard a funny grunting noise after that, and I couldn't stop myself—I took the last few steps so I could see what they were doing.

I stood completely still when I finally saw what my parents did in this room to make girls scream. Mum sat in a chair in the corner of the room watching my father having sex with a naked girl on a mattress on the floor. The girl's hands were tied together above her head, and her body jerked all over the place. Dad's hands squeezed her neck, and I knew he was making it really hard for her to breathe.

I wanted to yell at him to stop.

He was hurting her so bad.

I wanted to run back up the stairs and hide under my covers.

I wanted to leave this house and never come back again.

But I did nothing.

I watched my father.

And I hated myself.

I hated that I liked watching him hurt her.

I hated that I was glad he was hurting her rather than me.

2

─────────

King
Seventeen Years Ago
Aged 22

Rage was better than misery.

And blood was better than tears.

My president and I agreed upon that.

Jethro stood over Shark, who lay sprawled on the dirt out the back of the clubhouse, his angry red face glaring down at the club member who'd provoked his rage. "Did you really think you'd get away with peddling that shit on the side? You thought I'd never find out?"

Shark, the idiot, had been selling coke for the past month to a bunch of kids from the local high school. He'd skimmed some off the club supply and pocketed the cash for himself. At first, it had been such a small amount that it had gone undetected. But greed always won in life, and he'd taken enough last week for Jethro to notice. Our president's ruthless way of dealing with betrayal like this meant it had only taken him a day to find out who was responsible.

And here we were, watching Shark's punishment.

Or should I say, his torture, because Jethro was just getting started. By the time he was done, Shark wouldn't be recognisable. He also wouldn't be breathing.

Every cell in my body roared to life as I watched Jethro deliver the punishment. I hungered for this kind of violence, the kind inflicted as retribution, and although I wasn't the one to deliver it, I could taste the sweet victory of it as I zeroed in on the blood dripping from his mouth.

When Shark didn't answer him, Jethro smashed his heavy boot down onto Shark's face, grinding it harder into the ground. "Answer me!"

My restraint stretched close to breaking point. It took everything to hold myself back. To not push Jethro out of the way and shove *my* boot in Shark's face.

Shark writhed on the ground and tried like hell to push Jethro off him, but our president's strength was unrivalled. When Shark wasn't forthcoming with an answer, Jethro yanked him up off the ground and slammed him against the brick wall of the clubhouse.

He gripped the front of Shark's shirt. "You wanna know what we do to members who betray the club?"

Struggling for breath, with his face swelling and cut to shit, Shark managed to get out, "I swear I'll never do it again, Jethro. I swear!"

Jethro's eyes turned wild. Frenzied. Like a fucking madman—something I recognised and related to. "I don't fucking believe you!"

Without waiting for a response, he pummelled Shark's face until it was a bloody pulp. Two other members had to move into place to hold Shark up as Jethro unleashed his fury. Almost unconscious, the only sounds coming from him were grunts of pain and cries that turned to whimpers and pleas for mercy.

Jethro scowled at him in disgust. "Have some fucking self-respect and stop your fucking crying." He grabbed Shark's chin and pulled his face up. "It's time to settle in. We've got a long night ahead of us."

I'd been told what happens when a member is disloyal to the club, but this was the first time I'd witnessed it. It was also my first week as a prospect, and I knew I'd never make the same mistake as Shark. Fuck, I knew that before witnessing his death. I may have only been a prospect for a short time, but I'd been a hangaround for a while, and I knew I'd live and breathe for this club. I'd fucking live and breathe for anyone who was as loyal to me as I was to them.

"How was your day?" Ivy asked when I joined her in the kitchen of our tiny home later that night.

She stood at the sink, back to me, washing dishes, and my gaze dropped to her ass. Five years of that ass being mine, and I still couldn't get enough of it or of her. Getting engaged to her two years ago was one of the smartest things I'd ever done. The sooner I had a wedding ring on her finger, the better.

Keeping my eye trained on the short denim skirt she wore, I grabbed the tub of ice cream I'd picked up on my way home and a spoon from the rack where she was placing clean dishes to dry. I popped the lid and moved to where she stood, pressing myself to her back. Ivy had a thing for short skirts and loose tank tops that gave me perfect access to all my favourite places. Today she wore both, and my gaze dropped to her chest. She had on the pink lacy bra I loved, and my dick hardened while I thought about ripping it off her soon.

As I manoeuvred my arms around her, ice cream in one hand, spoon in the other, I answered her question. "Long." *And fucking satisfying.* "Here," I said as I brought a spoon of ice cream to her mouth. "It's your favourite." Ivy had an obsession with banana ice cream from Baskin Robbins, and I tried to feed it to her as often as I could. It made her happy, and I fucking loved seeing her happy.

"Mmm," she murmured after her first spoonful.

She stopped washing dishes as I continued feeding her. Hands still in the sink, she rested her head against my chest and gazed up at me.

After her fourth spoonful, she said, "It's been exactly three days since I've had ice cream."

"I know," I said around a smile as I scooped more from the tub for her. "Too long to go without something you love."

I bent my face to her hair. Fuck, she smelt good. I dropped a kiss there before lifting my head and sliding the spoon into her mouth again.

It was moments like these with her that I lived for. Ivy's moods shifted so fast some days that I couldn't keep up. Add to that my moods, and we spent a lot of fucking time arguing over stupid shit. As much as we tried, we were both too damn stubborn and unable to control our tempers to stop the unnecessary arguments.

Placing the tub and spoon on the counter, I slipped my hand down the front of her skirt and dipped my head again so I could kiss the bare skin on her shoulder. Not only had it been three days since she'd had ice cream, it had also been that long since she'd had my cock. Not by my fucking choice, though. If I had my way, I'd be inside her morning and night. And in-between if I could swing it, too.

"King," she grumbled, pulling my hands from her skirt, "I've got all these dishes to wash and then I've got study to do."

I glanced at the huge pile of baking dishes she referred to. "Why the fuck are there so many dirty dishes?" I'd known Ivy for eleven years and lived with her for four; she didn't love baking.

She turned in my arms, placing her hands on my chest. Bubbles from the sink soaked into my shirt and some floated in the air between us. But I wasn't looking at those bubbles; my gaze was focused entirely on the happiness radiating from my woman.

Smiling, she caught me up. "Our mothers spent the day with me. The girls, too. We made shortbread, white Christmas, rum balls, Christmas pudding, and a gingerbread house. You should have seen Skylar. I don't think I've seen her as excited for something as she was for that gingerbread house. Even Nik was happy to spend the whole day with us." My sister, Annika, had just turned seventeen and tried to spend as much time as she could with her dickhead boyfriend. She argued a lot with me and our foster mum, so it surprised me she'd stayed all day. Skylar, on the other hand, was only seven and desperately craved family time and attention, so I could imagine her eating up every minute of the day with everyone.

Time slowed while I captured everything good about this moment. From the first day I met her, Ivy had drowned out some of the bad in my world. I was eleven, she was ten, and she'd looked at me like she knew what wounds were etched into my soul. All I'd said to her was "Don't touch my shit, and I won't touch yours. And anytime you want to whinge about your life, I'm not interested. I already know that life sucks." That had been the day my foster mother's sister, Ivy's new foster mother, brought her over to our house and intro-duced everyone. She'd listened to what I said before replying, "Deal. And if you touch me, I'll kick you so hard in the balls they'll fall off." The way she'd said it was as if she truly believed that would happen, and for one brief moment, she'd flooded my mind with bright light, dulling the darkness in there.

I gripped her waist and lifted her onto the kitchen counter next to the sink. A second later, my hands slid up her thighs and under her skirt, and before she managed to protest, I had a thumb on her clit and my lips to hers.

Pulling one of her legs around my waist, I groaned into her mouth, "Fuck, I will never get enough of you."

She kissed me back, but her usual enthusiasm was missing. When the kiss ended, she said, "I don't have time for this, King. I told you that."

I rubbed her clit and slid a finger inside her. "You're wet for me so I'd say you should make the time for this."

Her lips flattened in the way that told me we were in for a fucker of an argument if I continued to push the point. Smacking her hands against my chest, she threw out, "Everything always revolves around what you want. What about what *I* want? Does that ever matter to you?"

Fuck, something had her worked up. Letting her go, I took a step back. "What's going on here, Ivy? What's pissed you off today?"

Her eyes widened. *"Today?* You make me sound like I'm a bitch who is always pissed off."

I raked my fingers through my hair, not wanting to get into this with her. Not tonight. Not after the events of the day that had me wired for blood. I'd come home hoping that some time with her would trip that switch.

"I'm not doing this with you tonight." I turned to leave the kitchen. To put some space between us.

I'd only made it two steps out of the room when she wrapped her hand around my bicep and yelled, "Don't you walk away from me! I want to know what you meant!"

I clenched my jaw and counted to ten, willing her to let

this shit go. She didn't, though, and I didn't make it to ten before she'd convinced me to have it out with her.

Spinning back around, I glared at her, resentment and frustration choking the air around us. Why did we always —*always*—have to hurl our pain at each other like this? Why the fuck couldn't we express ourselves without all this extra bullshit?

I slammed my hand down on the table next to us. "All right, let's get this shit out then."

She flinched before quickly recovering, every inch of her body tense and ready for battle. "I told you I have study and that I want to finish cleaning the kitchen, but no, you decide —and like always, it's *your* decision—that we're going to have sex. I'm sick of never getting a say, King. And I don't like that you accused me of always being pissed off. I'll admit I'm stressed with my study and work, but I'm not always going off at you about stuff."

I wanted to tread carefully with her, but she'd worked me up so much that I didn't have that in me anymore. "Almost every fucking day lately, I come home to a new fight with you, and the thing I've worked out is that whatever the fuck you're arguing with me over isn't actually the issue. So dig deep and figure out what it really is, and spit that shit out fast because I'm running out of patience for all of this."

She took a long breath and stared at me like she was trying to figure out which way to go now. Finally, she spat out, "Fuck you and your patience!"

A second later, she attempted to barrel past me out of the kitchen, clearly having changed her mind about wanting to get into this with me, but there was no way she was leaving until I got to the bottom of whatever her issue was. I was done with coming home to yet another tongue-lashing.

Scooping her around the waist, I lifted her and carried her into the living room. She kicked and fought me, but she was no match for my strength. Depositing her on the couch, I straddled her and pinned her in place so she couldn't escape. Gripping her chin hard, I stared into her eyes and demanded, "What's really going on?"

Winded, she fought for breath, remaining silent while glaring back at me.

"I've got all fucking night, Ivy. I'm not moving until we sort this out."

She continued to glare silently at me, until finally she exhaled and said, "You told your mum you don't want me taking that job at the hospital."

"Yeah."

"Well, it's the job I'm going to take, and I know you're going to make it hard for me to do that. And it pisses me off that you always do this and—"

I placed a finger to her lips to quieten her. "It's not safe for you to work there. Not when I can't guarantee I'll always be available to come pick you up when you finish your shift in the middle of the night."

"I don't need you to come and pick me up. They have security for nurses who work that shift. I'll be fine."

Ivy wanted two things in life. Me, and a job in nursing. She had both, but she'd decided to do further studies, which meant she wanted to switch jobs so she could work nights and have the days to study. She'd found a job, but I didn't like the fact she'd be walking out of work at 2:00 a.m. alone. Now that I'd been made a prospect, who the fuck knew when I'd be called out at night for club business.

"I don't know that for sure, and I won't allow something I'm not one hundred percent on."

"Oh my God, you can be an ass!" She pushed hard against my chest, trying to move me, but I resisted.

Taking hold of her arms, I held them by her side. "I'm not fucking putting you out there on the street for any motherfucker to do what they want to you. Do you have any idea of the kind of men who walk those streets?"

Her eyes flashed with wild anger. "Do *you* realise how impossible you're being? And that this is how you always handle me?"

"Now you're being dramatic. I don't *handle* you."

"Yes! You do! It's like you're saying I'm a weak woman who can't fucking look out for herself, and I'm over it. I'm not doing what you say this time, King."

My chest tightened at the loss of control I felt. Keeping her safe was *all* I fucking cared about. It was my goddam mission in life to never let hurt come to her again. Under my watch, she would never experience the kind of pain her parents had permitted. After they'd fucking rented her out as a child to men on weekends to do whatever they wanted to her, I'd looked out for her and dedicated time helping her find a way through that. And I'd continue doing that for eternity.

My hands crushed harder around her wrists, ensuring she couldn't leave. Not until I'd made her understand I was right. "You *will* do as I say, Ivy. And if you go against me, I'll take you out there myself and show you the kind of shit that goes on. You'll change your mind real fucking fast."

Her eyes bored into mine while she considered that. If hate were a physical thing, it would have been smashing into me. That knowledge scared the fuck out of me because it was the first time Ivy had ever looked at me this way.

Finally, she nodded and said, "Fine. You win." Jerking her wrists, she added in the coldest tone she'd ever taken with me, "You can let me go now."

My eyes searched hers, needing to read the truth in her agreement. "You won't take that job?"

"I won't take that job." Her voice turned flat, resigned.

I wanted to figure out how to get us both on the same

page happily, but right now I had the answer I needed, so that could wait for another time. And bringing up the fact that she sounded so down about it would only stir this argument more. Letting her go, I sat back. "Good."

She watched me for another moment before saying, "Get off me, King. I can't stand looking at you for another minute tonight."

I ignored her attitude. All I cared about was that she'd come around to my way of thinking. She'd get over whatever anger she felt soon enough.

She didn't waste time leaving the room, and as she went, she glanced back at me and said, "Don't bother coming to bed tonight. There's no way I'm letting you anywhere near me."

3

King
Six Months Later

"You're with me, King."

I eyed Jethro, watching him closely as he walked towards his bike. It had been just over six months since I was made a prospect, and today I'd been voted in as a full patch member.

Ghost scowled at me. He'd made it clear how unimpressed he was that Jethro had moved me up so fast. Usually, it took Jethro over a year to agree to a vote on a prospect.

Ignoring Ghost, I followed my president.

"Stick close to me," he said as he got on his bike. "We've got business to take care of, and then we're meeting Breaker."

Breaker, the Black Deeds president. That surprised me, because Jethro usually took his VP with him when he met Breaker, but I kept my surprise to myself.

Just under an hour later, we pulled into an out-of-the-way

construction site. A lone car waited for us, the owner perched on the hood. He turned as he heard our bikes rumble in.

"Dash," Jethro greeted him. "You've got the package?"

Dash narrowed his eyes at me before glancing back at Jethro, distrust clear in his gaze. "Who the fuck is this? We have a deal, Jethro. You come alone."

"King will be with me from now on." His tone signalled he wouldn't get into a discussion on this.

I had no idea who Dash was or what the fuck was going on, so I kept quiet.

Raking his fingers madly through his hair, sweat forming on his brow, Dash muttered, "Fuck, this changes shit, Jethro. If they find out—"

Jethro grunted his displeasure with the conversation as he scrunched a handful of Dash's shirt into his grip and pulled him close. "King's not spilling a word of this, but yeah, if they find out some other way, you're dead. If you don't do as I say, *I'll* fucking make sure they know about our little visits, so give me the fucking package and get on board with this."

Dash crossed his arms, a smug expression on his face. "You're full of shit. You've got nothing worth shit on me, and without the info I've got for you today, you can't prove a thing about Breaker."

Jethro bared his teeth as his lips pulled back in a sneer. "Show him what happens to men who don't honour their commitments, King," he barked.

Over the past six months, I'd been called upon numerous times to deal with assholes who tried to fuck the club over, but this was the first time Jethro had personally asked me to step up.

Not wasting a second, I swapped places with Jethro and landed my first punch. Adrenaline blazed through me, and my lust for violence took over.

I smashed my fist into his face repeatedly, barely registering his cries of pain as bloodlust filled my mind. While every one of my senses picked up on his pain, I needed only the visual and touch to keep me locked into what I was doing.

It was the blood, the agony on his face, and the feel of inflicting pain that got me off.

And that made me want more.

So much more.

Most days I walked the tightrope of controlling my urges. They had grown over the last six months since I'd deepened my ties to the club. If it weren't for Ivy and my family, I'd give in to them completely. My love for a few kept my madness in check, but it was in these moments with the club that I could surrender and own my insanity.

Dash was unrecognisable by the time Jethro pulled me off him. Swollen eyes glued shut with blood, broken bones, teeth missing, crooked nose, and a complete and utter sense of defeat made up the man who'd dared argue with the Storm president. The message was unmistakable.

As I fought to get myself under control again, Jethro crouched in front of Dash and said, "Give me the package, Dash, or else I'll let him loose on you again."

One of Dash's eye's cracked open to a slit. He rattled off an address for where he'd left the package, struggling to get his words out. When he was done, his body sagged more than it already had, like a deep silent sigh of anguish. I recognised his pain for what it was because I'd experienced the same pain at the hands of my father. It was emotional more than physical. Your mind could find a way to cope with physical pain, but it could never fully survive the emotional trauma another person inflicted on you.

Jethro called Ghost and had him retrieve the package. We waited in silence while he did so. Jethro retreated to his bike, and I rested against Dash's car while watching him. My mind swam with questions about why we were here collecting a package, but I knew not to ask. Jethro kept his cards close to his chest and pounced on anyone who dared question him over anything. I chose to trust my president, so while I wondered what we were doing, I never doubted it was for the good of the club.

Fifteen minutes passed before Jethro received the call that Ghost was in possession of the package. His eyes found mine as he ended the call. Coming my way, he said, "We're good to go. Just need to take care of one last loose end."

Dash.

I moved off the hood of Dash's car and waited for Jethro to tie up his loose end. Instead of doing that, though, he nodded at me, eyes going to where I kept my gun holstered and said, "This one's yours, King."

My hand slowly curled into a fist, more than ready to do as he'd said.

Dash would be my first.

For as long as I could remember, I'd hungered for the death of someone on my hands. It had been my father's blood I'd wanted. Even though I hadn't seen him since I was nine, and even though he'd finally been locked up for life two years ago, not a night went by where I didn't think about the ways I would end his miserable fucking life.

I had plotted his death in minute detail at least twenty different ways. I'd even started trying to figure out ways to break him out of prison just so I could taste his blood on my hands. *After I tortured every last part of his fucking body*.

"King," Jethro barked. "Now!"

Although he lay almost unconscious on the dirt, Dash made one final plea for grace. His words were incomprehensible. His attempt to save his life, futile. Once the Storm president made up his mind, he didn't ever waver. His actions drilled into me the importance of never backing down when enforcing a plan. I'd seen the loyalty he had from all club members and the way we looked to him for leadership because of his ruthless determination and decisiveness. Jethro was the reason Storm was a force to be reckoned with; the reason why so many in Sydney feared us. And that shit right there was the reason why I did anything and everything asked of me.

I never wanted to be in a position of weakness again.

I would *never* allow anyone to hurt me the way my father had.

I'd fight to my dying breath to protect the power my club had because it meant I too would have power.

Dash slowly gave in, surrendering, understanding what would happen next.

His eyes met mine, hopeless and tormented.

I felt anything but.

Reaching for my gun, I aimed it at his head and pulled the trigger.

My first kill.

The rush of power kicked in fast. A new type of high. One that obliterated so much of the chaos that flowed through my veins every minute of every day.

I'll never be the weaker one again.

4
<hr>

King

I often wondered what the inside of my head would look like if I'd been born to different humans rather than the mother-fuckers I was given. Would it be as murky as it was? Filled with as much grime and as many fucked-up thoughts? The nature versus nurture debate could probably be settled once and for all if people like me were given two lives with two sets of parents. But fuck, maybe I'd be the mess I was regardless.

Maybe killing was in my blood anyway. Maybe it was my fate. The only thing I knew for certain, after the events of this morning, was that killing was in my blood *now*. One taste had unlocked a whole new room in my mind, and the views were mind-blowing.

Jethro had watched me with a knowing look after I'd fired my gun and killed Dash. With a quick nod, he'd turned to walk back to his bike. No words were exchanged, but I had the understanding that he'd brought me with him for a reason. A test. One I'd passed. And then I'd passed another when we met with the Black Deeds president.

Jethro had threatened him over his club's violation of the territory agreements set in place years ago for drug deals done in Sydney. The package from Dash had confirmed that. When Breaker had refused to back down, Jethro didn't waste a minute before taking his life. I hadn't seen it coming— because it would stir a fuckload of shit for Storm—but I hadn't hesitated in backing him up. My instincts had kicked in fast, and I took care of the two club members Breaker had with him before they could retaliate and kill Jethro.

Three lives taken in one day.

That shit fucking lit me up in ways I'd never been lit up.

It cleared pathways in my brain that had been tangled my whole life.

I sensed a new purpose.

I finally knew my path forward.

"Why are you sitting over here all by yourself?"

I glanced up to find one of the club whores looking down at me with eyes that said she wanted my dick. I'd arrived back at the clubhouse an hour ago and searched out some peace and quiet in the corner of the bar. Lifting my almost-empty beer to my mouth, I tipped the rest of it down my throat before saying, "Because I want to be by myself." It didn't seem to matter how often I told her I wasn't interested, she kept circling.

The seductive smile she always used spread across her face as she straddled me on the couch. Making sure to press her pussy against my dick, she ran her hands up my shoulders to my neck before looping them at the back of it. "Come on, King, let me show you how much you're missing every time you say no to me. You think your woman can give it to you good? She's got nothing on me."

I clenched my jaw as I pulled her arms from my neck. "Get the fuck off me," I said slowly, harshly. "I'm not fucking interested in you, and if you ever say shit like that about my woman again, you'll fucking wish you didn't."

She took her sweet time moving off me, grumbling about what an asshole I was. It took everything in me not to shove her off, but I managed to keep my anger in check. By the time she'd done what I'd asked, Ivy had entered the clubhouse bar and stood in the doorway staring at me with the jealousy we seemed to be bogged down in these days.

Fuck.

I raked my fingers through my hair as I stood and walked her way. Her eyes remained glued to me as she angrily folded her arms in the way she did when I'd upset her. It told me we were in for another fucking fight. That seemed to be the story of our lives for the last six months, ever since that night I'd forbidden her from taking the night shift job she wanted. Ivy had wrapped her disappointment and anger at me up and kept it inside. She pulled it out every time I did something wrong and every time she *thought* I did something wrong. Like tonight.

"You finished work early," I said, moving close to slide my hand around her waist. Instead of the nursing job she'd wanted, she had taken a job in a nursing home with shifts that ended no later than 9:00 p.m.

She jerked out of my hold and smacked my hand away. "I would have stayed at work if I'd known what I was going to walk in on."

My patience for this old argument had worn thin, and my temper flared fast. "I don't fuck club whores, Ivy. You fucking know this."

"I don't fucking know this, King. All I know is what you tell me, but what I'm *seeing* is a different story," she spat back, eyes flashing with hostility.

"What you're seeing is nothing. She sat on me, she tried to fuck me, I said no. You can't keep throwing fucking accusations at me and expect me to keep defending myself when I'm not doing anything wrong. At some fucking point, you have to decide to trust me, and I'd like it if you got to that point soon because all this bitching and moaning is doing my fucking head in."

Her eyes widened, and she smacked my chest with both hands as if she was trying to push me away. I wasn't fucking moving, though. No fucking way. "I hate you sometimes. Why can't you understand what I'm going through? There are sluts everywhere here, and almost every time I come by, they are fucking on you. Can you not see how that makes me feel and why I'm struggling with this?"

"Jesus, Ivy, you're being fucking dramatic now. They might be here, but they're not fucking *on* me."

"They are!" she screamed, drawing attention to us. Her body was wound tight with all the emotions engulfing her, and I knew from experience that she would likely only get louder and more antagonistic the longer we argued.

I grabbed her arm and dragged her outside away from watchful eyes. Jethro had made it crystal clear he didn't want old ladies causing trouble in the club. I didn't need this on his radar.

"Let me go!" She fought me every step of the way, but I gripped her hard and forced her away from the building towards the shed around the side. The outside lights of the clubhouse threw a little light on the area, but I steered her to a darker spot for privacy.

When we were alone, I loosened my grip and said, "Can you calm down for one fucking minute and listen to me?"

"I do listen to you. It's you who doesn't listen to me." She said this with total conviction, the anger in her eyes shifting to something else. Sadness maybe.

I took a step back, hit hard by what I saw there. The last thing I ever wanted was Ivy sad. It was clear though that she wasn't happy and hadn't been so for at least the last six months. Fuck, maybe more. I would have sworn against what she'd just said, but she honestly believed I didn't listen to her.

Scrubbing a hand over my face, I contemplated how to react. Holding her gaze, I finally blew out a long frustrated breath and asked, "Do you really believe I would screw around on you?"

She blinked, seemingly unsure, and wrapped her arms around her body. My question managed to cut through the argument and give us the space to stop and think, to try and get our heads together and see things clearer. Fuck knew our tempers were our greatest flaws and did neither of us any favours.

"I don't want to," she said, her voice quieter, the hostile edge gone. In its place was the vulnerability that shot straight to my heart every time. This was the Ivy I loved.

I reached out and pulled her close, my hand cupping the back of her head. "Fuck, Ivy, what are we doing?"

She buried her face against my chest, not answering me. When her body shuddered with a sob, I wrapped my other arm around her waist and held her to me. Ivy didn't like crying. She said it made her feel weak. So I knew shit was bad if she was crying.

I pressed a kiss to the top of her head, her long dark hair whispering across my face. "I don't want to fight with you anymore. It's fucking killing us. How can I make you understand that you're the only woman I want in my life and in my bed? Tell me, and I'll do it. I'll do any-fucking-thing to make you happy."

She scrunched my shirt in her hands, thumbs digging into my chest as she sobbed. I hated it when she cried, too. It reminded me of all the times she wept when she first came to live with her foster mother. She cried back then because of the horrific things her parents had allowed to be done to her, and no fucking way did I want to be the cause of more tears.

I pulled away and took hold of her chin. Angling her face up to mine, I said, "Don't cry. I'll fix this. You've just gotta tell me how to do that."

She wiped the tears from her cheeks and took a breath. "I know you love me, but when I see those women near you, it does something to me. I know my jealousy is extreme, but I can't control it, King. I try, but I can't. And then you fire up at me, and that just makes it worse." She stopped for a moment, looking at me with uncertainty, as if she was unsure how to go on, but then she said, "You yell at me, and I feel like you don't hear what I am trying to say to you. You're so set on trying to make me bend however you need me to that you don't listen to what *I* need. I'm tired of being the one who always does the bending."

I knew our arguments were about so much more than whatever we were fighting over. This was the first time Ivy had given me any hint as to what that was.

"Are we talking about that night shift job?" I asked.

She sighed. "Yes. And other things."

"What other things?" *Jesus, just fucking tell me.*

Her forehead creased in a frown. "Don't get shitty with me again. I'm just trying to be honest here."

"And I don't want to have to pry this shit from you kicking and fucking screaming," I muttered, working like fuck to keep a leash on my impatience.

"You are such a fucking ass." She glared at me. "It's almost everything you do, King. You're demanding and always want things your way. You wanna be the one to drive when we go out, and drop me off and pick me up when I'm out with friends, and choose what mobile phone I get, and tell me when you don't want me to wear a certain skirt or dress when we go out... things like that. And on top of that, you usually assume you're right and don't always listen to what I have to say. It's too much. You need to let me be me. And you need to let me show you that sometimes I do know things."

Fuck.

The way she saw things was a whole lot fucking different to the way I saw it. "The reason I do all that shit is to keep you safe and protected—"

Wild energy rushed between us as her mood swung back to hostile. "So choosing my phone is to keep me safe? That's bullshit, and you know it. And again, you're not listening to me!"

Fucking hell, I had whiplash. Turning, I took a few steps away from her. I had to; otherwise, I'd lash out. Not physically, but verbally, and that would only move us further away from each other.

I paced back and forth a few times before coming back to her. My eyes met hers again, full of determination. I had to make her understand me. "All I've ever wanted was to keep you safe. Hand on my fucking heart, I do all that shit with that goal in mind. I know I'm bossy and demanding and a pain in your ass, and I wish I could tell you I'll change and things will be different and all that shit that men tell their women whenever they fight, but I can't. I'm not going to change because my goal isn't going to change."

She remained silent while she processed that, but Ivy had the kind of face that displayed all her emotions, and they all ran across it while she did her thinking. So much so that I knew I'd failed to make her see where I was coming from. "So that's it then? Things stay the same, you get everything you want, and I just have to make you happy?" She crossed her arms again in that same furious manner as before and waited for my response.

Give and take wasn't one of my strengths, but I knew I had to meet her somewhere in the middle. Fuck knew how, though, because I'd meant every word about not budging from trying to keep her safe. "I'm shit out of ideas for how to manoeuvre through this, but we're equals here, so no, you don't just have to make me happy. You have to be happy too. All I ask is that you're also safe." *And you let me do what I need to do to make that happen.*

She stared at me like I had two heads. "Fuck me, is that you compromising, baby?" Her lips twitched with the hint of a smile. It was her use of "baby" that really caught my attention. I couldn't recall the last time she'd used it; she'd been pissed off at me for that fucking long.

The way we watched each other changed. Softened. Anger faded as hope flared. "Don't get fucking used to it."

Edging closer to me, she said, "Those things I mentioned that you do, they don't always bother me." She took hold of the hem of my shirt with one of her hands. The other one stayed by her side. "I just want you to give me the choice, you know? Don't always barrel in all protective and shit. It makes me feel powerless."

Her last statement was the puzzle piece I needed. Everything she'd been trying to tell me finally fell into place in my fucked-up brain. Why hadn't I seen it before? Of course Ivy would lash out if she felt powerless. After having her power stripped from her as a child, it was the one thing she held onto tightly.

Fuck.

I knew I didn't have it in me to change completely, but I could try to rein my shit in for her.

My arms circled her so I could hold her close. "I love

you," I murmured, before my mouth found hers in the kind of kiss we hadn't shared for months.

Deep and slow at first, the kiss turned desperate and frantic as I backed her up against the clubhouse shed. Soon we were tearing at each other's clothes, the need to fuck overwhelming.

It had been months since we'd been like this. Sex had become a purely physical release for us—we got off as fast as we could and we moved on—but this, this was raw and carnal.

Ivy's clothes and my shirt landed on the ground. She undid my zip and pulled out my cock, eyes to mine. Pumping me, she bit my bottom lip and kissed me before saying, "I can't drag this out, King. I need you now."

Within a moment, I had her in my arms and up against the wall, her legs tightly around me. Thrusting my cock deep inside her, I growled, "Fuck!" before losing myself in the act completely.

I slammed into her furiously, needing my fill.

Her fingers dug into my back as she held on, blissful moans matching my groans. Ivy loved it when I fucked her like this.

My eyes closed as the pleasure built.

Up my spine and out to every nerve ending.

I needed more.

Craved the dark shit.

The shit I never touched.

Refused to touch.

Grunting, I grabbed hold of her hair and yanked her head back before sinking my teeth into her neck. I barely heard her whimpers. Between the brutal way I fucked her, the savage marking of her skin, and the roar of need raging through my head, I was oblivious to everything but my filthy desires.

I was a fucking time bomb waiting to detonate with the

hunger that breathed deep inside me. I never gave it air. Didn't want to inflict it on the woman I loved, but something had triggered inside me today, and I was helpless to stop the course I was on.

I was unravelling.

Coming undone.

Unable to stop myself from taking what I wanted.

It wasn't until Ivy bucked violently against me that I was dragged from the dark haze I'd allowed to take over.

My eyes snapped open.

Hers stared back at me with fear.

And panic.

My fucking hands were around her neck.

Choking her.

She clawed at me trying to loosen my grip, but my strength was too much for her. She could hardly fucking breathe.

My body had her pinned against the shed while I fucked and choked her. And I hadn't fucking realised it was happening.

"Fuck," I muttered, letting her go and stumbling back-wards once she was standing on her own, out of my hold. No other words came out. I struggled to fight the mess of thoughts in my mind.

How the fuck did that happen?

This was the shit I kept a tight fucking lock on. It was the shit my father did, not the shit *I* did.

I dragged my fingers through my hair, clawing at my scalp.

Fuck.

No.

Ivy collapsed to the ground, huddling into a crouch. When she had her breathing back under control, she looked up at me with confusion, completely stricken. "King," she started, her voice cracking. "What's going on?"

I stared at her, battling my way through the mental fog blanketing me. "That shit will never happen again." I never made promises unless I intended to keep them, and this was one promise I would never break. Jesus, *I* was the one who kept her safe. I would never be the one who hurt her.

Tears streamed down her cheeks as we watched each other, a deathly silence hanging between us. I wished she would stop looking at me with those eyes full of terror.

We stayed like that for what felt like forever. When she finally stood, she quietly dressed before wrapping her arms around her body and asking, "Have you done that before? With someone else? I mean, is that something you want in sex?"

I'd slept with a handful of girls before Ivy, but had never done that with any of them. I shook my head. "Never."

She moved closer to me, looking up into my eyes with a questioning look. "Did you like it?"

"Fuck, Ivy," I said, unsure of what to say. I did fucking like it; I was getting off on it like I'd never gotten off. But that didn't mean I wanted to do it again. What the fuck would happen if I went too far? I didn't want to think about that. The average male could play with it in their sex life, but I wasn't the average man. I was fucked-up and craved shit no one should ever crave. I'd likely go to the extremes like I did with everything else in my life. I couldn't chance that with her.

"Tell me," she demanded. "I need to know if I should be prepared for this."

My eyes searched hers, looking for what, I wasn't sure. An interest in being choked? Fuck that, I needed to shut this shit down now.

"It doesn't matter if I liked it, we won't be fucking doing

it again," I snapped. I couldn't stop the hard tone from colouring my words, and I didn't blame her for flinching, but fuck, it felt like we'd taken three steps forward tonight and then two back. Just when we'd sorted out one problem, I'd fucked up and caused a new one.

She turned silent again. I wondered what thoughts ran through her mind, but before I had a chance to find out, her lips flattened, and she muttered, "I'm going home."

I exhaled sharply as I watched her walk to her car. What a clusterfuck.

Needing a drink, I headed back into the clubhouse. I wouldn't be going home tonight. Ivy and I needed some space, and I needed to know she was safe from me.

5

King

I quietly watched Ivy from where I sat at my foster mother's dining table. Margreet had her best china laid out for today's lunch. Sunday lunch was a tradition in our family for as long as I had lived with her. I'd only missed five lunches in that time, but Ivy had made it to every single one. She and Margreet had a special bond. One I loved to watch, which I did now as I drank a beer.

They sat together on the couch, talking excitedly about something they were doing together next week. It was the first time in a week I'd seen Ivy light up. *Since I'd wrapped my hands around her throat and lost my footing with her*. We'd hardly connected during the last seven days. She'd pulled away, I'd been busy with club stuff, and I hadn't trusted that we could get through a discussion about it without ending up in another argument. So, I'd kept my distance.

Skylar wandered into the room and plopped herself on the chair opposite me. Sliding a piece of paper across the table, she asked, "Can you please help me with this?"

I took the paper from her. Dropping my gaze to read it, I said, "Mum or Nik can't help?" It was an assignment about her family.

"Mum said I had to ask you about some of it. The stuff about you."

I met her gaze again and nodded. "Yeah, okay. When's it due?"

"In two weeks."

I'd given my full attention to Skylar so had failed to notice Ivy walking my way. It wasn't until she ran her hand across my back and said, "We can stay after lunch and do it," that I noticed.

Our eyes met. The warmth I found in hers took me by surprise, and I returned it. Fuck, we needed this today.

Looking back at Skylar, I said, "You wanna do this today?"

"Hell no, but Mum said I couldn't leave it until the last minute this time."

"Skylar," Mum said in a warning tone as she joined us, "don't use that language please."

My sister pulled a face. "King swears all the time. It's not fair that I get into trouble for it when he doesn't."

My lips twitched as I tried not to chuckle. The hell I'd caused Margreet as a teen had equipped her with the necessary mental and emotional tools to deal with any misbehaviour from her other foster kids. She'd been tough as nails from the day I met her, but after raising me, she'd learnt how to be smart about it, too.

"He doesn't swear in my house," Mum said as she tied her apron, preparing to finish cooking the roast lamb and vegetables for lunch. Her gaze landed on me. "And he knows the rules and what will happen if he does." She looked back at Skylar. "Same as you do, young lady. Your decision to use that word just now has earnt you a half-hour deduction of your television time today."

Skylar groaned as she slouched in her seat. "That's not fair! That wasn't even a real swear word!"

"Don't argue with me, child," Mum said as she bustled into the kitchen. "You know full well that word is not permitted in our house. If you keep arguing, you'll lose another half hour."

As Skylar's mouth opened to argue back, I reached across the table and placed my hand over it. "Enough."

She shot daggers at me, but she shut her mouth and did as she'd been told. Snatching her assignment sheet off the table, she shoved her chair back and grumbled, "I don't need your help anymore," before stomping off towards her bedroom.

I leaned back against my seat, my eyes meeting Ivy's. She'd taken the seat next to me. "And you want kids?" I wasn't convinced we could handle them. Hell, we could barely handle our own relationship. Adding children to that mix could end us.

A slow smile graced her face, and she leaned into me, hands curving around my neck. "I don't just want kids, I want *your* kids. You're going to make the best father."

If we weren't sitting in my mother's home, I'd have pulled her onto my lap and kissed the fuck out of her. Instead, I brushed my lips across hers and said as quietly as I could, "We're never doing a week like this again, Ivy. This radio silence almost killed me."

She swallowed hard and nodded as her fingers splayed across the nape of my neck and threaded through my hair there. "I've missed you," she whispered.

I placed my hands on her legs before slowly running them up her thighs. It was a good thing she had jeans on, or I'd have seriously struggled keeping myself out of trouble. "I'm taking you home after lunch, and we're talking this out. And we're not doing anything besides talking until it's sorted."

Her brows arched. "Umm, it's not just me who has trouble keeping their hands to themselves."

Mum cut into our conversation when she called out from the kitchen, "Zachary, I need your help in here, please."

I kept my gaze trained on my woman as I called back, "I'll be there in a minute." Then to Ivy, I said with fierce conviction, "I love you."

With that, I stood and headed into the kitchen. The tension I'd carried with me for the last week hadn't eased completely, but it had lifted somewhat. I didn't feel like I was drowning in the ocean while ten fucking sharks circled me, which was how I'd felt while Ivy refused to come near me. I'd do everything in my power to ensure we never went through that again.

Mum lifted her chin up towards the top of her pantry. "Can you please get that sugar down from up there?"

"Why do you put it all the way up the top?" It beat me why women did anything half the time, but it seemed like sugar should live on a lower shelf.

Her lips flattened, and she placed her hands on her tiny hips. She may have been short and little, but Margreet King wasn't a woman to mess with. "Don't give me grief, Zachary. You know I don't use sugar very often."

"I wasn't aware of that fact," I muttered as I grabbed the sugar down for her.

"Thank you." She took it from me. "I've spent the last three months cutting it out of our diet as much as I could. Skylar's behaviour has improved dramatically since I did that. You should consider doing the same. The amount of sugar you and Ivy consume in soft drink is probably enough to kill you both one day."

I rested my ass against the counter while I watched her add a small amount of sugar to the batter she had in a mixing bowl, making fuck knew what. Probably her famous short-bread biscuits. Whatever it was, it would be good. That was a guarantee whenever Mum cooked.

Crossing my arms, I said with a grin, "Well, if it's not the smokes or any of the other sh— stuff, it'll be the sugar that'll get me in the end."

She shook her head while hitting me with the frustrated look I seemed to encourage. "I love you, but boy, you test me. I don't know why you won't give that filthy habit up. I've prayed to God ever since you took it up that he'll find a way into your heart and convince you to stop."

Fuck, she'd been praying for a long time then. I'd started smoking when I was sixteen.

"King quit smoking?" My other sister's voice floated into the kitchen, and a moment later, her dark eyes found mine. Settling against the counter next to me, she nudged my shoulder with hers. "I don't suppose you have a spare fifty you could lend me."

"Annika!" Mum looked up at her, horrified. "What do you need fifty dollars for?" She puffed out a breath in an effort to blow the stray hair that had fallen across her face. The only thing it achieved, though, was to shift the flour from her nose. The hair continued to bug her, but her hands were busy in dough.

I chuckled as I leaned across and moved the hair off her face, tucking it behind her ear. "What seventeen-year-old *doesn't* need fifty bucks, Mum?"

"Your sister does not require money for anything, so don't you be giving it to her."

Annika scowled at our mother. "Why do you *always* do this to me?"

"Always do what?"

"You never let me have anything!"

Hurt flashed in Mum's eyes as she watched her daughter. Not only had Margreet fostered us all, but she'd also adopted the three of us along with our brother, Axe. She'd gone without many things to give the four of us the kind of childhood none of us would have had otherwise. I knew from conversations I'd had with her over the past few months that Annika was pushing her harder than either Axe or I had. "It's a girl thing," she'd said. "We'll get through it." But by the expression she wore, I wondered how battered she'd be by the time they did get through it.

Before Mum could reply, I stepped in. "That's not fair, Nik. Mum's given us everything."

Irritation flared in Annika's eyes as she turned her angry glare towards me. "This has nothing to do with you!"

"I'm fucking standing right here in the middle of it. I'd say it has something to do with me."

"Zachary," Mum chastised, "enough with the swearing, please."

Annika barely allowed her a word in before launching a tirade at me. "I'm sick of you always butting in and trying to take over. You're not the dad of us, okay?"

"When you treat our mother like shit, I'm gonna step in. Deal with that. And stop being a bitch to her and start being grateful for what she does for you."

"Zachary!" Mum raised her voice in a way she didn't often do. If there was one thing she was known for, it was her ability to run a family without the use of yelling. She was a gentle woman who usually got her point across with calm but firm discussions. Right now, though, she appeared completely flustered, and I had to wonder just how much hell Annika had been giving her.

I raised my hands, signalling my surrender. "No more swearing. I know."

Mum exhaled a long breath and started to say something, but Annika cut her off.

"I'm not being a bitch. I just wish she would think about letting me have the clothes I want rather than clothes from the thrift store."

Mum untied her apron, a look of complete defeat on her fifty-year-old face. Glancing between us, she said, "I'm disappointed in the both of you today. I don't ask for much, but what I do ask for is respect while you are in our home. Lunch is ready, but I need a moment or two to myself. When I return, I expect you both to have yourselves under control so we can discuss our problems in a more civilised manner."

In other words, she needed to pray.

And we needed to sort our shit out.

After she left the room, I turned to Annika. "You know she can't afford the clothes you want, so why are you giving her so much hell for it?"

Six months after I'd come to live with Margreet, her husband died from a severe asthma attack, forcing her back to work. Raising four kids as a single mother meant there wasn't a cent spare most weeks. Neither Axe nor I had ever asked her for more than she gave, but I finally understood why Mum and Annika were clashing so much.

My sister's face crumpled into a mess of tears.

Fuck.

I was far from capable of dealing with this, but I pulled her into my arms and gave it a shot. "Nik, what's going on?"

She clung to me and cried for a good few minutes before looking up at me. "You don't understand what it's like for me at school. The girls are so bitchy, and because I don't measure up to their standards, they pick on me every single day. It's been like this since the middle of last year, and I can't take it anymore."

Her tone concerned me. It sounded like she was ready to give up. No fucking way would I allow that. "What do you need?"

That seemed to throw her. "What do you mean?"

"I mean, what will it take for you to feel confident enough to get to school every day this year and get the shit done that you need to get done in order to not fuck the rest of your life up by failing?"

Her shoulders slumped and she moved out of my embrace. "You can't fix everything for everyone, King. This isn't the kind of situation where you can just make a few changes and poof, it's all good."

I crossed my arms and planted my feet wide, ready to do battle with her. "Tell me what you need, Annika, and I'll make sure it happens. Sure, shit won't ever be 100 percent the way you want it to be, but there's gotta be some things we can do that will allow you to take care of business."

She threw her arms up in the air. "Oh my God! Take care of my business? What does that even mean? Is that biker talk or something?"

"Let me help, King," Ivy said, moving next to me. She didn't like to step on toes, so she usually stayed out of arguments, but I was fucking glad for any help she wanted to offer.

Thankfully Annika loved Ivy. "Please tell him that teenage girls are the meanest humans on the planet and that this is the kind of problem that even the almighty King can't fix."

Ivy smiled, but she didn't give Annika an inch. "I'll agree that teenage girls are mean, but you should never think that your problems can't be worked on, Nik. A few fashion and beauty tweaks, and you'll be fine. And I can tell you how to make them happen without costing the earth."

That caught Annika's attention. "Really?"

Ivy nodded. "Yes. Trust me, I've been through all the same stuff with my mum. I know the ways around this."

I wasn't sure why my offer of help didn't result in the same level of excitement as Ivy's, but however the fuck we got there didn't matter. The main thing was that Annika had her arms around Ivy, a huge smile on her face, and those defeated shoulders were gone.

Thank fuck.

My gaze met Ivy's in appreciation while I jerked my chin towards the kitchen door. "I'll be back soon," I mouthed. In other words: you sort my sister out because I have no fucking idea how to do that.

I went in search of Mum, finding her on the wooden bench in the garden she loved. She sat with her back hunched, hands curled around the seat gripping it tightly, head down. Everything about the way she sat led me to believe she wasn't doing so well.

I sat next to her, noticing for the first time the worn dress that hung from her tiny frame. Fuck, how had I missed her struggle? I'd been so wrapped up in the club and my problems with Ivy that I'd neglected the other woman I cared for most in the world. In that time, she'd not only been dealing with a teenage girl, she'd also been through a falling out with her closest sister.

"I'm sorry about before."

She looked up at me, surprise clear in her eyes. It wasn't often anyone got an apology out of me. "Thank you," she said softly, her voice laced with exhaustion.

"You need a break from the girls."

Her chest rose and fell as she took a deep breath. "I can afford neither the time nor the money, Zachary. And besides, your sisters need me. I can't just take off on a holiday whenever I feel like it."

She might not have been my birth mother, but we shared the same stubborn streak. I readied for a fight. "One week. I'll pay for it and stay with the girls while you're gone. Ivy will help. She's in there now helping solve Nik's problems. If she can manage that, she and I can manage them for a week." At the pursing of her lips, I added, "I'm not taking no for an answer, so don't even try to argue with me about this."

The time that passed between my offer and her response felt like forever. She watched me silently for the longest time before gazing out at her rose bushes. A few birds landed on the birdbath next to the rose garden, drawing her attention there while cold wind sliced through the air scattering chills over our skin. And all the while I thought about my life before her, which only added to the bite of the wind making me cold.

I'd had six month's experience with the foster care system and the streets by the time I landed on Margreet and Dale King's doorstep. While those six months hadn't been anywhere near as bad as living with my parents, they'd been fucked up. Three sets of foster parents who didn't know how to handle an angry nine-year-old boy, one filthy cop who'd handled me in ways a cop never should, and a fourth foster father who'd tried to beat the anger out of my system added another layer of damage to that already inflicted by Carl and Lois Brown, my biological parents. To say I'd been filled with mistrust was an understatement.

Dale had been a good father in the time we had before he passed away, but it was Margreet who found a way to connect with me. Compassion, love, and patience were things I never knew until I met her. I hadn't the first idea of what those words even fucking meant before her. She showed me and taught me how to love. And although I wasn't the best at it, I was far better than if she'd never been my role model.

Turning to face me, she murmured, "You were my most difficult child."

I wasn't sure where she was taking this. "And?" That wasn't news to me, so why voice it now?

She placed her palm on my cheek. "And look at you now."

My thoughts faltered, and my breathing slowed. Carl and Lois had fucked me up to the point that I didn't know how to accept kindness, and although Margreet had done her best, I still didn't know what to do with it most of the time. My mind was conditioned to expect and deal with cuts, bruises, beatings, burns, broken bones, and unimaginable other shit. Cruelty was the currency I dealt in. My brain misfired when presented with anything else. Sometimes I figured it out; sometimes I refused and clung to the familiar.

When I didn't reply, Mum nodded and said, "I'll go away for a week. Perhaps I'll go see Janet."

"No, I'm getting you a room at that resort in Port Douglas that you've always wanted to stay at." Janet, her sister, was a lazy bitch. She'd take advantage of Mum.

Her eyes widened, shocked. "That resort is far too expensive, Zachary. I'll just find a motel on the Gold Coast. I can lie on the beach all day and read."

I stood, and with a shake of my head, I said, "Nope, you're going to Port Douglas." *And I don't give a flying fuck how expensive it is.* She deserved it. Hell, she deserved so much more, but I wasn't a man who engaged in battles I figured I couldn't win. A week was all I knew I could push her for.

As I walked away from her, she called out, "Don't ever believe those voices in your head. They're wrong."

I paused for only a moment before continuing. She knew about the voices because I'd shared that information after I'd lived with her for a few years. I'd volunteered that the voices had helped me survive Carl's abuse, that they'd helped me understand why he inflicted it.

That I deserved it.

That I was a bad person.

I didn't hear the voices these days, and I didn't believe that I'd deserved Carl's abuse. Not anymore. But I did know I wasn't a good person. *She* was wrong about that, not me.

6
———————

King

"Is your mum okay?" Ivy asked later that afternoon when we arrived home.

Lunch had turned out to be full of laughter after Ivy and I ran interference with Mum and Annika. Skylar had even asked me again to help with her assignment. Peace had been restored in the King house. Fuck knew how long for, but we'd make the most of it while we had it.

I'd collapsed onto the couch as soon as we walked in our front door, pulling Ivy with me. The plan had been to have the talk I'd promised her, but that plan flew out the window the minute she was in my arms. Hell, it'd been more than seven days since I'd had her. I didn't care if all we did was kiss; I just needed to touch her.

I needed my hands on her body. Touch calmed me in a way not much else did. Fuck if I understood why, but it was how I knew things were okay in my world. A week without it, and I was climbing walls. Going out of my mind.

Ivy gave me a good five minutes of getting my fill before she pushed me away and asked about my mother. My dick was hard as fuck, and I could barely think straight while working out all the dirty shit I wanted to do to her, but she was right—we needed to talk.

I moved to the other end of the couch. At her questioning look, I muttered, "I'm too tempted to spread your legs and fucking devour you. I need to be as far from that pussy as possible."

Her lips pulled up at the ends in a smile as she stretched her legs out, rested them on the coffee table and pulled a pillow onto her lap. "I get it, you want me too much. I mean, who wouldn't?"

Although I'd proposed to her two years ago, and told her I loved her as often as I could, Ivy had no idea just how much I wanted her. I'd known her half my life; she was etched in my heart like no one else. Our lives were entwined, past and future. And my journey through life was something I couldn't imagine taking without her.

"Mum will be okay." I finally answered her question. "Thanks for your help with Nik today." It meant everything that she wanted to help my family. The falling out our mothers had experienced a few months ago had been hard on us, challenging our relationship in new ways, but she'd never once stopped being there for my mother and siblings.

"Always, baby."

Baby.

It lingered in my mind.

I had to find a way for her to want to call me that every damn day. I had to find a way to quieten the unpredictable thunder between us.

Fuck, I'd just put space between us when that was the last

thing we needed. I stood and closed that distance again. Scooping my arms under and around her, I lifted her and walked us upstairs to our bedroom.

Her eyes questioned me. "I thought we were talking."

"We are." I placed her down, sat on the edge of the bed and pulled her to stand between my legs. Taking hold of her hips, I said, "We've been engaged for two years, and I've been a patient man while you slowed the process down, but I'm done waiting. I want my ring on your finger, and I want it there within the next month."

Her mouth fell open. "Totally not what I thought we were going to talk about."

"We'll get to that, but I need to get this sorted before we move on." My eyes bored into hers, demanding an answer.

She tried to move out of my hold. When I gripped her harder so she couldn't, she placed her hands on mine and attempted to pull them from her hips. "Let me go, King."

I did as she asked and then stood. "Why are you stalling?"

Dropping her gaze to the ground, she bit her bottom lip and avoided my question.

I tipped her chin up so I could have her eyes again. "Talk to me, Ivy. What's going on?"

It took her a few moments, but she finally asked, "How can you still want to marry me when I can't even give you what you want?"

I had no idea what she was talking about. "What can't you give me?"

She crossed her arms so that each hand gripped the opposite forearm. Rubbing her hands up and down her arms in her nervous way, she said, "I know you like rough sex, and I do too, but I can't do the choking thing, King. I've thought about it all week, and—"

Jesus fuck, no wonder she'd pulled away. "That's why you've been distant?"

"I needed space to figure it out." She paused and took a deep breath, looking up at me with tears in her eyes. "I want to be able to give you whatever sex you want, and I thought maybe I could do it, but I can't. I'm sorry." The crack in her voice shattered through my soul reminding me I was a fucking bastard.

I needed to touch her, needed that contact, but I instinctively knew that *that* was the last thing Ivy needed. We'd been having sex for five years, and it had taken me a good three years to gain her complete trust. After her traumatic childhood filled with sexual abuse, sex had been hard for her. She wanted physical intimacy with me, but something as simple as my hands on her body had been difficult for her. Touching her during this conversation didn't feel like the right thing to do, so I pushed my needs aside in an effort to give her what she needed.

It was fucking hard not to pull her into my arms, though, when she stood in front of me crying.

"I don't need that. All I need is you, Ivy, however you want to give yourself to me." I watched her reaction closely, and when she looked at me like she didn't believe a word I said, I repeated with greater force, "I want *you*. I will never ask you to let me do that again or anything else you're not comfortable with. That shit should never have happened."

"But don't you see, King? It did happen, because rough sex is such an instinctual thing for you. I don't care what you try to tell me, you liked it. Why should I expect you to spend the rest of your life with me if I'm not willing or able to do things with you that you like?"

"That doesn't make any sense. That's like saying you should be willing to go fishing with me or spend hours working on cars with me simply because I like to do those things."

She finally stopped rubbing her arms and dropped her

hands to her side. "Those are things I *could* do with you if you really wanted me to," she said softly. "This isn't something I could ever do. When you started squeezing my throat the other night, it hurled me right back to the bad parts of my childhood." Her voice cracked again, and more tears slid down her cheeks. Madly wiping them away, she continued, "I can't... I can't go back there again, King. Not ever." Her last four words were barely audible—"Not even for you."

Ice slithered down my spine. I wasn't fucking losing her over this. No way would I allow that. I hated that I'd done this to her, and I would find a way to make things right again. But there wasn't any way in hell she'd be walking away from this relationship.

Unable to stop myself any longer, I reached for her. Sliding an arm around her waist, I pulled her body to mine. The way she came easily told me I'd done the right thing. "Do you remember the first time we had sex?"

She nodded. "Yes."

I traced a finger down her cheek. "Remember how you were scared out of your fucking mind? And how I didn't force you to do anything you didn't want to do?"

"Yes," she whispered, her gaze glued to mine.

Running my finger across her collarbone, I continued, "Let's back this shit up and forget last weekend. Let me show you just how right we are together. I haven't needed anything but what you wanted to give for the last five years, and I sure as fuck don't need it now. I'm more than fucking happy with what we have, Ivy. *You* are everything I have ever wanted, and I'm not letting you go."

Her entire body sighed. I felt it clear as fucking day. It was like she exhaled a breath she'd been holding for a long fucking time. Bringing her hands up to clutch my shirt, she said, "But—"

I pressed a finger to her lips. "No buts. I'm not backing

down on this. And I'm also not backing down on us getting married."

She watched me silently for a beat before slowly nodding. "Okay."

I then exhaled the breath *I'd* been holding.

~

I learnt a hard lesson the next day. One I'd already learnt at the hands of my biological parents. Somewhere along the way, I'd forgotten that lesson. I'd never fucking forget it again.

The worst kind of betrayal comes from those you love.

Ivy's foster mum, Bethany, and I had always been close. The falling out she'd had with my mum had been challenging for our families, but through it all, she and I had remained solid. Mum had encouraged it; the falling out wasn't her choice. They'd argued over some seemingly insignificant thing that had then blown up into the kind of argument most relationships struggled to come back from. Mum held out hope, but Bethany had stayed firm—she didn't want anything to do with her sister again.

After a night of endless sex, Ivy and I left home early that morning to head to work. I had a busy day ahead of me taking care of a few cleaning jobs Jethro had assigned me. He'd been using me for them a lot more lately. "Cleaning up people's sins and making sure no fucker finds out what they did is something you're fucking talented at," he'd said. What he really meant was that I never hesitated to do the dirty shit others didn't want to do. Some jobs called for a phone call, others, a bullet. I gave no fucks which, I just did it.

I'd kissed Ivy goodbye and said, "Call your mum. Tell her we've got news for her tonight."

She blasted a sexy grin at me. "I could just tell her over

the phone. That way we don't have to leave the house tonight, and you can spend the night between my legs."

While that option appealed, I wanted to do this shit right. Bethany deserved more than a phone call for this kind of news. I shook my head. "No, we do it together in person. I'll swing by home after work to pick you up. After we see her, we'll drop by Mum's and tell her and the girls."

"You know," she murmured before kissing me, "for an asshole, you can be thoughtful."

I smacked her ass. "I'll see you tonight." As I walked towards my bike, I called out, "And Ivy?"

She looked up as she got in her car. "Yeah?"

"Take a nap today if you get a chance. You're gonna need it." *Because the shit I want to do to you tonight will require some fucking stamina.*

She smiled knowingly before pulling out of the driveway. I sat on my bike and watched her drive away. Something had shifted between us last night. She'd opened back up to me and allowed me to peel back another layer of her. The thing with Ivy, though, was that it felt like I still had a thousand layers to get through. She had every piece of me, but I knew I didn't have all of her. And I fucking wanted every last piece.

I took care of two jobs that morning and was on my way back to the clubhouse when Ivy called. The way she stumbled over her words told me something was very wrong.

"King... shit... I, um, fuck...." Her voice trailed off before I heard crying.

Every instinct I had screamed at me to tread carefully, but I was never good at that. My preference was to invade and interrogate. I was the storm that refused to relent. "What's going on?" I demanded, my voice harsher than necessary, but fuck, she had me twisted up with unease.

"Don't yell at me!"

"I'm not fucking yelling, Ivy. I'm just—"

"Mum won't give us her support to get married," she blurted. "She wants me to leave you and move back in with her."

My body tensed for the fight it knew was coming.

"What the fuck?" I roared, trying desperately to control both the thoughts raging through my mind and my response to Ivy. "You spoke to her already? Without me?"

"That's not the point here, King."

She was right, it wasn't, but it pissed me off that she'd done what I asked her not to. I shoved my fingers through my hair. "What did she say?" Fuck, I'd go over there myself and sort this shit out if I had to. I refused to allow anyone to come between Ivy and me.

Her hesitation almost caused me to explode, but I managed to keep my frustration in. When she finally answered me, I heard every ounce of distress she was feeling. "She said that you've changed since you joined Storm and she doesn't want me to marry you if you stay in the club."

"How the fuck have I changed?"

"She didn't say—"

"You didn't ask her?"

"I didn't get a chance. King—"

"Why? What the fuck else did she say?"

"King! This isn't my fault! I hate that—"

Fuck it, I was going over there. "Don't worry about it, I'll sort this out."

"No! Don't you go over there! You'll just make it worse. Let me talk to her again."

"It's me she has a problem with, Ivy, not you. I need to go and see her and find out what's going on."

"Please don't go. I really think you'll just upset her."

"I'm going now," I said forcefully. "I'll call you once it's done." I hung up without waiting for her response. Before we got into a fight over it.

Half an hour later, I stood at Bethany's front door, fuming with anger over what she'd said. I clenched my fists by my side as I attempted to rein that anger in. This had to be a huge misunderstanding, one that a conversation would solve. Fuck, Bethany had always been there for me. Why would she turn on me now?

"Zachary," she said curtly when she opened her door to me. "I don't know why you are here. I've said everything I'm going to say to Ivy."

I stared at her in shock. And not fucking much shocked me anymore. Where was the kind woman who'd patched my cuts and bruises when I fell off my bike as a child? Or the woman who'd asked me to look out for her daughter at school when her friends turned against her?

I didn't wait for an invitation; I pushed my way into her house as I said, "And now you can say it to me."

Bethany's home had always felt warm to me. Welcoming. Between the multitude of quilts strewn across her well-worn floral couches, the white lacy curtains, lamps dotted all through the house, and dog-eared books piled in every spare cranny, Bethany's house was more than a building where she raised ten foster kids. It was the home those kids never had a shot at without her. The place they came home to after school, with warmed Milo and homemade cookies waiting on the kitchen table where their foster mum would help them complete their homework. A complete contrast to what they would have come home to at the hands of their own parents.

She sighed and closed the door after me, following me into the kitchen.

I turned to her when we reached the kitchen. "You don't want Ivy with me anymore. Why? What's changed? And don't give me any shit about you and Mum. That's got nothing to do with *me* and you."

Her lips flattened in distaste. Bethany and Mum had been

raised strict Catholics, and both hated my swearing. Usually, I tried to respect their wishes, but I didn't have it in me when I was this worked up.

"You've changed," she said, as if those two words would be enough to explain her stance. They were far from enough.

I pushed my shoulders back and demanded, "How?"

She motioned at the table. "Please sit, Zachary. I don't want to argue with you over this. I'd rather do it as civilised adults."

Fuck that. "I'm not sitting, Bethany. I just want you to tell me what you have against me being with Ivy."

Her eyes turned cold, shocking me again. It was a slap in the face, but it was nothing compared to what was coming. "I always sensed the danger in you, always worried that Margreet wouldn't be able to stop you from becoming who your father's genes had destined you to be. I'd hoped the love we gave you would be enough, but it wasn't. I can see that now. I can see that motorcycle club is no good for you, and that the evil there is infecting Ivy, too." She crossed her arms and straightened in a rigid stance. "I won't allow you to drag my daughter down with you into that cesspool of sin you've chosen to be a part of."

Her words sliced through me.

Painful.

They were like acid burning me.

Cruelty really was the currency I dealt in, though, so my mind and every muscle in my body fell into line and prepared for war. I was like a well-oiled machine moving into preservation mode in a cold and calculating way.

Ivy had always been Bethany's favourite foster child. The others had come and gone, but Ivy had stayed until she was an adult. Ivy was the only one who thought of Bethany as a mother. They were close as fuck, and while I'd always respected that, Bethany had to understand and support Ivy's choice to make a family with me.

Ice laced my words when I spoke next. "Ivy has made her choice, and you need to respect that choice in the same way she has always respected your choices and decisions."

She dropped her arms to her side, her body stiff and defensive. "I don't have to do anything, Zachary. I certainly don't take directions from you."

I clenched my jaw. "No, but Ivy does."

Her eyes widened. "Oh I see, you've turned into one of those men now. The kind who like to control and order their women around." Contempt crept into her tone when she added, "I should have known that would happen."

I wasn't that kind of man and never would be, but this was combat, and I wasn't above using whatever method I needed to win. "Ivy loves me, Bethany. She has for a good eleven years, and it's the kind of love that not even a mother can come between. You wanna try, be ready for me to unleash a holy fucking war on you."

My entire fucking body strained as violent anger raged through me. I would claw and tear and smash my way into getting what I wanted before I'd ever walk away from Ivy.

Bethany's nostrils flared as she took a step closer to me. "You can threaten me all you like. I'm not scared of you. I will fight for my daughter until the end because that's what a mother does. Now, I want you to turn around, leave my house and never come back. And get ready for your war."

I watched her for one more tense moment before leaving. That would have been the end of it for today, but it turned out we had one more round left in us.

Ivy flew through the front door just as I reached for the handle. Her wild eyes met mine. One look and she knew the situation had escalated. "Oh God, what did you do, King?"

I ignored the panic in her voice and wrapped my hand

around her arm. "I took care of shit, and we're leaving now." My voice was hard, my position unyielding.

"Ivy," Bethany called out, coming into view as she made her way down the hallway to where we were.

Ivy pulled out of my hold. "What's happened?" It was a plea, but deep down she had to know what had happened. I wasn't the kind of man to retreat, and her mother wasn't the kind of woman to abandon her child.

"Your fiancé has made it clear he won't be walking away from you, Ivy. I'm disappointed because I'd hoped my sister had raised a man who would choose to do the right thing, but it seems she failed—"

I turned on her, my chest exploding with fury and fire. How fucking dare she utter a bad word about my mother? Drawing close, I loomed over her, glaring down with daggers, and warned, "I would be very careful if I were you, Bethany. Do not drag Margreet into this. Say whatever the fuck you want about me, but you will never speak badly of her."

Her earlier declaration that she wasn't scared of me proved incorrect. She flinched and took a step away from me.

"King! Can we please calm down and talk this out?" Ivy begged me with her words and her body, but I was past talking. Her mother had been crystal fucking clear in what she wanted, and no amount of talking would change this situation. The only thing that would make her happy was Ivy walking away from me, and I would make fucking sure that never happened.

My eyes bored into Ivy's as I issued my final command. "I'm leaving, and you're coming with me."

She stared at me with shock. She knew what I meant. *Make a choice now. Your mother or me.*

Swallowing hard, she gave her mother one last pleading look. When Bethany wrapped her arms around her body and refused to budge, Ivy's face crumpled, and a tear slid down her face. More came, but that was after she took my hand and exited her mother's home.

The worst kind of betrayal comes from those you love.

I'd opened myself up to Bethany and allowed her to rip a piece of my heart out when she decided I wasn't good enough for her.

I was tired of learning my lessons.

There would be no more pieces of my heart shredded at another's hand. I would make damn sure of that.

7

King
Sixteen Years Ago
Aged 23
Six Months Later

Addictions were a habit that would leave you desperate and willing to crawl to your death for just one more hit.

They made you reckless.

Foolish.

Un-fucking-hinged.

I knew all about them. I was addicted to Ivy in ways that were beyond my comprehension. I looked at my behaviour some days and wondered who the fuck I was and what the fuck inspired me to do most of the shit I did.

But I knew why.

And still, I didn't change a fucking thing.

The day, six months ago, that I'd stood in her mother's house and forced Ivy to choose between us was my lowest point. I hadn't been able to think straight that day, let alone make rash decisions. All because I feared never having another hit.

Our relationship had almost become a casualty of my ultimatum. Ivy chose me and hated me for it every day for a good four months. *I* fucking hated me for it, but I couldn't bring myself to take the demand back. She spent her days and nights working and studying. I spent all my time at the clubhouse. We were ships in the night. And as far as our wedding was concerned, neither of us brought it up.

Without my drug of choice, I found another way to medicate myself and quiet my demons. I turned to violence and went on a four-month rampage delivering death and destruction for Jethro in his war with the new Black Deeds president, Zero. It had been a bloody and vicious war, and it honed my skills in the way only four straight months of day in, day out depravity could.

I hardly recognised myself when I looked in the mirror each day. Cold, soulless eyes stared back at me, void of any remorse for the things I did. Without Ivy to hold me at the end of the day, I forgot what compassion was. I had no need for mercy, so I dispensed with it.

My days held one clear goal: protect my club. And I became the master at it.

It took an argument with Margreet to pull me back into line. My mother saved me for the second time in my life.

It was the day that Jethro and Zero called a truce. I turned up at Mum's place that night, late and half-cut. I'd missed all her Sunday lunches for the past four months and skipped every dinner she'd asked us to attend. Ivy went to all of them, but I couldn't sit next to her at my mother's house and pretend shit wasn't fucked up. I couldn't sit under the weight of my mother's gaze and pretend I hadn't fucked up as badly as I had.

I stumbled into the house just over an hour late, heading straight to the kitchen in an effort to avoid Ivy. The only reason I'd turned up at all was that I needed my birth certificate for some bank account bullshit, and Mum had it.

"Zachary." Mum's voice sounded behind me as I bent over to search her fridge for something to eat.

I gripped the fridge door harder, willing her to leave it alone, but I knew she wouldn't. She'd blown up my phone for the past four months with demands for me to *come to my senses*, and I'd ignored all of them. This was her first opportunity to tell me exactly what she thought of everything I'd done.

Straightening, I turned to find her watching me, arms crossed over her chest, a stern expression on her face. "Do we have to do this?"

Her brows lifted. "You thought you could show up at my house, drunk, raid my fridge, grab your birth certificate and leave without me asking you to explain your actions? I raised you better than that."

I walked the couple of steps backward I needed to rest against the kitchen counter. Scrubbing a hand over my face, I blew out a harsh breath. "I'm not in the mood for this tonight."

"It seems you're not in the mood for a lot of things lately. Not for your girlfriend or your family anyway."

I narrowed my eyes at her, wondering how much she knew about my relationship with Ivy. Resting my hands either side of me on the counter, I said, "I've been busy with the club."

She pressed her lips together. "Don't insult my intelligence, Zac."

I threw my hands up and pushed off from the counter. "Fuck, Mum, what do you want me to tell you? Do you want to know how badly I screwed shit up with Ivy four months ago? That I'm a bastard who ordered his girlfriend to choose him over her mother? Or maybe you'd like to know how I fill my days doing anything that will drown out the shit that fills my head? You tell me, and I'll do my best to lay it all out for you in fucking detail."

I expected her to lay into me for disrespecting her, and I wouldn't have blamed her, but she surprised me when she uncrossed her arms and came towards me. "Well, that's a start at least. I can't say I have much tolerance for your language, but since I haven't heard your voice for almost four months, I'll take what I can get at this point."

Fuck, I was an asshole.

I dropped my head to each side, stretching my sore neck muscles before saying, "I'm sorry I haven't been around. I couldn't."

She nodded. "Ivy has kept me updated on what's happening."

"Really?" That surprised me. I thought she'd have locked that shit down deep and avoided talking about it at all costs.

"Well, I've had to drag it from her. You two are as guarded and stubborn as each other. I'm sure she's only giving me just enough to satisfy my questions, but it's more than I've heard from you."

"And Bethany? She still not talking to you?"

Sadness filled her eyes. "I haven't heard from her."

Fuck, I wanted to throttle that woman.

I jerked my chin towards the dining room where Ivy was. "How is she?"

"How do you think she is?"

My chest tightened at the thought of how my woman was doing. I hadn't touched her, kissed her or been with her in four months, and we'd barely spoken a word except to discuss household issues. We may as well have been housemates. We weren't even sharing a bed. I'd gotten to know the fucking couch better than Ivy over the past months.

When I didn't answer her, she nudged, "Go in and see her. I know she'd like you to."

I wasn't convinced. Scrubbing my face again, I shook my head. "No, I'll just grab my birth certificate and head out. I don't want to—"

It wasn't often my mother lost her temper, and when she did, I knew I'd *really* upset her. This was one of those occasions. Her steely expression more than caught my attention, but it was the way she snapped at me that glued my attention to her. "I don't know what thoughts are running through your head these days, Zachary, but let me tell you I'm not a fan of them. And I know I taught you how to show people you love them, so I'm uncertain as to why you're treating Ivy the way you have been for the last four months. You will not be leaving this house tonight until you walk yourself into that room and sit your behind down next to your girlfriend and engage in a conversation with her. Talk about the weather for all I care, but you look her in the eyes and show her that you're still in this with her. Because if you don't, you are going to lose that beautiful girl, and only God knows what that will do to the both of you. I do not want to lose my son to the evil in this world, and that is the one thing I *do* know will happen if you don't have the love of that woman behind you."

She *had* taught me how to show people I loved them, and it was because of the unconditional love we shared that I did as she said. She asked me to do something, I did it. That was one of the only rules I had for myself, and I wasn't about to break it now.

Ivy looked up the moment I entered the dining room. Her eyes met mine and didn't let go. She seemed uncertain and didn't say anything as I took the seat next to her. No one said anything; they simply stared at me waiting for my next move. I didn't care about them, though. Not right now. The only person on my radar was Ivy.

My gaze roamed over her, taking in everything I hadn't been paying attention to. Fuck, she'd lost weight, and she didn't have any spare to begin with. I ran a finger down her cheek as I noted the exhaustion lining it. She didn't flinch away from me. Instead, she appeared to welcome it, like she'd been waiting forever for my touch.

Before I could draw my hand away from her, she reached up and covered it with her hand. "King," she whispered, and my soul shattered.

I closed my eyes, unable to let the world in any longer. An ache like I'd never known consumed me. It bled into my bones, ate at my heart, and made me question why the fuck I'd allowed this distance between us to grow. Four fucking months wasted.

When I opened my eyes again, I shifted to the edge of my seat so I could be closer and took hold of her other hand. "I've missed you."

The brush of skin against skin shifted things in my head. Started clearing the confusion I'd existed in for months. When we were good, *I* was good. And while we weren't even close to good right now, her touch waved a white flag.

The conversation at the table started up again, allowing us the space to talk between ourselves. Not that I cared if my family listened to what we said. I barely noticed them there. All I saw and felt was Ivy and the desperate need sitting between us to fix the cracks we'd sledgehammered in our relationship.

She squeezed my hand. "Can we go home now?"

I nodded and pushed my chair back, more than ready to take her home.

Mum looked up with a hopeful glint in her eyes. "Ivy has

your birth certificate." *Of course she did.* I wondered how many times Mum had practiced the speech she'd delivered. She'd managed to hit my triggers, and thank fuck for that.

As we exited the house, Ivy squeezed my hand again. When I looked back at her, she said, "I'm driving. There's no way I'm letting you get back on that bike tonight." Her tone was forceful, but I saw the hesitation in her eyes. Her doubt slayed me. We might have lost our way for a while, but I'd never once considered the relationship over. It sucker-punched me that she didn't know where we stood.

I took her face in both my hands and backed her up against the house. A ferocious urgency consumed me—she had to understand I wasn't going anywhere.

"I'm sorry I've been a bastard and shit all over us, Ivy, but I'm here now, and I'm one-hundred-fucking percent back in this with you. You do what you need to do with your mother, mend that fence or whatever, but know this—I will never make you choose between me and anyone ever again. You want me, I'm yours. However you'll take me. Just fucking promise me you'll take me. I never wanna be out in the cold again."

Our bodies were smashed together, our breaths coming hard and fast, and my blood roared in my ears while I waited for her response.

She flung her arms around me as tears streamed down her cheeks. Her mouth crashed to mine, and she kissed me like she hadn't kissed me in years. She fucking breathed life back into me with that kiss.

We didn't need words.

We never had.

They just got in our way.

All Ivy and I needed was this.

We needed hands and mouths and to just shut the fucking world out while we showed each other our feelings.

And so my addiction only grew.

My drug of choice came back to me.

The problem with addictions is that in the end they always get you. They shred you, rip your life apart, eat you the fuck up and spit you back out. They consume you, and before you realise what's happening, you hit rock bottom, and you're left with nothing. You're out in the cold without any hope of ever getting another hit.

8

King

I surveyed the Christmas tree standing in my lounge room. "Jesus fucking Christ, Ivy, this must have cost the fucking bank." The tree touched the roof and felt like it filled half of the room. And the number of decorations on it was beyond anything I'd seen on a tree before. A fucking rainbow had vomited in my lounge room.

"Stop your bitching, King," Annika called out from the kitchen where I figured she was helping Ivy cook dinner. "You told Ivy to sort the tree so she sorted it."

It was Christmas Eve, and Ivy had insisted she wanted to start a new tradition of Christmas Eve dinner at our place. It had been two months since we'd patched up our relationship, and she'd reached out to her mother a few times, but Bethany didn't want anything to do with her. Not while she stayed with me. I'd done everything I could to try to fix the situation. Nothing worked. It pissed me off that this would be Ivy's first Christmas without her mother. However, I kept my anger to myself in an effort to keep the peace in my home.

I entered the kitchen expecting to find my mother having words with her daughter over her language. Frowning when I didn't see her there, I asked, "Where's Mum?"

Ivy glanced up from the potatoes she was chopping and leant over to brush a kiss on my lips. I slid my hand around her waist and down to her ass as she did this. The last two months had consisted of my hands on her and my dick in her as often as I could manage. We'd had a lot of time to make up for, and I'd made sure I showed her just how fucking much I wanted her. Shit was improving between us.

Mostly.

Her mother had managed to get her hooks into us without even trying. While I'd done what I could to fix the divide between Ivy and me, some cracks remained. My woman still held me at a distance some days. I wasn't giving up, though. Far fucking from it. Thank fuck I had decades ahead with Ivy—I was sure as shit gonna need them to peel back all her layers.

She smiled up at me. "Margreet dropped the girls off about an hour and a half ago. She said she had something to do so that our first Christmas Eve dinner here could be perfect."

Keeping my hand on her ass and her body against mine, I reached for the glass of whisky she had on the counter. I threw some down my throat as I watched her. "Did you have a good day?"

"Yeah. I finished wrapping all the presents, did all the laundry, made shortbread, and packed for our trip. Did you?"

She didn't want to know what I'd spent my day doing. My hands had gotten dirty today, taking care of club business. I let her go so I could pour myself a drink. "My day is done, and that's all that matters."

She frowned at me. Ivy never pushed me to share club shit with her, but that was because I usually gave her something. Nothing I shouldn't, but some story about what I'd done during my day. Since we'd reconnected two months ago, I'd shut down on discussing Storm business. Things had changed for me at the club—Jethro had me doing all kinds of things I'd never talk about—and all I wanted to do when I came home at night was get my fill of her. Sex at night balanced out the violence of my days, and it eased the tension that club problems knotted in my body.

Reaching for the hem of my shirt, she tugged it gently and asked, "Did you have a bad day?"

"No. I just don't want to discuss it."

Her frown deepened and hurt flashed briefly in her eyes. Letting go of my shirt, she turned back to the potatoes. I knew by the way she started a conversation with Annika about girl shit that she'd erected one of her walls between us again. She was blocking me out because I hadn't engaged how she wanted me to. This was classic Ivy, a game of silent treatment she liked to occasionally play. One that pissed me off. Not that her games played a huge part in our relationship anymore, but I'd noticed some shit creeping back in over the last couple of months.

Swiping my glass of whisky from the counter, I left the room and headed upstairs to take a shower. The peace and fucking quiet would help me get my shit together. That we still swung between good and bad so fast and easily did my head in. *Would we always be a hurricane of emotions like this?* I liked some fight in my woman, but the moods our relationship suffered exhausted me.

I pulled my shirt over my head as I took the stairs two at a time, dumping it in the laundry basket and then stripping the rest of my clothes from my body. Blood from a beating I'd given one of Storm's drug customers earlier had splattered on my jeans, so I kept them to the side. I'd wash those rather than leaving them for Ivy. I'd rather avoid her questions.

I rested my arms against the tiled shower wall, dropped my head and stood under the hot water for ten solid minutes to soothe my aching muscles. When I was done, I pulled on clean jeans and the black AC/DC shirt Ivy gave me for my last birthday, grabbed my dirty laundry and headed back downstairs.

Skylar smiled conspiratorially at me when I sat down on the couch next to her after loading the washing machine. "Are you avoiding Ivy?"

I scooped some popcorn from the bowl in her lap and eyed her. "You think she's still shitty with me?"

Her smile morphed into a full grin. "Yeah. Of course. She was complaining to Nik that you always eat her Fruit Loops and that you bring the stray cat inside when you know she hates that."

I grinned back at her. Skye and I always stuck together. Even when I pissed her off, she'd come through for me if I needed her. I'd been seventeen when Margreet fostered her; she'd been two. Six years of me looking out for her and helping Mum raise her meant we shared a special bond.

I shovelled popcorn into my mouth. "Don't tell her, but sometimes I eat those Fruit Loops just to piss her off." It usually ended with my hands in her pants. First came her complaints, then the sex.

Skylar raised her brows as if to say she thought I was an idiot. One day she'd understand the dynamics of sex, but if I had my way, that wouldn't be until she was at least forty. Until then I'd just let her think I had no clue about women.

"Do you think Ivy will ever let you keep Booey inside?"

The stray cat that had wormed his way into my heart a

year ago would never find his way into Ivy's good graces. For one, he was a cranky motherfucker. Even after a year, he greeted me with a hiss before demanding food. When he saw Ivy, she received more than a hiss. He didn't seem to like anyone but me. And two, she was allergic to cats. Booey, named by Skylar, was destined to live on my front step.

"I doubt it, Skye. He makes her sneeze too much."

"Can't she take allergy pills or something?"

I smiled down at her. The kid loved cats. Mum wouldn't have one at her place, so Skylar looked forward to visiting Booey and me. "It's not fair for me to expect her to have him inside."

She smooshed her lips together disapprovingly. "He needs a home. He's cold outside."

I ruffled her hair as I put my feet up on the coffee table. Jerking my chin at the cartoons on the television, I asked, "You watching this or can we find something else?"

Her eyes lit up. "You wanna watch wrestling?"

I nodded. "Yeah." I checked my watch. "Do you know where Mum was going?"

Her hesitation told me she did, but that it was probably supposed to be a secret. "She said not to tell you guys in case she couldn't make her agree."

"Make who agree?"

She took a deep breath and exhaled loudly, seemingly torn about telling me. "Fine, I'll tell you, but don't tell Ivy, okay?" At my nod, she continued, "She was going over to Bethany's to ask her to come here."

Jesus, she'd been gone awhile.

I pulled my phone out and dialled her number. It rang out, so I tried again. After doing this three times, I said, "I'll be back soon." Standing and motioning at the television, I added, "Find the wrestling."

I headed into the kitchen and said to Ivy, "Mum dropped the girls off about two hours ago, right?"

She had her hands in the sink, washing up. Glancing around at me, she nodded. "Yes." Then, taking in the concern on my face, she asked, "Why? What's wrong?"

"Skye said she went to see your mum. She's trying to convince her to come for dinner. But fuck, two hours... she should be here by now." My gut churned with worry that they'd gotten into it. The situation with Bethany was already bad; I'd be pissed off if that woman tore Mum to pieces more than she already had.

Wiping her hands on a tea towel, she came my way with a smile. "Maybe they're talking and sorting things out. God, I love your Mum. This is such a sweet thing to do."

I hadn't considered that option, but deep down I didn't believe it to be the case. Dialling Mum's number again, I put my phone to my ear and hoped to hell she answered and was okay.

When I stabbed at the phone, frustrated, Ivy said, "You want me to call Mum and check on them?"

"Yeah."

She rummaged in her bag and pulled her phone out.

No answer.

She tried again.

Still no answer.

Fuck it. "I'm going over there."

Ivy gripped my shirt. "That's not a great idea, King. Let me go."

I shook my head. "No, you finish what you're doing."

She followed me as I stalked out of the house. "King!"

Turning to face her, I said, "Ivy, I've got this. I'll be back soon."

Pursing her lips, she said, "You'll screw everything up. Please don't go."

Shoving my fingers through my hair, I demanded, "How the fuck will I screw it up? It's already screwed up. I just want to—"

"Mum called me today," she blurted before stopping herself and biting her lip in the way she did when she'd said something she regretted.

I closed the distance between us, my shoulders tensing as I waited to hear what she had to say. "And?"

"She just wished me a Merry Christmas, that's all," she said a little too quickly for me to believe that was all that had been discussed.

"Jesus, Ivy, just fucking tell me everything."

I saw the moment she decided to let it all out. Her expression flashed from frustration to anger to determination in the space of two seconds. Straightening, she said with force, "She told me how hurt she was about everything that's happened this year with your mum and with me. She misses me and wants to fix things between us. I'm going to see her tomorrow."

That last bit threw me—we were supposed to be leaving on our road trip tomorrow. But what really pissed me off was that she thought I'd screw this up for her. I planted my feet wide and crossed my arms, settling in for a long discussion. "You don't want me to go there now because you assume I'll fuck shit up?"

"Well, you did last time."

And there it was.

Would we ever move past my last transgression?

"I thought we'd moved on from that." My tone had turned cold. I tried like hell to curtail it, but when Ivy cut deep, I retaliated with ice.

She stared at me in silence, and I saw all the anger she still carried about this situation. I saw her judgement and her lack of faith in me. And when she finally spoke, I heard her resentment. "You might have, but I'm the one without my mother, not you."

Every ounce of self-control I had snapped. Anger rushed through my veins and required an outlet. I'd discussed this with Ivy until I was blue in the fucking face over the last two months. I'd apologised. I'd told her I'd do whatever she needed. I'd tried to fix shit with Bethany myself. There wasn't anything I wouldn't have done for her if she'd asked.

But she didn't fucking ask.

She'd cried and held me at a distance and played her games with me. And all the while, she'd told me we would get through this. And now she wanted to throw this shit in my face.

I turned away from her and punched the brick wall behind me. I'd fucking regret that later, but for now it was what I needed. I then stalked to my bike without even so much as a glance back at her.

She came after me, though. "So that's it then? You're just going to walk away from me?"

I spun around, anger rolling off me in waves I wasn't sure I could control. "It's safer for all of us if I get the fuck out of here."

She flinched. It was the first time she ever had. But she recovered fast and kept on coming. Slapping her hands against my chest, she yelled, "Do you want to hit me, King? Would that make you feel better?"

I took a step back from her, my jaw clenching. There was no way in hell I'd ever hit a woman. But I needed to get out of here before I started tearing our relationship apart more than we already had.

Fuck.

I turned my back on her again, but she grabbed my arm and pulled me around to face her. Wild fury blew between us. "I miss my mother! Do you even get that? Or do you just care that you have me where you want me, and fuck everyone else?"

"Of course I fucking get that you miss her! Where the fuck is this coming from?"

"I've been telling you for weeks that I wanted her here tonight, but you hardly even listened to me. I feel so alone, King. You never talk to me about this!"

"Fuck, you've told me twice that you wanted her here. Fucking twice! Not multiple times over weeks. And I don't talk to you about her because it only ends in you shutting me out for days afterwards. You tell me, would you want to bring shit up with me if you knew I'd stop talking to you and touching you for days on end?"

"I do not shut you out!"

I threw my arms up in the air. Why the fuck did we always —*always*—see shit completely differently? "The last time I spoke to you about this was three weeks ago. Do you know how I know *exactly* what day that was?" I paused for a beat before pointing my finger at her and continuing. "You came home from work wearing a flower in your hair. A pink rose. You were sad because your mum had left you that nasty message on your phone. Remember? So I made you get changed into that red dress that I know makes you feel good, and I took you to see that movie you'd been jabbering on about for days. The chick flick with the woman whose husband screwed around on her." I stepped closer to her and angled my face closer to hers. "You hated the fucking movie after all that, you hated the pork belly I bought you for dinner, and you cried when I asked you what the fuck was really going on. We talked about your mum and then you refused to talk to me or let me fuck you for three fucking days. I slept on the couch for three nights. Tell me you remember that, Ivy, because if I'm recalling this incorrectly, I'd really like to fucking know."

Before she had a chance to respond, Annika ran out of the house and flew down the front stairs, a look of complete terror on her face. Holding the phone out to me, she cried, "It's Bethany!" Sobs blurred her words. "Mum's been in a crash!"

The world spun, anger and fear colliding as I took the phone from her. "Bethany," I barked, "Tell me she's okay."

Silence.

Blood roared in my ears.

"Tell me!" I thundered. "Fucking tell me my mother is okay!"

A sob ripped through the phone. "Zachary...."

I knew.

I fucking felt it deep in my bones.

Gripping the phone harder, I demanded, "Where?" When all I heard were sobs and no answer, I repeated, "Where is she?"

"Oh, God... it was a drunk driver.... Margreet was turning out of my street when he hit her. Just smashed straight into the side of her car...."

I passed the phone back to Annika. I didn't want to hear another word that woman said. If it wasn't for her, my mother wouldn't be dead. If Bethany hadn't insisted on this fucking cold war with Mum and Ivy, none of this would have happened.

I had to go to her.

To Mum.

I had to see for myself.

Fuck.

It slammed into me.

Like a movie, my life with Margreet rolled through my mind.

The day I came to live with her.

The times she held me when the night terrors claimed me.

The days she collected me from school because I got myself into another fight, and still loved me anyway.

My last day of high school when she told me she was proud of me. And that she believed I could achieve anything.

I saw the Band-Aids, the cooked meals, the kisses, the time she gave, the sacrifices, and even the lectures.

Margreet loved unconditionally.

She fucking laid her heart down and let it bleed love.

She was my one person.

The one who, no matter what I did and what I fucked up, I knew would never walk away from me. *Would never hurt me.*

And now she was gone.

As I got on my bike, voices drifted in and out, faces flashed in front of me, and hands reached for me. I zoned the fuck out until Ivy's eyes came into focus.

"King! Where are you going?"

I blinked.

Where the fuck did she think?

I was going to see my mother.

And then I was going to rain destruction down on those who took her from me.

9

King
Three Months Later

Lifting the glass of whisky that had been placed in front of me on the clubhouse bar, I threw it down my throat in one gulp. I ground my teeth together at the burn and jerked my chin at Sadie for another one.

She lifted her brows but did as I wanted. Sliding it across the bar, she said, "This is your last. Jethro will have my ass for this."

"Why?" I demanded before draining half the glass.

"He told me last week to cut you back. Said he's given you a three-month pass, but now he's done. That it's time for you to clean yourself up." She nodded at the drink in my hand and added, "That's more than half a bottle you've drunk tonight, so I'm not giving you any more."

I emptied the glass and slammed it down before moving

off the stool. "Fucking asshole," I muttered. If I wanted to fucking drink ten bottles, I fucking would.

"King." Jethro's voice sounded behind me. "A word."

Turning, I scowled at him. "I'm busy, Jethro. What do you want?"

Anger slid across his face. "My fucking office!" he barked.

Less than a minute later, I stood in front of him and demanded, "What the fuck with the drinking? You slapping limits on any other fucker around here or just on me?"

Jethro never tolerated this kind of outburst, and tonight was no different. "You'd do well not to test me, King. Not after all the shit I've had to deal with over the last few months while you've been drinking yourself almost to death. I've let it go because you're dealing with your mother's death, but that was three months ago. It's time to get yourself straightened out."

"What shit are we talking about, Jethro? I've done everything you've asked of me. I've cleaned up a fuckload of messes for you and taken care of anyone you needed taking care of."

"The problem is that you've taken care of them a little too well. Your bloodbath across Sydney is starting to bite the club in the ass. We've got too much heat on us. You need to tone that shit down, brother."

"That bloodbath was at your request, *brother*."

His mouth pulled into a flat line. "If I say to tone it down, tone it the fuck down."

The tension between us crackled through the office. I'd had just enough to drink that I was willing to tell him to fuck off, but I hadn't had enough that I forgot my respect for him, so I backed down and nodded.

His hard gaze didn't ease. "We need to discuss Ivy."

"What about her?"

He studied me for a moment, like he was assessing how

to proceed with this conversation. His tense shoulders dropped and his gaze thawed. "It's no secret that I have plans for you, King. I recognised your strengths the day I met you, and I've been training you up ever since. The things you're capable of are things this club needs if it's going to hold its own, so I've worked to draw them out in you." He paused for a beat. "Those things are good for the club, but they're not good for Ivy."

I crossed my arms. "What the fuck are you talking about, Jethro?"

"I've been watching your relationship, and I'm concerned about what I'm seeing. Ivy used to turn up here happy to see you. You used to make all the time in the world for her. Sure, you two fought, but I never saw you lose your shit at her in a way that I feared for her safety. Something's shifted between the two of you, King. She's not happy, and you're angry with her all the time. And to be fucking honest, I think you'll go too far one day and hurt her."

My breathing slowed. His words rang with an honesty I didn't want to admit. My mother's death, and my subsequent quest to punish those I believed responsible had taken the kind of toll on my relationship with Ivy that I feared we couldn't come back from. On top of that, we were raising Skylar together after Mum's death. Between our work and family commitments, our anguish and my bitterness over Mum's death, we were crumbling. These days, we didn't fight so much as move through life disconnected from each other. I couldn't recall the last time we'd even mentioned our engagement.

The drunk driver who killed Margreet had disappeared, and I had been unable to track him down. Prevented from delivering the punishment he deserved, I'd fixated on the other person I blamed. Ivy's mother. It was a fucked-up mess because as much as I wanted to destroy her for the part she played, my love for Ivy stopped me. And so we existed in a toxic bubble of resentment, hate, love, and an inability to reach the other. Physically, we came together, but our sex had disintegrated to irregular, violent encounters.

Jethro was right.

Even I was concerned I'd go too far with her one day.

I blew out a long breath. "Fuck." Eyeing the man I trusted the most in the world, I admitted something I never admitted to anyone, ever. "I don't know what to do."

He watched me earnestly. "If you love Ivy, you'll walk away from her. You'll put her safety before everything else. The path you're on is a dangerous one, brother. Don't force her to deal with the repercussions of that."

I'd heard about Jethro's old lady, but since she was dead, I hadn't met her. The story went that they'd endured a violent marriage. I'd heard rumours he'd beaten her so badly one night that she'd ended up in a coma and died the next day. I had never been convinced the story was true, but listening to him now, I contemplated that maybe it was.

A knock on the office door ended our conversation, but I couldn't get his words out of my head for the rest of the night. By the time I arrived home three hours later, completely shitfaced after visiting a pub on the way, I was a wreck of confused thoughts and denial over the state of my relationship.

I could never give Ivy up.

She was mine, forever.

Fuck, but what if Jethro was right?

What if I did the unthinkable one day?

"King? Is that you?" Ivy's voice floated downstairs as I stumbled through the house knocking shit over as I went.

"Fuck," I muttered. "Yeah," I called up to her. I vaguely recalled that Skylar was at a sleepover with a friend. Thank fuck, because my crashing and banging would have woken her, and she had enough trouble sleeping these days. Mum's death had devastated her to the point it affected every part of her life but especially her sleep.

When I didn't hear from Ivy again, I figured she'd gone back to sleep. Probably hopeful that I'd leave her alone. But fuck if thinking about her all night hadn't given me a hard-on that I desperately needed her to take care of. I hadn't been inside my woman for a good two weeks, and I fucking needed her. Needed her touch.

I staggered up the stairs, tugging my shirt over my head as I went. Dropping it on the floor of our bedroom as I entered, I then reached for my belt. Fuck, Ivy lay naked on the bed, with the sheets kicked off. Every inch of her beautiful body displayed to me. And that sweet cunt I would never get enough of calling to me.

I moved faster, shedding my clothes, and climbing on top of her. She lay face down, and I spread her legs as I ran my hard dick along her pussy.

"King," she mumbled, sleepily. "Don't."

My mind, fuzzy from too much alcohol, tried to keep up, but my need for her controlled me. I ground myself against her, groaning at how fucking good she felt. "I need you, Ivy." I peppered kisses down her back. "I need this sweet fucking cunt."

She swatted me away. "Not tonight," she mumbled again.

Taking hold of her arms, I pressed them into the bed either side of her as I continued to grind against her. Jesus, I fucking needed inside her fast. "Yes, tonight. You haven't fucking let me near you for two weeks. Tonight, you're letting me fuck you."

"King!" She woke up and bucked under me. "Fucking stop it! I don't want to have sex with you tonight."

I was so fucking tanked and screwed up over the state of our relationship and everything I'd discussed with Jethro that her refusal pissed me off. Pushing my body forcefully down onto hers and gripping her wrists hard, I demanded, "When the fuck do you think you might want to fuck me again, Ivy? This year? Next year? Fucking ever? I'm getting tired of this game."

She jerked under me and started a full-force battle to shift me off her. When I refused to budge, she bit my arm and screamed, "Get off me!"

"Fucking hell!" I roared, letting her go. "Why the fuck did you do that?"

She scrambled off the bed, staring at me angrily. "Why the fuck do you think? You wanna force yourself on me, you should expect me to fight back! Just FYI!"

I moved off the bed and lurched towards her. "Don't be fucking dramatic. I wasn't fucking trying to force myself on you."

Her eyes widened. "Well, what the hell would you call it when a woman says no and her man doesn't listen?" She screamed her question at me, almost out of breath because she was that worked up.

I moved in close to her, backing her into the corner where she pressed herself against the wall like she was trying to escape me. "I'd fucking call it desperation. I'm so fucking hard for you, every fucking day, and every time I manage to get close to you, you shut me the fuck down." My eyes bored into hers. "At some point, you need to give me what I want."

She glared back at me. "Or what, King? You'll just take it?"

I glared back at her, my blood pumping hard, my head pounding.

Fuck.

How the hell had we gotten here?

How the fuck had I become this man?

I stumbled backwards, like I'd been punched hard in the gut.

I would never just take it from her.

Fucking never.

But would I have if she hadn't been able to fight me off?

Bile lodged in my throat, and my mind raced to catch up with everything happening.

Fuck.

I had to get out of here.

I needed to put distance between us and get my fucking head together.

I had to figure out if I was willing to put Ivy at risk again.

At risk of being hurt by me.

10

King
Fifteen Years Ago
Age 24

There were moments in your life that changed everything. Sometimes they were planned. Sometimes fate dealt them. As I leaned back against the clubhouse couch and forced the club whore's mouth down over my dick, I closed my eyes and drew in a long breath. This was a moment I would never forget.

Planned? Yes.

Life altering? Yes.

Fucked up? Fuck yes.

But then, fucked up was my style. So Ivy shouldn't have ever figured me for anything else.

I'd spent nearly six months working up to this moment. *After the night I almost forced myself on her.* Hell, I'd tried to do this in a civilised manner, but she hadn't accepted that. It turned out that although she'd thrown her walls up at me for months, she blanched at the idea of us walking away from each other. She'd refused to accept a break-up, declaring her love for me and promising to try harder. Never wanting to imagine a life without her, I'd allowed our dysfunction to continue. So here we were about to spiral into poison and a betrayal we were guaranteed to never recover from.

My only option to keep her safe.

Fuck.

Just the thought of what I was doing to Ivy caused my dick to shit itself and soften in the whore's mouth.

I pressed harder on her head. "Suck it, bitch. If you can't make me fucking hard, I'll find someone who can."

She glanced up at me with a scowl. "Screw you, King. I'm fucking trying here. It's not my fault if you can't get it up. How long's it been since you've had a decent blow job anyway?"

I eased my body to a sitting position and wrapped my hand around her neck. Squeezing her hard, I snarled, "You wanna keep that shit up about my woman, and I'll make fucking sure your ass is out of this club faster than you can open your fucking legs. I asked you to suck me off. I didn't fucking ask you to argue with me or speak to me." My fingers dug harder into her skin. "You think you can manage that?"

Fear crawled across her face. She nodded, but her previous confidence disappeared. When she answered me, her voice held the hesitation I could see in her eyes. "Yes."

Thank fuck for that. I needed this shit to happen now. There wasn't any time to fucking waste.

I let her go and sprawled back against the couch. I reached for the bottle of whisky that sat next to me, and took a long swig of it while she got to work.

Another club whore came into view, smiling down at me. "Sorry I'm late, King. I got sidetracked doin—"

I motioned for her to get her ass onto the couch next to me. "Just get your tits out and put them in my mouth." I didn't have time to listen to her bullshit.

The fact she didn't argue with me made my fucking day.

By the time Ivy entered the clubhouse bar where I lounged with my dick in one whore's mouth and my lips wrapped around another whore's tits, I'd zoned the fuck out. I wasn't getting off on any of it. Instead, I was counting down the minutes until Ivy found me.

My eyes met hers as she came to an abrupt stop. I didn't move. I simply kept sucking the tit in my mouth. Kept fingering the cunt riding my hand. And kept fucking the mouth wrapped around my dick.

Seven years flashed right before my eyes, though.

Seven years of loving Ivy.

Fuck, if we were really counting the years I'd loved her, it was more like thirteen.

I watched as the shock, anger, and utter disappointment hit her. I took in the way her face contorted, and her shoulders slumped for a moment before she squared them again and prepared to go to battle with me.

Always fighting me.

"You fucking bastard!" Her pain screeched out of her, slamming into me. I was deeply intimate with Ivy's pain, but this was a whole new type of hurt for her.

I had never once cheated on her. I knew she still wondered about it, because club whores could be summoned with the click of a finger, but I'd sworn my loyalty to her when I was seventeen. And I fucking lived by that loyalty. It was the one thing I believed in. The code I lived by. When I swore loyalty, I fucking meant it.

And yet, there I was.

Breaking that code and shitting all over the one relationship that meant the most to me.

Ivy's madness consumed her as she ripped both the whores away from me. Her eyes dropped to my dick before straying to my hand that had just been inside a pussy that wasn't hers. Her face curved in disgust and disbelief right before her hands pummelled my chest.

"How could you do this to us?" she yelled as she straddled me, still beating her hands against my chest.

Fuck, there was the fight I craved.

But it was also the fight that I knew would be the death of us eventually.

Ivy and I were on a path of destruction. We loved each other too much. Too fiercely. Too fucking savagely. We would never survive this kind of love.

Jethro had made me understand that. He'd shown me how I was slowly killing Ivy. We weren't a match made in heaven. We were each made in hell—our parents saw to that —and we would burn there together if we continued pushing each other to the edge of crazy.

I allowed her to continue her tirade, only stopping her when she slapped my face and yelled, "I gave you everything. Everything! And you knew how hard that was for me. You told me you'd never fuck us up!"

I gripped both her wrists and stopped her. "I told you last week I wanted to end this, but you didn't listen."

Her eyes widened. "And I told you I was willing to change, to work on us, because I love you. I thought that's what we were doing."

"No, that's what *you* were doing. I never agreed to that."

She tried to wiggle out of my hold, but I tightened my grasp on her wrists and held her in place. I needed her to take this in.

Her breathing grew ragged. She blinked rapidly to stop tears from falling. Ivy hated crying. That she was close to it now told me I was on the right track. I just needed to push her harder.

"Why are you doing this, King?" she begged. "I don't understand."

My chest tightened at her plea. *Fuck.* This was more difficult than I'd prepared myself for. "All we do is argue. I'm sick to fucking God of it." *And I'll probably kill you one day if we keep dancing this dance.* No fucking way would I allow myself to kill the woman I loved. I needed to know she was safe. *Safe from me.*

"You're not sick of it. There's something else going on here. I want you to tell me what it is." Her eyes implored me just as much as her words did. Ivy wasn't giving up without a fight. Because that was what we did. We fought not only over random meaningless shit, but we went to battle for each other. *For us.*

Jesus, was the threesome not enough to make her walk? To make her hate me? I clenched my jaw. "Ivy. We're done." My tone was low, full of warning. I needed her to take note. I did not want to have to speak any more lies to force her hand. Lies that would, by necessity, shatter her.

She yanked her wrists from my hold. Her eyes flashed with the passion that called to me. Fuck, how I loved Ivy's fire. "We are not done! We've been through too much together to ever be done, King. You might be an asshole and possessive as hell and fucked up, but you are also the man who has made me feel more loved than anyone ever has."

"If you really wanna know what's going on here, I'll tell you." Sucking in a deep breath, I steeled myself to inflict a level of hurt on her that would kill me to do. "I've spent thirteen fucking years propping you up, Ivy. You're weak. I need a stronger woman by my side. So you need to pack your fucking bags and get the fuck out of my life. This thing between us is over."

My words hit their intended mark. She froze as they sliced and suffocated her. And those tears of hers finally fell. She wasn't done with me yet, though. In true Ivy fashion, she had to have the last say. "I tried hard to be the woman you needed, King. I wasn't perfect, but I fucking tried. You are a hard man to love, let me tell you. Demanding, bossy, irrational, and I'm almost certain you're half insane. And yet I still loved you through all of that. Even your fucked-up needs when it came to sex weren't enough to push me away. I might have failed you there, but I fucking *tried!*" She jabbed a finger at me. "Fuck you for being a motherfucker who can't keep his dick in his pants. I thought you were so much more than that."

By the time she was done, black tears streamed down her face as her body shook with anger and hurt. She looked at me like I'd driven a knife through her heart. Like I'd pierced her soul and drained every last drop of love and trust she'd ever been able to find in her darkness.

The worst kind of betrayal comes from those you love.

I'd achieved my goal.

Ivy walked out of my life without a backwards glance.

I stood rooted to the spot watching her leave. Watching my reason for fucking living exit my life. And I vowed never to fall in fucking love again.

11
___

King
Eight Years Ago
Age 31

You couldn't fucking trust people.

Unfortunately, that was a lesson I had to keep learning over and fucking over—from the day I was born to today. This time the lesson came from a man I'd trusted with my life, obliterating any desire I might have had to ever put my faith in anyone again.

I'd dedicated almost a decade to Jethro, believing him and blindly following his directions. After I'd ended my relationship with Ivy, my focus had been completely on him. I'd descended into the pits of hell for him, taking care of the filthy shit he didn't want to.

I used to think Jethro was everything. He'd been Storm's president for fifteen years and had taken me in when I'd shown up at the clubhouse with a friend who wanted to join the club. I'd come for a drink and left with a burning desire to be part of a brotherhood unlike any I'd known before. Jethro taught me everything he knew about life and the club. Or so I thought. Turned out he'd only shown me the side of himself he wanted to. He'd kept hidden the fact he stole from the club and harassed members behind closed doors to get them to do shit he wanted. Shit that benefitted him, not the club.

Jethro sneered at me. "Giving up the presidency to you wasn't enough, huh, King? Now you're gonna kill me?"

I clenched my jaw. "You gave up the presidency because you're a lying, thieving motherfucker and wanted to keep the money you've stolen from the club more than you wanted to remain president. If you ever thought I'd simply allow you to make me president in return for my silence forever, you were mistaken. That shit will come out in the open tonight. But this between us now, this is for what you did to me and Ivy."

"What the fuck did I do to you and that bitch?"

I sucked in a deep breath and stopped myself from punching him. Why, I wasn't fucking sure. I had no reason to contain my need for revenge anymore. Tonight I would finally do what I'd been planning for the last week. "You pushed me into leaving her."

"Fuck, that was seven years ago. You're still holding onto that shit? And besides, I didn't push you into doing anything. That was all on you."

Rage breathed down on me. It threatened to smother me with its need for retribution. My skin crawled with anger until I finally snapped and allowed my darkness out to play.

Taking the few steps between us, I grabbed Jethro's shirt and yanked his body against mine. Our eyes met, and I showed him the thunder roaring in me. He may have thought he'd witnessed the depths of my crazy, but he hadn't. I kept the extent of my madness carefully concealed. Jethro would wish he'd never met it. Would fucking wish he'd never crossed me.

"You manipulated me, Ivy, and half the fucking club so I'd think leaving her was for the best. I bought into what you were selling. And what the fuck for?" I gripped his shirt harder. "What the fuck did *you* get out of Ivy leaving?"

Distaste painted his face. "That bitch was your one weakness. I simply helped you see that and deal with it. She was fucking tenacious, though. I'll give her that."

His words shattered my focus. "What did you do to her?" I demanded on a harsh breath. I would kill him slower for this. I'd find a way to draw his blood so it hurt ten times more than I had planned.

He only hesitated for a moment. Jethro liked people to know the shit he'd done. "No matter what I did to her or what I had club members do to her, Ivy never fucking ran to you and dogged on anyone. That bitch told me that even though she hated me and half the club, nothing would force her to leave your side. She said you two had been through everything together and she'd be there until the day you died." His lips flattened. "*That* was why you needed to get rid of her. She would have dragged you and the club down because you would never have been able to put the club first."

I saw fucking red. Without another thought, I smashed my head against his nose. As he reeled back, I roared, "No one makes decisions for me!"

Before he had a moment to recover and get his mind back in the game, I punched his face. He continued stumbling backwards, towards the brick wall in the filthy alley where I'd met him, while I continued punching him.

I'd unleashed my demons, and they weren't retreating anytime soon. They would see this through.

I lost myself to the violence. After being raised on a diet of brutality and cruelty, this savage fury was ingrained in me. It lived deep in my soul. *In my fucking bones.* I dedicated effort to keeping it locked up, but Jethro had hit the trigger, and I was helpless to stop it.

The one thing I knew without a doubt in life was that you should take the time to identify the monsters that walked among you and then do everything in your power not to wake them. If you did disturb them, that shit was on you.

By the time I was done with him, Jethro lay at my feet, a bloody mess of slashed skin, broken bones, and damage I hardly recognised as coming from my hands.

I took a few minutes to get my breathing under control and my thoughts back in focus. It'd take me hours to come down from this, but I needed to concentrate enough to call Hyde.

Hyde answered straight away. "You're done?"

"Yeah, brother, I'm fucking done. Just need your help getting rid of this body."

"Text me the address. I'll be there." He paused for a moment. "And King, you did the right thing. I've got your back on this."

I'd told Hyde of my discoveries regarding Jethro, and he'd helped me investigate to confirm. He'd wanted to watch the motherfucker die, had wanted to help, but this was something I needed to do on my own. That he'd taken my back wouldn't be forgotten anytime soon.

While I waited for him, I crouched down next to Jethro and allowed the memories of the shit we'd done together to come. I needed to do that. Needed to remember so I wouldn't make the same mistakes again. Promises made flashed through my mind, and I noted them too.

I wouldn't go down this path again.

I would never hand the gun to someone and load the bullets for them.

I'd rather aim that gun at myself and blow my own fucking brains out.

Betrayal was worse than death, and the only way to avoid it was to never trust anyone but yourself.

PART II

PRESENT TIME

12

King

I stood rooted to the spot staring at the woman who had haunted my dreams for over a decade. Hell, she'd haunted them even when we were together. Ivy wasn't a woman you simply forgot, not even in your sleep while she lay next to you.

I'd never wanted to forget her.

Nor had I tried.

I'd always welcomed the raging torrent of memories, even on the days they almost strangled the breath from me. They served as a reminder never to trust people or love again. Those memories were a tangled vine of Ivy, Jethro, Bethany, and my mother. Love, hate, lies, betrayal and death, all wrapped together in my head. Although I'd fucked up and fallen in love again after Ivy, I'd tried like hell to never go down that path again. Nothing good came from it.

"Hello, King. It's been a long time."

I'd stopped counting the days years ago. The years, however, sat between us, a harsh reminder of the choices I'd made. Choices she knew nothing of.

She watched me closely. When I found no words, because she'd caught me completely fucking off guard, she spoke again. "Are you going to say anything?"

The room had swallowed me. Consumed every thought I had. Jen's death—*her baby's death*—vanished from my mind.

I took a step towards her. "You look well."

Ivy would be thirty-eight soon. She looked all of thirty. The beauty she wore today was a far cry from the ravaged beauty she'd walked out of my life wearing. I'd never forgiven myself for breaking her.

"Looks can be deceiving."

My mouth turned dry, and I had difficulty swallowing. "What's going on, Ivy? Are you not well?" What the fuck did she mean by that? Was she not fucking well? My mind raced with the possibilities of what could be wrong. The thoughts flying at me, though, became one big fucking jumbled mess.

Nothing fucking made sense right now.

Why the fuck was she here?

"Nothing that would ever concern you," she snapped. "But I didn't come here to talk to you about that."

I restrained my frustration. Ivy always had liked to stretch me to breaking point. "Ivy," I warned. "I asked you a question."

The dull tone disappeared from her eyes. Resentment slashed the air between us as her hostility roared to life. "You gave up that right a long time ago, King."

Fuck.

Ivy was the lightning to my thunder. When she sparked, I rumbled. And she had just fucking sparked. The raging storm inside me exploded out. I couldn't hold it back any longer. "Answer me!" I needed to fucking know that she was okay.

She moved towards me, our bodies unbearably close. Her eyes were cold. The only time I remembered her looking at me with these dead eyes was the day I told her to get out of my life. "You don't get to demand answers from me, King, so don't fucking ask them. Now, if you want me to tell you what I know about the shit going down with your club, have Hyde take his gun off me."

"I'm fucking confused here, Ivy. You came here, knowing we'd be here? And what the fuck are you doing in the attic?" She would at least answer those questions before I made my next move.

"Yes, I organised this meeting. This is a house I own. And I waited up here because I didn't want all of your men pointing their guns at me."

More confusion snaked through my mind. It made no fucking sense for her to have organised this meeting. "Put the gun down, Hyde."

"You sure about that, brother?"

"Yes," I barked, not removing my eyes from Ivy. I didn't believe she would have a gun, but I wouldn't have believed she could have anything to do with the shit Storm was in, either, so it was best to take precautions. Watching her closely was the only one available to me. I knew she wouldn't talk until Hyde did what she wanted. Stubbornness was a classic Ivy trait.

"Fuck," Hyde muttered as he lowered the gun.

Ivy glanced at him before giving me her full attention once she was satisfied. "There's an attack coming. I don't know when, and I don't know how, but I've heard him talk about it for weeks. And it won't just be on your club, it'll be on your families, too. He wants them all dead." She stopped to take a breath. "He wants to wipe everyone and everything you care about off the face of the earth. And I believe he could do it."

He?

My jaw clenched. "Who?" I demanded. "Who the fuck are you talking about? And why?"

Her hard eyes refused to let me look away. "My husband. You took what was his, so now he wants to take what is yours."

Understanding smashed into me. But this puzzle was still a long fucking way off being solved.

"Fuck! Tony is the one behind all this?"

Hyde moved closer to Ivy, anger clouding his face. "What the fuck did King take?"

She looked at Hyde. "He took me."

I drew a long breath and then slowly released it. "How the fuck did I take you?"

I hadn't had any contact with Ivy since the day she walked out of our house. This bullshit her husband was carrying on about enraged me. Fuck, he'd killed a woman and her unborn child today because of it.

Ivy's eyes came to mine again. "You didn't, but he thinks you did. He thinks I'm leaving him because I never stopped loving you."

My chest tightened as my mind went into overdrive in an attempt to keep up with my rapidly-firing thoughts. I might have broken Ivy when I told her to go, but living without *her* had completely annihilated me.

I met Ivy when I was eleven.

I promised her forever when I was twenty.

I fucked it all up when I was twenty-four.

"Is that true?" I demanded.

I didn't want to know, but fuck, I *needed* to know.

She stared at me.

Didn't answer my question.

And then she blinked. "No."

Her lie blazed between us.

It was in her blink.

Ivy always blinked when she lied.

Fuck.

We could never repeat our history.

Never.

It would fucking kill us both.

"Round everyone up, Hyde. We're heading back to the clubhouse." I reached for Ivy as I issued the order. To her I said, "You're coming with us."

She attempted to shrug out of my hold. "No, I'm not."

I gripped her arm hard. "This isn't the fucking time to argue, Ivy."

Her eyes turned from cold to angry, and her body tensed. "I didn't come here for you to stop my progress with leaving Tony. I'm flying out of the country today, so take your damn hands off me and let me go."

I shook my head. "Change your plans. This isn't up for negotiation."

"I see you're the same old King you always were," she spat. "Always completely focused on what *you* want. God forbid what anyone else wants."

My fingers dug harder into her skin as I lowered my face to hers. "I'm not going to say this again, so listen up close. You came to me with information I need to check out. While I do that, you'll stay with my boys. And you'll do this will-ingly, Ivy, or else you and I are going to have a big fucking problem, and you won't like the outcome."

Her eyes widened a fraction. She seemed surprised. "You need to check what out? You don't believe what I told you?"

A headache clamped down over my skull. Too much shit had happened today, and I had a lot more to deal with now that I'd had this conversation with her. Ivy and I had history —a fuckload of it—but that didn't mean I would simply take her word for this. I may have loved her once, but I'd learnt a long fucking time ago not to let love get in the way. These days I ran on distrust and gut instinct. "Did you ever know me to be a man who didn't check shit out? Not even you could make me roll the fuck over and blindly believe something." I yanked her arm. "Now move!" I barked as the pain in my head intensified.

"God, you're a bastard!" At least she'd stopped resisting me and had taken a few steps towards the attic ladder.

"You already knew that. Were you expecting something different?" I wasn't the man she'd known. Not anymore. And if she thought I was a bastard back then, she had a lot to learn about who I was now.

She chose not to answer that. Instead, she gave me one last filthy glare before following Hyde down the ladder. When I reached them a few moments later, he had her by the arm.

His eyes met mine. "You want me to take Ivy back to the clubhouse?"

My natural instinct was to keep her as close to me as possible, but I fought that. I needed to be smarter here. I knew if she stayed with me, it would likely fuck with my thinking. "Yeah, brother. I'll meet you there. And can you send Nitro over to Nik's to bring her back to the clubhouse?"

He nodded and headed outside. Ivy didn't put up another fight. And she didn't look back at me. She simply allowed Hyde to direct her movements.

Everyone had cleared the house, leaving me alone, which was a good thing. I fucking needed the space.

I sucked in a long breath and exhaled it harshly. Fucking Tony Romano. I'd never suspected he was behind all the shit going on. I'd heard the stories about his and Ivy's marriage. That they were a volatile couple. It hadn't surprised me, though. Not with the history she and I shared. But what she'd told us seemed extreme. Fuck, Tony ran an empire; he didn't have time to be fucking around on a revenge mission.

Pulling out my phone, I dialled my sister Skylar. It went to voicemail. *Fuck.* She had a habit of missing my calls. Or fucking ignoring them.

I dialled her again, my chest tightening with the need for her to answer.

Voicemail again.

I stabbed at the phone to try her again.

She finally answered. "Jesus, King, I'm in the middle of studying for an exam here."

I ignored her attitude. "And I'm in the middle of trying to save your fucking life, Skye. Pack your shit up. I'll be there in about fifteen minutes to pick you up and take you to the clubhouse."

"Ah, that would be a no. I have too much studying to do."

I massaged my temple where my headache kicked at my head. "This isn't up for negotiation. Take your books with you."

"Why?"

Skylar's twenty-four years were her downfall. She was too young and too sheltered to understand the darker parts of life. That was entirely my fault because I'd raised her that way. I'd fight every fucking minute of every fucking day to keep her sheltered, but the sooner she grew up and realised I knew best, the easier my life would be.

"Because I said the fuck so," I barked, unable to keep my frustration in any longer. "Be ready when I get there."

Without waiting for her reply, I ended the call and dialled my other sister, Annika.

She picked up straight away. "Hey."

"Nik, I need you to pack up the kids and wait for Nitro to swing by your place. Some shit is going down with the club, and I want you all safe with me at the clubhouse tonight."

Silence for a beat. And then—"Is this you being overprotective or is it for real?"

"Fuck, between you and Skye...," I muttered. "I'm being deadly serious. Nitro is on his way. Be ready for him. I'll see you at the clubhouse."

Again, I hung up before she could attempt to argue with me. Today wasn't the fucking day.

Images of Jen crumpling to the ground after that mother-fucker put a bullet in her flooded my mind. Her eyes would haunt me forever.

The way they came to mine in disbelief.

The way they screamed her horror.

The way they condemned me for her child's death.

This really *wasn't* the day for anyone to fight me on any-fucking-thing.

This was the day for me to stand the fuck up and take control of this fucking city.

Jen was right in her condemnation. I may not have put that bullet in her child, but I may as well have. No fucking way would I allow that shit to happen again.

13

King

"Uncle Zac!"

Annika's daughter, Rebecca, threw herself at me after coming screaming down the hallway of the clubhouse to the office where I was going over shit with Hyde. Her little arms circled my legs as she hugged me, her blonde curls bouncing all over the place.

I scooped her up, and she wrapped her arms tightly around my neck while nuzzling her face in there too. For a tiny six-year-old, she was strong. "You been a good girl?"

She lifted her head and met my gaze, nodding with wild energy. "Yes!" Her eyes widened with expectation. "Do I get a treat?"

I narrowed my eyes at her, making her work for it. "You think you really deserve one? How good exactly have you been?"

Tiny fingers dug into my neck while she wriggled in my

arms. When she answered my question, she did it with her signature style of enthusiasm. If I had to describe my niece in one word, it would be spirited. A huge contrast to her brother, Keith, who was mellow and a little shy.

"I've been the best. Ask Mummy! I even put all the books you bought me away in the bookcase this morning!"

"Mmm... was that before or after Mummy asked you to?"

Devil's voice sounded from behind Annika. "King, hate to butt in, but Bronze just arrived."

My eyes cut to his, and I nodded. "One minute." Giving my attention back to Rebecca, I raised my brows signalling I was waiting for her answer.

Her little lips pressed together in the way they did when she had to tell me something she didn't want to. She then nestled her head against my neck again while admitting softly, "After."

Tipping her face up to mine, I said, "You promise to do it before from now on?"

Her curls bobbed as she nodded. "Yes."

I bent to deposit her on the floor. "I've got a new book for you, but if I hear you're not sticking to our agreement, I'll take it back."

The excitement in her eyes couldn't be mistaken. I fucking loved her love for books.

Annika placed her hand on her daughter's head while giving me her eyes. "Thank you."

"Where's Keith?" Even though he was eight, two years older than his sister, he didn't have her confidence when it came to being around people, so he usually shadowed his mother.

"He's coming in with Nitro. I guess they got talking about bikes." She sighed. "You know what he's like. He's got that love of bikes you always had." He did. And I knew it concerned her, but I ignored that. Keeping a man from his bike was like taking his fucking air from him. I encouraged Keith's interest in bikes whenever I could.

"I've gotta deal with some stuff. I'll come find you once I'm done. Skye's studying in my room if you wanna hang out with her." My sisters knew their way around the clubhouse, but Annika preferred the quiet, so I figured she'd choose my room over the bar.

"How bad is this, King?"

I'd been a member of Storm for seventeen years, and we'd been through some shit with the club in that time. I kept my family close, so we always stuck together in these times. While Skye grumbled her way through them, Annika just dealt. Always practical in her life, she understood the need to get on with shit and do whatever it took to survive. But that didn't make it easier for her. I knew that while her strength ran deep, the effort to achieve it was great.

"Bad. Skye will fill you in." I didn't want to discuss this in front of Rebecca.

She nodded her understanding and guided her daughter away from me. I watched them for a few moments. I didn't care what the fuck it took, I'd make sure they stayed safe. I always had, and I wasn't fucking stopping now.

"King!"

I turned to find Bronze watching me, a wild expression on his face. Jerking my head towards the office, I barked out, "Nitro, my office!" He was somewhere in the club; someone would pass that on. Hyde, Devil, and Kick were already there, waiting to get shit started.

A few minutes later, door closed, I faced the five of them. The air in the room swirled thick with expectation. We all wanted the same thing. Even Bronze. He might have been a cop, but he knew what had to be done. He and I had been through a lot together in the seven years since I'd recruited him, and the one thing I knew for sure about him was that he had zero tolerance for family members becoming casualties of war. I knew without even having to ask him that he'd stand by me and avenge the deaths of Jen and her child. It's what I'd done for him all those years ago, and while Bronze wrestled with his conscience over many things, his loyalty for that act was guaranteed.

I looked at him. "Where are the feds?" They'd pulled eyes off us yesterday, so they'd missed the events of today. That caused me to question the shit that had gone down. I didn't fucking trust anything at the moment.

"The team has been moved for now. Looks like you've managed to lose your tail for a while." At my questioning look, he added, "Trust it, King. I did some digging. It's straight up."

I decided to run with it just being a coincidence. Turning my attention to Hyde, I asked the question I'd been putting off since I arrived back at the clubhouse, "Where's Ivy? And has she said anything else?"

My body remained on high alert since the moment I'd laid eyes on her in that attic. Every muscle tense, I warred with myself over her. Fifteen years apart and yet I still felt that pull to her. I wasn't sure, though, what it meant. I hoped it only lingered because of our family history. I did not need to fuck myself over by wanting something that had no place in my life.

"I've got her with Winter. Told him not to let her out of his sight. And no, she didn't utter another word to me."

I nodded. Winter was a good choice. Glancing at Kick, I asked, "You took care of Jen?"

Another fucking question I didn't want to ask. I'd left him to take care of her body when we headed out to meet with Ivy.

"Yeah, brother. What's the plan there?"

I knew what he was asking. *Where are we going to bury her?*

I scrubbed my face, feeling every fucking one of my thirty-nine years, and then some. It was unbelievable to me—and not fucking much was anymore—that out of the two women I'd ever loved, one of them was now dead because of the other one.

"Jen's got no one in her life. You find somewhere for her and let me know. I'll be there." I was all she'd had in the end. She might have driven me fucking crazy, but she didn't fucking deserve this shit.

Discussing this wound me tighter than I already was. The headache pounding against my skull felt like it could explode the fuck out of my head, and the muscles across my shoulders bunched to the point of pain. In an effort to get shit moving so we could stop fucking talking, I barked, "I want all family members moved to safety. When this shit goes down, I don't want any of them around. Nitro, you and Devil take care of that while Hyde and I work out a plan to get to Tony." *And while Kick finds a place to bury Jen.*

Fucking hell.

"And Marx?" Nitro asked. "What do you want done with him?"

Marx was of no use to us anymore. "Stay with him tonight and then get rid of him tomorrow."

Nitro nodded his understanding. "Will do."

After everyone filed out, leaving Hyde and me alone, I said, "Choose three men and send them to Melbourne. Get eyes on Tony. I want to know if Ivy's telling the truth."

He watched me with the same level of fierce intensity that churned deep inside my gut. He'd stood by me years ago and watched as I lost my shit after Ivy left, so he had to understand what it meant for me to even question Ivy's honesty in this. "And if she is?"

My hands clenched by my side. "Then we end this once and for all. I don't give a fuck how it affects ties we have to anyone else. We'll send the fucking word out—Storm doesn't tread carefully anymore. They wanna take us on? They'll pay the fucking price regardless of whose ass they're kissing."

Hyde's nostrils flared and he exhaled sharply. "Agreed."

It wouldn't have mattered if he hadn't, but it made shit easier that he did agree. "I'm gonna check in with Skye and Nik."

He hesitated for a beat before asking, "You gonna call Axe? Zane?"

"Yeah."

I would be calling in every fucking favour ever owed to me. And I'd drag every chapter of Storm into this war with us if I had to.

But first, my family needed me, and they were always my top priority. We hadn't lived through the shit we had for nothing. Our bonds had been forged in hell, and they were strong. Unbreakable. We may not have been blood, but I gave no shits about blood. The only thing I cared about was that they'd always taken my back. For that, I'd give them my life if I had to.

I left Hyde and headed to my room. Mine was the one at the far end of the hallway. While the clubhouse was large, not every member had a room. I'd had mine for eight years, and my sisters weren't strangers to it. I hated that they were dragged into my shit. Especially after everything we'd all been through as kids. And I really didn't fucking want that for Keith and Rebecca.

"So how long this time?" Skylar demanded the minute I stepped foot in the room. She sat in the middle of the bed with her books spread out around her, pen tapping impatiently on one of the books. Annika sat in the armchair in the corner of the room with Rebecca sprawled across her while Keith hunched over a colouring book on the floor, completely engrossed in what he was doing.

"Skye," Annika said in a low warning tone. Always the peacekeeper, she often tried to intervene in whatever Skylar and I had going on. It was pointless, though. Skye and I were both stubborn and usually refused to back down.

Skylar scowled. "No, Nik, I'm over this. It feels like it's just one thing after another with Storm at the moment. When is this madness going to end? I just want to be able to live my life without having to worry about all this shit."

"It'll be over soon," I started, but my phone rang, cutting me off.

"Oh, that'll be Axe probably," Skylar said, waving at my phone as I yanked it out of my back pocket. "I already called him and told him you'd kidnapped us."

"Jesus," Annika muttered, glaring at Skylar. "Why do you always do this?"

Skylar returned her glare. "Do what?"

Annika sighed, and I sensed her exhaustion. I wasn't sure if it was over the argument or life in general. She'd been through a lot lately—stuff I wouldn't blame her for being worn down over. "Bait him. It's like you want him to lose his shit at you."

Fuck. These two were in a mood with each other. Not unusual, but I wanted as little to do with it as possible.

I stabbed at my phone to answer it as I said to the girls, "I'll be back. Don't kill each other while I'm gone." And then to Axe, I said, "Skye filled you in?" I exited the room as my sisters went head-to-head.

My brother's deep voice rumbled through the phone. "She told me you had them holed up at the clubhouse, but she didn't tell me why. You need me, brother?"

"Yeah, I need you. And I need Zane, too." I caught him up with everything that had happened.

"Fuck, man, I've been waiting for Ivy to come back. Didn't

figure it would take her this long. You think she's spinning shit? We both know how unstable she can be."

I raked my fingers through my hair. "I need to have a conversation with her about it."

"But you don't want to get that close to her, do you?"

Axe knew me better than most and having grown up with Ivy and me, he knew her well, too. He knew how dysfunctional our relationship had been, so he understood my need to distance myself. "At this point, it doesn't matter what I want. I have to do this for the club."

He was silent for a beat before saying, "I'll get there as soon as I can. Just dealing with a situation here, but I should be done with that by tomorrow, the next day at the latest."

After he promised to catch Zane up with everything, we ended the call. I exhaled sharply as I contemplated what I had to do next.

Ivy.

I had to have that conversation with her.

Alone.

Fuck.

Too much could go wrong in this scenario, but I knew there was no way she'd tell me anything if we weren't alone.

14

King

Winter had Ivy in the room we kept free for members of other chapters who dropped in. When I entered the room, I found her sitting in the middle of the bed glaring at him. She diverted her attention to me as I moved closer to her. Cold eyes met mine, and her lips flattened. "Finally," she muttered.

Anger rolled off her, but it didn't diminish her beauty. Fuck, if anything, Ivy had grown more beautiful in the fifteen years since I'd seen her. The long dark hair, olive skin, curves, and ass I'd always been attracted to were all still there, but age had enhanced everything. It added to her appeal. A bad fucking thing for me when I was determined not to fall again.

I jerked my chin at Winter, indicating he should leave. When I had Ivy to myself, I dragged a chair next to the bed and sat. "Why now?" I demanded, keeping my eyes fixed firmly on her face so I could assess the truth of everything she said. Not even her body would distract me from this task.

Her gaze roamed over me as she sat in silence, not answering my question. She liked what she saw; that was clear in the heat flaring in her eyes. I allowed her silence, and when she met my eyes again, I lifted my brows questioningly.

"You've aged well," she said. "Is there a woman looking after that body of yours?"

"Ivy, I didn't come here for a catch-up. I want to know what the fuck's going on with your marriage, and why after fifteen years you're suddenly dragging me into it?"

Her nostrils flared. "Oh, so we can discuss *my* personal stuff but not yours. Have I got that right?"

I leant forward. I didn't want to, but the pull was too great. "The only personal shit I'm interested in is whether your husband is out for my blood. And I want more details on this attack you say is coming."

Before I realised what she was doing, she scooted to the edge of the bed. Our bodies were only inches apart. Reaching out, she ran a finger down the scar on my face. "I'll never forget the day I first saw this scar," she murmured. "We were just kids then."

I quickly moved my hand to pull hers from my face, but her reflexes were faster, and she grabbed hold of my hand and held it to my scar. Her touch blazed against my skin. It was too fucking much. "Ivy," I warned in a low dark tone. "Don't do this."

She brought her face closer to mine. Not close enough that our lips touched, but close enough to fuck with my head further. "You're so hard now, King. You always were, but not so much with me. I guess fucking around on me and kicking me out really did change things between us. But I'll never forget you as that eleven-year-old who shared his ice cream with me after I ate all mine and wanted more. That was the King I loved."

I ripped my hand away and stood as I shoved my chair back. My eyes bored into hers as I barked, "Tell me about your husband!"

Adrenaline pumped furiously through my veins while I fought to remain in control of this situation. Even after all this time apart, she still knew how to push my buttons. I didn't fucking need her bringing up our past. The best way to deal with it was to ignore it because she'd pounce the minute she saw a reaction to anything she said or did. God fucking help me, though, I was struggling to ignore her.

Her lips pursed together as she stared at me with eyes full of hatred. I couldn't be sure, but I thought I saw hurt flash through them first. "Tony hates you. He feels like he's competed with you for twelve years, and he's had enough, especially now I'm leaving him."

It was time to really push her. The sooner we got this over with, the better. "That's bullshit, Ivy. I don't fucking buy it."

She didn't flinch or react in any way. She simply said, "That's your choice, King, but I'm not lying to you. I hate to think what will happen to your club, though, if you choose not to believe me."

Interesting.

She didn't blink.

But still, I needed to push a little more to be sure. "Tell me, why would you come here and warn me when you hate me so much?"

Again, no reaction. "You might be a cheating asshole who can't keep his promises, but I'm loyal to a fault. Regardless of how *you* treated me back then, Nik and Skylar don't deserve whatever Tony has planned. I'll always look out for those girls. They were family to me."

Every instinct I had told me to walk the fuck out of the

room and come back later when I had my shit under control. At this point, I was warring with my belief of every word she uttered, and my gut instinct to never believe anyone until I verified facts myself.

In the end, my gut instinct won out. "Where's Tony now?"

"He's either at work or at home tonight, but don't go looking for him yet, King. You need to spend time making sure everyone here is safe. And you should take as many men with you when you go. He's got security everywhere." She wrapped her arms around her body, a look of concern on her face.

I stepped closer to where she sat on the bed and lifted her chin up to bring her eyes to mine. "You're worried about me now?" Things weren't adding up. One minute she was angry and seemed like she wanted to inflict hurt, the next, she was trying to keep me safe.

She pushed my hand away and stood. "I'm worried for the people who have put their trust in you. They're the ones I want to keep safe. God knows I understand the devastation that trusting you completely can end in."

~

"You believe her?" Hyde asked later that night.

I threw some whisky down my throat as I scanned the clubhouse bar where we sat. It was quiet; most of the members were getting their families to safety. "I don't fucking know, brother. The Ivy I used to know wouldn't fuck with me, but I don't know her anymore."

"Why would she make that shit up?"

That was the question I'd been rolling around in my head for hours. "Revenge. But fuck, fifteen years is a long time to wait for that, so it seems unlikely. If I believe that, though, I have to believe she's telling the truth."

"But your gut is telling you something else?"

I drank the rest of my whisky. "Yeah." I hated to admit that, because I wanted nothing more than to finally have an answer to who was screwing with my club. I also wanted to believe that Ivy wouldn't lie to me, but mistrust filled me.

"So we'll keep her here until we know more, then?"

I stood to leave. "Yeah."

Until then, I'd stay the fuck away from her. If I had any hope of getting my club through this alive, I needed to keep Ivy out of my sight.

～

Kree opened her front door when I knocked on it late that night, and shook her head at me. "King, it's nearly eleven thirty, which is when most normal people are either in bed or about to be. I know you like to drop in unannounced, but your visits are getting later and later."

I'd been keeping an eye on Kree since she'd come to work for the club as a bartender. Her cousin Zane who I'd known for over fourteen years, had asked me to watch over her while he dealt with her abusive ex in Brisbane. After the night I stopped by last Christmas to give her some cash when I knew she was struggling, I'd come by regularly. It was a fucking mystery to me why, but being around her calmed me. And I'd needed some fucking calming over the last few months.

Ignoring her speech, I entered her home. "You should know by now I'm not like normal people."

She closed the door and muttered, "Yeah, but I'm still holding out hope for a change."

I made my way to her kitchen and the cupboard that housed my bottle of rum. She never argued with me when I left it here. Kree seemed to know what to bother arguing over and what battles to avoid. Smart woman.

I met her gaze and held up the bottle. "You want one?"

Sighing, she nodded. "Yeah, I could do with one tonight."

I didn't like the sound of that. "What's going on?" I glanced around the kitchen and added, "Why aren't your candles lit?" Usually she had a fuckload of them blazing in all rooms. It concerned the hell out of me that she'd burn her house down one day, but it concerned me more that she'd deviated from doing something she always did.

"It's nothing for you to worry about. And"—she shrugged —"I just didn't feel like burning them tonight."

She may have been smart, which I liked, but she was also fucking stubborn and proud. This wasn't the time for that. "Spit it out, Kree, and don't leave anything out."

Irritation flared in her eyes. Taking the drink I offered her, she downed almost half of it before saying, "I like you, King, but man, you are difficult. Sometimes a woman just wants to handle her own shit."

I took a long swig of rum. If her argumentative side was coming out to play tonight, I was going to need it more than I already did. "And sometimes a woman needs to know when to let a man handle it."

Silence filled the room while we watched and waited for the other to make the next move.

Finally, she reached into one of the kitchen drawers and pulled out a folder filled with paperwork. Dumping it on the counter, she opened it and passed me the top document. "My husband is being an asshole. That's what's wrong."

After I read the letter from her husband's lawyer, I growled, "Your husband is being more than a fucking asshole, Kree. Why the fuck hasn't Zane dealt with him yet?"

Her husband, Don, was using the law to draw her out of hiding by applying for a parenting order. There was no way

Kree would agree to this, which meant she'd have to fight him. As far as I was concerned, Zane simply needed to put a fucking bullet in his head. That would solve her problem once and for all. We'd discussed this once, and he'd told me he did things differently to me. I'd let it go at the time, but if he couldn't fix this for her, I would.

"Zane sent me that letter because Don's lawyers sent it to him, not knowing where I am. He told me not to worry and that he's dealing with it. But that doesn't make this any easier. I know Don, and he has ways of finding people." Her voice cracked as she spoke, alerting me to how worried she was. This was unlike Kree who was usually strong and calm.

I placed the letter back in the folder and shoved the folder in the drawer. "I'm moving you and the kids to the clubhouse."

Her eyes widened. "What? No. The kids don't need any further disruptions to their routines, King. They've finally started making some friends in the street. I don't want to take them away from that. Not again."

"It's either that or you guys stay here and wait for Don to find you. And besides, we've got club shit going on that also means you need to be moved. I'm not taking any chances, Kree."

"So this is one of those situations that I need to let a man handle?"

I scrubbed my face. "Fuck, don't fucking argue with me. Not tonight."

Something I said or the tone I used caused her to soften. "When?"

I finished my drink. "Now. Pack a bag."

The softness I'd manage to stir in her disappeared, replaced with a scowl. "You test me, King, that's for bloody sure."

With that, she left me alone while she packed and woke

the kids. Fifteen minutes later, we were on our way to the clubhouse, Kree sitting next to me with her arms crossed, signalling her annoyance, and the kids sleepily whinging in the back. I paid no attention to any of it. Keeping people alive consumed my focus, and I would do whatever that took. Whoever was fucking with my club would never have the chance to hurt someone close to me again. I'd make fucking sure of that.

15

King

Ivy turning back up in my life was fucking with my head. Fifteen years without her by my side, yet it felt like only yesterday I sat back with a whore's mouth wrapped around my dick while killing the love Ivy had for me. But the love *I* had for her had never died, and that was proving to be a mindfuck I didn't have the time for. Not when I had club business to take care of.

Splashing water over my face in the clubhouse kitchen, I attempted to shake off the exhaustion that came from no sleep and trying like fuck to put regrets from years ago out of my head. They swam there, circling like hungry sharks desperate to feed on me, determined to dominate my attention.

Regret would choke the breath from me if I gave it space in my life, so I made a point not to. I didn't dwell on shit, and I sure as hell didn't spend time thinking about the bad decisions I'd made. But as much as I'd tried over the years, the regrets I carried over Ivy refused to ease up. I'd made promises to her and then I'd poured gasoline over them and lit the match myself.

The mindfuck of it all was that as much as I regretted how it went down, I still believed it was for the best. I was certain that if we'd continued on the path we were on, we would have destroyed each other. Our love may have been pure, but it was as fucked up and dysfunctional as it came.

I scrubbed a hand over my face and took a good look in the mirror. Thirty-nine years of hard living had etched itself into my skin, as had the exhaustion that staked its territory in my life. I was fucking tired of the battles I was fighting. That Storm was fighting. Shit had to get better soon; otherwise, what the hell was the point of it all?

Movement to my right caught my eye, and I turned to find Skylar entering the kitchen.

"You look like shit," she said, her voice groggy from what I guessed to be too little sleep. Moving to the fridge, she grabbed out the milk before reaching for a mug and the coffee. "You want a coffee?"

I rested against the counter. "You gonna slip some poison in it?" She'd spent last night pissed at me, so I found it surprising we were even having this conversation. Skylar could hold a grudge for longer than anyone else I knew.

Her eyes met mine. "Now why didn't I think of that?"

"Because deep down in that cranky soul of yours you do actually love me."

"Mmm, let's not get too crazy here, big brother. Love is a strong word."

I crossed my arms and narrowed my eyes at her. "Okay, what are you fishing for this morning?"

"What? I can't offer to make my brother a coffee without having a reason?"

"You refused to even look at me last night you were that pissed off. And now you're coming to me with a sense of fucking humour and an offer for coffee first thing in the morning before you've even fully woken up. I'm not buying it, Skye. What's going on? What do you want?"

Her shoulders sagged a little. "Fine," she muttered. "It's not so much what I want, but what I need. I've got a tutorial on today that I really have to attend, and I'm figuring you're going to try to block me from going."

Fuck.

I scrubbed my face. "I don't want you leaving the club-house. Can you get the notes from someone?"

She shook her head. "No, this isn't about the notes. It's about being involved in the discussion that'll be going on today. I really need to be a part of it." She hit me with the look that told me to expect a guilt trip to fall from her mouth next. "Besides, you're paying for this course so I'd expect you to want me to be there for something this important. I mean, I know you don't want me to fail."

Jesus, she knew how to push my buttons. She always had. "I'll find someone to take you." At the smile that snaked across her face, I added, "Two things, though. One, if I'm going to put you at risk like this, I hope like hell your grades are good at the end of the semester or we'll be having words. And two, this coffee you're about to make me better be the best fucking coffee you've ever made me." It was going to be a long fucking day while I worried about her safety.

Her smile morphed into a grin that screamed triumph. "Two things, King. One, when have you ever known me to make a shit cup of coffee? And two, my grades will make you fucking weep they are that good."

Without waiting for my response, she turned away to make coffee. I watched her in silence, remembering the day she'd agreed to go to university. She'd fought me on it for a long time, but I'd refused to back down. Skylar was smart, and I wanted her to have the best life she could, so it was a no-brainer for me that I pushed her to study. The day that Silver Hell cunt beat her up, I stepped in and forced her to get her shit together. Between partying almost every night and drinking far too fucking much, she was slowly pissing her life away. The beating seemed to knock some sense into her, and it had made my fucking year when she'd finally said yes to uni.

Annika wandered through the kitchen doorway, tiredness etched into her face, a yawn escaping her mouth. She rubbed her eyes and mumbled, "I need some of that coffee, Skye."

"Mummy!"

Rebecca screamed into the room so fast she ran smack into a cupboard before bursting into tears. I pulled her into my arms before her mother could and held her tightly while she buried her head into my neck, crying. Smoothing her hair, I attempted to distract her. "Did you read any of that book I gave you?"

Annika's eyes met mine and she mouthed, "Thanks," as she waited for Skylar to make her coffee.

Rebecca sobbed for another minute before lifting her head and slowly nodding. "I read some with Mummy last night."

"Is it a good book?"

She kept nodding. "Yes." Her face crumpled and more tears streamed down her face. "My arm really hurts, Uncle Zac. I think I broke it." Her body shuddered, indicating a flare in her anxiety. Rebecca was an anxious kid at the best of times, but in moments of stress, her levels could rise fast.

I held her to me and exited the room that had grown noisy. Carrying her to my office, I closed the door behind us to create some quiet. Sitting, I rested her on my lap and met her gaze while taking hold of her arm. "It takes a lot to break a bone. I doubt yours is, but I'll give it a good look, okay?"

She didn't seem convinced, but she agreed with a quick nod. Her bottom lip quivered, though, so I quickly inspected her arm. The sooner I could confirm there wasn't a break, the sooner I could get to work on calming her down.

Meeting her gaze again, I said, "Good news, it's not broken."

She wiggled in my lap, the look on her face telling me she remained unconvinced. "But it feels like it."

I nodded. "I know it does, and I know you're scared, but have I ever let you down?"

Exhaling a shaky breath, she shook her head. "No."

I gently rubbed my hand up and down her forearm. "Do you know what will make it feel better?"

Hope flickered in her eyes. She'd stopped crying, but I knew the tears weren't far away if her fear took over again. "What?"

In one swift movement, I stood, scooping her into my hold as I did. Heading back towards the kitchen, I said, "My chocolate milk."

The hope in her eyes turned to excitement, and I knew that promise had done the trick. She scrunched a handful of my shirt in her little hand and said, "With extra chocolate like you did last time?"

I met her smile with one of my own and nodded. "Yeah, with extra chocolate. But this is between us, okay?" I never kept anything from Annika, but I liked Rebecca to think I did because it drew her closer to me, and that was a place I always wanted her to be. Close as fuck so I could always keep her safe.

Her smile grew and she nodded enthusiastically while leaning in close and whispering, "I won't tell anyone. I promise."

I cleared everyone from the kitchen and made her a hot chocolate with extra white choc chips melted into it and plenty of chocolate powder sprinkled on top, all served in her favourite Winnie the Pooh mug I kept here for her. We sat together at the table while she drank it, and I ignored the text that sounded from my phone so I could give her my full attention.

Glancing towards where the sound came from, she asked, "Are you going to check your message?"

I shook my head. "No, I'm busy."

Her forehead wrinkled as she frowned. "No you're not. You're not doing anything."

I leaned toward her. "I'm spending time with you, which means I'm very busy."

"But the message might be important."

I shifted the lock of hair that had fallen across her face and hooked it behind her ear. "There isn't any message to check that could be more important than hanging out with you. When we're done here, I'll check it, but until then, I don't want you to worry about that message again. You got it?"

Nodding, she blasted me with a smile. "Got it!"

"Good. Now, I want you to tell me all about the trampolining party you guys went to the other day."

"I already told you about it, silly!"

"I know, but I wanna hear all about it again."

She looked at me like I was the silliest person on the planet before sighing. "Okayyy, but you're probably gonna get bored."

I settled back in my seat and crossed my arms. "Never." I jerked my chin at her. "Now start talking, little miss."

She giggled. I didn't call her that very often, but I knew she liked it when I did, so I reserved it for when I was working hard to take her mind off something. It did the trick this morning. Ten minutes later, we were laughing over the funny stuff that happened to her at the party, her sore arm and anxiety completely forgotten.

This was the shit I lived for and was the reason why I'd bury Tony Romano for even thinking about fucking with my family and my club.

~

I leant back in my chair and rubbed my temples. A headache pounded against my skull, interfering with my ability to think. The painkillers I'd taken after finishing my conversation with Rebecca had started to kick in, but still, the headache lived and breathed pain that I didn't fucking need. Looking up at Hyde, I asked, "Where are we at with Tony?"

"Our guys are in Melbourne but are yet to get eyes on him. His men are busy, but he's nowhere to be seen."

"I'll talk to Ivy again. See if she'll share more information."

Hyde pressed his lips together, concern clear in his eyes. "You want me to do that? Might be safer."

I grunted. "For me or for Ivy?"

"Yeah, not fucking sure at this point."

I contemplated it but decided we had more of a shot at Ivy talking to me than anyone else. "I'll do it. You keep on top of our guys in Melbourne and let me know if they find him. And call Scott Cole. Tell him to get his men ready. I have a feeling we're gonna need them on this."

He nodded. "Will do."

Turning my attention to Devil, I said, "I need you with Skylar today. She's got a uni class on that she can't miss, so I need you to make sure she's safe there."

"I'm on it," he agreed.

I rubbed my temples some more. "And don't fucking let

her talk you into anything other than that, Devil. My sister has a knack for asking for the fucking moon and getting it."

His lips twitched. "You forget I've played a round of that with Skylar, King. She's not getting anything out of me today."

"Good." I pushed my chair back and stood. "Fucking hell, is the fucking air conditioning working?" I felt like I was burning from the inside out.

Nitro frowned. "You okay, brother?"

"Yeah, just fucking hot. Get someone to look at the air con," I barked, irritated as fuck. Between the heat and my headache, I could hardly keep a straight fucking thought.

"King, it's not fucking hot today. It's raining and cold. You sure you're not running a fever?" Devil said.

I scowled at him. "I'm fine." Turning to Nitro, I said, "You good to deal with Marx this morning?"

He nodded. "Yeah. I'll leave in about twenty to take care of that."

"You want someone with you?"

"No, I've got it covered."

"Good." I didn't want to pull anyone off what they were already doing.

Hyde opened the office door. "Text me if you need me."

The three of them left me alone with my headache and my thoughts. If I knew anything, it was that my headache was going to get worse before it got better. This fucked-up situation we were in pretty much guaranteed that.

"She's not eating much," Winter advised me an hour and a half later when I met him outside the room we had Ivy in. I intended to keep her there until I'd dealt with her husband.

"Keep an eye on that and let me know if she still refuses food later."

I entered the room to find her sitting on the bed staring out the window. Her back was to me, but it seemed she could still sense my presence as easily as she could fifteen years ago.

"What do you want now, King?" The flat tone of her voice didn't surprise me. Ivy hated being confined in small spaces. It stemmed from the horrific childhood she had when her biological parents sold her for weekends at a time to men who locked her up and abused her.

"Why aren't you eating?"

She remained silent and still for a few moments, simply staring out the window. Then she turned slowly and found my gaze. "Why do you care?"

"Just answer the question."

Her eyes narrowed at me. "No."

"No?"

She stood and came to me, stopping a couple of feet away. "I'm not answering your question until you answer mine. Why do you care whether I eat or not?"

I scrubbed my face. "Fuck, Ivy, you're still as fucking argumentative as you were years ago."

"And you're still an asshole."

"I never tried to change. Now tell me why you aren't eating. Are you just trying to be a pain in my ass or are you not feeling well?"

"Did you ever consider that maybe I'm just not hungry? That you kidnapping and locking me up has killed my appetite."

This fucking conversation was the last thing I had patience for. I decided to cut to the chase. "Where's Tony?"

My question caught her off guard, and she frowned. "What do you mean?"

I exhaled harshly. "I mean, where the fuck is he? He's not anywhere he should be."

Still frowning, she said, "As far as I know, he should be either at home or at work."

She appeared to be telling the truth, but my gut twisted with doubt over her honesty again. If she were anyone else, I'd push her a lot fucking harder.

I warred with myself over which path to take to get the information I needed. In the end, I went with my gut.

Gripping her neck, I walked her to the wall and held her against it, ignoring the shock in her eyes. "It's been a long time for us, Ivy, since we've spent any time together, and I can't fucking tell anymore if you're being honest with me or if you're lying through your teeth." I gripped her harder. "What I can't figure out is *why* you'd lie to me." Pressing myself against her, I continued to squeeze her neck and bent my mouth to her ear. "Are you lying to me?"

Her fingers clawed at my hand, trying to pull it from her neck. Her breaths weren't restricted, but my grip was painful enough to get her full attention and understanding that I wasn't fucking around here. When I eased the pressure a fraction, she coughed and croaked out, "I'm not fucking lying to you! Let me go!"

I kept hold of her but eased the pressure a little more so she could speak without coughing. "Not until I know for sure what the fuck is going on."

Her eyes burned with hate as she spat, "You wanna know what the fuck is going on here, King?"

"What?"

"Your fucked-up kink is what's going on. Are you trying to get off while interrogating me?" When I didn't respond straight away, she kept pushing. *Taunting.* "You're just like your daddy. Tell me, King, have you succumbed fully yet?

Have you turned into the kind of man your daddy would have been proud of?"

I clenched my jaw as her questions infected the air around us. What Ivy didn't know was that since her, I'd embraced both the darkness his genes had given me, and my kink. I never took it to the extremes my father had, but I was brutal when it came to sex. Women knew what to expect—I never hid my desires—and if they didn't want the shit I wanted, I never went back for more.

I'd accepted my needs a long fucking time ago, and chose to own my depravity rather than fight it. This was a button she could no longer push.

With one last squeeze of her neck, I let her go. "That's not gonna work today, Ivy. I'm not the man you once knew. Not anymore."

She either didn't know anything further about Tony's whereabouts or she wasn't going to share it with me. There was no point continuing down this path. I'd find another way to get this information.

As I walked towards the door, she called out, "So that's it, King? You come charging in here demanding answers and assaulting me, and then you just leave without another word? Without getting what you want?"

I glanced back at her. She appeared agitated that I was walking away. It reminded me of how shit used to go down between us. Me trying like fuck to avoid a fight, her throwing shit in my face, drawing the fight out of me. And here we were, still doing that same fucking dance.

Stalking back to her, I grabbed her throat again, pissed off at the attitude blazing from her. She might not have been able to provoke me before, but she sure as fuck had now. Playing her games wasn't something I ever enjoyed doing. "Let's get one thing straight—*I* ask the questions, you provide the answers. End of fucking story. And when I'm done with your husband, you'll go back to your life and I'll go back to mine." I shoved my face closer to hers. *"End of fucking story."*

The only fucking way to get through this was to throw that wall up between us that should never have been pulled down in the first place.

I exited the room and didn't stop moving until I'd left the building. Wild energy engulfed me. Energy I didn't know what the fuck to do with. My chest felt like it would explode and my fists craved violence. The fucking worst of it was that I couldn't figure out my thoughts. They ran through my head so damn fast I could hardly latch onto them, and when I did, they conflicted with each other. This situation was stirring up a lot of shit from the past—shit I'd buried so fucking deep that I never wanted to confront again.

Fuck.

My phone rang, dragging me from my hell.

Devil's name flashed across the screen. I swiped to answer it and barked, "Yeah?"

I listened to what he had to say as parts of my body I didn't even fucking know existed knotted into balls of tension. When he finished, I roared, "Motherfucker! I'll be there soon."

"What's wrong?" Annika asked, joining me outside.

I shoved my phone in my pocket and tried like fuck to contain my anger. It was a pointless fucking exercise, though, because nothing right now would do that. "Devil and Skylar have been in a crash. Some asshole rammed his car into them. Devil's okay, but Skylar's not."

Her eyes widened with worry. "Oh God, what, King? How bad is she?"

"Devil's not sure, but she's conscious and still being a smartass, so my guess is it's not life-threatening. But she's in a lot of pain and Devil is pretty sure she's got broken bones."

I raked my fingers through my hair as I forced some of the breath I'd been holding out. "I'm heading to the hospital now. Do me a favour and stay here. I don't need anyone else to be worrying about today, okay?"

She nodded. "Let me know how she is as soon as you know."

16

King

"Jesus fucking Christ, Devil!" I roared as I took in Skylar's injuries. I'd arrived at the hospital ten minutes ago and had almost lost my fucking mind in the time it took me to get from the front door to where Skylar was in the emergency room. My heart pumped furiously as anger surged through my veins. Tony Romano would fucking pay for this.

"King! It wasn't his fault." Skylar tried to move, but her injuries caused her grief, and all she managed to do was scrunch her face in pain.

I moved closer to the bed, which only brought her wounds into sharper focus, causing another wave of fury to fill me. Swelling and bruises covered her face, neck, and arms, but it was what I couldn't see that worried me the most.

Meeting Devil's gaze, I demanded, "What have the doctors said? How bad is this?"

Regret blazed from his eyes. "Fuck, man, I'm fucking sorry this happened."

Every muscle in my body tensed with the anger I couldn't control. "I didn't ask for a fucking apology, Devil. I asked what the doctors have said." I wanted to fucking punch him. Rationally, I knew it wasn't his fault, but he was all I had to direct my emotions at. Hell, I wanted to do more than punch him; I wanted to rip his fucking head from his body and beat the living shit out of him. But I didn't. I held my shit together and waited. For what, I wasn't sure. All I knew was that I would tear the world apart in order to inflict hurt on those who did this to her.

Skylar didn't give Devil a chance to reply. She fixed a filthy glare on me and said, "I'm right here, and I'm capable of answering your questions. They think my hip is fractured. They're going to do an X-ray to confirm and then I may need surgery. Other than that, they've given me some good drugs, and I'm fine."

I ran my eyes over the black and blue marks on her skin. "You're not fucking fine, Skye. You look like you've been through ten rounds with Rocky." I had to give it to her, though—my sister was a fighter.

"Don't exaggerate this, King. I mean, aren't you the one who taught me to suck shit up and not be a pussy?"

Ignoring her, I concentrated my attention on Devil. "What the hell happened?"

I took in Devil's only injury—a gash on his forehead— as he shoved his fingers through his hair and blew out a long breath. "I took the backstreets like we planned, but I don't know, somehow they followed us. We were on Cyprus heading to Main Street when they rammed us."

"You recognise them or the van?"

"I've never seen the van before, and the windows were

dark, so I couldn't see who it was. And they took off fast afterwards."

"Fucking hell," I muttered. "As if we don't have enough shit to deal with."

"You want me to get a start on trying to figure out who the hell was responsible for this?"

"Make some calls and get it in motion, but I don't want you leaving this hospital. I want your eyes on Skylar at all times." When his phone rang, I jerked my chin at the door. "Go take that. I'm staying for a bit."

After he'd left us, Skylar said, "Don't blame him, King," before bursting into tears.

I didn't need any more reasons to hate the people who did this to her, but I sure as fuck had another one now. My sister didn't cry easily, so I knew by her tears just how shaken she was. And that concerned me because it meant Skylar's anxiety could flare over this.

Touching her arm gently, I said, "I don't."

She glanced down at my hand on her and then looked back up at me, nodding. Her face crumpled as she tried to stop crying.

My skin felt like it could rip apart at any moment. There were too many fucking emotions thrashing around inside me. Emotions that I didn't know what the fuck to do with. Add to that the fact I wanted to pull Skylar into my arms to console her but I couldn't because fuck knew where she was hurt, and it was all fast becoming too much to deal with.

I removed my hand from her arm and clenched my fists by my side while I attempted to get my breathing and my thoughts under control. Easier said than done. I'd never been good at getting myself under control. With each passing second, I felt it slip further away.

Skylar's eyes widened in understanding. She'd seen me

here before. "King, don't.... Everything's gonna be fine. Just calm down, okay?"

I sucked in a deep breath before forcing it back out.

Everything was *not* going to be okay.

Not until I found these people and put them ten fucking feet under.

Skylar reached for my hand and squeezed it. "King, sit down and talk to me. Please."

It was the way she half whispered her request that did it. She'd never coped well when I lost control of myself. After I'd ended things with Ivy years ago, I'd raised her by myself for three years before Jen came into the picture. I'd had to get my shit together fast in those three years while Skylar and I figured out how to live together. One of the most important things I'd learnt was that she needed me in as calm a state as I could get myself. She was one of the only people who could bring me round fast when my rage threatened to take over.

I did as she requested and pulled up a chair. The emotions threatening to cage me in faded to the point where I could breathe again. They didn't completely disappear, though, and that was a good thing. I needed that shit to keep me focused on my goal.

Before we could say anything further, a nurse came in and told Skylar they were about to take her for an X-ray. After the nurse left, Skylar watched me for a few moments, seemingly assessing my state of mind. Finally, she said, "Devil told me Ivy's back."

I knew what she was asking without her having to say the words.

I nodded. "Yeah." I may have known she was looking for a reassurance that everything was okay, but I didn't have it to give her, so I said nothing else.

"Why?" Her question came out harshly. Skylar didn't

know why Ivy and I had broken up, so she'd always held a grudge against her, even though I'd told her not to. Turned out my sister's loyalty ran as deep as mine, even if I did manage to piss her off every chance I got.

"Skye," I said, my tone holding a warning. "Don't go there."

"Why not? That bitch fucked you up years ago, and I don't want her coming back to stick the knife in any further. Why are you even letting her stay at the clubhouse? You should have told her to go back to where she came from."

I exhaled a long breath and dropped my head into my hands so I could massage my temples that were slowly being massacred by a headache. Meeting her gaze again, I said, "She didn't fuck me up. I fucked her up. And I've been telling you that for years, so just drop it."

The wild, angry energy we shared took hold of her and she sat up, the anger grooved into her face. The swift movement delivered pain to her body, though, and she winced slightly before lashing out. "I get it—you're a bastard. But, King, anyone who gets involved with you knows that. They know what they're getting themselves into, and Ivy knew for a long time who you were. Stop blaming yourself for that breakup. And for the love of God, walk away from her now. Don't go back down that path. I'm going to be really fucking pissed at you if you do."

I leant forward, closer to her. "I'm not going back, Skye. Stop worrying about me and concentrate on yourself."

"Just let someone worry about you for once, okay?"

Her question gave me a moment of pause. It wasn't often she expressed herself this way towards me. Usually, we spent most of our time arguing. Her question cut through the tension between us, and I smiled. "You wanna worry about me, Skye?"

She rolled her eyes and lay back down. "Don't be an ass. You might annoy the hell out of me most of the time, but that doesn't mean I don't love you. I always worry about you. You give a girl a lot of fucking reasons to do that, so maybe just this once you could stop with the dumb behaviour and give me some peace and quiet."

I leant back in the chair and crossed my arms. "I'll make a deal with you. I won't pursue Ivy if you stop giving me hell about wanting you at the clubhouse."

She groaned. "Worst deal, but I'll take it."

"Thank fuck," I muttered.

My phone rang, interrupting us, just as Devil stepped back in the room. It was Hyde. "Any news?" I asked, phone to my ear, eyes on Devil. I nodded at him, indicating I was over my shit and that we were good. He returned my nod and sat down.

"One of Romano's guys just turned up," Hyde said. "Says he's got information to share with us."

I sat up straight. "I'll head back now. Stick him in a room and wait for me."

"Will do."

We ended the call, and I stood to leave, motioning to Devil to join me outside Skylar's cubicle. After I'd filled him in on the new developments, I made my way outside to my bike. I was fucking wired to have this chat with Romano's guy. I didn't trust it, though. For all I knew, he'd been sent by Ivy's husband to screw with us some more. If that was the case, I'd find a way to use him. By the time I was through with him, he'd fucking agree to do anything I asked.

Hyde watched me walk the length of the clubhouse hallway

to the office. He looked as worn out as I felt. This shit was taking its toll on all of us. Over a year of fighting off enemies would do that to anyone.

When I reached him, he said, "I've put him in a room with Kick."

"Good."

"Let's see if I can rattle him."

Hyde nodded again. "Also, Axe just arrived."

"Good. Get him in that room with me. Between the two of us, we'll break this motherfucker if there's any breaking to be done."

Kick's eyes met mine when I entered the room where he waited with the guy. He then turned to Tony's man who sat across from him and said, "You ever met King? If there's anything you want to change about your story, I'd do it now before he gets started on you."

The guy looked between us. The minute his gaze landed on me, he pushed his chair back hastily and stood, moving backwards fast until he hit the wall. Hands raised, he yelled, "Dude, I'm telling the truth!"

I stalked to him, not slowing to give him time to think about strategy or any of that shit. My body language screamed out my mood for anyone to read clearly. If it didn't convince him I wasn't fucking around, my next move would.

"You sure about that, asshole?" I asked, pointing my gun at him.

He nodded frantically, gulping for air as he tried to reassure me. "Yes!"

I aimed my gun at his leg and fired. "I don't fucking believe you!" As the guy screamed his denials while staring with disbelief at his bleeding leg, I barked, "Shut the *fuck* up and start telling me the truth!"

I yanked him back to the chair and shoved him down in it at the same time my brother joined us.

"I see you started without me," Axe said, deathly calm and steady as fuck. Axe could have been in the middle of a fucking ambush and he'd still be as calm as this. That's what years in the military did to a man.

I, on the other hand, was feeling as far from calm and steady as could be. Every fibre of my being blazed with the need for retribution and blood. For all I fucking cared, the guy sitting in this chair would pay for the sins of Ivy's husband unless he gave me something. I didn't give a fuck whose blood I got on my hands so long as at the end of all this, I had Tony Romano's.

Axe and I ignored the shit spewing out of the guy's mouth while he protested his innocence and bitched about the fact I shot him. We circled him, and as Axe slowly rolled up the sleeves of his white button-down shirt, I said, "You got all fancy for me, Axe. But white? For this?"

He kept his eyes trained on the guy while he answered me. "Had a work thing I had to take care of before coming here. Required something a little better than what I would have preferred to wear for this. Although, you didn't tell me we'd be doing *this* today. I may have chosen black if I'd known."

I jerked my chin at the guy in the chair, who divided his attention between Axe and me, his eyes and body language growing increasingly fearful. *Exactly how they should be.* "He just turned up here an hour ago, brother. Says he no longer works for Romano and that he has information he wants to give us." I stopped circling him and slammed my hands down on the table, staring the guy dead in the eyes. "But I'm not fucking buying it. And that's what you and I are gonna figure out now. Whether the shit coming out of his mouth is worth another bullet or not."

The guy yelled at me, "I'm not screwing with you, man!"

Axe looked at him. "What's your name?"

"Brant." He swung his head around to face Axe. "You've gotta believe me. What do you need from me to know I'm not fucking with you? I'll tell you anything you want!"

Axe considered that for a moment. It was part of his interrogation tactic. Where I went in like a bull-at-a-gate, he never lost control of a situation. It was fucking killing me not to slam this guy back up against the wall and shoot his other fucking leg, but I knew that between us, Axe and I would get the result we needed. I just had to let Axe do his thing and wait my turn, because eventually, it would come. Axe had to get the guy there first, though.

"How long have you worked for Romano, Brant?" Axe asked, moving behind him.

"Seven years."

"And now you're turning on him? Seven years is a long stretch of loyalty for you to throw out the window."

Brant's face twisted into a scowl. "If you worked for Tony Romano, you'd understand."

"Ah, but I don't, so enlighten me. Tell me why you're betraying him now." Axe settled his ass on the edge of the table and crossed his arms like he was readying himself to listen to a long story.

"When you first go to work for Tony, he makes you feel like you're part of his family. He invites you to his home for parties, he gives you expensive gifts, he treats your family like his and looks out for them. It lowers your fucking defences until the day he has you right where he wants you, fully at his mercy. After that, he forces you to do things you wouldn't wish upon your worst enemy, and he threatens your family if you don't do these things."

Axe stared at Brant like he was bored. "So?"

"*So*? I'm showing you why anyone would want out of the Romano empire."

Axe leaned his face close to Brant's. "No, what you're describing to me is what other men would consider a picnic in the fucking park, Brant. You're not showing me anything I don't already know about working for men like Romano. What I *don't* need from you is a fucking sob story about why you want out." His voice grew deeper, darker. "Tell me why you'd come here and chance King riddling your body with bullets after he gets the rest of his anger out in other ways. Because I'm telling you that if you don't, you're going to wish you'd stayed at that fucking picnic you had going with Romano."

My breathing slowed as I waited to hear Brant's next words. I focused every sense on deciphering his body language, tone, and what he said in my effort to figure out the truth of him. And all the while, my finger stayed glued to the trigger of my gun because if I decided I didn't like what he had to say, that gun would be in his face before he could draw another breath.

Brant looked up at Axe and swallowed hard. He took his time forming his words before finally saying, "For Ivy."

My mind exploded with questions, and I was unable to hold myself back any longer. Throwing our usual plan of attack out the window, I pressed my gun to Brant's temple. "Keep fucking talking, motherfucker, and don't hold any-fucking-thing back. The minute you say something I know to be incorrect, you'll have a bullet in your skull."

His shoulders bunched more than they already had, and his hands balled. *Good.* He tripped over his words trying to get them out. "Ivy has always been good to me. Always. And he never appreciated her. I've lost count of the number of times I've turned up to their house and found her beaten up. I tried to convince her to leave, but every time she tried, he found her, dragging her home kicking and screaming."

When he stopped talking, Axe said, "Go on. I feel like you're just getting to the good bit."

Brant glanced up at me. "When she told me your history and that she'd heard what Tony had planned for you, I encouraged her to bring that information to you, hoping you'd take her in and keep her safe from him. She wasn't sure you would, not after the way things ended between the two of you. I figured you would, though, because of the way she said you'd always looked out for her, right from when you were kids. I've been waiting to hear from her, but I never did. And then Tony was raided by the cops and went into hiding and I—"

"When was this?" I barked. *And why the fuck didn't Bronze know?*

"Two days ago." His shoulders sagged a little. "Fuck, tell me you have Ivy. That's all I care about, that she's safe. I'd never forgive myself if Tony had another chance to hurt her for something I encouraged her to do."

Brant knew my history with Ivy, which led me to believe him. Ivy had never been the kind of person to share personal shit with people, so for her to open up to him meant she trusted him.

I was the worst kind of asshole. I'd let all the bullshit I carried with me after decades of dealing with the scum of this world affect the way I treated one of the only women I'd ever loved. Ivy had come to me in good faith, and I'd taken that faith and shit all over it. Worse, I'd been a bastard and locked her up.

Fuck.

I was halfway out the door when I looked at Kick. "Find out everything he knows and bring it to me. And don't let him out of your sight. We'll keep him here until I'm sure we don't need him anymore."

Pulling out my phone, I hit Bronze's number, and when

he answered a moment later, I said, "One of Tony's men turned up at the clubhouse today. Says Tony was raided two days ago. Why the fuck don't I know about this?"

"Fuck," he muttered. "Give me half an hour."

"I don't have half a fucking hour, Bronze. Get it for me now!"

Hyde exited the office and came my way, fury etched into his face, as Bronze said, "Half an hour, King, and you'll say yes because there's something else you need to deal with right now that I'm just about to fucking tell you."

I had the distinct feeling that whatever Bronze was about to tell me, Hyde was, too. "What?" I demanded.

"Nitro and Marx have been arrested."

Looking around the room at church five hours later, I noted the grim expressions on everyone's face. *Fuck*. Shit was going south at a great rate of fucking knots, and I was experiencing something I never had—concern that the situation was spiralling into a clusterfuck I couldn't manage. There were too many fucking balls in the air, and I only had two fucking hands.

I directed my attention to Kick. "Before we get into this, have you found somewhere for Jen?"

He leant forward to rest his elbows on the table and nodded. "Yeah. Just waiting on your word for when it happens."

"Tomorrow afternoon." Ignoring the churn in my gut—the fucking guilt over Jen that never left—I turned to Hyde. "Tatum's coming in soon. You and I are going to nail her down with a plan of attack. And then we're gonna figure out how to deal with Marx."

He nodded. "Also, Ghost made contact with me. He wants to see you."

"I don't have time. You go. Take Kick with you." Ghost was one of the last fucking people I wanted to deal with.

"No, he said he's got something to share and that he'll only share it with you."

I rubbed the back of my neck and stretched it as another headache clamped down over my skull. "Jesus fucking Christ, does it never end with that motherfucker?" I exhaled hard. "Okay, you and I will take care of that tomorrow." I'd have to move shit around to make it happen, but the sooner I sorted him out, the better.

Looking around the room at everyone again, I said, "Tony Romano has disappeared. The latest info I have is that the cops raided his warehouse two days ago, but Tony was already gone. Bronze is digging up more info on that, but this is all we know for now. We need to find him fast, so keep your ear to the ground and report any little thing back to me that you hear, even if you think it means nothing. Keep your families safe until we've dealt with him, and don't trust anyone outside of the club. It seems Tony still has men doing his dirty work while he's laying low, and I don't want a repeat of what happened this morning with Devil. As far as what's happening with Nitro, Tatum is working to get him out, but Marx has talked. If you have anyone on the inside who we can use, come to me with it. We're working all angles, and I'll consider anything. And when I say anything, I fucking mean *anything*. I don't give a fuck who it affects. I want Marx dealt with so he never becomes a problem again."

After the meeting ended, I headed towards the front of the clubhouse, looking for Tatum. Unfortunately, I didn't find her. Instead, I found Detective fucking Ryland.

"We need to take a walk," he said, a smug look on his face and swagger to match.

Hitting him with a filthy scowl, I said, "I can assure you, Ryland, you're the last person I need to take a walk with."

His eyebrow arched. "You want your men to hear what I have to say to you?"

Could the motherfucker be any more of a prick? "I don't keep fucking secrets from my club. Spit out whatever the fuck you came here for and then leave."

"Righto then. As you're aware, I'm talking with Marx about the activities of your club. On top of that, I have other sources I've been having conversations with, and I'm piecing together the crimes you and your club have committed over the last decade and a half."

The headache that hit during church intensified, and the violent impulses I constantly battled consumed me. It took every ounce of restraint not to flatten him. Pulling out a smoke, I lit it and inhaled deeply while counting to ten. When I knew I'd pulled myself together enough not to tell him to go fuck himself, I said, "You're telling me this because?"

That smug look returned to his face, pissing me the fuck off. "Because I want you to know it's only a matter of time before I have everything I need to lock you up for the rest of your life. And after I do that, I'm taking your club down with you. Be ready."

With that, he left through the front door of the clubhouse while I watched him go, mentally filing through every option I had to sort him out.

As he exited, Tatum entered, shooting him a look that expressed her hatred of him. She and I had come a long way since the day I'd told Nitro to deal with her. His hesitation in doing what I'd asked had coloured my view of her, as had her tendency to express her thoughts of me, but I'd slowly come around to appreciating what she offered the club.

"What did he want?" she demanded. *Good.* She'd need that fight to help us get Nitro out.

"To tell me he's gunning for me and the club."

Her lips flattened. "Like you didn't already know that."

"Yes." As much as he angered me, though, his actions today provided me with information that would help us figure out how best to work against him. "It seems he's a little too invested in this, which will work well for us."

She nodded slowly, a thoughtful expression crossing her face. "True. At some point he'll cross a line."

I smiled for the first time today. "And you and I will be ready for him when he does that."

"You and I?"

"I want you to liaise with Bronze and keep on top of everything we know about Ryland. Do some digging yourself. Find out his weaknesses, his strengths, all about his family, everything you can. Figure out a way we can use the law against him, especially when he crosses that line."

"I'm surprised, King. I assumed you'd just remove him from the equation."

"I plan to. But not before I figure out what he knows, who told him, and who else knows. I'll need an in for all that, and he's going to provide it himself. Your brain is going to work out the how. But first, I take it you're up to speed on Nitro and Marx?"

"Yeah, and I've got some recommendations for you as to who to hire now that this has escalated. We need to get them in to see Nitro as soon as possible." The expression on her face turned more determined than I'd ever seen it as she added, "And I hope you've got some ideas as to how to stop Marx from talking again, because this is some shit you guys are in. I'll be fucked if my man is going down, so if you don't have a plan, I'm calling Billy in to help me with it."

Nitro had done well with her. She had exactly the right

amount of grit needed to survive club life. Jerking my chin towards my office, I said, "Join me and Hyde. We're going over all this now." Involving an old lady in club business wasn't something I'd ever done, but this situation wasn't like any we'd ever been in, so I was running on my gut and right now it was telling me to use Tatum for all she was fucking worth.

17

Lily

"I'm just saying that maybe you want to consider a one-night stand or something. You're not getting any younger, and at the rate you're going, I'm concerned your vagina will forget what to do when you finally decide to let a man in again."

I ignored my mother while continuing to lay the dining table. Acknowledging her, and continuing the conversation, would only encourage her to give me more unwanted advice.

"Lily, did you hear what I said?"

Placing the last set of cutlery down on the table, I looked up at her. "Yes, I heard you, but my vagina has special memory powers so you can take it off your long list of things to worry about." Honestly, the list she had was longer than my list of shit I'd like to do to my ex-husband before he died. And that was saying something, because *that* list was long and I was adding to it daily.

She twirled out of the dining room into my kitchen, her

long floral, boho skirt flaring. "Darling, I'm trying to be serious here. I've watched you navigate this single world for three years, which was fine because you were actually dating, but this celibate thing you're experimenting with is disconcerting."

My mother trying to have a serious conversation while twirling around the place was a daily occurrence in my life. I loved her dearly, but man, she was hard work sometimes. A patchwork of mixed and often conflicting traits, thoughts, feelings, likes and dislikes, Hannah Bennett was anything but dull. She often said the same about me, though, so I took great comfort in the knowledge I was just as much hard work for her.

I followed her into my tiny kitchen so I could grab the eggs and bacon I'd cooked for breakfast. "I'm thinking of extending my celibacy just to annoy the fuck out of you."

Her lips flattened and she shook her head at me. "Six months is long enough." She gathered the juice and coffee pot and took them into the dining room while continuing on. "I could set that dating profile I made for you to public. Mmm, maybe I will. You'll have a list of suitors by the end of the day."

I joined her and placed the food on the table while hitting her with a stern expression. "Don't you dare. And who says suitors anymore?" *And whose mother even kept track of their daughter's sex life like this?*

A smile lit her face. My mother was a beautiful woman, but when she smiled, she glowed. And she looked all of forty-five rather than the fifty-five she was. "I could call them beaus if you'd prefer."

And she would, if only to exasperate me. She liked to use flowery language and big words and long freaking sentences because she knew it irritated me. I was all about getting to the point and getting there fast.

Turning to face the lounge room, I called out, "Kids! Breakfast is ready."

Mum's lips flattened again. "Really, Lily, must you always yell?"

It's going to be a long day.

It was only 7:00 a.m. and I'd already dealt with a clogged shower drain, a cat that had clawed her way through the screen on my back door, and the cranky old man who lived next door and who always wanted to talk to me about my children at six in the morning.

I took a deep breath before saying, "I like to use the beautiful voice you gave me."

She always liked it when I engaged in positive self-talk. I mean, it wasn't that I didn't believe it, but I wasn't convinced today was gonna be a day for extreme positivity. Some days you just had to get through. They couldn't all be days of profound thoughts and actions, could they? Today was possibly gonna be a survive-rather-than-thrive kinda day.

The sounds of my children running through the house filled my ears. I counted to three in my head, knowing it would only take my mother that long to say what she always said.

"Children, the food isn't going anywhere. You don't need to run through the house."

Yep, without fail. She'd said it to my sister and me while we were growing up, too. You had to wonder if she ever got sick of saying it.

The whirlwind that was my children filled the dining room, and I watched as the three of them scrambled for their breakfast before they'd hardly taken a seat. Even Robbie, which was odd. He was my eight-year-old nerd who loved to read more than eat, but this morning he was all about the food, too.

I frowned at him. "Are you okay, baby?"

Zara stopped filling her plate for a moment and looked up at me. "He's on a mission to get back to his iPad."

I didn't have to ask him why. Robbie was currently obsessed with a YouTube science show, and they'd just released their latest episode.

Smiling, I said, "Ah, I get it."

Mum sat down and threw in her two cents. "Whatever is on that iPad can wait. We're enjoying our breakfast together this morning."

God.

Help.

Me.

She was in a mood for all her old-school ways this morning, and I was *far* from being in the kind of mood to just let her be. Usually I simply ignored her, but then again, she didn't usually start the day with a lecture on opening my vagina up for anyone who wanted in.

I sat next to my oldest daughter, Holly, who shot me a sympathetic look, and said, "Mum, we always have our breakfast together."

"Yes, but you always just let the kids leave the table whenever they want. I don't get to have breakfast with you very often, and for once, I'd just like everyone to take their time so we can catch up."

I tried not to laugh. And I also made a mental note to say no next time she asked if she could sleep over. I mean, my mother lived five freaking minutes away from us, yet she was acting like she lived in another state and hardly ever saw us.

"You know my thoughts on this. Please don't push me to defend them," I said. She and I often argued over the way I raised my kids. I didn't rule with an iron fist, and she would have preferred a little more of that style.

She finished filling her plate with food and stopped for a moment. "I'm not asking you to defend them. I'm simply asking for some time with my grandchildren. Is that too much to ask?"

If she was going to be so intent on being this dramatic, I was going to need a smoke.

Standing, I muttered, "I'll be back in a minute."

Holly glanced at me, stifling a laugh. When Mum started talking again, she quickly interjected, "Grandma, how did your date go the other night?"

Smart kid.

She knew the best way to divert the conversation when her grandmother was involved.

As I headed outside to the back patio, Mum called out after me, "I know you're going for a cigarette."

Seriously. Could. Throttle. Her.

I made another mental note: find her a man fast. She needed something to focus her attention on rather than my sister and me, and all the problems we apparently had.

After I took my first drag, I pulled my phone out of my pocket and texted my sister.

Me: Your mother is slowly killing me.

Brynn: Not my mother today. She's all yours. And BTW, I'm already dead. She killed me yesterday.

Me: How?

Brynn: She sent me a male prostitute.

I called her.

"What the fuck, Brynn? Are you kidding me? And why didn't you call me straight away?"

"Not a word of a lie, big sister. Be prepared. I'm pretty sure your turn is coming since you haven't had sex in six months. And I didn't call you because I was dead, remember?" She sighed. "What planet do you think our mother is really from? What kind of mother sends her daughter a fucking prostitute?"

I took a long drag on my smoke. There wasn't enough nicotine in the world to get me through this morning. "I don't care if you're dead, you still need to warn me about these things." I frowned. "Wait, did you fuck him?"

She laughed. "I thought about it. Instead, I made him play scrabble with me. We took a selfie and I sent it to Mum. I'm surprised she didn't tell you."

I almost choked on my own laughter. "Maybe you and I are the weird ones, babe. I mean, who the hell turns down sex for scrabble?"

"Sex with a prostitute is not the kind of sex I want in my life, thank you very much. But, I do have to confess the dude was hot, and I mean, fucking hot. And on top of that, he's a pro at scrabble. I asked him for a rematch."

"Did he say yes?"

"Kind of."

"What does that mean?"

"It means I had to agree to do something with him first."

"Jesus, stop dragging this out. Just tell me already. What?"

"He wants me to go fishing with him on the weekend."

This story was getting weirder by the minute. "So let me get this straight—you just met him last night and now you're suddenly hanging out with each other? I honestly think I'm existing in some alternate universe today."

"No shit, Lil, we got on so well. Like, he's so easy going and funny. I wish the guys I dated were this easy to get on with."

"Is this fishing thing not a date?"

She was silent for a beat. "No. He told me he likes to do it with someone, but that none of his friends like it."

"Well, dude must be hot. You hate fishing. Make sure you ask him how he selected his profession. I've always wondered why someone would have sex for cash. I mean, it's hard enough to have good sex. I can't imagine having shitty sex more than once a day."

"That's because Linc didn't know what the hell he was doing and neither have any of the guys you've dated since him. Maybe Mum will hook you up, too, and maybe the guy'll know what he's doing."

I finished my smoke as I said, "If she sends a guy my way, I'll put him to good use in my kitchen while I go take a bath and a nap."

"Hey, before you go, how did you go with Zara and the boy problem?"

"Ugh, did you have to remind me about that?" My four-teen-year-old was giving me grey hairs long before any woman should have them. Her obsession with boys was out of control. "I told her the only way she'd have a night-time date with that boy was with me or her father in attendance."

"You know, just because you didn't have these issues with Holly doesn't mean you can bury your head in the sand over this. At some point, you're going to have to let her out on a date."

"I do. She can go out with him in the daytime, but no fucking way am I allowing her out at night with him." It was beyond me how I'd managed to raise such different girls. Holly was all about study rather than boys, while I was fairly sure Zara didn't even know what a textbook looked like.

"What's the difference?"

"There's a huge difference! Babies get made at night."

"Oh, God, please tell me you aren't that naïve. Babies can get made during the day, too."

"Brynn, I'm not that naïve, but I know from what Linc and I did when we were kids that there's more likelihood of sex at night. I do not want Zara having a baby at seventeen like I did."

"Jesus, Lil, it doesn't matter what you and Linc did. The fact is that if Zara wants to sleep with this boy, she won't care if the sun is shining or not."

I knew she was right. God did I know that. But for the life of me, I couldn't get my brain to think any differently than it did, and it was screaming at me not to let my daughter out at night with a boy. I was so fucking terrified of my girls making the same mistakes I had. I'd managed to get Holly to sixteen without a pregnancy so far, and I'd do whatever it took to get Zara there, too.

"I'm hanging up on you now. And let me tell you that when you have a daughter, I'll be the first one to say 'I told you so.' Girls plus boys plus no sun equals babies."

She laughed. "Fine, be stubborn. I promise I'll be the good aunt who is there to make sure your kid is okay when she refuses to talk to you because you've turned into your own mother."

"I am *not* turning into my mother." *Good fucking God, I better not be.*

"Lil," she said softly, "you are. But I still love you. Just don't start sending me male prostitutes. I'll have to reassess the relationship if you start doing that shit."

The door to the patio opened and my ex stuck his head out.

"Shit, Brynn, I've gotta go. Linc's just turned up." *And I'm going to fucking kill him.*

"I'll get on my knees and start sending prayers up for Linc's life."

I ended the call and took a step toward the man who consumed way too much of my time these days. "Did you have a brain fart, Linc? Because I could have sworn I asked you to stop showing up at breakfast time without warning."

His face pulled into the scowl I could trace with my eyes closed I'd known it for so long. "Why you gotta be such a smartass all the damn time, woman? And why can't a man show up at the house where his children live whenever he has something for them?"

Oh, he wanted to get into it, did he?

I moved closer to him, fixing a shitty look of my own on my face. "One, don't call me woman. I'm not your woman, and I haven't been your woman for a good three years. Two, it's a pity the father of my children only wants to show up to visit said children when it suits him. And three, my bank account seems to be minus a few numbers this week, so if you have something for the kids, you suck. They'd rather have their excursion fees paid and their swimming fees paid and their—"

He raised his hands in defence. "Okay, I get your point, Lily. You don't need to go on. The money should be going in your account today. And for the record, you never used to be this bitchy."

I lifted my brows. *Fuck him.* "And you used to handle your shit."

Shoving his fingers through his hair, he muttered, "Fuck. I've had a bad month. There's not much work coming in, okay?"

"*Okay?* Are you kidding me? I get that things are tight, but would it have killed you to warn me? Or to pick up the phone and let me know that the cash was going to be late? Because let me tell you, this mama already has enough shit to stress over. So don't come at me, all casual and 'I've got presents for the kids' when I'm over here spending my nights trying to figure out how to pay the damn electricity bill because you didn't uphold your end of this parenting gig." *And not for the first time.*

He hit me with one final glare before turning to walk back inside, not another word on the matter.

I contemplated taking the day off and locking myself in my bedroom. If I didn't love my job so much I probably would have done that. Instead, I gave myself a talking to and went back inside. I had shit to get through today, and I refused to give Linc any power over my actions. I'd pep talk the fuck out of today if I had to.

~

"You good for tonight, hon? I mean, you look like you need some time with your girls, but if you wanna cancel so you can sleep, I'll understand."

I watched Adelaide, my bestie, shove her bag in her work locker and wondered just how bad I looked. It hadn't been the best morning so far, but I thought I at least looked okay. "If I look as bad as you're saying, I shudder to think how awful I'm gonna look by tonight."

She pulled her long red hair into a ponytail and shook her head. "Okay so you don't look that bad, but I know you well enough to read the signs that shit isn't right with you. Is Linc still being an ass?"

"Ugh. Ass doesn't cover it. I'm not sure why, after three years of doing his best to ignore me, he's suddenly always on my doorstep. He doesn't listen when I ask him to please give me some notice he's coming over, or even to ask if he can. And his child support payments have gone from bad to worse. I used to at least count on some money from him; these days I either get nothing or I get it late. That shit makes it hard for me to budget, you know?"

"Oh, honey, I know. You *know* I freaking know. Some days I want to scream at Jedd for what his bullshit support has done to my financial situation, but you know what? We're stronger because of these men, Lily. Because of them, we've had to figure out how to stand on our own and give our kids what they need. When it gets too hard, remember that and be proud of who you've become and what you can achieve on your own." She threw me a wink as she added, "And just know that there are good men out there and that one of them's going to rock your damn world one day." The wink was because after two years of being single, Addy had started dating Mr Tall, Dark, and Handsome, and he was rocking her world in ways it had never been rocked.

"Just ignore me, babe. I'm having one of those weeks. I'll get my shit together again soon."

Usually I didn't allow anyone or any situation to interfere with my mojo. Usually, I'd get my meditation cushion out, light some candles and meditate my way through this kind of stuff. Or I'd burn some oils, fill my bath and chant my way through it. But Linc had been screwing with me for too many weeks now, and I was all out of sync with myself.

"What you need is a girls' night out. I'll organise one. And maybe we'll find you a guy to blow your mind for even just one night." She whipped out her phone and shot a quick message off before I could stop her. Looking back up at me, she hit me with the huge smile Adelaide Sutton was well known for. "Quinn and Georgia are in the loop. We'll finalise plans tonight. And Lily? I have the *exact* right dress for you for this!"

Before I could say anything or stop her, she was out the door, and I was alone thinking about the *exact right* dress she had for me. It would be slutty and most likely red. Addy had a thing for red dresses. I was all for colour, but I just knew this dress was going to scream "fuck me all night long in any way you want and I'll be sure to blow you real good" from a mile away. I closed my locker and headed out to start my shift, putting all thoughts of the red dress out of my mind after I decided I'd definitely wear it. God knew, this celibacy thing had to come to an end. I needed to get laid.

"Lily! Wait up," my boss called out, hurrying to catch up. Falling into line, he said, "Fuck, it's madness here today."

I eyed the exhaustion lining his face. "You need to take that holiday you've been talking about for six months, Jackson."

"Don't get me started on that," he muttered. "The higher-ups keep pushing our workload. At this rate, I'll be getting around Greece with a fucking cane."

Hospital life was never slow. The problem was, though, that these days it wasn't just hectic, it was unbearably so. Staffing and funding cuts were killing us, to the point where I'd even started considering leaving the hospital to work for a physiotherapist friend who had her own successful practice. She'd been after me to join her for over a year, but I loved working with Jackson and Adelaide so much that I hadn't entertained the idea.

He shoved a chart at me. "I need you to start with this woman today. Her brother is causing me no end of fucking grief, and while I'm loathe to give him what he wants, I just want him gone."

I frowned. "What's going on?" It was unlike Jackson to get this worked up over anything. His patience and calm way of getting through work were what made him so good at his job.

"She had hip surgery yesterday, and he's in everyone's face about her recovery. One of the nurses mentioned phys-ical therapy was up next, so he's been harassing them to get us down there. Apparently, he wants to be there for our first session, but he's busy and doesn't have all day to wait around for us." Anger clouded his face. "Like we're not fucking busy ourselves." He exhaled loudly and muttered, "Fuck."

"I think maybe you need to take the day off. It's so unlike

you to get worked up over an asshole like this and to cater to his demands."

"The nurses want him gone too. I haven't met him, but I've been told he's menacing."

I nodded. "Okay, well with the mood I'm in this morning, he can menace me all he likes. I've had just about enough of asshole men."

His face turned serious. "Be careful, Lily. These guys aren't worth messing with. I don't need another Mackie case on my hands."

The case he referred to had caused our team no end of headaches. The father of a young girl had assaulted one of our physiotherapists when he'd refused to cave to the guy's demands. His treatment plan didn't fit in with the father's work schedule, and while we'd tried to accommodate that, we didn't do enough as far as the father was concerned. They'd had a roaring argument that ended in the father punching our guy. Jackson had been the one who had to answer to bosses and deal with the fallout.

"I'll tread carefully, but I won't allow him to walk all over me."

He sighed. "God help me." Shaking his head, he added, "For once, I'd just like to be given a team member who doesn't ruffle feathers."

I grinned. He didn't mean that, but I knew both Adelaide and I created headaches for him. "You'd be lost without me." I took a step away from him. "I'll do my best to keep the peace."

Ten minutes later, I entered the hospital room of Skylar King and came face-to-face with who I presumed was the guy Jackson had mentioned. And I could see why the nurses were keen for me to get him sorted and out of here.

King

"Finally," I muttered, watching the dark-haired woman who'd just entered Skylar's room. If I ran my club the way this hospital ran, we'd never survive. They didn't know shit about efficiency.

Her brows lifted. "I think you mean hello. Right?"

I wasn't in the mood for snark. Not today. "I always say what I mean."

"King," Skylar said, "can you lay off her? She's just doing her job and trying to help me."

The woman looked at Skye and smiled. "Hi, Skylar. I'm Lily." She glanced up at me. "And I'm just going to ignore your brother's attitude. I deal with teens every day, so I'm a pro at that."

I held her gaze, unable to let it go. She was throwing up a challenge, and fuck if it didn't stir something deep in my gut.

But right alongside that was irritation. I stepped closer to her. "I'm not someone to be ignored, Lily."

"Oh God," Skylar muttered, but I blocked her out, my entire attention on the physiotherapist. Not that I knew for sure that was who she was, but my patience levels were running low, so I hoped to fuck she was.

She stood taller, straightening her shoulders. "Well, like I always say to my kids, I won't ignore you if you treat me with some respect. But if you wanna hit me with bad manners and rudeness, you won't get much out of me."

I opened my mouth to give her my thoughts on that, but Skylar glared at me. She then turned to Lily and asked, "Are you my physio?"

Lily nodded. "Yes. I'm going to get you started on some rehab this morning and work with you until you go home."

"How long do you think I'll be in here?"

"Usually three to five days for this type of injury, but that depends on a lot of things."

"What kind of things?" I asked.

She looked at me again, her gaze a little less sharp. "Once Skylar is able to get out of bed unassisted, use the toilet, and shower herself, we can discharge her. She'll need someone to help her at home, though." Glancing at Skylar, she asked, "Do you have someone?"

"She'll stay with me," I said. "I'll take care of everything and make sure she has whatever she needs."

Lily's eyes cut to mine, flashing with something I couldn't quite read. Surprise perhaps? She watched me silently for a moment before nodding and saying to Skylar, "Okay, great. So the nurses have had you sitting in the chair. I want you to do as much of that as possible. It'll reduce the risk of bed sores and clots, and help you transition to standing. I'm going to visit you both morning and afternoon to get you up

and about, but we're going to take it slow, okay? It's important not to do too much too soon."

Skylar nodded. "Got it. Slow and steady."

"Right, let's get you out of bed and into the chair. Then
we're going to focus on you standing on your uninjured leg for
today. The goal is to try to get you on both legs tomorrow."

My phone rang as Lily helped Skylar out of bed, and I left
the room to take the call.

"Everything is set for us to visit Ghost this afternoon,"
Hyde said when I answered the phone.

"Good. Any news on Nitro this morning?"

"No. The lawyer Tatum recommended is seeing him in
about an hour, so we'll know more then."

Nitro and Marx had been picked up when Nitro was on
his way to get rid of the asshole. A fucking cracked taillight
had done it. Marx had been unconscious in the back seat,
causing the cops to grow suspicious, and because of Nitro's
club ties, they'd hauled both in for questioning. Fuck knew
what Marx had told the cops.

"I'll be there in about an hour or so. Make sure Kick's
around then. We need to discuss our plans to draw
Romano out."

"Will do," he said, and we ended the call.

When I stepped back into Skylar's room, she was
standing on one leg while Lily helped her. I slowed and ran
my gaze over the woman who would be helping my sister's
recovery. She had the kind of beauty I didn't see often, and
while it had a lot to do with her looks, it had a fuck of a lot
more to do with her energy. I'd take a beautiful face, long
legs, and a tight ass any day, but it was the way she stood up
for herself that got most of my attention. I didn't like a
woman arguing with me, but I respected the fuck out of a
woman who didn't let a man walk all over her. Sometimes

those two preferences clashed, but in the end, respect always won the battle.

"I'm guessing that you're gonna load Skye up with a rehab programme to do at home when she leaves here, and I'm also guessing her recovery would be helped along by seeing a physio," I said to Lily. At her nod, I continued, "How often do you recommend for that?"

She answered me while keeping an eye on what Skylar was doing. "A few times a week if you can swing it. The more the better. I can give you some names of physios I recommend."

I nodded. "I'd appreciate that." Looking at Skylar, I said, "I'm gonna head out now. Devil's on his way up to stay with you today, and I'll be back tonight. Text me if you need anything."

"Can Nik come to visit? I could do with the company."

"No. Devil will keep you company."

"Ugh. You are such a pain. I like Devil and all, but I'm fairly sure he's bored out of his brain talking to me."

"Yeah well, he's all you've got. You'll be back at the club-house in a few days hopefully."

The last thing I heard as I exited the room was her mutter, "Men. Do the guys in your life give you this much hell, Lily? Tell me I'm not the only one who has to live with this kind of stuff."

I didn't catch Lily's reply. My mind was already on the next fire I had to put out. I didn't give a fuck if Skylar felt like I gave her hell. All I cared about was protecting her.

∼

Lily

Do the guys in my life give me that much hell?

I laughed. "Where do I begin?" Honestly, I felt like maybe they didn't, because her brother seemed way over the top, but at the same time, I experienced as much frustration with Linc as she did with King.

I wonder what his first name is?

God, why was I even thinking about him? The man was rude and demanding, and I had no space in my head for people like him. But, good lord, he had something that sparked my interest. Tall and built with muscles for days, he'd commanded my attention as soon as I entered his space. His piercing eyes had hit me instantly. They looked like eyes that hid a thousand secrets. God, I'd even liked his dark hair that was a little longer and a little more unruly than I usually preferred. Not to mention his beard and tattoos. King looked to be everything in a man I'd never had but had always wanted to try. I'd found myself wanting to pull him into line for being so rude while also wanting to talk a whole lot more with him.

And that scar on his face.

I wanted to know who did that to him and why.

Skylar cut through my thoughts. "Are you married?"

I steadied her while she did the exercises I'd prescribed. She was fit, so I had high hopes for a speedy recovery. With any luck, she'd be out of here fast. "Not anymore. After twelve years of marriage, I discovered my husband was cheating on me. We're divorced now, but he still gives me headache after headache."

"Fucker. I'd cut his balls off. Like, literally. But then, I'm as crazy as my brother, so I'm not really a sane person when it comes to being crossed by people."

I liked her honesty and the easy way she allowed me to work with her. Some patients struggled with their rehab and fought it every step of the way. So far, Skylar had done everything I'd wanted her to. And it had impressed me that her brother seemed invested in her recovery. Family support was a huge key to success in this journey.

"Trust me, I dreamt about doing that to Linc. I've got three kids, though, and parenting from prison didn't seem like a good option, so I let him keep the balls. But let me tell you, this week, I'm this close to slicing them off."

"That's gotta be the worst—still having to have him in your life after what he did to you."

"It's definitely hard. And bittersweet some days."

She frowned. "How so?"

"Linc and I were high school sweethearts. I'd always thought we'd be together forever. The fact I still like the guy underneath all the bullshit means it hurts to have him around, knowing everything we'll never have."

"Yeah, I can see that."

She was beginning to tire with the exercises, so I manoeuvred her to the chair. "I think we might be done for now. How are you feeling about everything?"

Taking a seat, she said, "I'm over it already, but I know I have to do the work, so I'm not complaining. Please just tell me if there's anything I can be doing to speed everything up."

I took a seat next to her and smiled. I really did love her desire to do what needed to be done. "Time is a big factor in all this, Skylar. As is you continuing to do the exercises I give you. Please don't put any pressure on that leg today. Wait until tomorrow and I'll assess it then. I think, though, that you'll be ready for it tomorrow."

Another man joined us, blasting me with the kind of smile any woman would love sent their way. "How's she going, Doc?"

I returned his smile. He must have been the man King referred to as Devil. Interesting names these men had. I'd never had anything to do with bikers, though, so I had no idea about how they chose them. The only thing I knew about bikers was what I read in the newspapers, and lately their club had been mentioned a lot. That was how I knew what the name on the back of their jackets meant. "I'm not the doctor, but she's going well." Standing, I said, "I'll be back later this afternoon, but remember what I said about no standing on that leg."

I ran into Jackson twenty minutes later as I did my rounds. "You took care of that guy?"

"Yeah, all sorted."

"Thanks, Lily. That's one problem I can take off my list of shit to worry about today."

Speaking of lists of shit, Linc had sent me a text telling me the child support money would still be a couple of days away. If only I could take him off my list as easily as I'd taken Skylar's brother off Jackson's list.

I decided to put him completely out of my mind and not think about him today. Maybe instead, I'd think about King and that scar of his.

I wonder how he did get that.

And I wonder what he's like in bed.

I bet he's rough and demanding and bossy.

Oh, God.

Yes.

Oh, fuck.

No.

No, no, no.

Worst idea I'd had in a long time.

It was then I realised I really *did* need to get laid, because I was clearly losing my mind if I was imagining what it would be like to have sex with a rude man like King.

I had enough troubles in my life.

I didn't need to add asshole to my list.

19

King

There was no love lost between Ghost and me. Jethro had seen to that. He'd played us off from the very beginning, but by the time I'd figured that out, too much water was under the bridge for us to ever go back. Ghost had always eyed the Storm presidency, believing it should have been his. Jethro had other ideas. He marked the position as mine early on, and once Ghost worked that out, he'd gone out of his way to fuck with me. Ivy and Jen had been caught in the crossfire, but again, I hadn't learnt of that until it was too late.

Ghost had targeted them because Jethro told him to. Jethro had told a few club members to harass both of my women, but the difference with Ghost was that he'd taken it all a step further and tried to force himself on them simply because of his grudge against me. I'd never forgive him for that.

Sitting across from him at the jail later that day, it took a lot of fucking control not to reach across the damn table and choke the life out of him. After my last visit, I'd intended never to return.

"Spit it out, Ghost. Why are we here?" I demanded. "Have the feds come back?"

He shook his head. "No, not the feds." He paused for a moment, almost as if he was still deciding whether to share his information with us. Finally he said, "Tony Romano paid me a visit, and since all he spoke about was you, I figured you'd want to know."

"What the fuck?" Hyde muttered, leaning forward and resting his arms on the table.

I was as confused as Hyde. It made no sense. "What did he want?"

Ghost's smile was one of victory. He squared his shoulders. "I thought you might ask that, but if you think I'll just hand that kind of information over without getting something in return, you're mistaken."

Fucking Ghost. I'd known this was a fucking ambush when Hyde had said Ghost would only talk to me. "You wanna stay a member of Storm, you need to get that mouth moving, Ghost. That's the only fucking thing up for negotiation here."

Ghost's smile disappeared and hatred blared from his eyes. "At this fucking point, King, I couldn't give a fuck if you kick me out of the club. The only thing important to me is getting the fuck out of here. You make that happen and I'll give you whatever information you want."

"I've already got shit happening towards your release."

"And we both know you could be doing more. Stop dragging your feet and make this happen within the next couple of weeks."

He was right—I was dragging my feet. Helping Ghost get out of here was the last thing I wanted to do, but I'd given him my word, and I never went back on that. Not even when it was given to someone I despised.

"Done." I leant forward, my eyes boring into his. "Now start fucking talking and don't stop until you give me everything. I find out you skipped some shit, your release gets pushed back as far as I can make that happen."

Ghost's eyes flashed with the same hatred mine did. "And if you don't get shit done in a few weeks, I'll find a way to fuck you over."

Jesus, the motherfucker had a death wish. "Talk!" I barked, coasting close to my threshold of control.

His lips pulled up in a snarl, but he finally spilt what he knew. "Romano wants you dead, and he wants Storm wiped off the map. He has a wealth of knowledge about Storm's drug trade, who you buy weapons off, the shit Jethro was into…. Fuck, I don't know how the hell he knows this shit, but I'm telling you, if he went to the cops with any of this, every member of the club would go to prison. He even knows about Moses."

"Jesus fucking Christ," Hyde said, echoing my own thoughts. *We have a rat in the club.* "What did he want with you?"

"He offered me half a mill to turn on the club. Wants me to go to the cops with what I know."

"You expect us to believe you'd turn down that kind of cash? To help me?" I said.

"Not to help *you*, King, but to help the club."

"Bullshit."

The hatred in his eyes flared again. "It's not bullshit. Fuck, think about it. Why would I call you here and tell you this shit if I was gonna take the cash? I'd just fucking take it, talk to the cops and never look back if that was my choice."

My mind worked as fast as it could to come up with scenarios of how this could all play out, but with all the shit in there, it was a battle I was losing. Ghost had a point, but I still had my doubts.

"If I choose to believe you and you fuck us over, there's no coming back from that, Ghost. Not for you and not for your sister."

"Look," he snapped, agitation getting the best of him, "I've always been loyal to the club and I don't intend to change that. Best I can figure, Romano is fucking insane. I've got enough insanity to deal with in you. I don't wanna get into bed with another crazy asshole."

"What else did he say?" I pushed. "Nothing you've told us helps us in any way. We already knew Romano was coming after the club."

He contemplated that for a moment. "Now who's speaking shit?"

"What else?" Hyde almost bellowed. By the looks of him, he was as close to losing his shit as I was.

Ghost scowled at him. "Ivy is the key to all of this. He's fucking obsessed with her. You get to her and you'll get to Romano."

"See now that's where your info is fucked up, Ghost. We have her and she's telling us jack," I said.

Ghost's eyes met mine again, a flicker of confusion in them now. "She's with you? And Tony hasn't turned up looking for her? I find that hard to believe."

"He's disappeared," Hyde said. "Dropped off the radar to avoid the cops who raided him two days ago."

"And Ivy has left Tony," I added.

Ghost's confusion grew, and he frowned. "I don't see any of that happening. Not from what Tony said the other day. For one, I got the impression he's in with the cops, and two, I don't think he'd ever allow Ivy to leave him. I'm telling you, he's consumed by her. If anyone could cause Tony Romano to fall, it'd be Ivy. She'd be enough for him to not go into hiding from the cops because all he'd be able to think about would be getting her back."

Fuck.

I glanced at Hyde. "What do you make of all this, brother?"

"We need to head back to the clubhouse and go over it all. Pull Devil and Kick in on it and get their take on it. Bronze too."

"You also need to work on my release," Ghost said.

I eyed him. "I have a job for you before that happens." I detailed the club's problem with Marx and told Ghost to find someone to fix that problem.

He nodded. "I may already have someone in mind."

I stood. "Good. Hyde'll be in touch. Until then, sit tight and call us if you come across anything else."

As we left the prison, Hyde looked at me with determination. "I'm going to talk to Ivy."

My reaction surprised me. He'd wanted to talk to her the other day, too, but I didn't want to inflict him on Ivy. It was a gut-deep response. Hyde interrogated people the same way he took to them with his fists—he was savage and ruthless in his quest to extract information. As much as my head screamed yes to this, every fibre of my being refused to agree.

"No."

"You sure about that, brother? She could be our best bet to find Romano."

"No."

"You're too close to this. I might get more from her."

Fuck. "No."

"King, think with your head and not your dick."

He was a stubborn fucking bastard. He wouldn't let this go. "I'm not thinking with my fucking dick, brother." Or was I? I scrubbed my hand over my face. Jesus fucking Christ. "Just don't fucking hurt her."

His stubborn side showed itself. "If she has info the club needs, I'll go down swinging to get it."

No fucking way would I allow him to harm her. "I want in that room."

"King," his voice hardened, "you're not setting foot in that room. I don't give a fuck if I have to knock you out, I'm questioning her, and I'll do whatever it takes to save our club."

Fuck.

Shit was spiralling.

And I couldn't fucking stop it.

I felt ripped apart by my allegiances. I'd loved Ivy for a long time. Could I allow her to become caught up in this? Would I allow Hyde to do whatever it took to get her to talk?

Had I fallen that far down the fucking black hole that I no longer cared what happened to her?

I exhaled a harsh breath and met Hyde's gaze. "Just get it done. I don't want to fucking know the details."

20

King

I met Jen three years after I pushed Ivy away. I hadn't been looking for a woman to share my bed with, but she'd forced her way into my life and then into my heart. We'd met at a party thrown by a club member. She was drunk and had tried to fuck me in the bathroom. I was a lot of things, but I wasn't a man who took advantage of drunk women. I'd said no and left, but not before I'd found someone to get her home so some other asshole couldn't force himself on her. A week later, she'd turned up at the clubhouse to thank me for it. She'd called me a gentleman, and I'd laughed for the first time in a long fucking time. That had been the start of our journey down a dark, fucked-up path of jealousy, raging arguments, destructive behaviour, and resentments we never found our way through.

Sex had been our glue; Jen liked it brutal, and she quickly worked out that it kept me coming back for more. She understood that after a long day taking care of club shit, all I'd wanted to come home to was a woman who'd let me lose myself in her so I could wipe the day from my mind. She'd saved the fights for the daytime and the sex for the nights. It worked until she figured out I'd never love her the way she wanted. I'd loved her, but I'd never hand every last piece of myself over to anyone again, and Jen wanted to collect those pieces like fucking trophies. In the end, she'd cheated on me, and I'd walked away. The betrayal had stung because they always did, but I couldn't find it in me to hate her. I'd known the cheating was because I refused to give her everything I'd given Ivy. I could hardly fault her for my shortcomings.

I'd felt guilt more than anger.

I'd ruined another woman, another relationship.

Kick had found a place for her out by the creek she'd loved to visit. As I'd said goodbye, memories had rushed at me of the times I'd taken her there. Fuck, memories always carved jagged grooves deep in me. If I could have avoided it, I wouldn't have visited her grave. But I owed her that. I fucking owed her a lot more than that, but since I could never pay those debts, this was all I had to give.

I'd sat with her for an hour, and when I was done, I'd headed back to the clubhouse and spent the night obliterating every memory from my mind. Turned out Jen had been hell alive, and she was still hell for me dead. Kick dropped me at the hospital just after midnight. "No fucking way am I letting you on the road in this state," he'd said. What he didn't know was that there was no fucking way *I'd* ever allow myself on the roads in this state.

"King," Skylar mumbled early the next morning, prodding my arm. "When did you get here? And God, you smell like a brewery."

I was only half asleep in the chair by her bed. The night had been long and the ghosts had refused to leave me alone. I sat up and rested my elbows on my knees, stretching the kinks out of my neck. Sleeping in a hospital chair fucking blew. So did the headache pounding my skull. "We buried Jen yesterday afternoon." It didn't answer her question, but it told her everything she wanted to know.

Her face softened. "Oh."

I stood so I could also stretch my back. I felt like hell, but I was more interested in how Skylar was feeling. "How's the pain?"

"It's okay. The drugs are working." She paused for a moment before saying, "You know I wasn't a huge fan of Jen's, but I hate that she died like this. No one deserves that."

"Yeah," I agreed, but I didn't want to get into it. Didn't want to be having this conversation with anyone, because that meant I'd have to face the guilt again. "I'm going for a smoke. You want anything when I come back?"

The look she gave me told me she knew what I was doing. Skylar knew me better than anyone. It was one of the reasons we argued so damn much. She liked to see how far she could push me. Always had. But today, she let that shit slide. Nodding, she said, "Yeah, a coffee. I can't do the stuff they serve here."

When I stepped outside five minutes later, I lit a smoke and stared up at the dark morning sky. The colour of the clouds matched my mood. And the rolling thunder added to the symphony playing in my head. A symphony of fucked-up thoughts that wouldn't leave me the fuck alone.

For one mad moment, I wondered whether my father's mind had been as chaotic as mine. Was this how he crossed the line into insanity? Did the thoughts become too much to deal with that his mind cracked into so many pieces that he could no longer figure out right from wrong?

Could *I* fucking figure out right from wrong anymore? I

wasn't sure. Most days I didn't give a fuck, but every now and then, someone came along and tested that attitude. Ivy reappearing in my life was one big fucking test.

She and Jen had played on my mind all night, and my dreams had tortured me. It had been a long time since I'd had dreams like this. After I'd pushed Ivy away years ago, I'd spent a year dreaming of her, my father, my mother, and Margreet. The dreams had become nightmares I couldn't escape. I'd avoided sleep that year, and insomnia had plagued me ever since, but the dreams had disappeared.

Until last night.

Last night I dreamt of Margreet and the disappointment she felt over the choices I'd made in my life. Ivy and Jen had shown up in my dream, too, and told me I was going to hell after I was finished with this life.

Fuck.

I'd woken in a cold sweat, thoughts of hell still on my mind. I knew the only place I'd be going after this life was straight to hell. My father had made sure of that the first time he'd forced me to help him with his sick and perverted crimes. Usually it was my mother who helped him, but not that night. She'd been sick and unable to do what he wanted, so he'd dragged me out of bed and used me to lure the blonde teenager into his car. What girl wouldn't want to stop and help a nine-year-old who was alone on a street in the middle of the night? She'd never stood a chance between my sad eyes begging for help and my father's brute strength when he pulled her into the car.

He'd kept her locked up in our house for a week before he ended her suffering. I'd endured seven nights of her screams and his grunts. But that was only the beginning of it all.

I had the blood of five girls on my hands by the time I was ten. Three days before my tenth birthday, my father was arrested for assaulting a man at the pub he frequented. My early birthday present that year was my mother abandoning me at a hospital because she decided she couldn't raise me on her own. It was the best birthday present I ever received.

Jesus, would this shit ever go away? Would I ever stop thinking about my father? Would Margreet linger in my mind forever?

I took a long drag of my smoke, closing my eyes as it worked its way into my lungs. Why the fuck was I turning my actions over in my head? Questioning myself in ways I tried never to question myself. There was a lot of shit to deal with today. Thinking about this wasn't doing me any favours. All it did was fuck with my thinking. And that wasn't fucking useful. Not to me and not to my club.

I opened my eyes, took one last drag of my smoke before stubbing it out, and turned to go back inside. Another round of thunder cracked overhead, but I barely heard it. Thunder didn't come close to the noise of my mind.

"Good morning."

I'd been so lost in my thoughts I hadn't seen Skylar's physiotherapist standing in my path to the front door of the hospital. I'd almost run into her.

I nodded at the smoke between her lips. "If the way you're sucking that smoke back is any indication, your morning is as shit as mine."

"Yeah, that about sums it up. Kids."

My gaze dropped to her body. She wore the tightest fucking jeans I'd ever seen with a white T-shirt and black leather jacket. It seemed an odd outfit for a hospital employee to wear, but what the fuck did I know? Finding her eyes again, I asked, "How many you got?"

"Do you really care?"

She had me there. And yet, I was engaging in small talk, which I rarely bothered with, so there was some interest. "How many?"

A smile ghosted across her lips as she drew more smoke deep into her lungs. "I knew you weren't as big of an asshole as they told me. I've got three. Two teens and an eight-year-old. It's mostly my fourteen-year-old daughter who keeps my nicotine addiction fed."

I narrowed my eyes, assessing her more closely. "You don't look old enough to have a fourteen-year-old."

Her smile grew larger. "Well, now I like you even more. I'm old enough to have a sixteen-year-old."

"Daughter?"

"Yeah."

"Fuck, I wish you well."

Her brows lifted. "You have daughters?"

"No, but I've got experience raising girls." I jerked my chin at her smoke. "That's not gonna be anywhere near strong enough soon."

"Trust me, I know." She glanced at her watch. "Shit, I've gotta go. My boss will kill me if I'm late today." She rummaged through her bag and pulled out a breath mint before smiling again and saying, "Your sister did really well yesterday. She should be standing on both legs by this afternoon."

"Good. I need her home with me as soon as possible."

She slowed and fixed her gaze on me. "I like your dedication to family. I mean, unless you're some creepy stalker brother who keeps his sister locked away, but out of all the vibes I'm getting about you, that isn't one of them."

We watched each other silently for a few moments as more thunder rumbled overhead. And then she was gone, and I was alone again with my thoughts. Fucking worst place to be.

I had another smoke before going back inside to check on Skylar. Today was going to be a long one. And with a bit of fucking luck, one that produced some results in our efforts to track Romano and our rat down. But to get that shit done, I first needed to make sure my family was okay.

∼

Annika glanced up from the coffee she was making when I entered the clubhouse kitchen an hour later. "You look like hell."

"I fucking feel like it too." I jerked my chin at the kettle. "You got enough for another one?"

She nodded. "Yeah. I'll even take pity on you and make toast to go with it if you haven't had breakfast. You want vegemite?"

I lifted a brow. "What are you after, Nik?"

She pulled another mug from the cupboard. "Maybe I just think you need some TLC at the moment. I'm not the sister always wanting stuff, remember?"

She was right. Annika was the maternal type while Skylar was the complete opposite. Nik never asked me for much at all. I had to force my way into her life when I knew she needed me. Skye, on the other hand, was the sister who came looking for me when she wanted something. It had been the other way around before Margreet died. Her death altered our relationships, causing Annika to shut down on me, and Skylar to demand my attention constantly.

I moved closer to her and leant against the counter. "Vegemite sounds good." As she made coffee and toast, I asked, "Are you guys holding up okay here?"

She stopped what she was doing and gave me her full attention. "We're fine, King, but it's odd for you to even ask that. Usually you just want to tell us what to do, not ask us how we're doing. What's going on? And where's the brother I know and love?"

Scrubbing my face, I muttered, "I'm trying here."

She smiled. "We're good. The kids are running wild, but they get on well with Kree's kids, so at least there aren't any problems there."

Fuck, I hadn't made the time to speak with Zane about Kree's ex. He was due to arrive today, so I made a mental note to do that then.

I took the coffee she passed me. "I just came from the hospital. Skye's physio says she's doing well. She should be home in a few days."

Axe joined us, his gaze coming straight to me. "Zane's about five hours out. He's got all his gear with him."

Zane ran his own security firm, his team mostly all ex-commando, and had the best surveillance gear you could get your hands on.

I nodded just as my phone rang. *Bronze.*

"Bronze, you're not gonna hit me with bad news so early in the morning, are you?"

"Not bad so much as interesting. The info you have on Romano being raided by the cops is wrong. It didn't happen."

I gripped my phone harder. "He *wasn't* raided?"

"Correct. Whoever told you that is full of shit. He's not even on their radar at the moment. Well, not besides the usual level of interest they have in him that is."

None of this made sense. Why the hell had Brant fed us that bullshit? "Anything else?"

"Yeah," he said forcefully. "Why the fuck have you got the blonde grilling me on Ryland? I've got enough shit going on, King. I don't need her all over me too."

Tatum.

"I told her to investigate Ryland. He's too invested in this case, and at some point, he'll cross a line to get the result he wants. Tatum's gonna figure him out and she'll work with you on that."

"Fuck." He paused for a moment. "Fine, but just get her to back off a bit. She's a little too fucking enthusiastic."

"She's not gonna back off, Bronze. She'll do whatever it takes to get Nitro out and to get Ryland off our back. You'll just have to deal with her."

"Some days I regret agreeing to work with you," he muttered.

"Yeah well, we both know you'd make the same choice over if you had to." I eyed the toast Annika held out for me. "I've gotta go. Call me if you find anything else."

I ended the call and took the plate of toast off Annika, already going over in my mind what I'd just learnt. Axe's and Annika's conversation blurred into the background as I tried to figure out Brant's angle. He'd seemed attached to Ivy. More than fucking attached if I really thought about it.

I pulled out my phone again and called Hyde.

"I was in the middle of something," he grumbled, and I heard Monroe complaining too.

"Fuck, brother, you need to get Monroe out of town. I thought you'd moved her already."

"You ever tried to convince an argumentative woman to do something, King? I'm fucking working on it."

I could imagine the shit she'd given him. "Yeah, I can imagine."

"I was just about to get my dick sucked, so maybe you could move this along."

"Bronze has new information that contradicts what Brant told us. Romano wasn't raided by the cops. We need to talk to Brant again."

"Yeah. And I'll talk to Ivy again."

Hyde had interrogated her yesterday while I buried Jen. He'd let me know she hadn't come through with any further information, but I was yet to discuss it with him. I'd avoided it. Hadn't wanted to know how far he'd had to go with her.

"No, I'll have this chat with her." I'd allowed him one shot at her; I wouldn't give him another. Fuck knew I was wound tight because of it. *Because of my inability to wrap my mind around my feelings about Ivy showing back up in my life.* And that I just let Hyde at her like that? Fuck, that fucked my head up even more. Had I really become a man so hardened by the shit I'd lived through that I was willing to abandon someone I'd once loved?

"I figured you'd say that. I don't think she knows much more than what she's already given us. It makes sense, especially with what Ghost told you yesterday. I reckon Romano's fucking with us, brother."

"You think he sent Brant to feed us that bullshit?"

"Yeah. Brant played the Ivy card well, and I bet that was because Romano told him to. To get to you. Romano wanted to know if you had Ivy."

"I'll talk to Ivy. And for fuck's sake, lay the fucking law down with Monroe. I don't want her caught in this shit we've got going on."

Ending the call, I looked at Axe. "I've gotta take care of something, and after that, you and me are gonna talk to Brant again. And this time, we're not going easy on him."

He nodded. "Understood."

I left the kitchen and made my way to Ivy.

Winter sat outside her room, looking exhausted. He stood and met me. "She still isn't eating much, and I think she may be feeling sick."

I nodded. "Take a walk while I talk to her. You look like you could do with some sleep too, so I'll organise for one of the guys to give you a break today."

"Thanks, brother."

It had been two days since I'd seen Ivy, and Winter was right, she looked ill. She sat in the armchair in the corner of the room with her legs curled up under her and her head resting on the arm of the chair. Lifting her head, she said, "What now, King? Another fucking interrogation? I'm surprised you didn't send one of your men to do it."

I dragged the other chair in the room to where she was and sat in front of her. Resting my elbows on my knees, I ran my eyes over her. Hyde hadn't touched her, thank fuck. The only marks on her face were the bags under her eyes. Those damn eyes, though, roared with mistrust and anger. They threw out an accusation I found hard to stomach. It turned out that no matter how hard I tried to bury my fucking soul, it was still there. My fucking heart may have been frozen for years, but those eyes of Ivy's caused it to thaw, and that made me feel even more out of control than I already did.

When cornered like this—when forced to confront myself in ways I didn't want to—I drew upon the only response I'd ever known. I fought back with anger. When Ivy threw her hurt at me like this, I always threw mine back. And so it seemed, we never changed.

"Yes, another fucking interrogation. But only because I'm trying to keep you safe. Do you even fucking understand that?"

She sat up straight in the chair, her body rigid. "All I understand is that I came to you with information that was good and you've done nothing but thrown it in my face since I got here. And then you didn't even have the decency to come in here yourself yesterday to ask me what you wanted to know. You sent one of your men to do it. I know there's nothing between us now, King, but I honestly thought there was more than that. I thought I deserved better than *that*."

Fuck.

She did deserve better than that.

I shoved my chair back and stood, pacing the room for a moment, trying desperately to get my thoughts in order, before coming back to her. I couldn't fucking figure out what

I was thinking, what I was feeling. It was like my mind had been reprogrammed in the years after she left and now it was misfiring, unsure how to register everything being thrown at it. The only thing I truly knew was that we had to get through this and then go our separate ways again. I could not allow myself back into her life or her into mine. But fuck, getting us to that point felt like the hardest fucking thing I'd had to do in a long time.

The best way I knew to deal with shit like this was to avoid it. So I ignored what she said and focused on what I needed. "It turns out Brant's information was wrong."

She stared at me for a long few beats before blinking and muttering, "You're a fucking asshole. You can't even be bothered to discuss what I just said to you. I'm glad you cheated on me because I was better off without you in my life."

Her words sliced through me. Fuck knew how because I'd learnt a long time ago not to let people hurt me like that. But Ivy had always had a way of cutting deep.

"Tell me what you know about Brant," I demanded in a low dark voice. I needed to get this information from her and then get the hell out of this room.

She uncurled herself from the chair and stood. Coming close—too fucking close—she snarled, "I told Hyde everything I know. I don't know anything about Tony being raided, and I don't know why Brant would turn on him."

My breathing sped up as I fought all the emotions coursing through me. *Fought feeling them.* Needing to put space between us, I took a step back. "Tony wasn't raided. Brant lied about that. What I want to know is why."

The anger rolling off her burnt out a little, replaced by confusion. "I don't know why he'd do that. That makes no se—" She stopped talking abruptly, and I zeroed in on that.

"It makes no sense to you?"

By the way her mouth fell open and her eyes widened a

fraction, Ivy appeared bewildered by what I'd just told her. And that confused *me*.

When she didn't respond, I pushed her. "What's going on, Ivy? Why doesn't this make any sense to you?"

She wrapped her arms around her body and looked at me with anger again. "Nothing makes sense! I don't understand what's going on. And I feel like I'm going to be sick, so can you please get me a bucket or something in case I vomit?"

Her face had turned white, and I recalled what Winter had told me earlier. Gripping hold of her arms, I directed her back to sit in the chair. "Wait there, I'll get you something."

She curled into a ball and closed her eyes as she rested her head on the arm of the chair again. As I exited the room, I heard her murmur, "Thank you." It surprised the hell out of me and caused my guilt to rear its head. Although the only emotion that seemed to come from her was anger, I knew that was how Ivy coped with life. She'd used it when we were a couple, and it seemed she hadn't changed. But her "thank you" reminded me that at the core of that anger was a vulnerable woman. I needed to remember that and make allowances. The only way we'd survive this would be for one of us to back down, and I knew that had to be me. I wasn't sure I had it in me, but after everything I'd put Ivy through years ago, I had to fucking try.

21

King

"You think you could manage not to shoot him today?" Axe asked as we prepared to question Brant again.

I eyed Brant who sat at the table in the middle of the room looking nervously between Axe and me. "What? You don't like a little blood in your interrogation room?"

"I've told you everything. I'm not sure why we're doing this again," Brant said, fear clinging to every word that fell out of his mouth.

Axe moved behind Brant and bent so he could talk into his ear. "That's your first lie for the day, Brant. Don't let there be another or else King's gun will be the least of your worries."

Brant's eyes widened and he swallowed hard, but he took Axe's advice and didn't utter another word.

I took the seat opposite him. "You lied to us the other day, too. Your boss wasn't raided by the cops."

"No, he was. I know he was."

Interesting—he didn't frown or give off any body language that he was confused by what I said. I glanced up at Axe who remained behind Brant and jerked my chin to indicate the show was his for now. Axe knew how to hurt people without killing them. I struggled with that, so this part of the interrogation was his.

Axe wrapped an arm around Brant's neck and squeezed hard. When Brant panicked and attempted to pull out of my brother's grip, Axe said, "Easy there. You keep thrashing about like you are and you'll likely end up choked to death."

Brant's face reddened as he tried to suck in some breaths. He stopped fighting Axe and nodded his agreement.

"Good," Axe said. "Now, I'm going to ask you some questions, and you're going to give me straight answers. If you don't, this is going to get a whole lot uglier for you. Got it?"

Brant forced air out of his nostrils and nodded. He looked like he was about to shit his pants, and I had to wonder why Romano had used him for this dirty work. If he'd sent Brant to us, I suspected he'd chosen the wrong man, because Axe was about to break him and then, if needed, I'd finish the job off.

Keeping his arm firmly around Brant's neck, Axe continued, "We know for a fact that Romano wasn't raided by the cops. Why did you lie to us?"

Brant shook his head, and Axe eased his grip just enough for the asshole to splutter out his words. "I didn't lie! That's what Tony told me! I swear—"

Axe clenched his jaw as he squeezed Brant's neck again. "Bullshit." When Brant shook his head again and tried to claw Axe's arm from his throat, Axe tightened his hold even more and yanked him up out of the seat. Dragging him back towards the wall behind them, he growled, "Shit's about to get real messy for you, Brant. Start fucking telling the truth."

By the time Axe slammed him against the wall, Brant was fighting for breath. When Axe let him go, he raised his hands in a defensive manner and pleaded, "Stop! Ask me anything else. I'll tell you whatever you want."

Axe threw out his first question without hesitation. "Did Romano send you here to give us false information?"

"No."

Axe slapped him. "I'll ask that again. Did Romano send you here?"

Brant held his face where Axe had hit it. "No, he didn't. I came by—"

Axe slapped him again. Harder. "Why did you come here then?" His questions were rapid fire, giving Brant little time to think in between.

"Because I wanted to check on Ivy. You've gotta believe—"

Again, Axe slapped him. "I don't fucking believe you, Brant. Give me something I can buy into."

Brant's words came out fast, like he was tripping over them to get them out. "I was worried for her safety. I knew Tony would be going crazy looking for her, so I wanted to check that she was with you or that she was safe somewhere else. After Tony went into hiding—"

Axe gripped Brant's shirt with both hands and pulled him forward before slamming him back against the wall. Moving fast, he punched him hard in the gut and demanded, "Who told you Tony went into hiding?"

Brant doubled over, holding his stomach and trying to draw breath. "Fuck, man—"

Jesus, it was taking every ounce of my self-control to hold myself back. I wanted to get in there and punch every last breath out of the motherfucker so that he'd just fucking give us what we wanted. Instead, I paced back and forth, giving my brother the space to drag the information from him.

But, fuck.

Axe didn't allow Brant the opportunity to complain. He punched him again and roared, "Who the fuck told you Tony had been raided by the cops?"

Brant stumbled, almost falling to the ground. Doubled over, he yelled, "Tony did!"

Axe took hold of Brant's chin and lifted his face. A moment later, his fist connected with the asshole's cheek, knocking him to the ground. As Brant lay in agony, Axe crouched beside him. "Start from the beginning and tell us everything. I wanna know why you care so fucking much about Ivy's whereabouts, and how you came to have that conversation with Romano about being raided."

Brant stared at Axe with hatred while catching his breath.

Axe watched him in silence, waiting.

My brother's patience fucking amazed me. It always had. Even when we were kids, he'd had this level of calm that I envied. I'd never had patience for much. My father had seen to that. He'd wired my brain to respond with anger and swift retribution whenever I felt fucked over.

Finally, Brant started talking. "Like I told you the other day, Ivy has been kind to me, so I care about her. I don't want Tony to be able to hurt her ever again, so I've been helping her get ready for this attempt to leave. Tony called me the day she left, asking me to check on some stuff at work, and in that conversation, he told me he was laying low for a while because the cops had raided him. I swear to fucking God, that's the truth."

Axe remained silent for another few moments before saying, "You're in love with Ivy, aren't you?"

Brant's eyes darted between Axe and me. He seemed desperate not to have this conversation, but he nodded slowly. "Yes."

"And she loves you?" Axe asked.

"No, I don't think so." Brant stumbled over his words and glanced at the wall as he answered that question.

I stopped pacing and narrowed my eyes on him. Watching. Waiting for the truth.

"You're lying, Brant," Axe said. "You do think she loves you."

Brant stared at the wall, silent. When he answered Axe's question, he fixed his gaze on me. "I want her to love me, but she loves you."

Fuck.

Axe stood and turned to me. Jerking his chin at the door, he said, "We need a minute." When we were out of the room, he said, "He's not lying."

"I agree."

"My bet is Tony knows about this thing between him and Ivy. Probably figures that Brant knows where she is, and possibly thinks that if he believes Romano's in hiding, it's the perfect opportunity to go to Ivy. I'd say Romano has eyes on him and this clubhouse, and is waiting for him to leave here."

"So we put him back out there and wait for Romano to come to him."

Axe nodded. "Yeah, but we wait for Zane to arrive and get him to bug Brant's phone and put a tracker in it. You get Brant to call Romano so we can track him too."

"And I'll get him to mention our rat to Romano so he knows that I fucking know. And whichever club member suddenly disappears is our guy." I glanced down at my ringing phone. Holding it up, I said, "Can you finish with him while I take this?"

He agreed, and I answered the call. "Tatum. Any news?"

"Nothing. He's still on remand, and I'm still waiting to hear from you as to whether you've found a way to deal with Marx."

She was pissed off, and I wasn't a fan of her throwing that shit at me. "Because you're Nitro's old lady and because you're helping me with this, I'll let that shit slide this time, Tatum. But you come at me with that kind of attitude again and we won't remain friends very long."

"King, I don't give a fuck if we're friends or not. The only thing I care about right now is that Nitro gets out. You take care of that or I will."

"I'm in the middle of taking care of it for fuck's sake." Why the hell had I involved her in this? I wouldn't make that mistake again.

"Good. Let me know when it's done."

She ended the call, leaving me staring at my phone wondering how the fuck an old lady had managed to get under my skin like she had. I was annoyed as fuck at her, but I had to admit she had my respect for taking Nitro's back like she had.

Hyde came my way, a look of determination in his eyes. "Just heard from Ghost. He thinks he has a guy who can take care of Marx for us. Said he'll confirm ASAP. And Winter said to tell you that Ivy's not feeling any better."

"Call the doctor. Get him to give her the once over." I shoved my phone in my pocket. "Brant confirmed the truth in her story. I'm just about to see her again and let her know she doesn't have to stay in that room anymore."

"You think it's wise to let her go? With what's going on?"

I shook my head. "No, I'm not letting her out of here, but she's not a fucking prisoner."

"I'll let the boys know that's she's not to get past the front gate. And I'll get onto the doc now."

Five minutes later, I entered Ivy's room again. She lay on the bed, back to the door, and didn't acknowledge my presence. I walked around to the side she faced and found her staring at the wall. Sitting on the bed, I expelled a long-held breath and rested my elbows on my knees.

Neither of us spoke.

Not for a good five minutes.

There was so much to say, and yet, I couldn't find the words to express any of it. And she didn't appear interested in talking either.

Finally, I said, "I fucked up."

She didn't respond immediately, and when she did, bitterness filled the air. "Yeah. You did. And not just this time. But I'm not interested in an apology." A caustic laugh fell from her lips. "Not that you ever apologise. God forbid King should ever think anyone's worthy of a sorry."

I clenched my jaw, resisting the urge to reply to her sour words. "You can leave this room, but I won't allow you back out on the streets yet. Not until Romano is dealt with and I know you'll be safe."

Sitting up, she threw out, "You won't *allow* it? Why do you think you have any say in my life anymore, King?"

I'd avoided meeting her eyes, but I turned and looked at her now. "I mightn't have any say in your life, but this isn't up for argument, Ivy. You will not be leaving this building. Understood?"

Her lips flattened as she stared at me with loathing. She didn't answer my question, though. Just stared at me.

I jerked up off the bed and paced in front of it, attempting to sort through the shit I wanted to say. "Fuck, why can't you see what I'm trying to do? That this is in your best interest?" That she couldn't, or wouldn't, bewildered me.

She shot off the bed, coming to me with fire in her eyes. They burned with it. Getting in my face, she yelled, "Why can't *you* see that you don't always know what's in other people's best interests? You haven't changed, King! Always laying down the law as you see it, not once stopping to consider that I might have a different vision for my life." She slapped her palms on my chest and added, "Fuck you!"

My veins filled with fury, and I gripped her wrists. "You don't know me as well as you think you do," I thundered. "Not if you think I don't stop and consider every-fucking-thing about those I care for."

Her brows lifted. "Oh, so cheating on me was your way of considering everything, then? You're full of bullshit."

She tried to wiggle out of my grip, but I squeezed her wrists harder and pulled her to me. Our bodies, this close, was dangerous. The desire I'd always felt for her sparked to life, circling us, threatening to pull me under. Because that's where I'd end up if I let it take over.

The weight of my past actions sat heavy on my shoulders. I'd carried it with me for too long, some days almost suffocating under the pressure. Knowing I'd fucked her up had fucked *me* up. I'd decided long ago to carry it and never tell her the truth. It was better she continued believing I was an asshole. Better she kept me from her life.

But her outburst, and the way she kept looking at me with so much hatred, tripped me up. I wasn't sure I could stand that hatred for much longer. Not when Ivy was the person I'd loved the longest in my life.

I latched onto my own anger over this situation and used it to fuel my reaction. Glaring at her, I said, "I didn't come here to get into it with you. That shit is in the past, so let's move the fuck on and deal with important shit."

Her eyes widened, and from the way her face morphed from angry to hurt back to angry, I knew we wouldn't be moving the fuck on. Wild energy engulfed her, and she engaged in a full-out battle to disentangle herself from me. Shoving her hands against my chest and fighting me, she shouted, "That shit *is* important to me, you fucking asshole! That you would say that and think that, just shows me what a bastard you really are. Did you even really love me? Because I don't think you did! I think I was just another pussy to you. Someone who warmed your bed and fucked you whenever you wanted."

Her words tore me apart.

They ripped shreds of my soul from me. The soul I'd refused to acknowledge since I'd pushed her out of my life. But Ivy saying this shit to me? That caused my soul to rear its head and force its way back into view.

Fuck.

Motherfucking *fuck.*

I lost my calm.

I lost my fucking mind and allowed words out that should never have seen the light of day.

Letting her go, I roared, "I didn't fucking cheat on you! I did that for your protection, too. Don't you fucking get it, Ivy? I do everything for your fucking protection." My voice darkened as hurt consumed me. "And never fucking say that I didn't love you. I loved you more than any-fucking-one. You were never just someone to come home to and fuck. Hell, if that was the case, I would have left you when you kicked me out of your bed for months." I moved closer to her again, ignoring the emotions blazing from her. Ignoring everything but my own needs now. I fucking needed to get this shit out there. "Anything you wanted, I would have given to you. Anything you needed, I found a way to get. And when I realised the last fucking thing you needed was *me*, I took matters into my own hands. I never once cheated on you. Not until that night, and even then it wasn't real. I set it up to make you leave. To keep you safe from me. So don't throw accusations at me that are as far from the fucking truth as you can get."

She stared at me with shock and disbelief. Her chest

pumped furiously while she tried to steady her breaths. "You lied to me?"

One simple question with only one truthful answer.

But that answer had so many layers to it.

Where did you start when years of love and hate and hurt all piled on top of each other? How did relationships ever survive that? I had no fucking clue because I'd never managed to keep a relationship from crumbling under all those layers.

I didn't want to answer Ivy's question. Not without being able to give her the full picture. But what was the point? We were done a long time ago. There was no going back, ever. So I simply nodded. "Yeah, I lied to you."

Her silence hit me more than if she'd yelled and screamed at me. It always had. I didn't know what to do with silence. Didn't know how to engage with it. I did best with anger and violence. Come at me with either of those, and I'd find a way through it. But silence caused me to stumble and falter because it hurt like a motherfucker. My father had taught me that.

When she sat on the bed and turned away from me, her own hurt so deafening it blocked out everything else, I was done. I'd already said too much and didn't want to continue falling down the fucking abyss of our past. Exhaling hard, I said forcefully, "Don't try to leave the clubhouse, because you won't like the response."

With that, I stalked out of her room and outside to my bike. I needed to get out of here for a while. Fuck knew I had to put some distance between Ivy and me. And I wouldn't be hurrying back to her any-fucking-time soon.

22

Lily

I stared down at my phone, hoping I'd imagined the text flashing on my screen.

I blinked, trying to get the words to disappear.

Surely it wasn't real.

He wouldn't.

Fuck, he probably would.

My ex was that dumb, he would.

I blinked again, squeezing my eyes tightly, praying for the text to be gone when I opened my eyes.

Shit, it was still there.

"Motherfucker," I cursed.

I shot off a text to my sister in response to hers.

Me: I'm going to fucking kill him.

Brynn: Ooh, let me do it first.

Me: Do not let Zara out of your sight. She is NOT going on that date tonight.

Brynn: Hurry home, sis. She's already applying her makeup.

I called her. "I swear, I'm going to wrap my hands around his throat and squeeze every last fucking breath from him. And then I'm going to get a knife and stab him so many times that when they sentence me for my crime, they'll give me the death penalty even though they don't give that to anyone anymore. I'm going to make him fucking hurt for this shit. This is the last time Linc screws with me!"

I was on my way to see Skylar King, but realised I needed a moment, *or fifty*, to calm down before I saw her, so I spun around to head outside for a smoke first. I stopped abruptly when I came face-to-face with Skylar's brother.

King.

He watched me with an intensity that flustered me.

"Shit, Brynn, I've gotta go," I rambled into my phone, not giving her a chance to respond to what I'd already said. "I'll be home as fast as I can this afternoon. And thanks for the heads up." Ending the call, I shoved my phone into my pocket and took a step backwards, away from King. "Hi," I said, completely muddled by both the news Brynn had given me and the fact King was right there. I mean, he was so damn close and staring at me so intently that my thoughts had become a jumbled mess.

"Remind me never to piss you off," he said, that voice of his a deep rumble that did things to me. Things I wasn't used to from the men I spoke to. Goodness, he was dangerously sexy this close.

"Huh?" I had no idea what he meant. Especially not when all I could focus on was the way he watched me.

"The threat of strangulation and a stabbing frenzy."

"Oh, that. Right."

His lips twitched slightly, like he was amused by me. "Someone close?"

I let go of the breath I held. Thinking about Linc was enough to ease my nerves around King, because the anger he induced cleared my head of the disorientation King caused. "My ex is being an asshole." I remembered what King had said about having experience raising girls. "Tell me, would you allow your fourteen-year-old daughter out on a date at night?"

"Only if I had eyes on her at all times."

I frowned. "You'd stake out her date?"

He nodded. "Yeah. I know the shit that runs through a fourteen-year-old boy's mind."

"Oh, God." I yanked my phone back out and hit Linc's number. Looking up at King, who continued to watch me with that damn intensity I wish he'd let go of, I said, "One sec, I have to rip my ex a new one."

Amusement flickered in his eyes and across his lips again.

When the call went to message bank, I let loose on Linc. "You better get your ass over to my place quick fucking smart, Linc, and tell your daughter that you made a mistake by saying yes to her date tonight. If you don't fix this, I swear to God, you will regret it. I will find all the ways under the sun to make you regret it."

I stabbed at the phone when I was done and looked at King and demanded, "What?" when I saw the way his eyebrows had arched. "You think I'm a bitch to my ex? He deserved that, for so much more than just this! I'm sick and tired of putting up with his crap." My heart raced with anger and frustration. Why did I ever take this journey with Linc? He'd given me nothing but heartache and grief for years now, and I wasn't sure how much more I could handle.

King shook his head. "No, I'm just thinking 'good fucking luck' to your ex."

"Yeah, he's going to need it," I muttered before blowing out another long breath and changing the subject. "Are you heading up to see your sister?"

"Yeah. How's she doing today?"

"Good this morning. She managed to put weight on both legs, which I'm really happy with. I'm just going for a smoke before I do this afternoon's session with her. I'll see you there if you're still around. I have a list of physios for you to check out, too."

He nodded and continued on. I watched him walk away, wondering again about that scar on his face. Heck, there were a lot of things I wondered about that man. Things I'd never find the answers to. Things I would probably rather not know. And yet, I'd found my thoughts drifting to him since we met.

That's because you're the good girl who always falls for the bad boy.

It's time you got your shit together and found yourself a nice stable man.

Ugh.

I sounded like my mother.

Brynn was right.

I *was* turning into her.

~

"So you think she may be able to leave here in a couple of days?" King asked as I finished up Skylar's session.

I smiled at Skylar who settled herself on the chair next to the bed. She'd worked hard today, and I was more than happy with her progress. "Yes." I passed him my list of recommended physiotherapists. "Here's that list I promised."

"Appreciate it," he said, taking the list and perusing it. "There are only a few names on here."

"Yes." When he glanced back up at me, questioningly, I added, "I'm fussy with my recommendations. I would never give you the name of someone if I wouldn't personally use them."

"Good to know." He folded the piece of paper and pushed it into the pocket of his jeans. Then to his sister, he said, "I'll get the guys to set up a room for you with everything you want, so text me a list today." He glanced back at me. "Is there anything you recommend I get to make shit easier for her?"

Yesterday, I'd thought King a rude man. Maybe he was, but I couldn't help softening my opinion of him as I took in how much he cared for his sister. I'd worked with a lot of families in my role at the hospital, and sadly, I wasn't surprised anymore when it was clear some of them treated caring for an injured family member as the biggest burden they'd ever endured. That kind of scenario happened all too often. King was different. He cared deeply and by the looks of it, would do whatever it took to help Skylar recover.

I listed a few things I thought would help and had just finished when his phone rang. He checked the caller ID and said, "I've gotta take this," before stepping out of the room.

"Thank you for all your help," Skylar said, distracting me from watching King go. It was hard to draw my gaze from him though. When jeans hugged a man's ass the way King's did, it was almost impossible.

When I finally turned to Skylar, she watched me like she was entertained by me. Ignoring that, I said, "Absolutely."

Smiling, she shook her head. "I can never work out why women are so freaking attracted to my brother."

"It's his ass," I said, deadpan. "Because it sure isn't his friendly vibes or anything like that."

Her smile morphed into a laugh. "Honestly, I've watched women throw themselves at him, even when he turns assholey on them."

I shrugged. "What can I say? We women are screwed up when it comes to men. I've always liked the bad boys, but almost everything about your brother tells me he's more than just a bad boy. I'd take that ass, though."

She continued to laugh. "I like you, Lily. You just say it like it is."

I gathered my stuff to leave. I still had two more patients to see before I could go home and lay down the law to my daughter. "Between an ex I wanna strangle, three kids who cause me heart palpitations most days, and a mother who tests my patience with her crazy-ass way of living, I don't have the time in my life or the energy to say it like it isn't." I paused for a beat before smiling at her and adding, "I'll be back tomorrow morning. Do those exercises I gave you, okay?"

She nodded. "I wouldn't dream of not doing them. My physio is bossy and will give me hell if I don't."

"Yes she is, and yes she will," I agreed before exiting her room.

I'd almost made it to the lift at the end of the corridor when King came towards me, a look of deep concentration on his face. I had no idea what was going on his life, but from what I'd observed of him so far, it felt like he was dealing with something big.

His eyes met mine as we moved closer, and I did my best to ignore the way his attention stirred butterflies in my stomach. I'd never met a man like King before. He exuded power without even trying. It surprised me that I found this a turn on, because I'd never been about a man taking charge of me. But a girl had no freaking say over what got her excited, as much as she tried. And God knew, I'd tried.

"Thanks for all your work with Skylar."

The butterflies in my stomach flapped their wings all over the place as his voice vibrated across my skin.

I decided then and there that dangerous wasn't a strong enough word to describe King. If a man could elicit this kind of response simply from uttering a few words, I didn't want to imagine how I would react to anything more. It was a good thing his sister would be going home in a couple of days.

I smiled. "Just doing my job."

"Something tells me that you doing your job means a lot more than what it would mean for most people."

My breathing slowed.

Not many patients or their family members acknowledged the efforts I went to. Most just thanked me and moved on to the next phase of their recovery.

"Thank you. That means a lot."

His gaze swept down my body briefly before coming back to meet mine, and oh good freaking Lord did that cause a riot in my belly.

Dangerous? Freaking hazardous, more like it.

"I'll go through this list of physios this afternoon and will be back in touch if I need you."

With that, he left me to go back into his sister's room, leaving me staring after him wondering what he meant by getting back in touch if he needed me. His statement bamboozled me, but then again, maybe it was just his ass that did that.

"Shit," I muttered to myself. I had better things to do than stand here lusting after a man who probably went through more women in a month than I went through men in a decade.

~

I'm going to get through this weekend.

I'm going to survive my kids.

I'm not going to kill my mother.

I slid down the bath and submerged my entire body as I chanted positive affirmations that not even I believed.

I quite possibly might kill Linc.

That one rang true.

I'd had to drag him over this afternoon after I got home from work to retract his approval for Zara to go on a date tonight. He hadn't wanted to, because he hated not being the fun parent, but I'd threatened to report him for late child support payments if he didn't. Heaven knew why I hadn't already. When we'd divorced, I promised myself I'd do everything to keep his relationship with the kids close, and for some fucked-up reason that I couldn't let go of, I thought that not reporting him would help with that. He always came through with the money in the end, so while it could be stressful, it always worked out. If that changed, I'd definitely reconsider my stance.

I came up for air as a knock sounded on my bathroom door, followed by my sister's voice. "Lil, can I come in?"

"Yeah, but only if you have wine for me."

The door opened, and she held up a bottle of wine. "I have supplies."

"Thank God, because it might be the only thing that will stop me from committing a crime tonight."

She grinned as she sat on the edge of the bath and passed me the glass of wine she'd already poured. "I'm not sure if Holly has ever ushered me inside the house faster than she just did. Tell me everything." Brynn'd had to rush off to a massage appointment when I'd arrived home, so she'd missed out on all the drama with Zara and Linc.

I gulped some wine down and squeezed my eyes closed for a moment before taking another gulp. Opening my eyes, I took a deep breath and said, "Zara hates me, and I doubt she'll speak to me for a good month. Maybe a year. Mum stuck her nose in and told Linc off. They had a huge fight, which then led to me having a huge fight with Mum. She left in a huff, at which point I told Linc he'd pretty much reached my limit, and that if he didn't get his shit together and back me on parenting decisions rather than going against me in order to gain the kids' approval, then he and I were done." I took another deep breath and downed the rest of the wine in my glass.

Brynn refilled my glass. "What do you mean by you guys being done? As far as I'm aware, you're already done. Are you planning murder? Or is it code for something else?"

"Murder is definitely on my list of options, but I'd need to watch a heap more crime shows first to figure out how to get away with it, and honestly, when does a girl have time for that?"

Her eyes sparkled with amusement. "So, what then?"

I sighed and drank some more wine. "You know, I could really do with a smoke right about now, but I made a decision at lunch to give them up."

Brynn cocked her head to the side. "Lil, stop avoiding my question."

I stared at her, not wanting to admit the truth of the matter because I knew it could lead to an "I told you so" moment, and I really, *really* hated those moments. "Okay, fine, you were right—I need to stop letting him get away with so much."

"Which means?"

"Jesus, Brynn, why do you have to push me on this? I know what I have to do, and I'm gonna do it."

"I push you because your heart is too kind and I know you too well. You're angry with Linc today, but what happens when that anger subsides? Will you still be so ready to let go of your tendency to go easy on him? I just want what's best for you, and I don't think the way you two have been co-existing for the past three years is the best for you anymore."

"I agree." I took a sip of wine. "And that's why I told him we're doing things differently from now on. He's going to have the kids every second weekend, he's not going to drop by unannounced, he's going to pay child support on time, and he's going to take the kids every alternating Wednesday night. And on those Wednesday nights, he's going to help the kids with their assignments rather than just doing fun stuff with them."

Brynn's eyes widened. "You guys worked all this out this afternoon?"

I nodded. "Yes, and I'm serious about making it happen. I can't go on in this super-stressed state anymore."

"Good," she said, standing.

"Where are you going?"

She jerked her head towards the door. "I'm going to check in on Zara. When Holly called, she said Zara was asking for me. I just needed to make sure you were okay first."

I frowned. "Holly called you to come over?"

"Yeah, she said shit had gone down and she figured you'd need me. You raised some good kids, babe."

"If only they all still loved me like that."

"They do. Zara will come around."

As she exited the bathroom, I called out, "Wait! Is tomorrow your fishing date with the prostitute?"

She looked back at me. "Yes, but can we not refer to it as a date? It's just fishing."

"We both know it's not fishing."

"We do not."

"We do. And by the way, what's his name?"

She poked her tongue at me. "I'm not telling you." She closed the door and left me alone.

"I'm going to find out!" I called after her, laughing as I thought about my sister ending up on a fishing date with a prostitute our mother ordered for her. It was the kind of story that people just wouldn't believe. And it was the exact kind of story that helped me through my days. Thank God for having Brynn as my sister. The hilarious shit she got up to always made me laugh and eased my stress a little.

23

King

"Don't let him out of your sight," I said to Devil over the phone early the next morning. I'd pulled him off watching Skylar so he could track Brant.

"Has he made contact with Romano yet?"

Devil and Kick were tailing Brant who we'd let leave the clubhouse fifteen minutes earlier. Zane had bugged Brant's phone so we could keep track of him and also listen to his calls.

"No."

Hyde entered the surveillance room Zane had set up and eyed me. "Ghost just made contact again. The guy he thought we could use to deal with Marx has been moved, so he's not an option anymore. Ghost is working his contacts to find someone else."

"Fuck," I muttered. "Go through everyone we know again

and see if we can do this without Ghost. We need this dealt with as soon as fucking possible."

Hyde nodded and left as Axe met my gaze. "Do you know what Marx has given the feds yet?"

"Not yet. Bronze is working on that, but they've locked the case down tight apparently, so he hasn't been able to access the info."

"I've got a guy who might be able to help. I'll mention it to him."

Zane cut into the conversation. "Here he goes."

The room turned silent while the three of us listened to Brant's call with Romano.

"Where have you been?" It was Romano.

"I'm in Sydney. I've been looking for Ivy for you."

Silence followed for a moment. *"Did you find her?"*

"No, but I found out something that might interest you."

"Keep talking."

"I visited the Storm clubhouse, thinking Ivy might have gone to King. She hasn't, but they're knocking themselves out looking for whoever's been fucking with them. I heard one of the guys mention something about a rat in the club."

I'd threatened his life if he didn't come through for us with this, and it seemed he'd taken me seriously.

"And what the fuck makes you think I'd have any interest in that?"

"I figure if the guy's working with you, feeding you information, you might wanna look out for him. Warn him or something."

Romano laughed, his contempt bleeding through the phone. *"They're looking in the wrong place."* He paused before saying, *"Get your ass back to Melbourne. I've got shit for you to do."*

Zane glanced at me as the call ended. "Romano's playing with him. He's gotta know where Brant's been."

I nodded. "Agreed. And now we wait for him to come for Brant."

"That comment about you looking in the wrong place, though," Axe said, "That didn't sound like a play."

"Yeah," I said, "I'll get Hyde to extend the search." I met Zane's gaze again. "You need to deal with Don." *Kree's husband.*

His movements slowed, and he gave me his full attention. "I am."

"No, you're fucking about trying not to step on fucking toes, Zane. That's not dealing with anything. Don needs to be removed from Kree's life for good."

"I don't *remove* people like you do, King, and you know that. I've got a plan in place that should neutralise the threat to Kree."

"Should?"

His jaw clenched. "It will fix the problem."

"When? Because if this fucking problem isn't fixed in the next couple of days, I'll take care of it."

"Fuck." He rubbed the back of his neck as he swore. "Give me a week. If it's not done then, it's all yours."

I contemplated that. Kree and the kids were safe here, and I had enough other shit to take care of so this was probably the best option. Against my better judgement, though, I nodded in agreement. "A week. Make sure it's done."

Winter stuck his head in the room as Zane went back to what he was doing. Eyeing me, he said, "We need to get onto the doctor again. Ivy's getting worse."

Fuck.

After the argument I'd had with her yesterday, seeing her was the last thing I wanted to be doing.

"How?" I asked. "And has the doc given you any idea when he can make it?"

"She hasn't left her room since you said she could. I've

been checking on her, and there's blood on her sheets. When I asked her about it, she refused to discuss it. Doc said he'd come by this afternoon. He was swamped yesterday. But I don't think we can wait that long."

"How much blood, Winter?" For all I fucking knew, it could be something as simple as a nosebleed.

"The amount of blood I'd be worried about if she were my sister."

"Jesus. Okay, I'll deal with this."

I made my way to the room we'd allocated Ivy and entered it without knocking. Concern sparked through me when I found her hunched over on the side of the bed.

"Do you need a doctor?"

She took her time looking up at me. When her gaze met mine, she nodded. Standing, she came my way, clutching her stomach. "Yes, I think so."

Pulling out my phone, I hit the number for our club doctor. "What's wrong?" I asked her, putting the phone to my ear.

Her mouth opened, but all that came out was a scream of pain as she doubled over. It was then, as her hands grabbed hold of my shirt, that I saw the pool of blood on the bed sheet.

Winter had been right to be worried.

It looked like Ivy had lost half her fucking blood.

"A miscarriage?" I stared at the doctor, hating every word coming out of his mouth. "So you can't save the baby?"

He sighed as he pulled the gloves off his hands and threw them in the bin. "There is no baby to save, King. She'd already lost it. Two weeks ago. But it was an incomplete miscarriage. That's why she's still experiencing cramping and bleeding. She needs to go to the hospital for a D&C."

I glanced beyond him at Ivy sitting in the bed staring at the wall in front of her.

Fuck.

My fucking chest hurt just looking at her.

Ivy had wanted three kids. It had been all she'd talked about at one stage while we were together. She'd picked out three girl names and three boy names to cover all bases. When I'd asked her why the fuck she wanted to bring children into this fucked-up world, she'd smiled at me and said we would do it right. That she and I would be the best type of parents. The complete opposite of our parents.

I nodded at the doctor. "I'll take her now."

Moving past him, I went to her. "I need to get you to the hospital."

She ignored me for a few moments before finally turning to look up at me. "He never wanted children. Not like you did."

I clenched my fists by my side. There was something in her tone, something that made me ask, "Why did you miscarry?"

A sob escaped her lips, and her hand flew to her mouth as tears slid down her cheeks. When she answered me, the words choked out of her. "He beat me until I passed out. When I woke up, I was bleeding."

It took everything in me not to roar with anger. Not to drive my fists into the wall. Instead, I scooped her into my arms and made a promise I intended to keep. "He will pay for this, Ivy. If it's the last fucking thing I ever do. He will fucking pay."

Her eyes found mine and held them as she slid her arms around my neck. I struggled for breath while she did that. It was all too fucking much.

Her pain.

Her body in my arms.

Her fingers on my skin.

And when she whispered, "Thank you," through her sobs, and nuzzled her face into my neck, I knew I'd do anything to put an end to her husband's life. I'd fucking bleed if I had to.

24

King

"You look like shit."

I looked up from the drink I was staring at to find Kree watching me with a look of concern. She'd broken the silence I'd managed to find in the clubhouse bar. "It's 2:00 a.m., Kree. Why are you up?"

She slid onto the stool next to me and reached for my glass of whisky. After she took a long gulp, she said, "I can't sleep here. I need my candles and crystals around me. I'm agitated without them."

I moved around to the other side of the bar as I said, "I'll send the boys out to get your shit tomorrow. You need your sleep." Grabbing a glass, I poured another whisky and placed it in front of her. "Drink that."

Her lips curled into a smile. "You don't like sharing your drink, King?"

I ignored that and moved back around the bar to my stool.

I wasn't in the mood for fucking small talk.

We sat in silence for a good few minutes before she broke it again. "You wanna talk about it?"

I eyed her. "I thought you didn't wanna know the shit in my head."

"I don't, but you've got a lot of stuff going on, and I figure you need to get that shit out. And I also figure you're not the kind of man to talk about any of it." She took a sip of her drink. "I'm not saying I want specifics, but you *need* to talk about it. You might just blow the place up if you don't."

I watched her for another moment before nodding. She made a good fucking point. Since I'd learnt of Ivy's miscarriage yesterday, my mind felt like it had fractured. I'd moved through the motions of getting her looked after and then bringing her back here, but after that, I hadn't been able to bring myself to see her. I'd spent the rest of yesterday and all of today out looking for Romano. The motherfucker still managed to elude us. Not even Brant had drawn him out. Nothing was fucking going in our favour, and fuck knew I needed to get some of that shit out of my head.

I emptied my glass and poured another one before turning to face her again. "I've fucked a lot of things up in my life, Kree." I paused and exhaled a long breath. "I don't wanna fuck this up, but shit's heading south every hour." I stopped talking and knocked back some whisky. I was wrong—I didn't need to get into this shit with her. I didn't need to get into it with anyone. I just fucking needed to stay focused on my goal and get it done. Talking about it didn't help anyone.

"We've all fucked stuff up in our life. You shouldn't be so hard on yourself."

The longstanding tension in my shoulders made itself known. I'd lived with it for so long I hardly felt it anymore, but every now and then the pressure became all I could feel.

I dropped my head for a moment and then glanced sideways at her. "You ever fucked anyone over? You know what guilt feels like? And I mean the kind that twists your gut so fucking much that some days you can't fucking breathe."

"I don't know that kind of guilt, but I'll tell you something—if you're the kind of man who can admit his mistakes, you're the kind of man who can be forgiven."

"I'm not looking for forgiveness."

"Well, maybe you should be."

"Why?"

"If you don't, this kind of stuff will eat you up and kill you." She leaned closer. "And when I say you should look for forgiveness, I mostly mean from yourself. You need to show yourself the kind of love others would show you if you asked for it."

"Fuck, Kree," I muttered, taking a swig of my drink. "I'm not asking for love or fucking forgiveness. I own my shit. I did it, and I'll fucking live with it."

"Yeah well, you're *not* living with it, King, if you're sitting here in a bar asking me about guilt at 2:00 a.m. So have a think about *that*, okay?"

I was fucking done with this conversation. Moving off my stool, I said, "Let Kick know what shit you want from your house tomorrow. He'll get it."

She called after me as I left, "Think about it. I'm not always right, but I'm right about this."

She wasn't right, not if she thought I needed forgiveness. Men like me didn't deserve that.

I made my way to the kitchen but got distracted by the door to Ivy's room. The light coming from under the door shed a tiny sliver of light into the dark hallway, catching my attention.

Against my better judgement, I closed the distance to her room and entered it.

She was lying on the bed, staring up at the ceiling, but

turned her head to look at me. No smile, but the hard edge to her seemed to have disappeared. Now, she just looked broken.

My chest squeezed.

Fuck.

I sat on the bed and held her gaze. After a few moments, I asked, "How are you feeling?"

"Tired mostly."

"Do you need anything?" Winter had been keeping an eye on her and had told me she still wasn't eating much.

"No."

The lifeless tone to her voice worried me. Ivy used to shut down on me when something devastated her, and this was the tone I knew well from those times. It was the sign she was tapping out, and I'd be fucked if I'd allow that.

My jaw clenched as I thought about all the shit her husband had put her through. "How many times did he do this to you?"

Her eyes closed and she rolled to her side and curled into a ball.

"Ivy," I demanded, my voice harsher than I meant, "tell me. How many times?"

She shook her head. "Don't, King. I don't want to talk about it."

"What? Three times? Four? Five?" My voice grew louder as my desperation to have this conversation intensified. I needed to fucking know. "How many fucking times?"

Her eyes snapped open and wild, angry energy blazed from her. "Why? There's nothing you can do about it now, so there's no fucking point going over it!"

"There *is* a fucking point because I'm going to make him pay. Tell me."

She stared at me for a long beat, and I wondered if I was going to have to drag this information from her, but finally she said, "I've had six miscarriages. Four were because of him."

I shot up off the bed and paced the tiny room. "Fucking hell! I will fucking wrap my hands around his throat and take his last fucking breath."

Ivy sat up on the bed, resting against the wall. Her exhaustion clothed her, and I fucking hated him for that too. "Just let it go, King. I'm not going back to him. He can't hurt me anymore."

I stopped pacing and directed my gaze back at her. "You've got that fucking right—you're never going back to him. And I won't fucking rest until I make sure he can never touch you again."

A long sigh fell from her lips. "Can you please pass my painkillers and the glass of water that are on the table?"

I did as she asked and then sat on the bed again, watching her closely for a sign—*any sign*—that she was going to be okay. When she looked at me after taking her drugs and said, "Remember the miscarriage I had when we were together?" I knew that was my sign. Somehow, we'd moved past the standoff we were at.

I nodded. "Yes." *I'll never fucking forget it.*

Ivy had fallen pregnant a couple of months after the night I'd almost forced myself on her. It had been a rare night where we'd connected again and the sex had been good, like old times, rather than rushed and just a release for each of us. I'd held hope the pregnancy would bring us back together, but six weeks later, that hope had been killed and she'd pulled away from me again. It had been one of our darkest moments together.

A tear slid down her cheek. "I was a bitch to you after that."

She had been, but so much other shit had already gone on

between us, that by then, we were both at fault. "It's in the past, Ivy. We both did some fucked-up shit."

More tears fell and she wiped them away. "Yeah, but I shouldn't have pushed you away and treated you so badly. I'm sorry for that."

Regret sat heavy in my chest as I thought about that time in our lives. There'd been so much confusion and so many misunderstandings, and if I could take that shit back, I would. But I wouldn't change the fact we weren't in each other's lives anymore, because that was the only thing that actually made sense. We would have destroyed each other if we hadn't made that break.

I stood as I said, "Get some sleep."

Leaving the room, I didn't look back.

Never fucking look back was how I lived life, and now was not the time to change it.

25

King

"You're going to be fine," Lily said, trying to assure Skylar, who looked anything but convinced she was going to be fine.

I was taking her home today, and she'd just spent the last fucking ten minutes freaking out about how she was gonna cope without the support she'd had while in hospital. Lily had to be one of the most patient women I'd ever come across. The way she remained calm with my sister impressed the fuck out of me.

Panic crossed Skylar's face. "I might not be! King still hasn't been able to find a physio off your list who can fit me in. What am I gonna do without you, Lily?"

"Jesus," I muttered, losing *my* patience, but Lily's eyes cut to mine and she hit me with a look that told me to rein it in.

"I'm going to give you my phone number, okay?" Lily said to Skylar as she sat next to her on the bed and held out her hand for Skylar's phone. "And if you need to chat or need me to talk you through anything at all, you call me."

Skylar passed over her phone and fuck if Lily's offer didn't calm her down a little.

Lily keyed her number in, handed the phone back, stood and then said with a level of bossiness that Skylar responded to, "Right, up you get. I've got another patient I have to see, and your brother looks like he's about to lose his shit if you guys don't get moving soon."

My brows arched as I met Lily's gaze. Her serious expression disappeared and a ghost of a smile flickered across her face. It didn't last long, and as soon as she turned back to Skylar, it was gone, but it sparked a smile of my own.

I watched as she helped Skylar up, all the while talking positive shit to her. It reminded me of how Margreet used to encourage us as kids and how she always had the ability to stay focused and calm, even when we gave her hell. Lily's words blurred into the background as my gaze drifted down her body. Fuck, she owned some serious curves and a tight ass. The kind that usually gave me a hard-on. If I wasn't knee-fucking-deep in club shit at the moment, I'd have paid more attention to those curves by now.

"King!" Skylar's voice sliced through my thoughts, drawing my focus back to the situation at hand. "I'm ready to go."

I nodded as I continued eyeing Lily. When I made it back up her body and found her watching me, she blinked and immediately dropped her gaze before turning to Skylar and mumbling a goodbye. A moment later, she exited the room, confusing the hell out of me as to what the fuck just happened.

"King, can you take this?" Skylar asked, passing me her iPad.

I packed it into her bag and gathered her shit while she

sat in the wheelchair the wardie had waiting to take her downstairs. We were on our way to the elevator when Hyde called.

"I've got some good news finally," he said. "Ghost has someone organised to take care of Marx."

"When?"

"Tonight."

"Let Tatum know. The less she feels the need to ring me, the better."

"Will do."

"Any news on Romano?"

"Nothing yet. I do have news on Ivy, though."

I followed the wardie and Skylar to the lift. "What?"

"She's looking for you."

"And?"

"She's harassing the fuck out of Winter about seeing you."

"Tell her I'm busy, Hyde." Seeing Ivy was the last thing on my agenda for today.

"You ever tried to tell Ivy something she doesn't wanna hear? She's fucking stubborn."

"Yeah. I know." *Did I fucking know.* "She can wait."

"Fuck," he muttered.

"You get Monroe out of town?"

"She left this morning. I hope to fucking hell we get this shit sorted soon because she's headed down to Melbourne to see Charlie who's staying with Tenille. Those women could kill each other if left together for long enough."

I gripped my phone harder. "We need to make a new plan to get to Romano. I'm on my way back there now. Get Axe and Zane in on this too."

As I ended the call, I eyed Lily ahead. "I'll meet you downstairs, Skye," I said, leaving her with the wardie while I cut a path to where Lily stood going over her files.

"King," she said, glancing up from her work. Her eyes held uncertainty, wariness maybe, but they also held the kind of warmth I didn't often come across in my world. And again, it reminded me of Margreet.

"Will you work with Skylar on her rehab?"

She shook her head. "No, I don't do private physio work. Have you got many left to call from that list I gave you?"

"I've called them all. None have any spare appointments."

She frowned. "Oh. I thought Skylar said you still had some left to try."

"You saw how anxious she is about this shit. I haven't told her they're all busy. I was hoping you might be able to squeeze her in."

"No, sorry, like I said, I don't do any work outside of the hospital." She shifted her weight onto one leg, drawing my attention down those legs again. Fuck, I really needed to get laid. I needed to drive some of this fucking tension out of my body.

Forcing my gaze back up to her face, I said, "I'll pay you whatever you want."

She opened her mouth to respond, but quickly shut it again. Then she said, "I honestly don't have time between my kids and work. Sorry. There are plenty of good physios out there. You'll find someone."

With that, she gave me one last smile and walked away, leaving me staring after her wondering why the fuck I was annoyed she'd said no. There had to be hundreds of physiotherapists in Sydney.

"Fuck," I muttered to myself, stalking towards the lifts. I'd find someone else. Skylar didn't need Lily.

～

"I've spent days looking into Ryland and can't find any dirt on him," Tatum said an hour later when she found me in the clubhouse bar. I hadn't been in the clubhouse for longer than twenty minutes, and hadn't had a moment of peace in that time.

"Keep digging. Everyone has dirt."

"I'm telling you, King, he doesn't."

"Fuck, Tatum, he will. Just keep fucking looking." It had just gone midday and the bullshit I'd already dealt with today left me little patience for any more. From issues with cleaning jobs we had going on, to a drug shipment being delayed, to club members growing restless with the Romano situation not being handled yet, to Tatum being on my ass about this, I was ready to call it a fucking day and go in search of pussy to dull the roar in my head.

She hit me with the cool gaze she often reserved for me. "I should have known you'd fob me off. You've been doing it for days." She turned to leave, throwing back, "I'll get Billy to help me on this."

I reached for her, wrapping my hand around her wrist and pulling her back to me. Every ounce of frustration and anger I felt over this fucking situation and her attitude spilled out as I growled, "You do that, and you won't like my response. This shit stays club business. The minute you make it something other than that is the minute you're out in the fucking cold." My eyes bored into hers. "Understood?"

Her cool gaze quickly turned stormy. Yanking her arm from my grip, she continued to drive my blood pressure up, hostile as fucking ever. "No, not understood. You can take your threats and shove them up your ass, King. I'm not scared of you."

"I'm not trying to scare you, Tatum. I'm just letting you know how shit will go down if you choose a path that's not in the club's interest."

She glared at me for a moment longer before stalking out of the office.

Fucking hell. The last thing we needed was Billy getting involved in this. I had to keep this contained in order to keep the club safe. There was far too much shit buried that needed to be kept that way, and the more people involved, the more likely some of it wouldn't stay buried.

I dialled the lawyer we'd hired to get Nitro out.

"King. What's up?" I appreciated that he always got straight down to business.

"I need to see Nitro."

"I can get you in tomorrow morning."

"Book it."

"Will do. I'll send you the details."

Hyde entered the office as I ended the call, his body as tense as I felt. "Ryland's back."

I blew out a harsh breath. A fucking frustrated-as-fuck breath. "Jesus fucking Christ."

Hyde nodded. "Yeah. You want me to tell him you're not here?"

"No, I need to know what the fuck he's here about today. Has Tatum left?"

He nodded again. "What happened there?"

"She's ready to get Billy involved. I've organised a visit with Nitro tomorrow. He needs to keep her on a fucking leash."

"Might be easier said than done with her. And Nitro's not gonna be happy if we threaten her in any way or do something to keep her quiet."

"I've already threatened her. If Nitro keeps her quiet, I won't need to go through with it." Without waiting for his input on that, I asked, "Any luck on the rat yet?" He and Zane hadn't turned up any good leads yet.

"Still nothing, but I've got some of the guys out knocking

down doors to find this motherfucker. It won't be long now. Also, nothing new on Brant either. He might be back in Melbourne, but Romano hasn't made contact with him."

"He will. Keep Devil and Kick on Brant for when that happens," I said as I exited the office. "And organise Church for tomorrow morning. I want to see where everyone's at."

I made my way outside to where Ryland was waiting for me. He watched me come towards him with the same satisfied expression he'd worn the other day. The one I would wipe from his face when I was finally done with him calling the shots.

"King, are you having trouble sleeping? You look tired."

Maybe I'll just fucking deal with him now and be done with it.

"What the fuck do you want now, Ryland? I'm busy and don't have time for all your visits. Either charge me with something or get the fuck off this property."

He smirked. "I see my presence agitates you, which is completely warranted with the shit I'm digging up on you. I just dropped by today to let you know the investigation is progressing well."

I clenched my jaw as the overwhelming desire to smash my fists into his face consumed me. The whole fucking scenario of how I'd remove him from this earth played out in my head in a rush of seconds, but I managed to control my thirst for his blood. "And now you've told me that, you can back the fuck up and leave."

"Nitro sends his regards. Mind you, he doesn't talk much, that one. No worries, though, Marx does enough talking for the both of them."

I took a step closer to him at the same time Hyde joined us, warning, "King. Not a good idea, brother."

He was wrong. It was the best fucking idea I'd had in a long time.

Fuck.

I stepped back. "If that's all, Ryland, I've got shit to do."

He hit me with another satisfied grin. "I bet you do. I wouldn't bother trying to cover up all your skeletons though, King. It's too late for that."

As we watched him leave, Hyde said, "He's fucking with us, brother."

My head throbbed with the beginning of a headache. "Yeah, but I'm not convinced he doesn't have some shit. We need to call Cole in on this now. We need all the fucking help we can get."

He nodded. "I agree."

"You organise that while I check in with Axe to see if he's been able to find out what Marx has given the feds."

I found Axe a few minutes later, chatting with Skylar in my room that we'd set up for her. They were laughing over something, and it caused me to slow down for a moment. Axe hadn't been around much over the last few years while he'd been dealing with some personal shit, and I knew Skylar missed him. He'd always had a calming effect on her. Hell, Axe had a way of quieting any fucked-up situation. He also had his own way of fucking shit up if it was called for, but right now, I knew his presence soothed her fears,

"Did you find me a physio?" she asked when she realised I stood watching them.

"Still working on it."

"Oh God, there's not going to be anyone available on such short notice. I just know it." Her voice wavered with anxiety, something she'd struggled with since Margreet's death.

"Hey," Axe said, in the deep lulling rumble of his that usually worked on her, "it's all going to work out okay, Skye. There are plenty of physios around."

The anxiety I'd heard in her voice flashed in her eyes as she glanced between Axe and me. "Can you please go and take care of it now, King?" She paused for a moment before adding with an almost begging emphasis, *"Please?"*

I jerked my chin at Axe. "I need a moment with Axe first and then I'll get on it."

Skylar reached for Axe as he stood. "Don't be long. And can you bring me some of that chocolate when you come back?"

He nodded with a smile before meeting me outside. Closing the door of her room, he asked, "What's up?"

"Did you get hold of the guy who might know something about what Marx has told the feds?"

"Yeah. Just waiting for him to get back to me. He said to give him a couple of days, so I'm expecting to hear something soon."

"Let me know as soon as you do."

"Will do." He pulled a pack of gum from his pocket and shoved some in his mouth. "What's the go with the physio? Surely it's not that hard to book one?"

"Fuck," I muttered. "None of the ones the hospital physio recommended are available. I haven't told Skylar that so don't mention it to her. We'll have to take our chances on an unknown and hope like fuck they're good."

"What about the hospital chick? Skylar hasn't stopped talking about her. She'd help ease Skylar's anxiety."

"She said no."

"And since when do you ever take a no? Just make it happen." He nodded at the door to Skylar's room. "I better grab this chocolate she's after and get back in to her before she loses her shit. This whole situation is fucking with her head."

He left me alone with my thoughts, which was a dangerous place to be. This situation was fucking with all of our heads.

I entered Skylar's room again and found her sitting on the

bed crying. She glanced up at me and wiped her tears away. My fucking heart squeezed at the difficulty she was experiencing with everything going on. I had to fix this.

Holding out my hand, I said, "Skye give me your phone."

Her brows pulled together. "Why?"

I motioned with my fingers for her to just do as I'd asked. "I want Lily's number."

The way her shoulders relaxed told me I had to do everything I could to get Lily to say yes. Axe was right that she would help Skylar's anxiety.

She passed her phone as she swiped more tears from her face. "Thank you," she said softly. "I know I'm a pain in your ass and that I don't make any sense with all my worry, but I'm really grateful for everything you're doing."

"Fuck, if it wasn't for the shit I've got going on, you wouldn't have been in that accident, Skye. This is all my fault."

She sighed and rested her head against the wall. "I don't blame you, King. And you've really gotta stop taking the blame for every bad thing that happens in our lives."

Before I could respond, Annika joined us. "How's the patient?" She smiled at Skylar. "The kids are dying to get in here, but I told them you need some time to settle in first. I'll do my best to keep them away for as long as I can, but I can't promise anything. They're going a little stir-crazy being cooped up here."

A smile tugged at Skylar's lips. "Oh God, please let them come in. We can go stir-crazy together. And besides, I need some little slaves to do stuff for me."

Annika laughed. "Perfect. It'll get them out of my hair. I might even get a nap in this afternoon." She glanced at me. "What are you taking the blame for now? I heard you guys talking when I came in, but I didn't hear what it was about."

"Nothing," I muttered, not wanting to get into that conversation again.

"It wasn't nothing," Skylar said. "I was telling King he needs to stop taking the blame for the bad stuff that happens to us."

"Oh," Annika said, nodding. "She's right. I mean, you might be the almighty King, but you're not responsible for everything."

I ignored them and held up the phone. "I'm going to call Lily."

As I stepped out of the room, Skylar called out, "We're going to finish this conversation one day."

It wasn't a productive conversation, so I had no desire to finish it, let alone engage in it. Instead, I dialled Lily and waited for her to answer. She didn't pick up, though. It went to message bank, which I didn't bother with. I dialled again. Same thing happened. On the third try, she finally answered.

"Shit, sorry, Skye, I was in the middle of dealing with a teenage girl who thinks it'd be a good idea to follow in her mother's footsteps and give up her virginity at an age where she doesn't fully comprehend that babies can come from sex. And an asshole ex who still doesn't understand that he wouldn't get as much hell from me if he just held up his end of this parenting gig. I'm going to need copious amounts of wine tonight to get through this day. Why do men make our lives so hard some days? I know that if he backed me up on this with her, she'd be more inclined to listen to what I'm saying."

Her outburst cut through the shit in my head in a way not much did. I didn't know what the fuck it was, but she somehow managed to jolt me from my thoughts, easing some of the tension in my body as she did so. It was a welcome fucking distraction. One I didn't have time for, but one I would indulge just to have a few minutes of peace from my thoughts.

"Take something from him that he values. He'll do whatever the fuck you want after that."

Silence. And then—"King? God, I thought it was Skylar calling. Just ignore everything I said. I'm rambling. Shit. Wait. What do you mean by take something from him?"

"What does your ex get from you that he values?"

A few moments passed in silence where I figured she was thinking about my question. "He likes to come over to my place a freaking lot, but there's no way I can take that from him. I've tried telling him to stop, but he just keeps coming whenever he wants. Besides that, I don't know..." Her voice drifted off before suddenly she said, "Oh, I know! He still has access to the couple's gym membership my sister got for me years ago. I'll take his name off it."

I frowned. "You let your ex use a gym membership you pay for?"

"I don't pay for the membership. It's her bestie's gym, so they give it to me for free. Linc is vain as fuck, so it'd kill him if I stopped letting him use it."

I had zero clue what would possess a woman to let her ex use her like that, but in my experience, people did shit for the strangest fucking reasons, so I wasn't touching that. "Cut him off. He'll come crawling back to you begging for it back and willing to do whatever that takes."

She turned silent again before saying, "You're a smart man. Thank you."

I'd been called a lot of things in my life, but smart wasn't one of them. The compliment felt odd, but fuck, it put a smile on my fucking face. "I've dealt with enough assholes to know how to use them to get what I want."

"Take the compliment, King. Now, what can I do for you? I'm presuming you called for a reason."

I was unsure how her ex managed to coerce her into shit; she seemed switched on to me. But then I knew better than anyone how love led you down paths you never intended to take. "I need you to take on Skylar's rehab."

"I'm sorry, but I really can't fit her in. My kids are a handful at the moment and work is kicking my butt."

"There has to be something I can offer you to make you say yes. Name it."

"You just don't back down, do you?"

"No. Not when I want something this much. I'm not sure how close you and Skylar got, although with the way you answered my call, I'm guessing you guys got friendly, but she suffers from anxiety. It's flaring pretty badly due to the accident and what she has to do now. Just the mention of your name eases that anxiety a little."

She exhaled. "I really wish I could say yes, and I want to, but as much as I try to figure it out in my head, I just don't see how I can work her into my schedule."

The headache Ryland caused pounded harder against my skull. "You're busting my fucking balls here, Lily. Have a think about it. I'll get back to you soon."

Without waiting for her reply, I ended the call. I'd give her the rest of the day, and then I'd strongly encourage her to come around to my way of thinking. There was no way she wasn't taking on this job.

26

Lily

I closed my eyes, sunk further into the warm bath and took a deep breath before clearing my mind of all thoughts.

I exhaled.

Inhaled.

Exhaled.

Fuck, who was I kidding? Meditation wasn't going to work tonight. Not after the day I'd had. But the bath *was* helping, which was a relief. It was only Monday, and I already wanted this week over with. Zara still refused to talk to me and had defied me last night by slipping out of her bedroom window to spend time with her boyfriend. I'd realised she was missing when I'd gone to say goodnight at nine o'clock. Linc had been less than helpful, refusing to end the date he was on to come and help me find her. In the end, it had been my mother who had saved the day. She'd called Zara and talked her into coming home. She'd actually surprised the heck out of me with the patience she exhibited. That patience hadn't been there when I was a teen. I liked this older version of her, even if she drove me crazy trying to fix what she perceived as my problems.

I checked the time on my phone. Just after ten. Time for bed. The kids were finally all asleep. I'd checked Zara's room at least five times to make sure she was there. She wasn't freaking escaping me again. I'd never been the kind of parent who tracked their kids' phone, but I was seriously considering getting one of those spy apps for her phone.

Ugh, I was turning into someone I didn't recognise. Suspicious and helicopter-y. But as much as I tried to fight these tendencies, I failed. Zara was my baby, and I had to protect her.

I hopped out of the bath and dried myself off as I got lost in parenting thoughts again. *Story of my life.* I'd just figured out how to help Holly with one of her problems when a sound outside jolted me to full alert. It sounded like someone knocking on my front door, which made no sense due to the time of night.

God, I hoped it wasn't an intruder. Although with the mood I was in, I wouldn't hesitate to take them on.

I debated my options of getting dressed versus wrapping the towel around me before I went to investigate. I figured I'd rather not approach an intruder wearing only a towel that barely covered my ass, and had decided to throw some clothes on instead when the noise sounded again.

Jesus, they were going to wake the kids. I did not need to be dealing with tired, cranky kids if they were woken. I quickly secured the towel around me, doing my best to cover my butt, grabbed my phone, and yanked the bathroom door open. I'd taken two steps when my phone vibrated with a text.

Unknown number: Lily, let me in. We need to talk.

Me: Who the hell is this? And do you realise it's after ten?

Unknown number: King.

What the what?

Me: Goodness, stop freaking knocking. You'll wake my kids up. IT'S LATE.

King: I'll stop knocking when you let me in.

Men!

I marched out to the front door and checked to confirm it was him. I mean, I knew it would be, but checking was a habit.

It was most definitely him standing out there dressed in the jeans and leather that made me weak at the knees.

Shit.

Opening the door, I stepped outside, pushing past him so I could close the door, and then grabbed his arm and pulled him with me to take our conversation away from the house. I then turned to him and, eyes wide, whisper-yelled, "How did you get my address? And why do you feel it necessary to drop by unannounced so damn late? I thought you were an intruder!"

My heart hammered with bewilderment.

King was here.

It was late.

I was wearing a towel.

What the freaking heck did he want?

And oh God, why did he have to affect me so much?

Focus, Lily.

This is not the moment to lose your shit.

The street lamp threw just enough light over us for me to see his eyes skim over my body before meeting mine again. "I have a guy who's skilled at finding people. Let's just leave it at that."

My eyes bulged some more. "Umm, no, King, let's *not* just leave it at that. That's too casual for me. And I feel a little violated, to be honest. What else is your guy skilled at? Should I be expecting—"

Before I knew what was happening, he slid his arm around my waist, lifted me and walked me back to my door and inside my house. Once we were in, he let me go and quietly shut the door behind him. It happened within seconds, completely throwing me off-kilter. Looking down at me with those intense eyes of his, he rumbled, "I needed to know where you lived and he could help me with that. That's all. Now, do you wanna put some clothes on for this conversation?"

Holding my towel in place, I stared at him, almost at a loss for words. If I'd felt bewildered before, I wasn't sure what to label how I felt now. Being manhandled by King had shaken all my thoughts and emotions into disarray.

I need a smoke.

Shit, I gave them up.

You can start not smoking again tomorrow.

But clothes first.

Grab the smoke on the way.

Shit.

Pointing at him, I said, "Stay here. I'm going to get dressed. And for the love of God, if you wake my kids, I *will* hurt you."

I waited for his response, but he gave none. Well, none that was clear. He simply continued watching me in silence, waiting. It threw me further off balance. I liked it when people didn't beat around the bush, but this was a whole new level of not wasting breath on words that had no importance. And with King, I would have preferred a little more insight into what he was thinking.

Leaving him, I hurried to my kitchen in search of my handbag that held the pack of smokes I hadn't dumped yet. My hands shook a little as I lit it, but I ignored that and took a long drag. I hated that it was exactly what I needed. What I *really* needed was to find a way of dealing with stress that didn't involve cigarettes, but that was a job for tomorrow. Tonight, I had only one thing I needed to do, and that was to get through this conversation with King without agreeing to his demands.

His request to help Skylar had been rattling around my brain all day. It had taken willpower to say no to him in the first place because I could do with the cash he offered. I mean, who turned someone down when they told you to name your price. I *had* turned him down, though, because I didn't want to get any closer to King than I already was. Not only did the man intrigue me, I was more attracted to him than I wanted to admit. And with what I had going on in my life, I didn't need to get distracted by a man.

After I changed into my jeans and a T-shirt, I went back to him, ignoring the way his gaze travelled my body again. I liked his eyes on me, but I certainly wasn't encouraging it. "If you came here to ask me again to work with Skylar, you should just leave now. I won't be forced into doing this."

"You don't strike me as the kind of woman who can be forced into doing anything."

Frowning, I asked, "So you're not here for that?"

"I am, but I wouldn't use the word force. I don't make it a habit of forcing women into shit, Lily."

I lifted my brows. "So what word would you use, because

it feels like you're trying to push me into this. Especially since you came here tonight rather than calling me in the morning to discuss it."

"We weren't getting anywhere over the phone, and this couldn't wait until tomorrow. I've spent the last hour trying to calm Skylar's anxiety over the fact she won't have someone coming to see her tomorrow. I'm here now to fucking beg you to work with her." His eyes flashed with determination as he added, "And I'm not the kind of man to beg for anything. But she wants you, and I'll do whatever it takes to make that happen."

My fierce resolve not to cave to his demands crumbled at the sight of him standing in front of me begging for my help. There was no doubt in my mind as to his sincerity. I didn't know this man, but from everything I'd seen of him at the hospital, I knew he cared for his sister. And if there was one thing in this world I respected more than anything, it was someone who would do whatever it took to provide and care for their loved ones.

"Shit," I muttered. "Shit, shit, shit."

The tension he carried in his shoulders appeared to loosen as he lifted his brows and said, "So that's a yes?"

Against my better judgement, I nodded. "It's a yes. I'll start tomorrow after work." I couldn't believe the words falling out of my mouth, but I also couldn't stop them. It was like he'd cast a spell over me.

"Thank you," he said, the hard, determined tone vanishing from his voice. I didn't know him enough to be sure, but his words seemed to be laced with relief and gratitude. He definitely didn't appear as strained as he'd been at the beginning of the conversation.

"Right, so now this is sorted, can I please go to bed? I've had a long day and need some sleep."

He nodded. "I'll text you the address."

As he turned to leave, I said, "And King?" He glanced back at me. "Don't make it a habit of calling on me late at night. I'm not a fan."

His lips twitched with a smile that didn't quite form. "I have no fucking idea how your ex gets away with the shit he pulls on you."

With that, he was gone, the rumble of his bike signalling his departure a couple of minutes later. I was left staring after him, hoping that working with Skylar didn't also mean seeing a lot of him. King had a way of contradicting himself that revealed more about him each time we talked. With each new layer I discovered, I couldn't help liking him more. And that could prove bad for me, because while being attracted to him was one thing, liking him more than I already did would be a whole other situation to deal with.

I hardly slept that night. I couldn't get King out of my mind. Every time I closed my eyes, I saw his eyes, his lips, his scar and those muscles of his. And I heard the growl of his voice, because even when King talked to you in an everyday conversation, his voice held a trace of the growl I suspected lived deep in him. The growl that would be kryptonite to a woman.

By the time I finished work the next day and drove to his clubhouse, exhaustion had claimed me. Thank goodness Brynn had an early day on Tuesdays—she'd offered to cook dinner for us all at my place tonight so that when I got home, I could put my feet up and relax. I'd be having an early one tonight, and if King stopped by late again, I'd freaking tell him where to go.

His men let me through the gate, and I continued along the driveway to find the parking space near the front door that they'd kept free for me. I passed a line of about ten parked bikes before I arrived at my destination. A few bikers eyed me as I passed them. None smiled. I didn't expect them to, but I also didn't expect them to look so serious. I should have anticipated that, though, because King was the most intense man I'd ever met, so it made sense his men would be the same.

The Storm MC clubhouse was huge. Black paint covered the entire building, with not a window in sight. My gaze was drawn to the Storm MC sign painted on the building high above the front door. I found it all to be a little intimidating —entering the world of bikers who I knew nothing of except for what I'd read in the papers. But King had won me over with the way he cared for Skylar, so I trusted him enough to do this.

"Lily," a voice I knew called out as I exited my car.

Turning, I found Devil standing at the front door. I'd spoken to him a few times at the hospital and quite liked him. Where King seemed fierce, Devil seemed a little lighter. He definitely smiled more.

Locking my car, I headed his way. "I found the place, but I've gotta tell you, you guys are kinda hidden in here. I like the forest you built around your clubhouse." I'd almost driven straight past the property due to the trees hiding it from the street.

He grinned. "It keeps the assholes out." He jerked his chin towards the front door. "Skylar's been hanging out for you all day."

I knew this to be true. She'd texted me five times throughout the day with different questions about her recovery. King hadn't been exaggerating when he'd said she was anxious.

Devil led me inside, down a maze of hallways to Skylar's room. It surprised me how quiet the clubhouse was. I'd kind of expected with the size of it, that there'd be a lot of bikers inside, but I saw only four men along the way. They were all as subdued as the men I'd passed outside. I wondered if they ever smiled and had fun.

Skylar's eyes lit up the minute I stepped into her room. "Thank God you're here."

As I moved further into the room, I wondered what it was usually used for. Completely masculine with photos of bikes on the walls, men's clothing hanging in the open wardrobe, and filled with dark wood and leather, I guessed it to be one of the bikers' rooms. *Do they live here?* That seemed a strange idea to me. Did their families live here? I couldn't imagine wanting to live here if I were married to one of the men.

"Do you need me to get anything for you?" Devil asked, cutting into my thoughts.

I smiled at him and shook my head. "No, I'm good."

"Just yell out if you need me," he said. "I'll be down the hall in the bar."

"You guys have a bar here?"

He grinned. "Yeah. Stop by on your way out and have a drink with us."

"God, if only I could. I've got three kids waiting for me at home, of which one is a fourteen-year-old who's trying to kill me with her boy-crazy ways. I've gotta be at full capacity to deal with that, so alcohol is reserved for later in the night after I've survived her."

He frowned. "Surely you're not old enough to have a four-teen-year-old."

"Trust me, I feel sixty some days."

Winking, he said, "Well, sixty looks good on you."

I turned to Skylar after he left. "He seems like he'd be a lot of fun."

She shifted in her chair. "Yeah, I really like Devil. He's not as serious or bossy as the other guys."

I eyed the chair she sat in. "We need to get you a different chair and a stool."

"Why?"

"That one is too low. And a stool will help with swelling." I dumped my bag on the bed and dragged the spare chair in the room close to her. Sitting, I said, "Now, talk to me. Tell me what's concerning you, and we'll talk through it all so you know why stuff is happening and how you can move forward without so much worry."

Her face crumpled and tears streamed down her cheeks. "I feel so stupid to worry about all this, but I'm stuck here while King won't let me go home and I'm in pain and I don't want to do anything to hurt my hip and I hate asking people for help and..." She shuddered as a loud sob escaped. "I just feel out of control with everything going on and I'm worried I'll never get back to how I was before."

My heart ached for her. I saw this kind of stress in many patients, especially those like Skylar who weren't prepared for an operation and the recovery they'd have to go through. I reached for her hand and squeezed it. "Let's take all that one at a time. I'm going to get you through this, Skylar, and you *are* going to make a full recovery. However, you're going to have to make me a promise."

She blinked through her tears. "What?"

"I need you to promise me that you'll trust me completely and believe that I know my shit. If I tell you to do something, you'll do it. You can ask me all the questions under the sun, but at the end of the day, you will do what I say, because you know that I know my shit. Okay?"

A small smile peeked out from under her tears. "God, you're going to fit in around here."

"Yeah? Why?"

"Because you're just as bossy as my brother."

"Well, let's not go that far. I can be bossy, but I'm pretty sure I've got nothing on King." I stood. "Now, repeat after me—'you know your shit, Lily'."

Her small smile morphed into a larger one. "You know your shit, Lily."

I nodded. "Right, let's go over what I want you to do each day, and then I'm gonna get you up and take you for a walk."

We went over the list of activities I wanted her to do, and then I took her for a short walk around the clubhouse. She seemed scared of walking, so I focused on getting her more comfortable with her crutches. By the end of our session, her anxiety levels had dropped and she appeared more confident in her ability to get through her recovery.

"Thank you so much for saying yes to this," she said as I picked up my bag to leave. "I know King was probably really pushy about it, and I'm sorry about that, but I'm so glad to have you helping me."

"Yeah, he was pushy, but that's what brothers are for, right?"

"True, but I do know how he can be, so sorry."

"All good." I headed for the door, glancing back at her before I exited. "You good for tonight?"

The smile that spread across her face was what I was looking for. "Yes."

"Good. I'll stop by after work again tomorrow."

I headed down the hallway to leave, but I managed to take a wrong turn at some point and ended up in an area of the clubhouse I hadn't seen yet. As soon as I realised I'd gone in the wrong direction, I turned to go back. And ran smack bang into a hard back as a voice boomed, "Mace, where the fuck are those headache pills?"

King.

He'd stepped out into the hallway at the same time I'd turned around, and I'd run into the back of him. In an effort to steady myself, I reached out and gripped his arms.

"Goodness, someone has their cranky pants on," I muttered, letting him go as I found my balance again.

Turning, he stared down at me, his cranky mood clear in his eyes. "Are you finished with Skylar?" His question came out as a bark, matching his mood.

Jesus, I didn't have the energy to deal with his bad temper. "Yes. I'm just leaving now, but I got lost in your hallways."

He took that in before turning away from me, and barking out again, "Mace! Get your ass here. I need those pills and I have a job for you."

"Do you speak to everyone that way? 'Cause I gotta tell you, I wouldn't get my ass here if you yelled at me like that."

His head whipped back around to face me as he demanded, "What did you just say?"

I didn't miss the way he winced, as if he were in pain. "I said that I wouldn't get my ass here—"

Irritation flashed in his eyes. "I know what you said," he snapped, rubbing his temple.

"Oh for God's sake," I muttered, rummaging in my bag for the peppermint oil I always carried. "You are freaking moody today. Come here."

A guy joined us, looking anything but confident. Shoving a box of Advil at King, he said, "Sorry, King, I couldn—"

King cut him off with a snarl. "I don't want your fucking excuses, Mace."

Good Lord, I didn't like this side of King.

Mace glanced between King and me. "What job do you want me to do?"

"Lily needs help finding her way outside."

I shook my head. "Not yet." I held up the bottle of peppermint oil. "First, I'm going to fix that headache of yours."

King looked at me like I'd lost my mind. "I have pills for that. Mace'll get you to your car."

"Those pills will do jack for you, King. Get your ass into a chair and let me work my magic." Mace's eyes widened, and King looked like he was about to blow a gasket. Before he could argue with me, I added, "You have nothing to lose by letting me do this, and I can guarantee you'll be thanking me later."

Mace backed away slowly. "I'll come back when you guys have finished."

King's eyes never left me as he said, "Don't go too far. This won't take long."

Mace nodded and took off. I didn't blame him. King did not appear to be impressed with anything at the moment, especially not with me. I should have just left his cranky ass to rely on Advil, but I knew that wouldn't work as well as what I could do for him, so I persevered and kept reminding myself that I too could be a moody bitch when a headache was ripping my head apart.

I peeked into the room he'd exited and found it was an office. Nodding towards it, I said, "Sit," making sure to use the bossy tone I usually reserved for my kids.

His brows lifted, but he didn't argue this time. A couple of moments later, I stood behind him and massaged some oil into his forehead, temples and then the back of his neck. As soon as my fingers touched him, I knew this was one of my worst ideas ever. And I had a lot of freaking bad ideas. But this one took the cake. Touching him and being this close to him caused my belly to flutter all over the damn place. I couldn't remember the last time a man made me feel this way. Shit, it had to be because I hadn't had sex in six months. That long without it would probably make my belly flutter over any man.

Liar.

Shut up.

He's hot.

Ah no, he's moody as fuck.

Yeah, but he's still hot. You would fuck him in a heartbeat.

My fingers froze in the middle of massaging the oil into his neck.

I totally would fuck him.

Shit, shit, shit.

King stretched his neck from side to side. "You finished?"

"No," I blurted, taking hold of his neck to stop his movement. "Sit still."

He pulled away from me and stood. "We're done," he said, his tone signalling that this wasn't up for discussion. He didn't know me, though. Everything was always up for discussion. Especially when I knew I was right.

Straightening my shoulders, I said, "We are not done, King. Your neck and shoulders are so hard and tight. I've got something to rub into them that will help with that."

He glanced down at my bag sitting on his table. "How much shit do you carry in your bag?"

"Clearly lots of shit that you need." I couldn't work out why he was being so bloody difficult about this. "Look, I'm just trying to help you because you seem to be in a lot of pain. Are you always this obstinate when someone tries to help you?"

Scrubbing his face, he muttered, "Fine," before sitting back down.

Finally.

Getting him to do what I wanted was almost as frustrating as getting Zara to do something.

I grabbed my hot pepper muscle stick out of my bag and unscrewed the lid. I then placed my hand on his shoulders and gently massaged him through his shirt, feeling for knots. He needed more than this muscle stick.

"You need a massage," I said, figuring I was wasting my breath.

"I don't have time for a massage."

"Yeah, I figured you'd say that, but you should make the time. You'd be a new man after a few massages."

"Fuck, Lily, can you just get this shit rubbed on so I can get back to work?"

I could have seriously throttled him and his moodiness. Instead, I decided to get this done and get the heck out of there. Tapping his back, I said, "Take your shirt off."

He took a few moments, but he did what I said, pulling his black T-shirt over his head and dumping it on the desk. I wasn't prepared for what I saw next. A huge tattoo covered his back, the same image of a skull and wings that I'd seen on this building. It wasn't the tattoo that caused me to falter, though. The scars on one side of his back caused that. Some were hidden under the tattoo, but there were many that weren't. It looked like someone had taken a knife to that part of his back and tried to slash it to pieces.

What had King lived through to end up with so many scars on his body? My heart hurt just to think about it.

Pulling myself together, I ran the stick over his shoulders and upper back. The heat from it would help relax his muscles. I would have preferred to place a warm towel over his back after applying it, but I figured I had zero possibility of getting him to agree to that. So instead, I used my hands and massaged the balm into his skin, trying to get extra heat in that way.

As I worked my way up his neck, he dropped his head forward and groaned.

Holy shit.

That sound coming from King did things to me.

Really freaking good things.

If he didn't really need this, I would pack up and leave right now.

I did not need him to be doing those really freaking good things to me.

But *he* needed this, so I stayed.

He ended up allowing me to massage him for a good ten minutes before growling, "That's enough," and abruptly standing. Grabbing his shirt, he threw it back on before facing me. "Pack up your stuff and I'll walk you out."

I frowned, unsure why he was being so brusque with me. This was different to the crankiness of earlier. It was like he couldn't get me out of here fast enough. "Did I do something wrong? I thought the massage was good."

His features hardened. "I've got shit to do."

I stared at him, incredulous at the way he was treating me. "Fine," I muttered, throwing my stuff into my bag and slinging it over my shoulder. "Let's go."

He led me through the clubhouse, out to where I'd parked my car. We didn't say a word to each other, and he grunted at anyone in his way to move. This was the asshole King that my boss had warned me about that first day in the hospital. I'd never met a man like him, and I really didn't like him when he acted this way.

He pushed through the front door of the clubhouse and held it open for me to exit. Our eyes met for a moment as I passed by, but still, no words were exchanged. It wasn't until I was halfway to my car that he finally said something. "Thanks for what you said to Skylar today."

I slowed.

And turned.

The tone of his voice had softened, as had the hard lines on his face.

My brows pulled together as I asked, "You spoke with her

after I finished?" That made no sense, though, because he'd been in the office at that time.

He shook his head. "No."

I walked back to where he stood. "I'm confused, King. How do you know what I said to her?"

His eyes bored into mine. "I stopped by to see you during her session."

"But you didn't come in."

"You were laying down the law with her, and she needed to hear that, so I didn't interrupt. Fuck knows she doesn't listen to me when I tell her the same shit."

"I'm hopeful she listened to me."

"She did."

I smiled. "Good. I'm glad." I took a step back. "I'll be over again tomorrow afternoon to see her."

He nodded, but didn't say anything further.

As I drove down the driveway to the gate, I peered in my rear-view mirror and found him watching me. God, he was a complex man. One minute, so rude and gruff, the next, not as hard and much more likable. I had to wonder how the people in his life put up with him. I wasn't sure I could ever put up with a man like him.

27

King

I rubbed the back of my neck as I listened to the shit pouring out of Bronze's mouth. None of it was anything I wanted to hear.

I cut him off. "It's fucking bullshit, Bronze. I want Nitro out of there, and I want you to find out what the fuck is going on with that now that Marx is dead."

"I'm telling you, King, they're not releasing him anytime soon. Ryland is gunning for you harder now than he ever was. He's convinced you're behind Marx's death. And as for you getting in to see Nitro, forget it. They're not letting anyone in to see him."

Fuck.

Everything had turned to shit yesterday morning after Marx had been found dead in his cell. My visit with Nitro had been cancelled, as had Tatum's for later in the week. The lawyer hadn't been able to find out much, and then Billy had stuck his fucking nose in after Tatum involved him. I needed Nitro out of there fast.

"Why am I paying you, Bronze? If you can't fucking do what I need done, I'm just sinking cash into a black fucking hole of no return. Get this shit sorted."

I ended the call and slammed my phone down onto the desk. This day was going from bad to worse. After a failed lead on Romano's whereabouts this morning and then one of my men being beaten up in his home, I could have done with some good news for once. The headache Lily managed to ease last night had come back full force.

"King, are you okay?"

I lifted my head to find Ivy standing in the office doorway, watching me with concern. Since her attitude towards me had thawed three days ago, she and I had engaged in a few conversations. I'd done my best to stay clear of her, but we ran into each other randomly, and she seemed to want to talk.

"Yeah. You?"

Her mouth pulled into a frown and she stepped into the office. "You don't look okay."

I scrubbed a hand over my face and blew out a long breath. Frustration over the whole fucking situation of her husband coming after my club caused me to lash out. "Yeah well, that's because your husband is fucking with me. It'd make my life a whole lot fucking easier if you'd give me some helpful information about where the hell he is."

The ice I'd managed to thaw days ago returned to her gaze. "I've told you everything I think would be helpful. Maybe you should just let me leave here and go find him for you."

"You're not leaving here until I know you're safe, so don't bring that up again," I snapped, still unable to control my frustration.

"You make no sense half the time! Snapping and snarling all over the place, contradicting yourself. But then, that was always the case between us, so I shouldn't expect any different."

She thought *I* made no sense? If only she could have seen shit from my perspective, she would have understood the whiplash I'd felt over *her* actions. Fuck, it just reinforced that I'd made the right choice years ago. I decided to shift the conversation because we weren't going to agree on this. "Are you feeling okay?" I'd checked in with Winter each day who kept an eye on her for me, so I knew she'd been recovering well.

The ice in her eyes frosted some more. "Did you seriously just ask me that?"

Jesus, we were going from bad to fucked-right-up. "Fuck, Ivy, did I seriously ask you what?"

"Were you implying that I wasn't feeling well and that's why I said you make no sense? Because I *am* feeling okay and that *wasn't*—"

"When I ask you something, I'm not fucking hinting at something else." I grabbed my phone and moved towards the door, crowding her. "We're done here."

She glared up at me. "Yeah, we are."

I watched her as she walked away from me, wondering how the hell to best deal with this situation between us. The past was best kept there, and I would do that, but in the meantime, we had to co-exist under the same roof without these misunderstandings. But fuck, even when we were getting on, disagreeing with each other our go-to move.

I exited the office as I continued to contemplate a solution; however, Axe met me on the way to the room we'd set up for surveillance, and interrupted all thoughts I had.

"I finally heard from my guy. Marx retracted everything

before he died. They've got nothing on Nitro or the club as far as he's concerned."

"So they have no reason to continue holding him?"

"Not unless they have something else on him." He paused for a beat. "There's more, though, that isn't good. They're investigating Bronze for ties to the club. That's why he hasn't been able to access any information."

Fuck.

"Have they got anything solid on him?"

"It appears so, but that's not based on fact. It's just the feel my guy got when he talked to his contact. I've asked him to keep searching."

I stabbed at my phone, dialling Bronze. When he picked up, I cut straight to the point. "Sara sends her regards." *Our code to let him know he was compromised.*

"Fuck," he muttered. "Twenty minutes."

I ended the call and glanced at Axe. "I've gotta take care of this. I'll be back in an hour or so. Let Hyde know."

"Will do," he said as I left him to return to my office.

Moving fast, I opened the safe and grabbed out the package I'd hoped never to need. I placed my phone in the safe and grabbed out my burner that wouldn't signal my location to anyone. I then quickly made my way out to my bike and headed to the meeting point Bronze and I had designated years ago. It pissed me off that I had to let him go. But there was no way I'd leave him out in the cold with his dick swinging in the wind. Not after everything he'd done for me.

I'd started working with Bronze seven years ago after his wife, Sara, had been killed in a hit-and-run accident. I liked to deliver justice to those who killed that way, and I had, but not before I'd used what I'd learnt about the driver for my benefit. I'd known Bronze for about two years when his wife died. He'd investigated the club a few times and for some reason that was still unknown to me, he'd gone easy on me each time. So when I went looking for a cop to add to my payroll, Bronze had been my first choice. His wife's death made it possible for me to convince him to say yes. I'd offered up the name of the killer and my assistance when he took vengeance, in exchange for his agreement to work with me.

"What the fuck's going on, King?" he asked as he slid into the booth at the back of the noisy, out-of-the-way café where we'd started our working relationship all those years ago.

"You're being investigated for ties to the club. I don't have hard facts yet, but I don't doubt it's true. It also accounts for why you can't get any information at the moment."

He dropped his head into his hand and swore before looking up at me again. "So this is it then?"

I nodded. "Yeah." Sliding the package I'd brought with me across the table, I said, "Here's the agreed cash, burner, ID and list of contacts you can use to disappear."

"I have to see Hailee—"

"No," I said forcefully. "You need to walk out of here, get on a fucking train and get the fuck out of Sydney. And you need to never come back. They'll fucking crucify you if they can prove the shit we've done over the years."

"How the fuck can they prove any of that shit? Have any of your guys talked?"

I clenched my jaw, hating every fucking minute of this. "We have a rat, but I don't know who yet. We're working on that."

"So you find him and you take care of him."

"Fuck, Bronze, you of all people know it's not that fucking easy. Sure, I can take care of him, but the damage has been done. You're a target, and they won't stop coming for you just because their source is dead. They'll find someone else. They'll investigate the hell out of you until they can pin something on you." I leant forward. "You need to leave now, and you need to leave fast."

His face morphed into a canvas of anger and bitterness. "I should never have—"

I stood, done with this conversation. "There's no fucking point looking back. That shit can't ever be changed. I'll make sure Devil takes care of Hailee. And I'll take care of Matty."

I walked out of that café with a new, fiercer determination to find the motherfuckers who were intent on bringing down my club. And whoever was behind Bronze being targeted would die at my own hands. Slowly and fucking painfully.

28

King

"We've found the guy who beat Mace up," Hyde said after I arrived back at the clubhouse and filled him in on Bronze. It was the best fucking thing I'd heard all day.

"Let's go then."

"Who do you wanna take?"

"Just you and me." I had enough fury burning through me to take on ten of these cunts. Hyde and I could manage one on our own.

He swiped his phone off the desk and stood. Stretching his neck from side to side, he said, "I'm gonna fucking enjoy this."

Adrenaline surged in my veins. "You and me both, brother."

Forty minutes later, I kicked down the back door of the house where our target supposedly lived. Storming into the place, I followed the sound of a man's voice in one of the bedrooms. Hyde followed me, his violent mood matching mine.

We found the motherfucker sitting on his bed, talking on the phone with his back to the door. Our approach was quiet enough that he didn't hear us coming. The fucker was talking loud enough to not hear much else regardless of how noisy we were.

I moved close to the guy, hooked my arm around his neck and squeezed the fuck out of him while Hyde ripped his phone away and crushed it beneath his boot.

The guy tried to fight me off, clawing at my arms and taking swings at me, but I was so fucking jacked up and ready for this, that nothing would stop me. Stepping back, I dragged him off the bed and then twisted him to face me so I could slam him up against the wall. My fists took over at that point, and I channelled every ounce of fury coursing through me into punch after punch. By the time he slumped to the floor, blood splatter covered me and a good patch of the wall behind him.

Hyde rummaged through the guy's belongings while I stood staring down at the asshole. He glanced across at me and said, "You gonna take it easy for a moment? We still need to talk to him."

Crouching, I ignored Hyde and lifted the asshole's chin. "Alan, open your fucking eyes."

He leant to the side and spat some blood from his mouth before cracking one eye open. "Go fuck yourself."

My fury roared to life again, and I grabbed his shirt with both hands, dragged him up and shoved him across the room into another wall. "Who the fuck sent you to beat one of my guys up?" I demanded as I stalked to where he lay sprawled on the carpet.

Groaning as he tried to sit, he muttered, "He was yours? Fucking deserved it."

Before I had a chance to react, Hyde stormed across the room and kicked him in the stomach. "Yeah, motherfucker, he was ours." He bent and reefed the guy up to a sitting position. "Now, who the fuck are you working for?"

Alan tried to smile, but his face was so battered he hardly managed it. But I heard it in his voice when he said, "You can fucking kill me if you want, I'll never tell you."

"Careful what you wish for," Hyde snarled.

"Sit him against the wall," I said as I reached into my back pocket for the pliers I'd brought with me. It was either them or the knife, and today I was in the mood for a little teeth pulling.

Alan did his best not to show fear as I crouched in front of him again, but it flickered in his eyes. I held up the pliers. "How much do you like your teeth, Alan?"

"Fuck you," he said, before spitting in my face.

I saw red.

It fucking blinded me.

My taste for blood roared stronger than it had in a long time.

Hyde gripped Alan's jaw and held his mouth open, while I took hold of his front tooth with the pliers. "You want to keep this tooth, start fucking talking."

His face flashed with horror. "Fuck, man! I don't know who it was! I swear."

I didn't hesitate—I ripped his tooth out, the crunch of it satisfying as fuck, while he writhed on the floor, trying to escape Hyde's hold.

"Oh fuck, fuck, man... fucking hell!" Alan chanted his words as if they would make everything better. Nothing would make it better for him now, because even when he gave me what I wanted, I had no intention of leaving this house until he had suffered for what he'd done.

Grasping another tooth with the pliers, I demanded, "You like this tooth, motherfucker?"

He tried to fight Hyde and turn his head away, but failed. He was a mess of blood and fear, and I figured I almost had him where I needed him.

Turned out I was a lot closer to that than I realised. He mumbled something I could barely make out, so I let go of his tooth and said, "What?"

His chest heaved with what appeared to be relief when Hyde also let him go. "It was Tony Romano. He paid me."

I dumped the pliers on the floor so I could pull him up. Sitting him in the armchair next to the bed, I barked, "Now is the time to keep talking. Otherwise, I swear to fucking God, I'll yank every last fucking tooth from that mouth of yours."

He only hesitated for a moment before spewing the information out. He couldn't get it out fast enough. Romano's men had hired him and one of his mates to take out as many of our club members as they could in the next week. His goal at Mace's this morning had been to kill him, but Mace's neighbour had interrupted him before he could finish the job. Unfortunately they had no way of contacting Romano's men to set up a meet that we could intercept. The deal had been for them to wait to be contacted again. We discovered too late that their houses had been bugged so Romano's men could keep watch of them. That meant they now knew we'd found these guys. They were useless to us.

Hyde's face turned thunderous as he shoved a pen and piece of paper at Alan. "Write your friend's name and address down. And make sure it's the right fucking address."

Alan scribbled the information as Hyde pulled rope from the bag he'd brought with him. We tied the asshole up, ensuring there was no way in hell he'd be able to escape. Grabbing the paper with the address on it, I looked down at Alan and said, "Sit tight. We'll be back once we've paid your friend a visit." I failed to mention the fact that neither of them would live to see another day. That information would be my gift to him when I returned.

"King, you crazy motherfucker! It seems you've finally gone and pissed someone off enough for them to come at you," Nash Walker said later that afternoon when he and some of the Brisbane chapter arrived.

I threw some of the whisky sitting in front of me down my throat. Hyde and I had spent the last hour in here drinking after taking care of the two assholes sent by Romano. The buzz filling my veins was exactly what I fucking needed.

Scott Cole joined us, and I motioned for Kree to pour a round of drinks for everyone. "Heard you and Hyde got your hands a little dirty this afternoon," he said.

I drained my glass. "Not fucking dirty enough as far as I'm concerned."

The bar filled up as Griff, J, and Havoc eventually found their way inside, and my men returned from a long day out dealing with club business.

It had been eight days since Jen and her baby had been murdered. Between keeping the club running, ensuring the safety of our families, and chasing our fucking tails trying to find Romano, we'd hardly drawn breath. All of us were wound so fucking tight that we were close to breaking point. Cole and his boys arriving gave us a breather from the stress.

As the sounds of laughter and loud, alcohol-fuelled discussions filled the bar, Axe motioned for me to follow him and Zane outside. The rain that had fallen all day had subsided, but thunder continued to roll through the sky, with the occasional flash of lightning.

"I just heard back from my guy, and he was right that the cops have stuff on Bronze. They've been watching him for a few months and also have a source who's been feeding them information. You think he'd turn on you for them?" Axe said.

I shook my head. "No. He's gone."

"Gone?"

"We'd always agreed that if shit came to this, I'd set him up with cash, a new identity, and a network to help him disappear. I did that today. He's long gone."

"And his family?" Zane asked.

Neither of them knew Bronze's story, so I filled them in on how we came to work together before adding, "Devil is with Bronze's sister, and I've let him know what's happened. He'll make sure she and her family are taken care of. Bronze knows that."

"I hope you're right about him," Axe said. "He could cause you a lot of problems if you're not."

"Yeah, he could. But he won't." Bronze and I may have had a lot of fucking disagreements over the last seven years and gone head-to-head often, and he may have been on the other side of the law to me, but we were connected in ways no one knew about and would never know about. That was as per Bronze's wish. Those ways hadn't been planned, and I'd never done the things I'd done for him as a strategic move to keep him in my pocket, but I knew deep in my bones that because of what I'd done, Bronze would never turn on me or the club.

I watched as a car drove up the driveway towards us. Narrowing my eyes, I tried to figure out who it belonged to. It was almost 6:00 p.m. and I wasn't expecting anyone.

Lily.

Skylar was expecting her.

My belly tightened.

Fuck, the physiotherapist with a body made for fucking.

Every time I saw her, I noticed something new about her. Yesterday it had been the way her neck flushed when she was cranky and bossy. And fuck had she ordered me around. Anyone else who tried to pull that shit on me wouldn't make it through the front door of this clubhouse again, but there were two things about this woman that altered that consequence. One, Skylar needed her, so I chose to put up with her attitude. And two, there was something about Lily's smart mouth that turned me the fuck on. However, as much as I may have wanted to fuck her senseless, I wouldn't risk putting Skylar's rehab at risk. Women did some crazy fucking shit after I screwed them. I wasn't interested in anything but sex, and I could get that anywhere, so I'd keep my dick in my pants where Lily was concerned.

But that was easier said than done when she was standing in front of me. And when she'd massaged me yesterday, I'd gone to fucking war with myself over wanting her. I'd given her ten minutes to rub that shit into my skin. It was nine minutes more than I could handle. As I'd walked her out, I'd decided to find some pussy to work that need out of my system. But club business had gotten in the way, and I never got around to that. So here I was, a good two weeks since I'd been laid, thinking about all the ways I'd make a woman I'd never fuck, come.

"Fuck," I muttered, "I've got shit to do."

Ignoring Axe's and Zane's confused expressions, I turned and headed back inside, not stopping until I made it to my office. Sitting at my desk, I pulled out the bottle of whisky I kept in my drawer and took a long swig as I thought about going in search of a club whore. While neither of the ones here today were my preference, that didn't matter. Both were good with my needs and more than willing to let me fuck them how I wanted.

I shoved the whisky bottle back in the drawer and stood

to leave when the half-opened office door creaked open some more. "King? Are you in here?" The door opened all the way and Lily smiled up at me. "Sorry to barge in, but I have some information to give you. I saw you outside so wanted to catch you now in case you leave while I'm with Skylar."

I stared down at her, taking in the tight jeans she seemed to like to wear. Her long dark hair was long enough to cover her tits, but today they were on fill display because she'd swept her hair up into a ponytail. Fuck, my dick jerked to life as I thought about running my tongue down between her breasts while I wrapped my hands around her throat.

"King?"

"Yeah." I dragged my eyes up to her face and found her watching me intently, her face flushed. "What information?"

She thrust some papers at me. "Just some recommendations for furniture and other things that would help Skylar's recovery. Mostly, she needs a different chair to sit in. The one she has is too low. And she also needs a stool to keep her feet up."

I took a step back to rest against the desk and look over the information. She'd detailed the items and listed places where I could get them. Glancing at her, I said, "Thanks for this. I appreciate it."

She smiled again. "If you need help with any of it, just call me." Moving next to me, she reached for one of the pieces of paper. Pointing at it, she said, "And this guy? I know him well, so if you mention my name, he might give you a discount." Handing the paper back to me, she frowned. "Are you okay?"

Jesus, she was closer than I'd prefer, but I didn't shift away from her. Not when she smelt so fucking good. "Yeah. Why?"

"You're grimacing. Have you got another headache?"

I was grimacing due to her proximity, not another

headache, but before I could answer her question, she dumped her bag on the desk and madly searched in it for something. Pulling out her bottle of peppermint oil, she said, "Here, let me rub some more into your temples."

Grabbing her wrist to slow her, I shook my head. "I don't have a headache."

She stopped and looked down at my hand around her wrist, before looking back up at me. "Oh, okay. That's good." Her words were a little breathless, which only fucked with my dick some more.

We watched each other in silence for a few moments, until her phone rang. Digging it out of her bag, she pursed her lips together and said, "Sorry, I have to get this. It's Linc."

I nodded, expecting her to take it outside of the office, but instead, she put the phone to her ear and said, "What's up, Linc?"

As she listened, her face twisted with what I assumed to be frustration. Holding her free hand up in the air, she said, "Hold up a minute. You agreed to help the kids with their homework and assignments, so why are you guys at the movies?"

Linc said something, to which she replied, "This is bull-shit. And it means that I'm going to be up late with Zara tomorrow night helping her, because her assignment is due on Friday. If I'd known you had no intention of working on that tonight, I wouldn't have let them sleep over. I could have split the assignment time over two nights that way."

I watched with amusement as Lily waved her hands all over the place throughout the rest of the conversation. She was pointing and jabbing her fingers as if he were standing in front of her. When the call ended, she looked at me with wide eyes and said, "Oh my God, I could kill that man! Do you know what he's done now?"

I tried not to laugh. "What?" I asked as I crossed my arms over my chest and settled in to hear what she had to say.

Dropping her phone back into her bag, she said, "He's arranged tickets for them all to go to some motor racing thing on Saturday night. It starts in the afternoon, and he wants them from lunchtime."

"Is this a bad thing?"

Her eyes widened some more. "Yes! Well, I mean, it's awesome he wants to spend time with them. I'm all on board with that. But, Robbie has karate on Saturday. He'll have to miss it now, and *that* is bad. Linc shouldn't have organised stuff without asking me first."

"Why is it bad for Robbie to miss karate?"

She exhaled loudly as if I'd asked the dumbest question. Or maybe it was just complete frustration; I couldn't be sure because I didn't know her tells. "My son's coordination isn't the best, and he doesn't really love sport. However, he likes karate, and it's been so good for him. Plus, he's come out of his shell there and made friends, which is something he struggles with at school. He'll be disappointed to miss karate, but I know he won't say anything to his father because he doesn't like to rock the boat where Linc is concerned. On top of that, his instructor told me they'll be going over some important stuff this week, and I don't want Robbie to miss out on it."

"Can you take Robbie to karate and then drop him off to Linc afterwards?"

She pulled a face. "No."

"Why not?"

"Because my car isn't working at the moment, so I can't get him there."

"But you can get him to karate?" She wasn't making a lot of sense.

"Well, I can get him to karate in my sister's car, but she

needs her car straight after that so I wouldn't be able to then get him to Linc."

"Is that your sister's car you're driving today?"

"Yeah."

"What's wrong with yours?"

"It needs new brakes. My mechanic can't fix them until next Monday, and I don't know of any other good mechanics."

I mentally ran through everything I had on tomorrow and worked out I could spare one of the boys for a while. "I'll send someone over to your place tomorrow to fix them. Just leave your keys somewhere outside and text me where they are."

Staring at me like I'd just offered her the world, she said, "Oh wow... are you sure?" I didn't miss the way her body visibly relaxed, some of the tension she'd been carrying now gone.

I uncrossed my arms and stood. Moving around the desk, I said, "Yes." Grabbing the bottle of whisky from the drawer, and two glasses from the cabinet behind me, I poured two drinks. Passing her one, I said, "Here, you look like you could do with this."

I'd half expected her to argue with me, but she didn't. Instead, she took the glass and downed half of it in one go. Wiping her mouth, she nodded. "I most definitely did need that." She then threw the rest back before placing the empty glass on the table. Meeting my gaze, she said, "If I didn't have to drive home, I'd beg you for more."

The thought of Lily begging me for shit wasn't a thought I needed in my head, so I changed the subject. "Did you pull your ex's name off your gym membership?"

A smile spread across her face. "I did. He mustn't have been to the gym since I did it, though, because he hasn't called me about that yet." She paused for a moment before adding softly, "Thank you for that tip. I need to stop letting him walk all over me with some stuff."

I drank some of my whisky. "Yeah, you do."

She picked up her bag. "Thanks for the drink and everything. Are you sure you don't need some more peppermint oil before I go see Skylar?"

The last thing I needed was her hands on me. "I'm good." Jerking my head towards the door, I said, "Go."

Blasting me with one last smile, she nodded. "I'll text you about my keys tomorrow."

I scrubbed a hand over my face after she left. Christ, I really fucking needed to get laid now.

29

Lily

"Cheers!" Adelaide grinned at me as she raised her glass. "And now it's time for us to find you a man who will fuck that celibacy out of you."

I returned her grin and nodded. "Hell yes!"

After dropping Robbie to Linc after his karate class, I'd called my bestie and begged her to take me out for the night. It was the perfect opportunity; it wasn't often I had a Saturday night to myself. Addy had rounded up the girls and we'd arrived at the club just over an hour ago. I had enough alcohol in me that all my problems didn't seem like problems anymore. Fuck, even Linc could call me and say pretty much anything without pissing me off.

After I'd taken a long gulp of my cocktail, I eyed Quinn who sat next to me. "Are you still seeing that butcher? The one from the butcher shop with all the hot dudes." It was my favourite butcher to buy meat from. I swore they had a policy of only hiring sexy men with beards.

Mmm, beards... King had a beard.

Shit, where did that thought come from?

Stop kidding yourself. You've been thinking about that man for days.

Quinn waggled her brows. "Yes, and he's fucking good in bed. Let the record show how much I love you, babe. I had plans with him for hot sex tonight, but I cancelled that for you."

"Aww, you loves me, Quinny," I gushed as I leant my head on her shoulder for a moment.

Our other friend Georgia laughed from across the table. "I love it when Lily gets drunk. She gets that smooshy, lovey vibe going."

"Yes!" agreed Addy. "I love watching her hit on guys when she's all smooshy. They bloody fall at her feet."

"Girl, they do that even when she's not drunk," Quinn said.

Adelaide laughed. "She's been celibate for so long I'd forgotten that."

"I'm right here and can hear everything you're saying," I said.

Quinn smiled at me. "And you're all smooshy, so you don't really care what we're saying."

"True," I said and then drank some more of my cocktail, smiling like a loon.

My phone buzzed with a text.

"Oh for fuck's sake, that better not be Linc," Adelaide muttered.

"I'm ignoring it if it is," I said, checking the text.

King: Your brakes still good?

My tummy did somersaults. We'd been exchanging texts since he had one of his guys fix my brakes. Mostly he checked in on my car, and I checked in on Skylar. So nothing fun, but I couldn't deny I got a thrill every time I saw his name pop up on my phone.

Me: I guess so.

    King: You guess so?

    Me: Well I'm not out driving around at the moment. I'm getting trashed and looking for a man.

He didn't come back with a reply, which disappointed me.

"Who was it?" Adelaide asked as I stared at the phone, willing him to send another text.

"King."

"Who's King?" Quinn asked.

"The sexy biker dude who fixed her brakes," Adelaide said.

I looked up from my phone. "We met when his sister was in an accident. I worked with her after her op."

My phone buzzed again.

King: Watch out for the assholes.

    Me: May have had too many drinks to spot them.

    Me: But I'm not looking for a husband here.

    Me: Just need someone who knows what he's doing for a night.

Again, no reply.

"Ooh, Lily, what about this dude coming our way?" Quinn practically bounced in her seat as she smiled at the guy and motioned for him to join us.

He was definitely good-looking. I could tell that much through my alcohol haze. And tall, which was always important as far as I was concerned.

"Hello, ladies," he said, settling himself between Quinn and me. Nice strong voice, which was another tick.

"Umm, girls," Adelaide said as she slid off her seat. "I need the ladies. Who's with me?"

Quinn and Georgia quickly slid off their seats, too. "Be back soon, Lil."

The hot dude watched them leave before turning back to me with a smile. "I take it they didn't really need to go to the ladies."

"Correct. They're keen for me to get laid tonight, and it looks like you might be just the guy to take care of that for me." I threw the rest of my cocktail down my throat.

His smile grew. "I like your style." He nodded at my empty glass. "What are you drinking?"

"A Margarita please."

"Don't go anywhere, gorgeous. I'll be right back."

I tracked his ass as he walked to the bar. *Nice, but not as nice as King's.*

I got lost in thoughts of King's ass when my phone buzzed again.

King: Don't accept drinks off anyone.

Me: Oooh Mr Bossypants is in the house.

King: I'm serious. Fuck knows what shit they'll drop in there.

Shit, he was right. And I'd just let a guy buy me a drink. I glanced across at the bar to see if he'd been served yet. Squinting, I located him still waiting for the bartender. My gaze dropped to take in his hand on the ass of the woman standing next to him. She giggled at something he said and then leant in close to whisper in his ear.

I sighed. I'd met my first asshole for the night.

Well, he could buy me a drink, but I would not be drinking it, and I sure as heck wouldn't be sleeping with him tonight.

I went back to texting King.

Me: So I just met my first asshole. Ugh. Tell me how Skylar is and take my mind off the fact I may not be getting any sex tonight.

King: She's having a rough night. Anxiety high today.

Me: You think I should call her? Would that help?

King: No. Go get drunk.

Me: OK, but let me know if you need me.

A few minutes later, the guy with the drinks came back to the table, smiling at me like I was a sure thing. Sliding my drink in front of me, he said, "So I didn't catch your name before."

"Dude, I saw you chatting with the blonde in line while you got the drinks. I'm thinking you should go back to her because I'm not interested anymore."

He glanced back at the bar and then at me again. Plastering a confused expression on his face, he attempted to spin the truth. "Oh her, she was all over me. I couldn't get rid of her."

God, did men really think women were stupid?

"So grabbing a woman's ass is how you try to get rid of them?"

He scowled. "Fuck, lady, are you always this bitchy?"

My phone rang, King's name flashing across the screen.

I answered it as I said to the dude, "I'm only this bitchy when a man tries to fuck with me. So take the drink and do your best to find some other woman to fuck with."

With one last scowl, he picked up the drink and left me.

King's voice rumbled through the phone. "That the asshole?"

I sighed again. "Yes. You know, I'm not convinced I'm cut out for this finding-a-man bullshit. I don't do well with getting all pretty and flirting in the hopes a guy will like me. I'd much rather rock up wearing my sweats and find someone who can appreciate my personality. That would be a whole lot freaking easier, and I wouldn't have to wade through all the assholes who just like my tits." I wasn't sure if it was the alcohol in me or the fact I liked talking to King that made me vomit all those words, but either way, I was helpless to stop them.

He was silent for a beat, and then surprised me when he said, "Not all men are assholes, Lily. Keep looking. They'd be fucking idiots to only want you for your tits."

My tummy did somersaults. "You know, King, you can say some really nice shit sometimes."

"Yeah, well maybe you could tell Skylar that." Weariness crept into his tone when he mentioned Skylar's name.

"What's going on? I told you I'd come over if she needs me."

Silence again. And then—"She needs you."

He may have said that Skylar needed me, but by his tone, I had to wonder if he did, too. Or maybe that was just me being drunk.

I slid off my chair. "I'm on my way."

"I'll send someone to get you."

"No, I'll just catch an Uber."

"Lily," he started, but I cut him off.

"King, no. I'm getting an Uber. It'll be faster than me waiting for your guy."

"Be careful," he muttered before hanging up.

I wasn't sure what he meant by that, but I didn't waste time trying to figure it out. I went in search of my friends and let them know where I was going, and less than ten minutes later, I was on my way to see King. Actually, I was on my way to see Skylar. But the fact I'd also get to see King caused my core to clench. I'd had just enough drinks tonight that it was anyone's guess what I might say to him. Or what I might beg of him.

Skylar was in bad shape when I arrived. Anxious, in pain, and in a foul mood with her brother, she had me a little concerned as to how I was going to calm her down. King stood in the doorway of her room watching us for a while, until Skylar told him to leave us alone. After that, it didn't take me half as long as I thought it might to soothe her worries and lull her to sleep. She didn't like taking drugs to help her anxiety, but tonight she agreed to a sleeping pill. I figured if she could just get some sleep, she may wake refreshed enough to deal with things better.

It was after midnight when I left Skylar's room and went looking for King. I wasn't quite as drunk as I had been when I arrived, but I was still relaxed and feeling quite floaty—the complete opposite of King's tense state.

I found him sitting at the desk in his office. The room was dark except for the glow of light from the lamp in the corner of the room. King sat in the office chair, a half-empty glass of whisky in his hands, and all the troubles in the world on his shoulders.

Why did I always want to fix men? Well, not so much fix them, but help them when they were down. I'd had this nurturing streak for as long as I could remember. Even back in high school when I met Linc, I wanted to help him. My instinct to nurture was the reason why I still let him get away with a lot of stuff. He'd been struggling for the last year after losing his job and trying to find regular work, and on top of that, his father was really ill, so I cut him some slack. He may have cheated on me and hurt me, but I wasn't the kind of person to play tit for tat.

Looking at King sitting in the dark, his body rigid and his expression grim, I felt that burning need to nurture. It made no sense to me since I hardly knew him. And while King didn't strike me as the kind of man who people took care of —I imagined he was the one who always did the taking care of—I wanted to offer him something. Even just a conversation.

He met my gaze, his face not softening even a little. "What?" It was almost a bark. A demand. I wouldn't have stood for it with many people, but I made allowances for King. He'd shown me enough good sides of himself that I'd tolerate his bark.

Entering his office, I walked to the desk and wiggled my ass onto it so I sat next to him. King didn't argue; he sat quietly watching me. But he didn't look happy.

"You should pour me a drink," I said.

He slowly lifted his glass to his mouth and emptied it. "You don't need another drink."

I raised my brows. "How do you know what I need?"

He placed his glass on the desk. "I don't, but I know it's not that."

I eyed the bottle of whisky sitting on the desk, on the

other side of him. Deciding he wasn't going to give me what I wanted, I leant across him to grab the bottle.

He hissed and muttered, "Fuck," which I ignored as I unscrewed the lid and poured some whisky into his glass.

Focusing my gaze back on him, I drank some of the whisky before saying, "Skylar took a pill. She should sleep all night."

"Good."

I drank some more of my drink. "You're a man of few words, King. Normally I like that about people, but I kinda wish you'd say more."

His jaw clenched as he watched me intently. King had a way of making me feel like he was undressing me with his eyes, even when his gaze never left mine. Maybe it was my soul he was undressing, not my body. Whatever it was, it awakened a part of me that had been asleep for far too long.

I didn't just want his eyes on me; I wanted his hands.

His mouth.

His tongue.

God, I wanted that body of his to take mine in ways it had never been taken.

Just for one night.

Tonight.

He picked up the bottle of whisky and took a swig. "I'll get one of the boys to take you home."

I shook my head. "No, I don't want to go home. I want to stay here with you."

His body stiffened more than it already was. "No." His denial was harsh. And final. But I'd had enough to drink to ignore it.

I placed the glass I was holding down and pressed both hands to the desk either side of me. Putting all my weight on my hands, I lifted my ass so I could slide across the desk, closer to him. The red dress that Adelaide had insisted I wear, barely covered my thighs, and his gaze finally dropped to my legs.

"King," I started, as I tried to swing my leg closest to him around to settle in between his legs.

He stopped me, though. Placing his hand on my thigh, he held my leg down. "I said no." Forceful again. I couldn't work out why he was so against this. What man said no to a woman who was practically throwing herself at him?

I narrowed my eyes at him. And then I asked him the strangest question that I knew the answer to even as it fell out of my mouth. But damn it, the alcohol loosened my tongue, so I had little control over what I said. "Are you gay? Or do I just not do anything for you?"

Before I knew what was happening, he moved to stand in between my legs, wrapped one hand around my throat, and growled, "You don't wanna go there with me, Lily. I am not the kind of man a woman like you fucks."

My heart and soul roared to life as my veins pulsed with desire.

Oh God.

He was exactly the kind of man I needed to fuck me.

I needed wild, uncaged and raw.

I'd had enough humdrum, monotonous sex to last me a lifetime.

I ached for the kind of encounters that left me breathless.

My heart racing.

Alive.

I didn't want to know what was coming next.

I craved thrills and surprises.

To be jolted and rocked and pushed into tasting life like never before.

I wanted a man so hungry for me that he'd lose himself to his animal side.

This man would give me all that. I saw it in his eyes.

Heard it in his voice. Recognised it in the way he held himself and moved.

"No, you're not," I agreed, because it was the truth, "But I can't get you out of my mind. Just give me one night. I just need one night where I don't think about all the shit I have to deal with in my life." I curled my hand around his wrist. "And I think you do, too."

He inhaled sharply before exhaling the breath and running his gaze over my body. All the while, he kept his hand around my neck. He didn't speak, but everything about him told me what I needed to know.

King wanted to fuck me.

I'd never had to encourage a man to sleep with me, nor had I ever really been the one to initiate sex. I loved sex, but I wasn't overly adventurous with it or confident when it came to asking for what I wanted. However, I really wanted it tonight, so I tried to force his hand.

I reached for his belt and undid it. I almost had his zip down when he let me go and stepped away from me.

Eyes flashing with fire, he growled, "This isn't fucking happening, Lily. You need to get off that desk and go the fuck home."

"Why?" I demanded as I slid off the desk so I could move close to him again. "I felt you, King. You want this as much as I do."

His control finally snapped, and he backed me up against the desk. Taking hold of my throat again, he said, "You have no fucking idea what I want. If you did, you'd run and never come back." He paused, lowering his gaze to my chest. His eyes lingered there for a long few moments, which only served to make me more needy. I didn't care if he thought I should run from him. I wanted him to devour me. When he met my gaze again, he said, "You need to leave before it's too fucking late for both of us."

I gripped his biceps. "I don't know what you mean, but I don't care. I'm not leaving."

He dropped his head and rasped, "Fuck." It took him a few moments to lift it again, and when he did, I sucked in a breath at the change in his eyes.

I'd never had a man look at me the way King was.

It was indecent.

Dark desire blazed from his eyes.

I had no doubt he wanted to consume me in every way possible.

Spinning me around, he pressed me against the desk. One hand roughly grabbed my waist while the other slid around my neck again. Pulling my head to the side, he growled against my ear, "Do you know what I like to do to women, Lily?" My gasp encouraged him. "I'm rough in every way you can imagine. I'll strip you and fuck you without a fucking care for your comfort. I'll take what I need, over and fucking over, until you're raw from my hands, my mouth, my dick." His voice dropped lower, darker. "And when I'm finished, you won't hurry back for more."

My mind and body burst with anticipation. I wanted every single thing he'd just said to me. He'd already made my heart beat faster than it ever had. Now I wanted him to do filthy things to me.

When my only response was a moan, he reached for the bottom of my dress and roughly yanked it up. While my mind rushed to keep up with his actions, he had his hand in my panties and his fingers inside me.

"Oh God," I whimpered, my legs struggling to hold me up while his fingers worked me towards an orgasm. I was so wet and ready for him that it wouldn't take long.

His mouth remained against my ear. "Do you like pain, Lily?"

My legs swayed. "I don't know."

His thumb roughly circled my clit while he reached deep inside me, blowing my damn mind. "You've never had it while being fucked?"

"No."

"Fuck." That dark tone returned to his voice. It had a deliciously scary feel to it, and I wasn't sure whether to actually be scared or not. He ground himself against me while pushing me harder against the desk. The bite of pain that caused heightened my pleasure, surprising me. "I *will* hurt you if I fuck you. Are you ready for that?"

I could hardly get a handle on my thoughts, let alone utter any words. When I didn't respond to him, he turned me to face him and gripped my cheeks, his wild eyes demanding my attention. "Answer me. Are you ready for me to hurt you?"

Panting, I nodded. *God, I was ready.* "Yes."

His eyes searched mine, looking for what, I wasn't sure. He swore again, growing angry. "You have no fucking idea what you're asking for."

I opened my mouth to tell him he was wrong, but he dropped to his knees and grabbed hold of my legs as his tongue found my pussy. I almost died at that point. I was sure of it. King almost killed me with pleasure. He thought I wasn't the kind of woman who fucked men like him. I'd argue with him over that until I was blue in the face. I was the kind of woman who had never fucked a man like him, but I'd never known what I was missing.

His fingers dug into me as he gripped me harder.

His lips, tongue, and teeth devoured me.

Thoroughly.

He ate me like I was his last meal.

His moves were savage and crude.

The sounds he made were carnal.

And when I came hard, my entire body shuddering with the kind of pleasure I'd only ever dreamt of, he stood and looked at me with ferocious energy. "You'll never be ready for me." Shoving my panties at me, he ordered, "Get dressed. I'll take you home."

With that, he stalked out of the office, leaving me staring after him in shock.

He was wrong. And if he thought his warnings would make me run a mile, he'd have to think again.

30

King

I sucked on my smoke, dragging the nicotine deep into my lungs. It hit the spot, but only for a brief moment. I'd hardly slept in the past two weeks, and instead, was fuelled by whisky, cigarettes and an unrelenting need for vengeance. But that shit was starting to take its toll. We needed an end to the madness we were stuck in. Kick and I were about to pay a visit to an old friend who we hoped would share some useful information that wouldn't end in us hitting another fucking dead end.

"You want anyone with you and Kick?" Hyde asked, joining me outside the clubhouse.

Shaking my head, I dropped the cigarette and stubbed it out. "It'll only take two of us. We'll meet you and Cole at the drop-off point after. He organised for the rest to get there first?" We had a shipment coming in today, and we weren't taking any chances with it. Romano had fucked with our business for long enough; he would not be fucking with it any longer. I'd organised for some of my guys to get to the drop off early to ensure there were no surprises from Romano, and had asked Cole to send his men ahead too.

"Yeah, he's taken care of that."

Kick came our way. "We ready?"

I looked at Hyde. "Keep me updated with any news on Nitro."

"Will do," he said, turning at the sound of approaching footsteps.

I glanced around and met Axe's gaze. "You good for today still?" I asked.

"You may change your plans after I tell you Romano has been arrested."

I frowned. "Is this true or some bullshit story again?"

"True. I've just confirmed it. Not sure yet what they've picked him up for, but my guy's looking into it."

"Let me know when you hear back from him." I looked at Hyde. "Check in with our men down in Melbourne. Find out what's happening at Romano's headquarters. Our plans for today don't change, but we need to find out where they're holding Romano and who we can use to get to him."

Axe and Hyde left us, and Kick and I were almost to our bikes when a white Holden station wagon drove towards us. As it drew closer, I realised it was Lily. My gut tightened at the memory of Saturday night when she'd thrown herself at me. *Fuck.* I did not need that in my head when I was about to take care of club business. She was a fucking distraction I couldn't afford. And yet, I'd struggled to remove her from my thoughts since I'd driven her home that night.

The feel of her cunt.

The taste of her.

The sounds she made when she came.

I'd wanted nothing more than to lay her out and fuck her raw.

She'd fought me, and almost fucking shattered my restraint, but I hadn't given her what she'd wanted. Hell, she had no idea that what she thought she wanted wasn't what she'd get from me. We hadn't exchanged words on the drive to her place afterwards, and I hadn't been sure she'd show up for Skylar's session today, but thank fuck she had.

She parked her car and walked to me as Kick continued on to his bike. Today she'd swapped her tight jeans for black tights that were covered with long black boots to her knees. As my gaze got stuck on her legs and those boots, I took in the stiletto heel on them. Jesus, she wore that shit to work?

"King." Her voice cut through my thoughts, and my eyes found hers.

"You're early." Usually she came by after work, not around lunchtime.

She smiled, and it hit me in the gut. Lily's light fucking shone bright. Why the hell did she want to fuck me and allow my darkness to taint her? "I have the day off work and am taking the kids and their grandmother out for dinner, so I wanted to see Skylar now. How was she yesterday?"

"Much better. Did she text you? She mentioned she would."

"Yes, she did, but I'm always interested to hear it from a family member's perspective when I'm working with a patient. Sometimes it's different, you know?"

I heard everything she said, and understood it, but failed to respond, because everything else about her caused my mind to stray to the memories I had of stroking and sucking her pussy. The feel and taste of her was lodged in my brain, and I craved more.

"King, are you listening to me?"

Fuck.

"Yes," I snapped, pissed at myself for wanting her. I didn't fucking think about women in this way anymore. Not since I'd sworn off getting involved with anyone after Jen.

She pressed her lips together as she reached into her bag. "Okay, well I'm gonna head in there now to see her. But I wanted to give you this." She shoved a bottle of peppermint oil at me. "For when you've got a headache. Just rub some into your temples, forehead and the back of your neck." She closed her bag and took a couple of steps towards the clubhouse before adding, "Use it whenever you've got your cranky pants on too. It might work wonders."

That smart mouth of hers was a shot straight to my dick. Not the kind I usually preferred, but fuck, I couldn't deny how much I wanted to fill that mouth with my cock.

"Kick," I called out, "I've just gotta take care of something before we leave."

Without waiting for his response, I stalked inside and made my way to Skylar's room. I had something I needed to discuss with Lily about Skylar's recovery, and she'd taken off before I could do that.

By the time I reached my destination, Skylar and Lily were deep in conversation.

"What's Linc done now?" Skylar asked, her eyes alight in a way they only seemed to be these days when Lily was around.

"Ugh, he keeps coming over to my place even though I've asked him not to. He's doing my head in."

"Don't let him in, babe."

"I haven't been, but this morning he let himself in with the key I didn't know he still had."

"Oh God, you need to get that key off him or get the locks changed."

Lily nodded. "I'm getting the locks changed. I just have to

wait until my pay comes in on Thursday. Honestly, though, it's a freaking expense I don't need."

"Has King paid you yet?"

"Yes, but I've put that money aside to pay for Zara's braces. I'll just wait until I get paid later this week."

"Do you want me to hit King up for more cash?"

"No! He already paid me way more than he should have. You know, for a grumpy guy, I think your brother has a soft side under all that bullshit he's got going on. I've never come across a man who looks after his family the way he looks after you."

"Shit, you're not into him, are you?"

"I'm not gonna lie, he's got the best ass I've ever seen, but I don't have time in my life for a man. The last time I dated, it distracted me from my kids, and I promised myself I wouldn't do that again."

I decided not to interrupt them, and instead, put the peppermint oil in my office before going back to Kick. As I passed Skylar's room on the way back outside and heard them laughing, I was reminded again that not fucking Lily was the best decision I'd made since I'd decided to hire her. Skylar needed the friendship more than I needed to get laid. But that ex of hers needed to be pulled into line.

31

Lily

"Mum, I'm on my way now. I'm sorry I'm running late, but I got tied up at the bank talking to the guy about consolidating my credit card debt."

My day off that was supposed to be relaxing had turned into a big fat mess of stuff not going right after I'd left Skylar. To say I felt a little frazzled was an understatement. Especially after Linc had called and asked me if I'd go out with him and the kids for a family dinner on Saturday night. I didn't know where he was going with this, but it didn't feel like anywhere good. If I said no, the kids would get upset because they loved us all being together. If I said yes, it could give Linc the wrong idea. Why was there no manual for divorced couples to consult in times like this? There freaking needed to be one.

"Darling, don't stress and don't speed. You know my

blood pressure goes through the roof when I think you're speeding."

"Mum, you have low blood pressure." Jesus, my mother was a drama queen at times.

"Well, Lily, I can assure you it is high when you put me under pressure."

"Fuck, Mum, how am I putting you under pressure? I'm not speeding. I promise." I tacked the promise bit on the end there because she liked it when I made her promises. She didn't much care if they were broken; she just liked to think people were working hard for her benefit. My mother liked attention. I still wasn't convinced I actually came from her.

"Please don't swear. You know I don't like it."

I'd had enough of this conversation. We weren't getting anywhere with it. "I gotta go. The cops are probably out doing random checks on people using their mobiles while driving, so I better hang up before they catch me."

"Oh my goodness, why aren't you using your hands-free?"

I was, but I liked to freak her out sometimes. "Shit, Ma, I see a cop. Hanging up now."

By the time I got home, she may have had a stroke from her high blood pressure.

I was the worst daughter.

I was going to hell for the grief I gave my mother.

I pressed the accelerator a little harder in an effort to get home faster so I could make sure she didn't have a stroke.

Jesus, now you're buying into her drama.

I sighed.

This was one long-ass day. And it was only going to get longer because I still had to get through dinner out with my mum and the kids. What I needed was to think happy thoughts for the rest of this drive home. I'd fill my well with happy, then I'd do dinner, and then I'd have a long bath. With some wine.

King.

Shit, shit, shit.

Why did my mind instantly go to him when it searched for happy?

Because he made you very happy the other night, Lily.

My legs squeezed together as I remembered his mouth on me, his fingers inside me, and his tongue working me. The man was skilled, that was for damn sure. Not to mention skilled at saying no. I couldn't figure him out. And I still couldn't get him out of my mind.

I indicated to turn into my street and a few moments later, pulled into my driveway, surprised to see two bikes parked outside. I parked in the garage, grabbed my stuff and hurried inside to find out who was here. And came face-to-face with King when I stepped inside my home.

Coming to an abrupt halt, I frowned. "King?"

Good God he looked good today. It was in the way his clothes clung to his body. I'd always had a thing for black tees stretched across muscles, and he wore one today. My eyes were also drawn to the tattoos covering his arms, his fingers, and the small patch of chest I could see. I couldn't drag my gaze from them.

"We're almost finished and will be out of your hair soon," he said, confusing me.

I finally looked up at him. Ignoring the way he watched me with heat—the kind that made me squeeze my legs together again because it reminded me of the way he'd looked at me the other night—I asked, "What do you mean? What are you nearly finished?"

My mother bustled in at that moment, smiling the smile she reserved for men she really liked at King. "King, while you're here, do you think you could possibly check the oil and water in my car please?"

My eyes bulged. And I finally lost my shit after holding it

in all freaking day. "Umm, can someone please explain what universe I've stepped into here?" I looked at King and asked, "Why are you in my house?" before looking at my mother, and asking, "And why are you casually asking him to check your car like you guys are good mates?"

King's lips twitched as an amused expression crossed his face. "I'm changing your locks."

I stared at him. His answer hardly answered any of my questions. "Why are you changing my locks?"

Mum stepped forward, almost in between King and me. "Lily dear, King filled me in on the news that Linc still has a key, and he told me you asked him to stop by and do the locks. I don't know why you didn't tell me about Linc. I swear, that man—"

I grabbed King by the wrist and dragged him into my bedroom. I would have preferred to drag him anywhere but my bedroom; however, it was the only room in the house where I could be guaranteed privacy. Once I had him in there, I closed the door behind us, placed my hands on my hips and demanded, "How do you know about Linc? And why would you lie to my mother about me asking you to change my locks?" I held up a finger, letting him know not to talk yet because I had more questions. "And while we're on it, how did you even know I wanted my locks changed? Did Skylar tell you? And why would you think it was okay to just drop on over and change them without asking me?" My eyes widened as one more thing crossed my mind. "And fuck, why would my mother just let you in?"

I was out of breath by the time I got all that out, and sucked some air in as I waited for his response.

He didn't speak straight away, but rather, just stood there watching me with that same amused expression of a few moments ago. And then—"That's a fuckload of questions."

"Yes! And I'd like answers to them please."

He opened his mouth to speak, but the door to my bedroom flung open, interrupting him.

"Lily, I really need—" My sister's mouth snapped closed when her eyes landed on King. "Oh, my," she said, looking him up and down, "You must be the hot biker dude I've heard all about. Lily wasn't kidding when she said you had muscles to die for."

I wanted the floor to open and swallow me whole, which was a strange thing for me. I didn't tend to get embarrassed easily, and not with men. If I liked a guy, I didn't hide that from him. But for some reason, I didn't want King to know I'd been discussing his level of hotness with my sister. I felt shy with him, which *really* freaking confused me.

You didn't feel shy with him the other night.

Oh God, shut up. I was drunk.

Thanks to what my sister had just revealed, and the thoughts of Saturday night now in my head, I blushed. I, Lily Bennett, a thirty-three-year-old woman, stood in front of a biker I wanted to have sex with, and freaking blushed. And he didn't miss it. I knew this because heat flared in his eyes again as he watched me do it.

I threw up my hands. "You all need to leave. Now! I need a moment."

Brynn reached for King's arm and dragged him out of the room while informing him, "When Lily needs a moment, it's best to give it to her. Trust me on that."

Once the door was closed, and I was alone, I collapsed onto my bed and exhaled loudly. I felt all mixed up. Muddled. My life had turned messy, and the train I was on seemed to be hurtling so fast I couldn't get off. The thing was, though, it had been this way for a long time, and I hadn't felt so flustered with everything before. This was a new development, and I couldn't tell what caused it.

I walked into my ensuite and splashed some water over

my face. Staring at myself in the mirror, I mentally repeated some affirmations that usually calmed me.

I am fearless.

I am doing my best.

I am kickass.

Shit.

It was King.

He was the new development in my life.

It didn't matter how many affirmations I repeated, they wouldn't get rid of this nervous energy that seemed to be camped out in my tummy.

Why did I like him so much? I mean, the man was moody *all the time*. He was impatient. He yelled a little too much for my liking. He was demanding. *So freaking demanding.* He argued with me over stuff that really didn't need arguing over. I mean, I specialised in helping people with headaches, so he should just let me help him with that. There were a lot of things not to like about him.

But damn, there were a lot of things I *did* like that I had no control over liking. Why did God insist on giving us no control over who we were attracted to? I blamed God for this either way. Because, quite freaking honestly, if I could choose, I'd choose *not* to want King. He was hard work, and that was the last thing I needed in my life.

The sound of my bedroom door opening and then clicking shut startled me. Bloody Brynn never did pay much attention when I told her to give me a mome—

King appeared in the doorway behind me.

I gripped the vanity harder and tried like hell to quiet the swarm of butterflies flapping in my stomach. It was a useless exercise, though, because they kept on flapping as he stood there watching me.

"I'm not finished having my moment," I finally managed to get out.

He didn't move, just continued watching me. "I heard you telling Skylar about your ex and the locks. I didn't lie to your mother. She just didn't listen to what I said. I can't tell you what possessed her to allow two men she didn't know into your house, but I'm not going to stand here and say I shouldn't have done it. You needed locks. I could make that happen."

"I'll tell you what possessed her. *You*." I turned to face him. "You are the bossiest, most controlling and demanding man I know. And you're good-looking. My mother didn't stand a chance."

His nostrils flared as heat filled his eyes again. Closing the distance between us, he slid his hand around my waist and pulled me hard against him. "I fucking swore to myself I wouldn't touch you again, but you're hell on a man's restraint." He dropped his gaze to my neck as he brought his free hand up to grasp it. Circling his thumb over my throat, he said, "The taste of you is burned into my memory, and for the fucking life of me, I want more."

Having him this close, our bodies pressed together, was too much for me. My mind, already a mess, burst into a thousand streams of thoughts. My skin pebbled with just as many feelings. But every last one of them disappeared the moment he slipped his hand into my pants to find my pussy. His eyes didn't leave mine for a second. They took in the pleasure I experienced with each stroke of his finger.

The world fell away as King stripped every last thought from my mind.

"Fuck," he growled when I bit my bottom lip and moaned. His strokes became rougher, and our bodies moved together as he reached deeper and worked me harder. The pain from his fingers digging into my neck barely registered.

I was floating.

Soaring.

So high.

And then, in a flurry of fingers and lips and tongues, I careened over the edge into more pleasure than I ever thought possible. It wasn't until I came down from the high that I fully realised we were kissing. I'd processed that fact when he first claimed my lips, but I'd been completely lost in the moment that I kissed him without thought. With King, I didn't think; I felt. And it felt so good that nothing could break that moment.

Needing more, I moved my hands to his face, clutching him like I was afraid he would disappear any moment. He seemed to like the way I held him because he growled again and deepened our kiss. His tongue dominated mine as he consumed all my senses.

I never wanted this kiss to end.

I wanted a lot more, and I didn't want it from anyone but him.

His body jerked suddenly, and he let me go. Taking a step back, he muttered, "Fuck." His eyes were a raging storm of emotions as he said, "I didn't come here to fuck you."

Breathless and with my thoughts all still in a jumbled mess, I said, "You haven't fucked me."

He scrubbed a hand over his face. "I may not have had you with my dick, but I've had my mouth, fingers and tongue all over that sweet cunt of yours, Lily. I've made you come twice. That's close enough to fucking you."

"I want more."

"You don't." Even while he said that, I knew by the way his eyes wandered down my body that he wanted this too.

"Why do you keep saying that?"

"Because I have nothing to offer you but the kind of sex that will fuck you up."

"I'm not looking for a relationship, King."

"And I don't have one to promise you, but you're not

listening to me—I'm not into your standard sex. The shit I want... you wouldn't."

I moved close to him. "And you're not listening to me. I want you to fuck me up. I want it rough. I want you to leave me raw. I want pain. I've only ever had sex a few ways, and I'm bored with that. I want to try it your way."

He took all that in and watched me silently while he processed it. I thought I saw the moment where he lost the war with himself—the moment where he would agree to what I wanted—but then he shook his head once and forced out, "No."

Before I could argue with him again, he stalked out of my bedroom, the door slamming behind him.

32

King

Tatum hit me with a foul glare. "I'm going to pick him up. If he wants to come back here after, I'll bring him."

I shoved my fingers through my hair, feeling every ounce of frustration she was causing me. We'd just got word that Nitro was finally being released, and she insisted on challenging me over who would collect him.

I jerked my chin towards the front door of the clubhouse. "Go. But tell him I want to see him today. Or tonight. I don't give a fuck which, but make it within the next eight hours."

She continued glaring at me as she picked up her keys and phone. Without another word, she exited the building. Thank fuck Nitro was getting out; I wouldn't have to deal with her anymore.

"You think you two will ever get on?" Kree asked as she wiped the counter of the bar where I sat.

"I doubt it. She's too fucking stubborn. I don't know how the fuck Nitro puts up with her."

Kree slowed her movements. "From what I've seen, you've chosen women with a stubborn streak in the past too. It's funny what love does to us."

Love fucked people up. Of that, I was sure. She was right, though—I'd fallen for women who challenged me endlessly. Never again.

And fuck if Lily didn't slide into my mind then.

It had been two days since I'd changed her locks and almost fucked her. It was getting harder to turn her away, so I'd made sure I was nowhere around when she came to see Skylar yesterday. And I'd do the same today. Hell, I'd do it every day going forward. Lily was an illicit pleasure I wouldn't allow myself.

When I didn't respond to what she'd said, Kree changed the subject. "Hyde told me I might be able to go home soon. That you guys are almost finished dealing with stuff. How long do you think that'll be?"

"Hyde wouldn't have said that, Kree. You've misunderstood." We still had to take care of Romano, and fuck knew how long that would take. I wasn't about to make her a promise I couldn't keep.

"What wouldn't I have said?" Hyde asked, taking the stool next to me.

Kree looked at him. "I thought you said I'd be able to go home soon."

"Fuck no. I said home was looking good, meaning we're all itching to get back there."

I kept it to myself, but I also wanted her husband taken care of before she left here. I'd mentioned it again to Zane, who'd told me he'd have news for me on that in the next couple of days. He'd gone past the deadline I'd originally set, but with everything going on, I'd let it slide.

My phone rang, taking my attention off the conversation.

Axe.

"Tell me you've got something good for me," I said. We'd been waiting to hear more about Romano since he'd been arrested, but there had been radio silence on that.

"It's good, but not completely what you're after. Still nothing on where Romano is or what they're doing with him. Shit has been locked tight on that. But Zane and Devil have found your rat."

He was right—it *was* good news.

My entire body thrummed with anticipation.

I was way past the point of ready to deal with this motherfucker.

"Who? And where is he?"

"It's Tate. They've found him in Gosford and are on their way back to the warehouse with him. I'll let you know when they've arrived."

Fucking hell. Tate was Storm. He'd turned nomad years ago after we'd had a disagreement. But I wouldn't have figured him for a fucking rat.

I eyed Hyde after ending the call. "Devil and Zane have our rat. It was Tate."

He scowled. Hyde and Tate had never gotten on. "That motherfucker will pay for this shit."

I nodded, my mind already churning with a million fucking questions for the cunt. "Yeah, he will." Moving off my stool, I added, "I'm gonna go have another chat with Ivy. See if she can shed any light on this."

I found her a few minutes later, lying on her bed, staring at the ceiling. She didn't look at me when she realised I stood in the doorway, but rather she kept staring up as she said, "I want you to let me leave. Tony isn't a threat to me anymore." Her voice revealed her bleakness, but that wasn't new to me. I'd watched her mood shift over the last week, from hot-tempered to this resigned attitude. She hadn't argued with me in the past seven days. She'd pretty much kept to her room and stayed quiet. I'd avoided her because I didn't want us to get into shit again. But this new mood concerned me.

Resting against the doorjamb, I crossed my arms over my chest. "He's a threat until he's dead."

"I have somewhere I can go. Somewhere he won't find me."

"Where?"

"A friend." She finally looked at me. "Please, King. I need to get back to my life, and I can't do that here." She sat up and swung her legs over the edge of the bed so she faced me. "I thought maybe we could find a way to get on after I was sick. You seemed to let your walls down a little when we talked. But now I can see we'll always argue over stupid things. It's just who we are, but I don't want that in my life. It's too hard, and I'm too sad over everything to keep fighting with you."

Fuck.

I hated seeing her like this. It stirred something deep inside me that was long buried. Something I'd left behind and forgotten after one too many betrayals when I was younger.

Compassion.

I used to feel it, and maybe I still did every now and then, but only for the very few I allowed close. This feeling teasing its way out from the depths where I'd shoved it differed, though, to anything I'd allowed in the last fifteen years. It disturbed me in its intensity. I didn't want to feel it. Had no need for it in my life. But I couldn't fucking ignore it because it was right there as I listened to Ivy. In my chest and my gut and my head. It just fucking sat there, waiting for me to do something with it.

"Where's your friend?" Just asking that question filled me

with misgiving. I didn't want to put her back out there where her husband could hurt her, but fuck, keeping her here was killing her light. Maybe I had to let her go.

"He's in Sydney."

"Who is it, Ivy? I need to vet him before I consider this."

She stood and walked to me. "You don't need to check him out. He and I have been friends for years. You just need to stop thinking you're responsible for my happiness. I'll admit, I came here with a lot of hate in my heart. I hadn't fully let go of what happened between us, but I feel like I'm starting to. And for the first time in years, I feel hopeful about my life. Tony kept me down for so long that it fucked with my thinking. This time away from him is helping clear my head." She paused and moved even closer to me. Smiling up at me, she placed her hand on my cheek and said softly, "You don't have to take care of me anymore, King. I can do that myself."

It could have been her touch, or maybe the way she looked at me differently to how she had since she'd been here, or fuck, it could have been my screwed-up thinking while talking to her, but I found myself agreeing to something I never thought I would. "You can leave. Not today, though, but probably tomorrow. I've got something to take care of first."

She moved her hand from my cheek and smiled. "Thank you."

The moment caught me by surprise. This was the Ivy I'd loved. Softer, open, laid bare. Vulnerable. When there were no walls between us, anything felt possible. I liked the sense of calm and ease that brought with it.

I nodded. "I have a question for you. Did you know Tony had a club member in his pocket?"

"No. Why?"

I straightened, uncrossing my arms. "We've found a rat,

and I know Tony had someone feeding him club information, but I don't know if that information was coming from just one person or whether there are more out there I need to be looking for."

She shrugged. "I didn't know about this, sorry. But it wouldn't surprise me if he had more than one. Tony has always been anal about knowing every little detail about everything, so it'd make sense that he wouldn't just rely on one person."

"Fuck," I muttered.

"I'm sorry you have to deal with this, King. It's all my fault." Her voice cracked as tears fell down her cheeks.

My arms were around her before I even thought about it. Pulling her close, I cupped the back of her head and pressed it to my chest. "Don't ever fucking apologise for shit you had no control over. This is all on Tony. Not you."

Her arms circled me, and she held on tight. "If I'd never married him, this wouldn't be happening to you now."

If I hadn't fucked our relationship all those years ago, she wouldn't have married him. This was on me, not her, and I'd be the one to fix it.

~

Just under three hours later, I stared at our rat as he sat tied to a chair in the middle of our warehouse. Nervousness blazed from his eyes as he watched me. *Good.* He should have been fucking nervous, because what I had planned for him, he wouldn't have wished on his worst enemy.

Dragging a chair over, I sat in front of him and yanked the gag from his mouth. "What's it been, Tate, three years since we've spoken?"

He swallowed hard a few times, seemingly relieved to be rid of the gag. "Not fucking long enough."

I felt surprisingly calm considering the anger raging through me and what I was about to do with it. But that was usually the way when I knew what was coming. It was only when shit crept up on me, catching me off guard that my crazy took over. I wasn't sure which I preferred, but if I'd been put on the spot and forced to decide, I'd have to say this way was my preference. Having had the time to contemplate in painstaking detail every hurt I would inflict doubled my pleasure.

Every blow.

Every bruise.

Every cut.

The mental imagery was painted by the strokes of my wrath and tended to by my burning need for retribution. Sometimes that need was so strong and so violent I believed it wasn't just about the matter at hand. I never forgot a wrong, and they had a way of adding up in my head. Every now and then, someone suffered at my hands when I was dancing to the beat of decades' worth of hurts.

Today I had my fucking dancing shoes on.

"So you've been talking to Tony Romano about us. And the feds. Anyone else I should know about?"

His lips pulled up into a scowl. "I've got nothing to say to you, King."

I arched a brow. "Really?"

He didn't reply to that. Just sat there staring at me.

And still my calm state remained.

I lifted my gaze and looked at Hyde who stood behind him. Next to him was Devil. Behind me were Axe and Kick. Everyone was impatient for this to happen. Everyone but me. For once, I was enjoying taking it slowly.

"King."

I turned at the sound of Nitro's voice and found him walking my way. Standing, I took a step towards him, but thought better of my plan and, without warning, faced Tate again and punched him hard in the face, knocking him and the chair backwards. His head hit the cement floor with a hard whack, activating bright lights in my brain. Bright fucking lights of joy.

I then gave my attention to Nitro, grinning. "It's about fucking time they let you out."

"Yeah, brother." He looked around at everyone before focusing his gaze on Tate. "So he's our rat?"

I nodded. "He is."

Nitro grunted as he stalked to where Tate lay sprawled on the ground. Pulling his knife from its sheath, he cut the ropes securing Tate to the chair, gripped his shirt, and yanked him to a standing position. Then, faster than I'd ever seen him move, he walked Tate backwards and slammed him against the brick wall. "Motherfucking cunt!" he roared. Pummelling him, he bloodied Tate up until his face was almost unrecognisable.

I gave him a little time to get that shit out of his system. Fuck knew, if I'd been locked up, I'd wanna beat the shit out of the guy who may have had something to do with keeping me there. Plus, I derived great satisfaction watching the pain Tate experienced at Nitro's hands.

"Stop," I ordered, joining them. "We need him conscious for most of this."

Nitro punched him a couple more times before letting him fall to the ground. Raking his hand through his hair and jabbing a finger at me, he demanded, "When we take Ryland down, he's mine."

I nodded. "You get first shot at him, brother, but we share in that one, too. I'm saving some special shit for that cunt." Looking down at Tate, I said, "Now, this one... he and I are gonna have some fun."

Reefing him up, I moved him back to the chair and forced

him down on to it. He grunted in pain as I settled him there. I gripped his face hard and bent to look into his eyes. "Do you know what one of my favourite sounds in the world is?" I squeezed his cheeks harder, zeroing in on the agony that caused. "That right there. Those little whimpers of pain. They light some dark shit up in my head." I released his face, shoving it away from me before I sat on the chair across from him again. "However, I really would prefer to hear you detail everything you've given Romano and the feds, and you should know that if you don't, I'm going to fuck you up in ways that will paint my mind the blackest of black. I will draw that shit out for days, weeks maybe. I'll string you up here and drop by every night to remind you why you wished you'd just given me the information." I leant forward, my face hardening. "I don't fucking appreciate club members who turn their back on their brothers. I will make you bleed, and then the club will get their shot at you. By the time we're finished, you won't know your ass from your mouth, up from down, white from fucking black." I sat back and crossed my arms over my chest. "On the other hand, you give me what I need, and we'll take it easy on you."

His eyes darted around the warehouse, between everyone here. I saw the fear in them, but I wondered how much more I'd have to push him to trigger that completely. I trained my men well—they didn't give in to their fear easily. And Tate used to be one of my men, so fuck knew how many hours this would take.

He met my gaze again and spat some blood. "Do your worst, King. I'm not giving you what you want."

I nodded. "Okay, if that's the way you wanna play this, I can go along with that." I stood and looked at Nitro. "Strip him and hang him upside down. I'm going to get everyone some food. When I get back, we'll play."

~

It took me eight hours to break him. And a lot of fucking torture. But I finally got the information I wanted, and I now knew what we were up against with the feds. He'd given them more than he gave Romano, and what he'd given them would fucking crucify us.

After I'd dragged every last piece of information from him, I stood silently watching him, contemplating what would convince a club member to turn on their brothers. It was something so foreign to me that I couldn't even begin to wrap my head around it.

He lay on the ground at my feet, his body riddled with bruises, swelling, deep gashes, and blood. Every one of us had their turn at him, but now he was all mine, and while I was mentally exhausted from the day, my body was raring to go.

It tasted blood.

Knew what was coming.

Wouldn't fucking stop until Tate's last breath had been taken from him.

I crouched next to him. "Why did you do it?"

His breaths were laboured, and I knew he would struggle to answer me, but Goddammit, I wanted a fucking answer.

I forced one of his eyes open and demanded, "Why the fuck did you do it?"

He wheezed and attempted to open his mouth. It took him a bit, but he managed to get out, "Cash."

Cash?

He fucking betrayed his club for some fucking cash?

I hadn't expected that answer. Hell, I didn't know what I expected, because I just couldn't fucking understand any motivation to do what he did. But cash felt like an even bigger fuck you than any other reason.

I pushed up out of my crouch, angry. Angry as fucking shit. It was the kind of anger I would struggle to get out of my system.

"Fuck!" I roared, slamming my boot down onto him.

I kicked him over and over, trying desperately to rid my body of this fury.

Time slowed, or maybe it raced.

I had no concept of it while my depravity consumed me.

I kicked and beat and slashed his last breath out of him.

For the club.

For me.

For the fucking code of loyalty he'd shat all over.

When I was done, I stared down at his lifeless form and started calculating the next step for the club. He'd screwed us over, but we weren't down for the count yet. Not even fucking close. We were just getting started.

I took a shower, dressed in clean clothes and headed out to my bike after calling Kick to let him know Tate's body needed to be disposed of. It was nearly 10:00 p.m. and I was wired. I needed to take the edge off, and the best way to do that was to fuck it out of my system.

I had two options.

Find a club whore to take care of that or finally get my fill of the pussy I couldn't get out of my mind, to hell with the consequences.

33

Lily

"So you're going fishing with him again?" I asked Brynn as I wandered through my house cleaning up, the phone wedged between my ear and my shoulder.

"Yes. You know what's weird? I kinda like it with him."

"Ah, that's because he's hot. I don't think it has much to do with the fish." I picked up the last sock on Robbie's bedroom floor and straightened. "Are you sleeping with him yet?"

"Lil, he's a prostitute. I don't sleep with men that bang a hundred women a week."

"A hundred? You have to be kidding." I had no idea, though. Maybe she wasn't. God, I was so naïve when it came to some things. Marrying your childhood sweetheart, having three kids and a busy job would do that to you. I just didn't have the time or the energy to learn all the ways people had sex or how many people a prostitute slept with in a week. I really needed to change this.

Brynn laughed. "I was exaggerating. Anyway look, I have to hang up and do some shit before I go to sleep, but can I drop by in the morning and grab your picnic set?"

"Sure." I made a mental note to buy her one for Christmas. My sister was the least domesticated woman I knew. It wouldn't occur to her to buy one.

"I love you."

I traipsed into the laundry to put a load on before I went to bed. "You better."

"Hey, why does Linc have the kids tonight? I thought he was only having them every second Wednesday night?"

"I have no clue. It's like he's decided all of a sudden to try to be the best dad in the world. And he's being super nice to me, too. I'm actually a little worried about where he's gonna take this."

"You think he wants to get back together?"

"Maybe. I hope not, though, because I do not need the headache of saying no to him."

"Oh, God."

Oh God was right. Linc didn't seem to understand the meaning of no. When he wanted something, he just kept pushing until he got it.

Our conversation was interrupted when someone banged loudly on my front door. I almost jumped out of my skin at the noise.

"Shit, Brynn, I gotta go. Someone's knocking on my door."

"Who the hell would.... Oh, you think it's the hot biker?"

Yes, I did, and if it was, he'd be getting a stern talking to. "Yes. I'll see you in the morning."

I ended the call and stalked to the front door. "King, if

that's you—" My words instantly dried up the moment I laid eyes on him.

Holy. Shit.

I gripped the door to steady myself.

King was here to fuck me.

He didn't have to utter a word for me to know that; I knew it simply by looking at him.

Hunger radiated from him in a way I'd never seen it radiate from a man.

Taking a step inside, he grabbed me by the neck and pushed me up against the wall while kicking the door closed. He pressed our bodies together as his eyes bored into mine. They were as dark and demanding as he was. King wasn't voicing his request. His eyes were doing all the asking.

"Yes," I said, my voice all breathy.

His grip tightened around my neck and his nostrils flared as he forced a breath out. My answer seemed to anger him. But then, his mood already seemed darker and more intense than usual. When his mouth claimed mine, I experienced that ferocious energy firsthand.

He didn't just kiss me; he ravaged me.

Whatever emotions were running through him ran through that kiss. It was savage, and it stole my attention like nothing ever had. It drove all thought from my mind and demanded my submission.

King wanted control of me.

When he came up for air, his eyes sought mine again and he finally spoke. "This"—his fingers dug into my neck where he held me—"is what I need. Can you give me that?"

The air was thick with need, raw and edgy. Both his and mine. But what enslaved me was the danger bleeding from him. I had no idea what I was truly agreeing to, but I was helpless to say no. I'd told him I wanted his fucked-up sex, and I hadn't been lying.

I nodded. "Yes."

A hiss escaped his lips before he surrendered to what he wanted.

Finally.

Lifting me, he threw me over his shoulder and carried me into my bedroom. He dropped me on my bed and ordered, "Clothes off and then kneel on the end of the bed."

With my heart beating fast and my hands a little shaky, I did as he said. He switched my lamp on and stood at the end of the bed watching every move I made. I'd always liked King's eyes on me, but this took that to a whole new level.

When I'd stripped down to nothing, he reached for his belt and undid it. Working it, he formed cuffs that he restrained my wrists with. After securing the belt in place, he slid his zip down and removed his jeans. He then lifted his tee over his head and dropped it to the floor.

King stood naked in front of me, and my gaze travelled the length of his body. He was a masterpiece, a masculine powerhouse of hard muscle and brute strength. I shivered, thinking about what he would do to me. And when I saw his piercings, my core clenched. Both his nipples were pierced with silver hoops, as was the skin at the base of his cock. It was a pubic piercing. I knew that because one of my favourite singers had one, and I'd read the articles about how good they were during sex.

Moving closer, he said, "Turn around and place your hands on the bed."

I held his gaze for a beat longer than he preferred, and he ordered gruffly, "Now."

Turning, I obeyed his command. I had to use all my upper body strength to hold myself up due to my hands being bound together, and I knew instantly that this would soon become hard. I didn't have long to think about that, though, because King's hands landed on my ass, consuming my complete attention.

His touch surprised me. It wasn't rough, but rather gentle as he ran his hands over my ass cheeks and then down the backs of my legs. When he got to my knees, though, his gentle touch disappeared.

Gripping my legs just above the knees, he separated them. With my ass in the air and my legs apart, I felt exposed to him in a way that both thrilled and bewildered me. He was pushing me to do things I'd never done. And we were only just getting started. My mind raced, wondering how much further he would push me. But not for long, because as soon as he'd parted my legs, he took hold of my bottom and bent to lick my pussy.

He licked the entire length of it while a deep growl vibrated from his mouth.

My body quivered as pleasure jolted through me.

The pleasure built as his tongue entered me and his mouth worked my pussy.

Oh God, I desperately wanted to grip the sheet, but I couldn't. And the longer he spent with his mouth to me, the harder it became to hold myself up. My wrists, arms and shoulders burned with the effort it took not to collapse. When I reached the point where I didn't think I could stay up any longer, I dropped my elbows to the bed, but King had other ideas.

He lifted his face from my pussy. "Keep your arms up."

"I can't—"

He cut me off, his voice harsh. His order final. "Up."

When I didn't move straight away, he grabbed hold of my hips and yanked me backwards, towards him. It all happened so fast I didn't have time to think. Caught off guard, my face landed on the bed as he dragged me, burning my skin with the speed he moved. When he had me at the end of the bed, he flipped me onto my back and stood with his legs caging mine in.

Placing his hands on the bed either side of me, he brought his face close to mine. Eyes flashing black, he demanded, "Do you want me to fuck you?"

I nodded. "Yes."

"Did you listen to me when I told you it would hurt?"

"Yes."

He grabbed my face. Squeezing me hard, he said, "I don't think you took it in." Easing the pressure of his grip, he said, "So I'm going to tell you again and give you one last chance to walk away."

"You don't need to tell me again. I remember."

His jaw clenched. "I'm getting close to breaking point here, Lily. You need to be sure."

I didn't know whether to be excited about his breaking point or scared of it. God, he wasn't like any man I'd ever been with. But that was the point. "I'm sure."

He tightened his grip on my face again, the pain sharp. "When I tell you to do something, you do it. And you don't fucking talk back to me. We clear?"

I couldn't talk while he held me like this, so I nodded.

Letting my face go, he ordered, "Back on your hands and knees."

When he had me where he wanted me, he took hold of my ass again and buried his face back in my pussy. He then proceeded to edge me close to orgasm before pulling me back by withdrawing from my pussy. He did this over and over until I could barely concentrate. My body ached and burned. It also sang with bliss. The alternating sensations were a kind of ecstasy I never knew existed. And King knew exactly how to use them both to work me into a state of frenzy where I begged him to make me come.

He didn't, though. Just as I thought he was about to give

me what I wanted, he flipped me onto my back and undid the belt, freeing my wrists. I stared up at him, breathless and needy, so relieved to have the belt removed. His eyes met mine, but it was as if he didn't see me. It was like he was completely lost in this experience.

He moved onto the bed, over me, and dipped his head to suck on one of my nipples. His hands skimmed down my body to my legs and he spread them out, pushing them hard against the mattress. He kept hold of them there, his mouth still on my breast, while he ran his dick along my pussy.

My back arched as I flung my arms out and turned my head to one side. I'd used all my energy holding myself up, and pain still burned in my arms, but this felt so good.

I needed him inside me.

Now.

I reached for his face and pulled it away from my breast. "I need you to fuck me," I begged.

His jaw tightened and a vein pulsed in his temple. Letting go of my legs, he took hold of my wrists and brought them together on the mattress above my head. His fingers bit into my skin, and I winced at the pain. That drew his attention. He seemed to like it.

"I am nowhere near ready to fuck you," he growled as his eyes ran over every inch of me. Keeping hold of my wrists with one hand, he brought his other one down to my pussy. Roughly pushing what felt like three fingers deep inside me, he said, "We've got hours ahead of us before you'll get my dick, and the more you beg me for it, the longer I'll make you wait."

He wasn't giving me what I wanted, but God if he wasn't giving me what I needed.

I'd been waiting forever for a man like King.

One who would challenge and dominate me in this way.

A man who pushed me out of my comfort zone.

King spent the next two hours stripping away my comforts—the pieces of myself I held onto tightly so as not to make myself vulnerable. Because even though I was naked, my soul was still fully clothed. Opening myself up during sex and laying my needs and wants on the table was something I'd never done. Not since the one time I'd told Linc a fantasy of mine and he'd told me there was something wrong with me for wanting that. I'd protected myself after that. Had stayed safe and not dug deep within to ask if I was getting what I needed.

I'd used sex as a way to be close to someone else. I'd never used it to get close to myself.

King undressed my soul.

He took what he wanted from my body, was brutal with me, but in the process, my essence was laid bare.

I connected with my core.

My feminine centre.

And I realised it wasn't wrong to want the things I wanted.

By the time King was ready to fuck me, my mind and body were exhausted but awakened and ready for him. He found a condom and then came back to where I lay on the bed. Every inch of my skin hummed for him as he slid an arm under me and pulled me up.

He positioned me so my head hung over the side of the bed. He then wrapped both hands around my neck, just under my jaw, and pressed upwards, restricting my breath slightly. His eyes were focused completely on my neck. There was something about it that put him in a trancelike state.

Without warning, he thrust inside me. He moved so ferociously that he almost forced me off the bed. It was his hold of my neck that kept me from that.

I clung to the sheet while he slammed into me. His movements were slow to begin with; he was more into the choking than the fucking. I couldn't get enough of either. I also couldn't get enough of his piercing. It hit my clit every time he pushed inside. The pleasure was so intense I decided that if I never had sex again, it wouldn't matter because this was the best of my life.

"Fuck," he roared, moving faster and loosening his grip on my neck.

I found his eyes and didn't let go.

I wanted to watch him come.

Needed to see the moment this man lost himself completely.

But as he fucked me harder and faster, I drifted into my own trance.

I was so close to falling over the edge into absolute bliss.

My skin blazed with the need to get there.

My body begged for it.

My brain shattered completely.

I was reaching.

Crying out.

Aching.

Somewhere in there he let go of my neck, yanked me back fully onto the bed, and pounded so hard into me that I ended up with my head against the headboard.

I came first.

He wasn't far behind me, but by then I was adrift and only vaguely aware of his thunderous growl of release.

King had fucked me thoroughly and sleep claimed me fast.

34

Lily

I rolled over and cracked an eye open to check the time on the clock beside my bed. It was just past six in the morning. The morning after King fucked the hell out of me.

God, I could hardly move. The man had made good on his promise of rough sex. He'd dedicated time to every inch of my body, giving both pleasure and pain. I wasn't sure how I'd get through the day after last night.

I managed to leave my bed and throw on a T-shirt and panties before heading out to the kitchen to make a coffee. I was disappointed King had left without saying goodbye sometime during the night, but reminded myself it was what we'd both agreed to. No relationship, just sex.

I was lost in my thoughts when the door to my back patio slid open and King stepped inside.

I jumped. "Holy shit. Way to give a girl a heart attack." Frowning, I added, "I thought you'd already left."

His eyes slowly ran down my body before meeting my gaze. "Just getting my shit now and leaving."

The flare of excitement I'd experienced when I realised he was still here turned to another round of disappointment. "Oh okay. Do you want a coffee before you go?"

He shook his head. "No."

"Lily." My sister's voice floated from the front door to the kitchen. A moment later, she joined us, her eyes widening as she took in King. Her mouth spread into a huge smile, and she said, "I see you broke the drought."

King shifted his gaze from me to Brynn and then back to me, but didn't utter a word.

"Yes," I said as I pulled a mug down from the cupboard. I didn't want to get into a discussion about my sex life right now. "You want a coffee, Brynn?"

"I would love one. A coffee with you and King sounds like the perfect start to my day."

"He's not staying." I glanced across at him, finding him still watching me. His gaze caused butterflies in my tummy. God, I needed to get a grip. He was just the guy who broke my drought. Nothing more.

"Oh really?" Brynn asked. "You're leaving so early?"

Before King could answer her, my mother appeared on my back patio.

God help me.

She slid the back door open and came to an abrupt stop when she spied King. The smile that filled her face matched the one on Brynn's when she'd found King in my kitchen. Entering the house, she said, "I see I no longer need to get that dating profile of yours up, Lily."

I seriously wanted to bang my head on the kitchen counter.

Looking back up at them all, I said, "I'm only going to say this once—yes, I had sex last night, but no, it doesn't mean

I'm dating." I directed the next bit to Mum. "And that doesn't mean you should go hiring me a prostitute or go filling out dating profiles for me. I'm quite capable of finding myself a man when I decide I want one."

Mum looked a little put out. Waving her hands dismissively at me, she said, "I beg to differ on that last bit, my darling. You haven't so much as looked at a man in six months. I think you are most definitely out of practice."

"She's not out of practice," King rumbled, unleashing another round of butterflies in my tummy.

When he pulled out his keys, I asked, "Are you leaving now?"

"Yeah."

"I'll walk you out."

He shook his head. "No, stay with your family." And then he was gone.

Brynn and Mum both stared after him. "Don't feel like you need to stay with us," Brynn said. "Go say goodbye to your man."

"He's not my man, Brynn. It was just sex."

Mum's lips flattened. "Oh Lily, it isn't just sex when a man looks out for you like King has."

"Yes Mum, it is. And it was." *And I already want more.*

Brynn narrowed her eyes at me. "But you like him, yes?"

There was no point lying to her. My sister saw through all my lies. "Yes, but he—"

"No buts, Lil. Life is too short for buts," she said.

"It's also too short for wasting time on something that will never happen. And King is most definitely in that category."

It was great sex. Amazing freaking sex. But it was time to go back to being his sister's physiotherapist and nothing more.

⁓

"You're doing so well," I said to Skylar at the end of her session that afternoon. "We can probably look at cutting back our sessions to a couple of times a week now."

She sat in the armchair in her room, feet up on the stool King had gotten for her. "Sure, if you think I'm ready."

I smiled. "I do. I'm going to write you up a new plan of exercises, and I'll drop back to visiting you Mondays and Thursdays." My reasons were based purely on Skylar's needs, but it wouldn't hurt for me to visit the clubhouse less often.

As I packed up my stuff, she said, "Thank you for being so amazing, Lily. I don't think I could have gotten through the last couple of weeks without you."

She'd come a long way, both physically and mentally. And I had no doubts she could manage her recovery on her own now, with just check-ins from me to make sure all was progressing well.

I slung my bag over my shoulder. "You've absolutely got this. And you know I'm just a call or text away if you need me."

"Hey, are you going to see King on your way out?"

I nodded. "Yes."

"Can you tell him I've decided we should have tacos for dinner."

"Sure. Is he cooking?" I threw in that last question as a joke. It seemed unlikely to me that King would be making dinner.

She laughed. "You sound surprised. And yes, he is. He spent some time with me this morning and told me he wanted me, Axe, Annika, and the kids to all have dinner together tonight. I have no idea what's gotten into him, but I like that he wants to hang out. It's been too long since we've had family dinner together."

I headed for the door. "I'll let him know, and I'll email through your new exercises."

"Thank you," she said as I left the room.

Anticipation filled me as I walked the short distance to King's office. I had no idea if he'd be there, but I hoped so. I wanted to pay him back for the locks he'd installed the other day. I also just wanted to see him and talk to him. It was crazy since I'd never have him again, but I couldn't help myself. I liked spending time with him.

He glanced up from his desk when I entered the office, his eyes spending time on my body before meeting my gaze.

"Hey," I said, my voice full of hesitation even though I was trying hard not to show the awkwardness I felt over the situation. We'd experienced some highly intimate moments together last night and it confused me to go from that back to the business relationship we'd had before then. I had never had a one-night stand before. All the sex I'd ever had was part of a relationship, so this was new territory for me.

"How's Skye doing?"

Okay, back to business. I could do that.

I took a deep breath to centre myself. "She's really good. I'm going to cut back to seeing her twice a week from now."

His brows drew together. "Why?"

"Well," I started to say, but my voice cracked with nervousness. Swallowing hard, I continued, "Her progress is good, and she doesn't really need me to be with her so much now. She can manage her exercises well without me. I'll just swing by and make sure she's continuing to improve. And, well, it'll save you money you don't need to spend."

"I want to spend the money, Lily. Don't cut back the sessions."

The gravel in his voice hit my core, electrifying my skin. I didn't know whether to read between the lines with what he said or not.

"Okay," I agreed softly, wishing I had a lot more experience with men so I was better able to navigate whatever this was between us. "Oh also, she said to tell you she wants tacos for dinner."

He nodded, but didn't reply to that, just continued watching me.

Becoming flustered under his intense gaze, I smoothed my skirt when it didn't need smoothing. And blurted out, "How much do I owe you for the locks? I'll bring the money by tomorrow or if you need it sooner, I can drop back later with it. Or put it in your bank if you give me your details. However you want—"

"You don't owe me anything."

"No, I do, King."

"You don't." His tone turned hard, his statement absolute. I didn't care for that tone.

I stopped smoothing my skirt and straightened my shoulders. He would not be getting the last word on this. And he sure as heck wouldn't be refusing my money. "You took time out of your day and brought one of your men with you to do the job. You paid for the locks. You also checked my mother's oil and water. I appreciate all of that. What I don't appreciate is the way you bulldoze me when I approach you about some things. I always pay my own way in life, and I would like to pay for my locks. I'd also like to pay for your time, but I'm guessing that would be pushing for too much where you're concerned."

He stood, his jaw tight, his shoulders tighter. Walking around the desk, he went to the door and closed it. He then moved behind me, his body to mine. He caged me in so my legs were pressed hard against the desk, my hands flat to it, my ass tilted back as I bent forward.

With one hand around my waist and the other inching up my leg to reach under my skirt, he growled against my ear, "*I* appreciate the fuck out of many things in life, Lily, one of them being when a woman doesn't argue with me. You won't be paying me a cent and you won't mention those locks again." He slipped his hand into my panties as he nudged my feet apart. When he pushed his fingers inside my pussy, he added, "Do you understand?"

I didn't want to understand, but his ways were persuasive to say the least. I still had some fight in me, though. "No, I don't. We hardly know each other, so I'm not sure why you want to pay for my stuff." It really made no sense to me. I'd never met a man who randomly paid for my shit. Hell, I'd never even had a date pay for my meal. And I'd paid Linc's way for many things for a long time.

His fingers stroked me expertly, and I squeezed my eyes shut as the pleasure engulfed me. "This doesn't feel like not knowing you," he rasped, grinding his dick against my ass.

Oh God. It really didn't. And that was the source of my confusion. Gripping the desk, I said, "I don't know what we're doing, King. We said one night."

His mouth pressed harder against my ear, his teeth grazing my skin. "You fucking came undone last night. You want more than one night."

I couldn't argue with either of those statements. I wanted so much more sex with him. But where would that lead? King had made it clear he didn't want anything more than to fuck me, and I thought I could get on board with that, but now I wasn't so sure. Not after the amount of time I'd dedicated to thinking about him today. Not to mention that every time I closed my eyes or had a moment to myself, images of him fucking me filled my mind.

"Lily, stop thinking," he ordered as he lifted my skirt. "Tell me you want this."

My body fought my mind, and in the end, won the war. "I want this." The words fell from my lips before I could stop them, but I wouldn't take them back. When his hands were on me like this, and his mouth was promising me dirty things I never knew I wanted, King owned me. All I could do was go along for the ride and pray I came out unscathed when he was done with me.

He didn't waste a second once I'd given him what he wanted. He grabbed hold of my neck and forced me down over the desk. My skirt was pushed up over my ass, my panties ripped from me. The sound of a condom wrapper filled the air as he slid his zip down. One hand came back to hold my neck. I couldn't see him, but every noise he made, and the speed with which he worked told me he was as desperate for this as I was.

He slammed into me.

There was no gentle from King today. He took what he wanted with a savage energy that pushed me over the edge from wanting this to needing it like I needed air.

I didn't want gentle.

I wanted what he offered, any way it came.

And I knew that would be my downfall in the end because I'd never wanted sex this much.

Every part of my body ached from what he'd done to it last night, and his rough treatment now only added to that pain. But God if I didn't love every second of it.

It didn't take either of us long to come. When he was finished, he moved away from me, disposed of the condom and zipped himself back up all while I tried to get my bearings. My panties lay torn on the carpet, so I pushed my skirt down and straightened my top. As I ran my fingers through my hair, fixing it, my hand brushed across my neck and I grimaced at the pain I felt there. King had left bruises both times he'd had me.

His eyes met mine before dropping to my neck. He didn't comment, just clenched his jaw as he stared at me. I wasn't sure, but it seemed to anger him, but then, he was always in some kind of mood, so who knew what stirred his disapproval.

A knock on the door cut through our silence. "King, are you in there?" It was a female voice I didn't recognise, and my tummy knotted as I thought about him with other women. The thoughts came from nowhere, slamming into me and causing my head to spin.

I took a deep breath and picked up my bag, determined to clear my mind of whatever was going on in there.

You have no claim on King.

You need to remember that.

Oh God.

Why did I think this was a good idea?

Jesus, get your shit together, Lily.

"Fuck," King muttered, raking his fingers through his hair. He stalked to the door and yanked it open. "I'm busy. Can you give me a moment?"

"I'm leaving," I said, walking to the door.

King stepped to the side and glanced at me. My eyes, though, were on the dark-haired woman standing in the hallway watching me with great interest.

"Hi," she said, "I'm Ivy. I'm sorry to barge in when you two were in the middle of—"

"No, it's good." I turned my gaze to King. "We were finished."

Ivy looked between King and me, her expression changing into something that seemed a little dark. Jealous maybe. I wondered who she was to him for her to have that reaction. She covered it quickly, though, and smiled at me. "Great, because I need some time with him."

Oh.

Okay, so they were close.

With one last glance at King, I exited the office and

hurried to my car. My cheeks heated with the foolishness I felt over my reaction to Ivy. I was like a damn teenager jealous over her crush. It was crazy behaviour, and it surprised the heck out of me. I didn't do crazy. I did calm, rational and sensible. I was the woman who spent her life looking after her family, being the responsible one, and not getting sidetracked by men who drove her to act in ways she never had before.

I would go home and I would get my shit together.

And I would put King out of my mind completely.

35

King

I watched as Lily rushed out of my office. *Fucking hell*. After having her last night, I'd intended to move the fuck on and never go back for seconds. Not because I didn't want her again, but because I *did* want her again. Lily stirred a hunger in me I hadn't known for almost a decade. Not only did I want to fuck her, I wanted time with her. I liked talking to her. Hell, I liked fucking arguing with her. But I'd sworn years ago never to go down that path with a woman again, so I needed to keep my hands off her. That was turning into something I didn't seem able to do.

"Who's that?" Ivy asked, drawing my attention back to her.

"Skylar's physiotherapist."

She brushed past me into the office. "Yes, it looks like it," she said as she looked down at Lily's panties on the floor.

I ignored the chill in her tone. After our conversation the

other day, I'd thought we were good, but I should have known Ivy and I would never be good. "You ready to go?" I was honouring my promise to let her leave, and had agreed to take her to the train station.

"Yes, but I can catch a cab if you're busy."

"I'm not busy."

We watched each other in silence for a few moments. I was filled with misgivings about allowing her to leave, but I wouldn't go back on the agreement. Romano was behind bars, and she'd assured me she had someone who would help her disappear. She was the happiest I'd seen her since she'd turned up over two weeks ago, and I wanted that happiness to continue. Being here with me only made her sad and angry. It was time to let her walk out of my life again.

My phone rang, breaking our silence.

Axe.

I put the phone to my ear. "What's up, brother?"

"Ryland has been replaced as head of the case against you and the club. I'm still waiting on further info, but it looks like he's been suspended."

"Why?"

"It seems he's on someone's payroll. Not sure on that yet either, but I'm working on it."

"Fuck," I muttered.

"Yeah. My thoughts exactly. I'll let you know as soon as I know something," he said, ending the call.

"Is everything okay?" Ivy asked.

I shook my head. "No. I'm going to get one of the boys to run you to the train station. I have something I need to take care of."

Her smile faded, but she said, "Okay, thanks." She walked to the door, glancing back at me briefly to say, "Thank you for taking care of Tony for me."

After I'd organised Kick to take Ivy where she needed to

go, I rested my ass against the desk and took a moment to get my thoughts under control. Shit was changing and not in good ways. Ryland being replaced wasn't great. It was better the devil we knew with him. Fuck knew who would take over. Also, we were still in the dark as to Romano's location. The feds had him tucked away somewhere safe. And while I'd agreed for Ivy to leave, I would worry about her until we had her husband sorted. On top of all that, the club was struggling with everything going on. We were stretched thin trying to keep business running as usual while also working like fuck to fix the shit we were in. Add to that the fact I'd sent all family members away, and my men were starting to grow restless. I needed to pull us all back into line and get us ready for the next part of this battle.

I headed out to the clubhouse bar in search of Hyde. Finding him drinking with Nitro, I sat with them and detailed where we were at with Ryland as well as my thoughts on the unrest in the club. I then said, "We need a club get together tomorrow night. Something to bring us all back together and on the same page."

Hyde nodded his agreement. "I'll organise it."

"We also need a new plan to allow for everyone to have a couple of days off to visit their families. We've got Cole and the Brisbane boys here. They'll boost our numbers to make that possible." I looked at Nitro. "Can you get a roster sorted for that?"

"Will do."

I couldn't put my finger on what it was, but something had my gut churning. Something didn't fucking feel right, and I needed to figure that shit out fast.

~

I surveyed the clubhouse bar late the next afternoon, taking in my men. They'd started drinking just after three, and I'd let them all know our plan going forward. It was exactly what they needed to hear, and I watched as the tension eased with the knowledge they'd have time with their families soon.

"Everyone seems much happier," Annika said, joining me at the table where I sat in the corner. "It's amazing what some alcohol will do."

I drank some of my beer. It wasn't the alcohol that had caused this turn in mood. It was the brotherhood. It was always that. But I'd found unless someone was part of it, they struggled to wrap their head around just what the club meant. Every one of us would lay down our life for our brothers. Sometimes, though, the battles we waged took their toll. It was at those times we had to draw close and trust in our brothers to get us through. That was what today was about.

"How are the kids?"

"They've had enough, King. How much longer do you think this is going to go on?"

"They were okay at dinner last night."

"That's because you were there. They love you being around."

"I don't plan for this to take much longer, Nik." Axe had a lead on Romano's whereabouts, and we were following up on that. I was hopeful to have him dealt with in the next day, but I didn't tell her that in case shit went south.

"Good." She stood to leave. "One other thing—I really like Lily. She's such a great influence on Skylar. You did good there, big brother."

I finished my beer before heading out, too. I wasn't hanging around tonight. My head was all fucked up, so I needed some space to figure some of that out. I grabbed my shit from the office and dropped in on Skylar to check on her.

She glanced up at me from the bed where she was doing some study. "Ooh King, I'm glad you came by. Lily left her phone here." She held it out to me. "Can you please take it to her. She's probably stressing, wondering where it is."

I took the phone, but I wouldn't take it to Lily. I'd get Kick to run it over to her. "I'll get it to her," I promised.

Skye smiled, and I admitted to myself how right Nik had been about Lily's influence on our sister. Her anxiety had levelled out and she hadn't argued with me in days. "Thanky-ou," she said.

I pulled up a chair and spent some time chatting with her. Half an hour passed as she told me about her progress with Lily and the study she had to catch up on. We laughed and joked around with each other, and it felt like the easiest half hour I'd had in too fucking long.

"Something's going on with you," she said as we laughed over something silly she'd done that morning.

"What?"

"I don't know, but last night you wanted dinner with us all and now you're just sitting with me cracking jokes like I'm not sure I've ever seen you crack them." Her face softened. "It's nice, King. I like seeing you smile."

I stretched my neck. "I'd say it's because I haven't had a headache for a couple of days."

She narrowed her eyes at me. "Maybe. Whatever it is, I hope it continues. You need some happiness in your life."

"Okay," I said, standing, "I've got stuff to do, so I'm gonna head out. You need anything?"

"No, I'm good. Just please don't forget to get Lily's phone to her."

As I walked out to the bar to find Kick, Lily's phone rang. Her sister's face popped up on the screen.

I answered the call. "Yeah."

"King?" My gut tightened at Lily's voice. Jesus, she had this fucking effect every time I spoke with her.

"You left your phone with Skylar."

"Oh thank God. I thought I'd lost it. I'll come back and get it. Thank you."

"I'm on my way there with it now." *Fuck.*

Silence.

And then, softly and so fucking sweet it hit my gut again —"I really appreciate that."

Christ, I'd never done sweet. But hell if it didn't get me hard.

"I'll see you soon." I stabbed at the phone to end the call and shoved it in my pocket.

Fuck, I got myself into some shit sometimes.

Lily's sister answered the door when I arrived. "King," she greeted, a huge smile on her face, "Come in." She practically pulled me into the house and to the kitchen where their mother was pulling a roast out of the oven.

"You're just in time for dinner," Hannah said. I knew her name was Hannah because she'd spent a good twenty minutes telling me about her family the day I'd changed Lily's locks. In that time, I'd learnt everything from what an asshole Lily's father was to how they'd decided on Lily's name to their favourite holiday spot to the fact Hannah was desperate to marry her two daughters off because she didn't want them to end up alone like she was. Where Lily was straight to the point, her mother was wordy, and where Lily was practical, her mother seemed frivolous.

I placed Lily's phone on the kitchen counter. "I'm just dropping this off."

Hannah pulled a face and waved me off with one hand. "Don't be silly. We have plenty of food. And besides, you will kick yourself if you don't try Lily's famous roast beef." Her face pulled into a smile as she lowered her voice and shared what seemed to be a secret, "She's also made a caramel slice that the kids love. And I have to say it really is her best dessert. My girl is an excellent cook, but sometimes her desserts are kinda so-so. Not this one, though. This one you will want to stay for."

"You mean you don't love my baked cheesecake, Mum?"

I turned to find Lily standing behind me, a playful smile on her face.

"Oh Lily, I was just trying to let King know that tonight he really should stay for dinner."

Lily's gaze met mine, her smile still in place. As her eyes dipped down to take in my body, she said, "Stay." And fuck if that didn't make me wanna stay.

Ten minutes later, we were seated around her dining table. It was a rowdy dining table and it threw me back years to when I sat around Margreet's dining table with our large family. Lily's kids were hesitant with me at first, but when her middle daughter asked me what it was like to ride a bike, they warmed to me fast. By the time we'd finished dessert, they'd asked if I would stay and watch *Thor* with them after dinner.

"Kids, King probably has to get back to the club. He doesn't have time to watch a movie," Lily said, looking at me with an expression I couldn't quite read. She seemed a little unsure of shit, and I didn't blame her. I had no fucking clue what we were doing here either.

"I'm good," I said as I jerked my chin at Robbie. "Go get the movie set up. I'll be there in a minute."

"Awesome," he said as he ran out of the room. The girls hit me with smiles, too, and then followed him. Hannah and Brynn were busy in the kitchen, leaving Lily and me alone.

"You don't have to stay and watch the movie," she said, fidgeting with the tablecloth.

"Do I strike you as a man who does shit he doesn't want to do?"

The uncertainty disappeared from her face and she smiled. "No, you do not."

I stood. "You watching it with us?"

"Ah that would be a no. I've already seen it like four times. I'm going to go take a bath while you babysit."

"Fuck," I muttered. "I did not fucking need that mental image when I'm about to hang out with your kids."

She grinned. "Enjoy the movie, King."

I left her and made my way out to the living room where the kids had the movie ready to go. This night had turned into the strangest fucking night, but I couldn't deny it felt good to be with Lily and her family. Even when Hannah joined us and didn't shut up during most of the movie, I felt more relaxed than I'd felt in years.

Lily was still in the bath two hours later when the movie finished. The kids scattered to their rooms, and Brynn and Hannah had gone home a little while before the movie finished. I turned off the television and went looking for Lily.

Leaning against the doorjamb of her bathroom, I crossed my arms over my chest. "Have you been in there all this time?"

She cracked an eye open and shook her head. "No, I did some laundry first and got some stuff ready for tomorrow."

"What's happening tomorrow?"

"The girls are both hanging out with their friends while I take Robbie to karate and then to the science centre. It's gonna be another long-ass day."

"Today was long?"

She sighed. "Every day is long, King."

Fuck, guilt hit me over pushing her into adding to her long days by working with Skylar. "Maybe you should cut your sessions back with Skye."

She sat up, and my eyes were drawn to her tits that were now on display above the bubbles. "What is this?"

I frowned. "What is what?"

She pointed her finger between the two of us. "*This*. You having dinner with my family and then watching a freaking movie with my kids. You being nice to my mother. God, you being nice to *me*. Where's the moody man I know so well? And why are you saying I should cut back my sessions when you told me just yesterday not to?" She stood and got out of the bath, coming to me, water and bubbles dripping everywhere. A fierce expression had settled on her face. Jabbing me in the chest, she added forcefully, "You are so freaking confusing!" Then grabbing her towel, she wrapped it around herself and walked into her bedroom.

I reached for her arm and yanked her back to me. "I don't know what the fuck this is, but I can't stay away. That smart mouth of yours, and sweet fucking ways turn me the hell on. And your family? I like them. They're honest and real, and you don't fucking find that often anymore."

Her eyes searched mine for a long few moments before we got to what was really doing her head in. She pushed out of my hold like she was trying to keep some distance between us. "You made it clear you don't want anything but sex, and I figure you're not just getting that from me. Which is fine. I'm not saying it's not. But I'm not into that, King. I thought we were just going to sleep together once, and I was good with that. Kind of. But then I met Ivy and I realised I am so far from good with it, it's not funny. So you should go back to doing what you were doing before you met me, and we should call it quits."

Fuck I liked a woman who got to the fucking point and didn't play games with me.

I pulled her close again. "We need to get a few things straight. One, I'm not fucking Ivy. That's an old relationship that will never be revisited. Two, I'm not fucking anyone else. And three, there is no fucking way you and I are calling it quits." I gripped her waist and backed her up against the wall. "I wasn't looking for a relationship, and I can't say it's high on my priority list, but I also can't say I don't want to keep seeing you. What I *can* say is that I don't want to see anyone else." My mouth brushed her ear as I added, "You are the only woman I want to fuck."

Her hands came to my chest and she tried to push me away. "King—"

I refused to budge. Taking hold of her face, I angled it up to mine. "I'm not letting you walk away from this, so don't even think about that."

Her eyes widened. "So what, you'll just force your way into my life?"

"I won't need to. You want this as much as I do. And fuck, the way you opened up to me when I fucked you, you can't deny how good that sex was."

She contemplated that before scrunching my shirt into her hands. "Has anyone ever told you how infuriating you are? Because you are. And yet, all I wanna do is kiss you. It's freaking maddening to me how you manage to get away with shit." And then, before I had a chance to kiss her, she pushed me away and escaped my hold. Walking to her wardrobe, she threw over her shoulder, "FYI, my body is still sore after you fucked the hell out of it, so there won't be any sex for you tonight. Plus, my kids are here tonight, so there's that, too."

Fucking hell, this woman.

"I didn't come here for sex, Lily."

She dropped her towel, giving me half a minute with her

body before she covered it back up with a T-shirt. *Nowhere near fucking long enough.* "So are you staying or are you going? I'm good with staying, because I like having you to cuddle up to."

I jerked my chin at her bed before pulling my shirt over my head. "Get your ass in there."

She grinned. "Now there's the King I know." And then she made my fucking day by doing what I said.

36

Lily

I wasn't sure what I'd agreed to with King. All I knew for sure was the man was pushy with a capital freaking P. The other thing I knew for sure, and I was surprised as hell at, was that he could get through a night in my bed without trying to fuck me. That's not to say he could go a night without having his hands all over me, and his body pressed as hard to mine as possible, but I had to give him credit for respecting my wishes.

I woke up this morning wrapped from head to toe by his arms, torso and legs. When I tried to move, he tightened his hold on me. The weird thing was he was still asleep. It seemed King liked to look out for those around him while he was sleeping just as much as he did while he was awake.

I managed to wiggle my way out of his embrace and get up to use the bathroom. Entering the bedroom when I was finished, I found him awake, arms rested behind his head, watching my every move. "Morning," I said.

"Morning." Those eyes of his held a smile I wasn't sure I'd seen before. It was subtle, but it was there. And I liked it.

"I'm going to make a coffee. You want one?"

He nodded. "Yeah."

I hit him with one last smile before leaving the bedroom. Thoughts of what I was going to tell my kids about him sleeping over filled my mind as I headed into the kitchen. I'd dated a few guys after divorcing Linc, but none of them had ever stayed the night, not even the couple of relationships that lasted longer than a few months. I'd never been comfortable having them sleep over, and I had to wonder why I'd thrown all those hesitations out the window for King. Maybe it had to do with the fact my kids seemed to really like him. Or maybe I really was that distracted by the man that all common sense eluded me.

I'd just filled the kettle and switched it on when Linc's voice sounded from the back door. "What the fuck, Lily? You changed the locks?"

I stalked to the door and glared at him through the glass. "Yes, I did, to keep you out. You don't live here anymore, Linc, and I've asked you multiple times not to come by whenever you want or let yourself in. So I changed the locks."

"Fuck. Let me in, woman."

Oh my God, he did not just call me that. "Don't call me that! I am not your damn woman."

"Lily, for fuck—" He abruptly stopped talking as his gaze was drawn to something behind me.

Turning, I found King watching Linc with a murderous expression.

Oh goodness.

Shit, shit, shit.

"Who the fuck is that?" Linc demanded.

King's nostrils flared. He stepped forward, closer to me, and I knew simply by looking at him that this situation was about to go bad.

Placing my palm on his bare chest, I said, "King, let me deal with this."

His jaw clenched, his eyes coming to mine only briefly before locking back onto Linc. Ignoring my request, he growled, "You need to pull your head in and apologise to her."

Linc scowled at him. "She's my fucking wife, mate."

"And that's why you're standing out there and I'm standing in here," King said. His shoulders were like rocks. "Back the fuck up, apologise, and then leave."

Linc rattled the door. "Open this fucking door, Lil, and let me in."

Before I could say or do anything, King slid the door open and stepped outside. I knew that if I allowed this to continue between them, someone was going to get hurt. And I was fairly sure it wasn't going to be King. Moving as fast as I could, I got in between them and pressed my hands to their chests, trying to keep them apart.

Glancing madly between them, I said, "You two both need to take a step back. I have three kids in this house, and I do not want them to wake up to a punch up." I glared at Linc and added, "Especially not one involving their father."

Neither backed down straight away. It wasn't until I pushed both of them that King came to his senses and took a step back.

I looked at him. "Thank you." And then to Linc, I said, "The locks have changed. Deal with it. We've been divorced for three years, Linc, and we're never getting back together. I am not your wife anymore, and you can't keep dropping in here whenever you want. I'm not going to say this again. And also, you should know that I took your name off my gym membership, too."

He stared at me like I had three heads. "You're fucking kidding, right? We've been together since we were kids, Lil. Suddenly you meet a new guy, and I'm out in the cold?"

I expected King to get involved again, but he impressed me by staying back and letting me handle this. It was clear from his body language, though, that if I wasn't able to deal with Linc, he'd be more than happy to step back in.

"You cheated on me, Linc! Remember that? This has nothing to do with King, and everything to do with me finally figuring out that I need to set some boundaries with you. I can't expect you to respect me if I don't respect myself enough to do that." I jabbed a finger in the air at him. "Things will be changing around here, and that includes your freaking child support payments. I'm not accepting any bull-shit from you going forward."

"You've turned into a bitch, Lily," Linc said.

King lost his shit at that. Moving to Linc, he grabbed him by the shirt and threatened, "You call her a bitch again, you and me are gonna have trouble." He then shoved him away and guided me back inside, closing the door after us.

Linc got the message after that and stormed out of my backyard. His car screeched away from the house soon after. Less than a minute later, I burst into tears. Crying over Linc wasn't something I was in the habit of doing, but dealing with his shit had become a heavy burden to carry. Usually I just got on with it, but there was something about having King's support that affected me. I didn't feel so alone with this now.

"Fuck," King muttered, pulling me into his arms. "Don't let that asshole get to you."

His arms around me felt good. Soothing. I buried my head against his chest and took a moment to gather myself. King was right—I wouldn't let Linc get to me—but it didn't hurt to let my emotions flow rather than bottling them up like I had been.

I took a deep breath and lifted my head, looking up into King's eyes. "Thank you."

"I didn't do much, Lily."

I smiled. "You did."

The last three years as a single mum had been a hard slog, but if I were honest, the few years before that were just as hard, even while still married. People often said to me how difficult it must be to raise my kids on my own, and sure, it was, but what they didn't realise was that even when you were in a marriage, it could sometimes feel like you were doing it all alone. Linc had checked out of our marriage long before he'd cheated on me. He also hadn't been the kind of man who was always there for me as a husband or a father when I needed him to be. I'd learnt to rely on myself pretty early on. King didn't understand that in the short time I'd known him, he'd come through for me in ways my husband never had.

"Morning," Zara said sleepily, wandering into the kitchen. She eyed King, and I waited nervously for her reaction. I needn't have been worried. She hardly acknowledged his presence before grabbing a drink of water and wandering back out of the kitchen.

I made our coffees and as I was finishing up, King moved behind me, placing his hands either side of me on the kitchen counter. With his mouth to my ear, he said, "I need you tonight. Can you make that happen?"

I nodded, my body shivering just thinking about it. "Yes."

My need matched his, and I would do whatever it took to make that happen.

～

"I owe you big time," I said to Brynn over the phone later that day as I watched Robbie geeking out over stuff at the science centre. We'd had a busy day between grocery shopping, housework, karate and now the science centre. Brynn had just agreed to babysit the kids tonight so I could spend time with King, but I was wondering if I'd even have the energy that sex with him demanded. The man was brutal in both how he fucked and for how long he fucked.

"I'll sleep over so you don't have to worry about getting home at a certain time. And then tomorrow we can go to that farmer's market I've been wanting to go to for ages."

"Ugh," I groaned. I was so not a market girl, but Brynn loved them and was always trying to get me to go with her. "Really? That's how I have to pay you back?"

"Is King not worth the market?"

She had me there. Sex with King was worth all the markets. "Fine," I grumbled. "We'll do the market tomorrow. And you can tell me all about your hot fishing date on the way." We hadn't found the time yet to talk about her date with the prostitute. I was hanging to hear all about it. "Did you ask him how many women he bangs in a week?"

She laughed. "Let's just say we had other things to do rather than talking about that."

"Oh my God, Brynny! You fucked him?"

"That will have to wait until tomorrow to be discussed. You need something to look forward to if you have to go to the market."

"You are so right, but this is gonna be the longest wait of my life."

"Okay, I've gotta go. I'm going to cook the kids something special for dinner, so I'll be at your place from about three, okay?"

"Sounds good. They'll be excited," I said before ending the call.

Robbie came running over to me, excitement plastered over his face. "Can we stay for at least another half hour? They're doing a special show soon, and I really wanna see it."

I smiled. "Of course, baby."

He threw his arms around me and hugged me. "You're the best mum!" And then he was gone again.

I would miss his affection when he grew out of it. I definitely missed Zara's. She still hadn't completely forgiven me for the boyfriend thing, but she'd definitely calmed down over it. That kinda made me nervous, though, because I wondered why. I made a mental note to follow up on that tomorrow. I couldn't afford to let my guard down for one second with that child.

But for the rest of today, I was focused on myself and getting laid. I sent King a text to let him know tonight was on.

Me: Babysitter sorted. Let me know what time to come over.
   King: Any time after seven.

I started to type out a sexy reply, but then deleted it. King didn't seem like the kind of man who made time for sexting. I thought about it some more and decided to hell with it, he could just choose not to reply if he wasn't into it.

Me: I can't stop thinking about your hands around my neck.

He didn't come straight back to me. It took him about five minutes, but I figured I hit the mark by the reply I got.

King: Fuck

    Me: And I really liked your belt around my hands.

Again, five or so minutes passed before he texted back.

King: I'm in the middle of shit

I stared at the message, a little unsure of what he meant.

Me: And?

This time he didn't text, he called and got straight to the point when he said, "I'm dealing with club business, and your texts are distracting as fuck."

    I grinned, loving that I'd stirred him up. "Are they getting you hard, King?"

    "Fucking hell," he muttered. "That's a fucking understatement."

    "So I shouldn't send you any more? Or what about a boob pic?"

    "I have to go. Don't send me any more shit. I'll see you tonight."

    The call ended, and I sat on the chair watching my son having a great time while I grinned like a loon. Somewhere along the way, life had gotten really freaking good.

~

Sometimes in life, you didn't see things coming. They blindsided you. I'd had a few of those moments in my life—when my father had walked out of it right before my twelfth birthday and the day I'd caught Linc cheating on me. Each of those times, my sister had been there for me. We'd got each other through the heartbreak of our father leaving, and then she'd gotten me through my break-up with Linc. We shared a connection I held dearer than almost anything in my life. With Brynn by my side, I felt like anything was achievable and any situation could be survived.

I had never imagined a life without Brynn.

Could never imagine it.

That afternoon, I was blindsided for the third time in my life.

Robbie and I arrived home from the science centre. His friend who lived next door waved at him as we pulled into the driveway, so he left me to go see him. I slung my bag over my shoulder and exited the garage into the house. Brynn's car was parked in my garage, so I was surprised to find the house in silence. She usually blasted music while she cooked. Maybe she'd decided not to cook after all.

"Brynn, where are you?" I called out as I walked to the kitchen. "I have some goss to share with—" I came to an abrupt halt as I entered the kitchen.

Oh God.

No.

I was seeing things.

My heart raced as I stared at my sister lying on the floor with blood oozing out of her.

I screamed. I know I did, but I couldn't hear it.

I scrambled to the floor to pull her into my arms.

I couldn't think straight.

"Brynny, no!"

I sat with her head in my lap, clinging to her. Willing her to not die.

Gulping down breaths, I suddenly realised I should check for a pulse.

There was a pulse.

With shaky hands, I reached into my bag and pulled out my phone. Somehow I called 000 and got through the call.

"Brynn!" I cried out as if that would magically fix her.

My chest hurt.

I couldn't do this.

I needed Brynn to get me through this.

I dialled King. It was instinctual. There was no thought process. Somehow I just knew he was my person. *He* would get me through this when my sister couldn't.

He answered on the third ring. "What's up?"

I gripped the phone hard and tried to talk, but the only sound that came was a wail.

"Lily, what?" he demanded. "What the fuck has happened?"

"It's Brynn… She's been shot. I need you."

"Fuck. I'm on my way."

I couldn't breathe.

My heart was going to explode out of my chest.

My sister could not die.

I couldn't do life without her.

Hurry, King.

I need you.

37

King

I paced the hospital corridor early Sunday morning, my mind working out how I would avenge the shooting of Lily's sister. There was no doubt in my mind this was Romano's doing. And that shit was on me. I hadn't taken enough precautions to keep Lily and her family safe. I thought I had, but clearly I fucking hadn't. Her sister wouldn't be lying in a coma if I had.

Fuck.

I shoved my fingers through my hair and stopped pacing as I watched Lily walk my way. Empty eyes met mine, and I swallowed hard. Her arms circled me and she clung tightly as she sobbed. I held her for as long as she needed. I gave her that now because I wouldn't be giving it to her later. This would be the end of the road for us. No fucking way was I putting another woman's life at risk simply because she was in my life. Lily would never become a casualty of my war.

"Thank you for staying with me all night," she said softly when she let me go. "I couldn't have gotten through it without you."

I nodded, but I had no words for her. Not when the only words that would be honest enough were—*this is my fucking fault.*

"I'm going to take Mum home. The doctor has given her something to help her sleep." Another sob escaped her lips as her hand flew to her mouth. "I've never seen my mother so distraught." Her eyes pleaded with mine for answers when she added, "It will kill her if she loses Brynn."

I knew she wanted me to say everything was going to be okay, that Brynn would pull through and they'd go back to life as they knew it, but I couldn't. That had never been my experience in life, and I wouldn't lie to her just to make her feel better. Lies only helped in the short-term; they just made shit worse after that.

"I'll take you home," I said, needing to give her that before walking away from her. I'd already organised for some of my men to watch her mother's house. Once I'd dealt with Romano, I'd be completely gone from her life, and she'd be safe again.

"Thank you."

Forty minutes later, she glanced at the bikes outside her mum's place as I pulled into the driveway. "Who's here?"

I parked the car and looked at her. "I've put some of my guys here to watch over you."

She frowned. "Do you think whoever did this will come back?"

I knew she thought it was a robbery gone wrong, and I would have liked to let her continue thinking that, but I couldn't. She had to be prepared in case shit did go down again. "I don't know, but they may. Hopefully it will get sorted, and the guys won't be here long."

Her eyes widened. "Oh my God, King. Are my kids safe?"

"Yes. These men are my best, Lily. Military trained. You're safe."

Her shoulders sagged. "Thank you," she said before brushing a kiss over my lips. "I really would be lost without you right now."

Fuck, I was a bastard. I wanted more of that kiss. It would be my last taste of her. Gripping the back of her neck, I pulled her mouth back to mine and kissed her for a long fucking time. It was rough and demanding, and she gave that to me even though her world had turned upside down. Even when she was struggling just to breathe, Lily gave. I didn't deserve a woman as good as her in my life.

We woke her mother, and I got them both inside. Linc was there with the kids, and I stayed out of his way. As little as I thought of him, Lily would need him, and I hoped to fuck he came through for her.

We got her mum into bed, and then I helped Lily shower and dress before settling her in bed, too. When I brushed a kiss across her forehead and stood, she frowned. "Are you leaving?"

I nodded. "Yeah."

"Why?"

I rubbed the back of my neck. "I've got shit to take care of."

"Oh, okay. Do you know what time you'll be finished?"

"No." It came out hard, but I couldn't help that. I had to shut the fucking feelings I had for her down, and hard was the only way I knew how to do that.

She frowned again. "King, what's going on?"

"I don't have time to get into it. I have to go."

She was silent for a beat. "Well, I'm going to head back to the hospital in a few hours. I'll call you then and see where you are."

"Don't call me. I'll be on my way to Melbourne."

She sat up, her features filled with confusion. "I don't understand what's happening here. Why are you going to Melbourne? And when will I see you again?"

I took a step back at the same time I clamped ice down over my heart. When I answered her question, I let that ice coat my words. "You won't see me again. This is over between us." *This has to be over between us.*

I stalked out of the house without waiting for her response. By the time I reached the car, I'd switched to battle mode. The only thought in my head was that I had to obliterate Tony Romano's operation. Something I should have done a lot fucking sooner.

"King!" Lily called out, running out to the car. "Wait!"

My jaw clenched as I opened the car door. "Go back inside, Lily. This isn't up for negotiation."

She stood on the other side of the door, staring at me with shock. "I don't understand. Why?"

I ignored the tears streaming down her face. Refused to see them. *I'm doing this for her.* "Because you don't belong in my world, and I don't belong in yours. Now go the fuck back inside. We're done."

She flinched as if I'd punched her. And then she stared at me like she didn't know who I was. Wrapping her arms around her body, she moved away from the car. She didn't utter another word.

As fast as we'd begun, we were done.

And I was reminded once more that the journey through life was best taken alone.

BONUS SCENE 1

KING

This scene takes place after Nitro's Torment. You may have already read it from a Christmas bonus I wrote, but I'm including it in case you haven't read it yet.

"You gonna fuck that one or can I have her tonight?" Jacko asked as my gaze trailed after the hot piece of ass I'd been watching all night.

My eyes cut to him. He sat opposite me on the couches in the middle of the clubhouse bar. He'd had a long day and he was fucking wasted. Lifting my beer to my mouth, I tipped it back and took a long slug. I then said, "You'd be lucky to get your dick hard enough to show her a good time, brother. But be my guest." It wasn't like we had a shortage of whores to choose from.

He frowned as he leant forward. "You got a piece on the side, King? It's not like you to share like that."

I scowled at him. "You want her, go fucking get her now, otherwise she's off the table," I barked.

He didn't hesitate another second, leaving me alone.

Fucking finally. I rubbed my neck as I tried to relax. Trouble was, I was hard as fucking rock. Had been for months. Usually, sex eased my tension, but even that wasn't working lately.

Fuck.

I pushed up out of the couch and left the bar to head into my office. Being Christmas night, it was quiet at the clubhouse. Even at just after nine p.m. The few members around were either drunk or busy with pussy, which suited me because I craved some peace and fucking quiet after the rowdy day I'd been subjected to.

I found what I was looking for in the office fast, grabbed my shit and headed out to my bike. It was time Kree Stone and I had a talk.

***

"King," Kree said breathlessly after she opened her front door to me.

My eyes dropped briefly to take in the tiny denim shorts and the loose-as-fuck white top she wore. The shorts revealed long thin tanned legs that went on for miles while the top hung so low I copped an eyeful of tits and a lacy pink bra, as well as a collarbone that revealed how thin she really was. Her hair was piled messily on top of her head and her face was bare of makeup. She was missing all the jewellery she usually wore at the clubhouse, which also meant she was missing the fucking jingle-jangle noise that followed her throughout the clubhouse.

Our eyes met and I caught the flash of irritation in hers. I wasn't sure if it was because I'd come over so late on Christmas or whether she was pissed off that I'd checked her body out. Not that I gave a fuck either way. Taking a step towards her, I pushed my way inside her house. "We need to talk."

Without waiting for her to speak, I walked down her hallway towards what I figured was her kitchen. The door clicked closed behind me, and she muttered softly, "Sure, come on in."

When I reached her kitchen, I turned to face her, ignoring the glare she was sending my way. "Jesus, Kree, you'll burn your fucking house down with all these candles."

They lined her hallway on shelves higher than my head and filled her kitchen and dining area, too. As I glanced around the room taking them all in, I also noticed the plants she had lined up along the windowsill and scattered around the room. There had to be at least ten plants in there. I should have picked her for a fucking greenie, though, with the vibe she had going on. Kree was into herbs and crystals and talked in what felt like another language half the time with her discussions on star signs and moon phases and shit. Also, she'd been known to speak her mind occasionally, but usually she was too fucking soft as far as I was concerned. But fuck, she was the best damn bartender we'd ever had, so that was all that mattered to me.

"Haven't yet," she said, her voice firm. "What's so urgent that you need to barge into my home at nearly ten on Christmas night?" The hint of fire I heard in her voice surprised me, but it shouldn't have. With everything I knew about her, I knew she would go to the ends of the earth to protect her home and everyone in it. Someone forcing their way in—even someone she vaguely knew through work—wouldn't be something she'd be comfortable with.

"I've been talking with Zane." *Her cousin.*

She stiffened at that and blinked once, but full fucking points to her for maintaining her cool. "And?" Even her voice didn't waver.

I reached into my pocket and pulled the envelope out that I'd brought with me. Dropping it on the kitchen table, I said, "He told me what's going on." Lifting my chin at the envelope, I said, "That's for you, and I don't want any of it back."

Frowning, she picked up the envelope. It was when she looked inside it that her carefully maintained composure finally shattered. "Fuck, King," she said as she looked from the envelope to me. "I can't accept this. It's too much."

I scowled as she tried to hand it back to me. Shaking my head, I said, "No, it's not. You need it. I don't."

She opened her mouth to argue, but a little voice carried through the air, calling out to her. "Mummy, I don't feel so well." A moment later, a boy entered the room, coming straight to her and wrapping his arms around her legs.

I knew his name to be Tommy, and his age to be four. I also knew his father to be a cunt who Tommy and his younger sister, Mara, needed protection from.

Kree crouched low and took Tommy's face in her hands. Concern etched her face as she said, "Do you feel like you might vomit, baby?"

He nodded his head. His face was so white I figured she probably had less than a minute before he made good on that. She figured it, too. Scooping him up in her arms, she hurried out of the room with him, leaving me alone while trying to soothe him with love.

My fucking gut tightened at the image of mother and child.

Fuck.

I raked my fingers through my hair.

Fucking Christmas.

If I could wipe this fucking season off the calendar, I fucking would.

Ten minutes or so passed before Kree came back to me. Anguish covered her face. "I can't accept that money, King."

"Why?" I challenged her.

"It's too much. There has to be at least five thousand in that envelope."

"Ten thousand," I corrected her, ignoring the way her eyes widened in shock. "And you still haven't given me a good reason."

She swallowed hard. "I don't want to owe you." Wrapping her arms around her body, she added, "I never want to owe anyone ever again." That was when her voice cracked. I knew the reason for that, too, but I didn't bring it up. Kree struck me as a proud woman; the last thing she needed was me throwing her past in her face when she was trying desperately to leave it behind.

I picked up the envelope and placed it in her hand. "Take it and don't fucking argue with me. We both know you need it. I'm not going to mention it again, and you don't owe me," I said with force. "And one other thing, I'm switching your shifts around at work so that you don't have to work as many nights anymore. Those kids need you at home."

With that, I stalked down her hallway, not waiting for her response. My body crawled with the need to get out of there as fast as I fucking could.

Good deeds weren't my fucking thing.

I rubbed the back of my neck again, feeling the beginning of a headache forming.

Motherfucker.

I needed to screw my way through tonight and fuck this tension out of my body.

Hell, I needed to fuck my way into oblivion and forget every-fucking-thing about Christmas.

BONUS SCENE 2

KING

This scene goes with the events of Devil's Vengeance after King discovers Jen's betrayal.

Tightening my grip on the glass of rum I held to my mouth, I drained the last drop of alcohol as I watched Jen make her way towards me. The anger that had worked its way deep into my bones over her betrayal flared like fucking fireworks —loud, bright and fucking overwhelming. But then, this dance of anger and forgiveness wasn't new to us. Throughout the five years we'd been together, we'd fucking danced that tango almost daily. It had fuelled our relationship. Until it didn't, and we were left with wounds we'd never recover from, and a whole lot of fucking regret.

"You finally came home," she murmured as she inched closer to me.

I dropped my gaze to watch her close the distance between us, knowing her next move before she even made it. To most people, Jen was an unpredictable mess of chaos and bad decisions, but not to me. Probably because I lived and breathed chaos myself.

Pressing my hand against her stomach to stop her, I clenched my jaw and bit out, "You're not gonna like what I have to say."

She didn't surprise me when she ignored my warning. Pushing my hand away from her stomach, she took the last step she needed to ensure our bodies touched. When she responded to what I'd said, her voice held a smoky promise. "It wasn't what you said that kept me around for five years, King. It was always what you did that held me captive."

My eyes closed for a moment while I waited for her to take hold of my dick. This was all classic Jen. On the other hand, me allowing her to make her move was not my signature style. But then, this whole fucking situation was unlike any I'd ever been in before. And it was fucking with my head in ways I barely fucking comprehended.

Her warm breath fanned across my cheek as she moved her mouth to whisper in my ear while she slid her hand into my jeans. "You can tell me to leave all you like, or try to kick me out, but we both know that you and I have something special. Something that you're powerless to walk away fr—"

Rage swam in my eyes as I squeezed my hand around her throat and pushed her face away from mine. My breaths pumped furiously from me, and we stood staring at each other in silence, her eyes wide with shock. "What we fucking have, Jen, is something as far as fucking possible from special as you can get."

She attempted to pry my fingers from her throat, her efforts growing desperate when she realised I had no intention of loosening my grip. Sucking in the little breath I granted her, she begged, "King!"

Our relationship flashed through my mind, just like it had for the past few days while I'd contemplated the path forward. Her actions and disloyalty had carved the kind of hole in me that could never be patched or filled or fucking healed. This wasn't something that could ever be fixed. In one night, she'd managed to wipe five years worth of trust and love.

I walked her backwards and shoved her against the wall, finally letting her throat go. Ignoring her gasps for breath, I said, "I came home to tell you that you can stay here for the rest of your pregnancy if you need to. After the baby is born, you get your shit together and find your feet, and then I want you the fuck out of here and out of my life."

The way her body froze told me she hadn't expected that. Her strangled words confirmed it. "After everything we've been through, that's how you're going to end this?"

I tracked the tears falling down her cheeks before meeting her gaze again. "The tears don't fucking suit you, Jen. And they sure as hell won't make me change my mind. You should know that by now."

Her face twisted into an angry scowl as she scrubbed her tears away. "I can't fucking believe you! Five years ago, I cheated on you and you hardly blinked an eye. But for *this* you never want to see me again?"

I rubbed my hand over my face. Rehashing the past wasn't something I saw any point in, but she was forcing me there. "We both know why you cheated."

She moved her face closer to mine. The crazed glint in her eyes gave me a clear indication that this conversation wasn't going to end anywhere good. "Go on, King, tell me why I cheated. I want to hear the words from your lips."

If she were anyone else, pushing me like this, I'd put a fucking knife to her throat. My guilt over the shit I'd put her through stopped me from doing that. Instead, I worked hard to keep my temper in check. That, and the fact there was a child's life at stake here. "Jen," I cautioned her, my voice a low rumble. "Step the fuck back and think about what you say to me before you fucking say it."

"No. Tell me," she pressed, playing a dangerous game she knew all too well.

We were fucking swimming in heat and a toxic level of hatred and bitterness. A lethal combination. I took a deep breath as I did my best to ignore the way my clothes clung to my body. It was suffocating, but nowhere near as suffocating as Jen's insistence to dredge this crap up. "You do not want to go down this path. Not with me. Not tonight." With that, I stepped away from her and turned to make my way back to the bottle of rum sitting on the kitchen counter.

"You don't want to talk about your precious Ivy? Of course you don't. You never do, because you fucked her up more than you fucked me up, and you never want to think about *that*, do you?"

Her words were like venom spilling all over the place, infecting everything they touched. Unfortunately, they were the trigger that unleashed my anger in waves that could never be contained.

"There's a lot of fucking things I never wanna think about, but that shit? I think about it every fucking day of my life," I bellowed as I spun around and stalked back her way. With one swift motion, I had her pinned to the wall again. She recoiled as my fury thundered out of me. "I can't fucking escape it, because it's buried so fucking deep inside of me that I couldn't rid myself of it even if I tried. You think I didn't love you, but you have no clue what love is. You don't know what it looks like, tastes like or smells like, and you sure as fuck don't understand how to give it. So don't fucking come in here and throw accusations around that you have no business even thinking about."

Wild energy engulfed us as we each dealt with the situation in our own way. My breaths came hard and fast while I watched and waited for her response.

"I hate you," she spat. "I hate that you still don't see me for everything I am and for everything I could give you. I hate you for thinking I don't love you, when all I ever fucking wanted was to love you. I was a naïve teenager when you dragged me into your world, and I fucking adored you. We could have had the world, King, but *no*, you were so fucking hung up on *her*. You couldn't see straight because of her, and you still can't. Well, fuck you. I don't fucking want you anymore. I deserve better than you."

"I fucking see you, Jen. And I don't like what I see. And I sure as fuck don't like what I now know about you."

Everything about her screamed hatred, from her ugly glare to the hard set of her shoulders. But for one quick moment, disappointment flashed across her face as my words dealt a blow. "I thought that you might be able to dig deep and find a way to forgive me. But no, you've proven once again what a cold and heartless bastard you really are. I made a mistake, King. A fucking mistake that I wish I could go back and change."

"That's the thing about mistakes, Jen. You can't go back, and you can't undo them." I sucked in a long breath. "And the thing I've learnt is to never fucking forgive them." Turning, I strode to the counter, grabbed the bottle of rum and threw over my shoulder, "Don't ever fucking mention us getting back together again because that shit is never going to happen." Without a backwards glance, I exited the kitchen and then the house. The murderous energy consuming me demanded release, and I knew I had to get the fuck out of there before the blinding rage took over and I did something I had no control over.

***

"I'm not sure why you think coming to my home so late at night is a good thing," Kree muttered after she opened her front door to me an hour later.

"It fucking beats me, too. But you calm me," I said as I ignored the scowl she gave me and entered her house.

"Yeah, well maybe you could text me first. That way I could have your favourite chair and a drink ready for you by the time you arrive," she grumbled sarcastically, following me into her kitchen.

Facing her, I held up the bottle of rum I'd brought with me. "No need, I brought my own," I threw back, waiting for her comeback. If there was one thing I'd learnt about Kree on my four visits to her place over the last couple of weeks it was that she was fast and liked to give as good as she got. It was probably the reason why I kept coming back—she was a breath of fucking fresh air.

Lifting her brows, she said, "So thoughtful. I'll find you a glass before I get your chair ready, shall I?"

Moving to the cupboard where I knew she kept her glasses, I said, "Sit. I can pour my own damn drink, and besides, you look like hell, woman. Like you could do with a drink, too."

"Just what every woman wants to hear, King."

I poured our drinks while watching her take a seat at the table. Narrowing my eyes at her, I said, "Are you fucking eating? You look like skin and bones."

She sat cross-legged on her seat and scooped her hair into a messy bun while hitting me with a dirty look. Everything about those moves only accentuated how thin she was. "You know, just because you gave me some money doesn't mean you can show up here any time you want. It also doesn't mean you should feel encouraged to comment on my weight or my looks or any part of my life."

I screwed the cap back on the rum bottle and passed her drink over. I took a long sip of mine and eyed her over the rim of the glass. "The cash is long forgotten, Kree. My concern for you is not. Do you need more money?"

"God no!" Her eyes widened as the words flew out of her mouth. She then downed half her drink, pulling a face as it burned. "Fuck," she muttered, staring at the drink like she was remembering something. When her eyes found mine again, she said, "I'd forgotten how fucking awful rum is."

A smile briefly touched my lips. Kree intrigued me because she was different to most women I met. She was a mix of feisty, brave, tough and soft, as well as a contradiction of wise and naïve. And as far as I'd figured out, she wasn't after cash, sex or help, which was unusual in my experience.

Taking a seat at the table, I stretched my legs out in front of me while almost draining my glass. When I didn't say anything, she said, "Now that you've told me how *I* look, do you wanna know how *you* look?"

I shook my head. "No." But I knew she would tell me anyway.

Placing her half-finished drink on the table, she leant forward. "You look like you just went a round with one of your worst enemies. Without the wounds, that is." She paused for a moment. "Did you come here to talk about that, King?"

I exhaled hard and scrubbed my face. "I don't know why the fuck I came here except like I said, you calm me, and I need some fucking calming right about now."

She held my gaze like I imagined she would with her kids when she was about to tell them something important. "You don't say much when you come here, but you say enough for me to know you need to talk. To be completely honest, I don't want to be the person you talk to, because quite frankly the last thing I want to know is the shit you've got going on in your head. But, it's late and I'm ready for a shower and bed, so if you need to talk, can you hurry it along?"

I stared at her for a long beat before skimming my gaze over her body. She wore tiny shorts that showed off her long tanned legs, and a tight red tank top that was glued to her tits. I hadn't been kidding when I told her she looked like skin and bones, but even that couldn't hide her beauty. The thing about Kree, though, was that her mind interested me more than her body.

Shifting in my seat, I rested my elbows on my knees. "I didn't come here to talk."

She watched me quietly for a moment before saying, "I'm not fucking you, if that's what you're after."

My mouth spread out into a smile, and the tension coursing through my body eased a little. Fuck knew how she did it, but every fucking time, without fail, she managed to help me get my shit under control. Standing, I said, "If I wanted to fuck you, Kree, you'd know. And trust me, we wouldn't still be sitting here fucking talking about it." I lifted my chin at her. "Go take your shower. I'll see myself out."

I didn't wait for her reply. I simply left the way I came in. Minus the desire to take a knife to Jen's throat.

ALSO BY NINA LEVINE

USA TODAY BESTSELLING AUTHOR

ACKNOWLEDGMENTS

I need to send out huge thanks to my team for their work on this book -

Jodie O'Brien - my beta reader and assistant and all round cheerleader. Honestly, I'm fairly certain none of my books would get written without Jodie's ongoing support. She knows my patterns, she knows how shit always goes down with my deadlines, and she always steps in at exactly that moment I need someone to tell me that I can do this. I'm notoriously bad about hitting my deadlines right at the very last second. Every book has one day where I work on average 29 hours straight to get it finished, formatted and uploaded. That's the day Jodie pep talks the fuck out of me and makes me believe I can take on the world lol. She stays up late with me and she gets up super early to check in and see if I need anything. King's book required a lot more than just one of those pep talks, though. This book has been the biggest struggle of my writing career to date, for many reasons. I'll be honest and tell you I wasn't sure some days if it would ever get finished. It felt hard. Super fucking hard. Hard enough that I actually contemplated what I would do if I never published a book again. If you're a writer and you've been struggling with writer's block, I'm here to tell you that I truly believe it is a thing, but I also believe there comes a point where it becomes a story you tell yourself and buy into. My block stemmed from burnout, grief and physical pain, but there did come that point where I totally bought into it. The day I stopped that was only a few weeks before I published this book. I then sat down and wrote up to 5k a day to get her done. Jodie, you were there with me every step of the way, and I will be forever grateful for your friendship, encouragement and support. And girl, we have our girls weekend to look forward to now!! TWICE because of King's Reign!!

Becky Johnson - my beautiful, kind, giving and amazing editor. You made this book possible, Becky, and I thank you from the bottom of my heart. I am so thankful for the way you put up with my deadline bullshit. I'm also grateful for your friendship and support. I am so very glad Jodie convinced me to ask you to work with me all those years ago.

Trisha Wolfe - girl, I am so glad I found you last year!! And the day you said you'd beta read King's book for me was a fangirl down moment for me! Thank you so much for reading and supporting me through the writing of this book. I can not wait to finally meet you later this year! (For any readers reading this, check out Trisha's books if you love dark romance! She is one of my favourite authors, and one of the only authors I drop everything for to read her books when they're released. Her writing is stunning.)

MM - thank you so much for guiding me on police procedure and helping me get that part of the story right. But besides that, thank you for being such a light when I see you or speak with you. Whenever I think of you, I see that gorgeous smile of yours. We really should hang out more <3

Letitia Hasser - my beautiful and talented cover designer. Thank you for nailing these covers for me! I love them so much. You are so amazing to me - thank you for everything.

My Stormchasers (Levine's Ladies) - you girls! Gah! I fucking love you all to the moon and back! The amount of support you offer me blows my mind. There aren't enough words to express my gratitude for you all. Thank you <3

My bloggers - So many of you have been with me from the beginning, and for that, I FUCKING LOVE YOU! And to my newer bloggers, so glad you found my books! Thank you for absolutely everything you all do <3

Eliahn - you may never read this, beautiful girl, but in case you do, I am seriously blessed to have been given a daughter as amazing as you. I never expected to have the relationship with you that I do. You love me unconditionally, you don't hold grudges, you give it to me straight but with kindness, you look after me when I'm struggling, and you buy me Thai for dinner when I'm on my long deadline day even though you would prefer anything but Thai. You are my person. You and Jodie. You girls make me love me better when I'm with you.

KING'S PLAYLIST

Did you know I have a playlist for every book I write? They're on Spotify here.

King's list:

To Be Alone by Hozier
Bloodstream by Ed Sheeran
My Sacrifice by Creed
Best of You by Foo Fighters
Sympathy For The Devil by Guns N' Roses
With Arms Wide Open by Creed
Let's Hurt Tonight by OneRepublic
Choke by OneRepublic
I Love You Always Forever by Betty Who
Still Falling For You by Ellie Goulding
Remedy by Adele
Water Under The Bridge by Adele
River Lea by Adele
It's Gotta Be You by Isaiah
Spaces by One Direction

Long Stretch of Love by Lady Antebellum

One Great Mystery by Lady Antebellum

Smooth by Florida Georgia Line

Beautifully Unfinished by Ella Henderson

Hard Work by Ella Henderson

Long Way Down by One Direction

Over You by Daughtry

Waiting For Superman by Daughtry

Start of Something Good by Daughtry

No Surprise by Daughtry

Torches by Daughtry

Go Down by Daughtry

Baptized by Daughtry

I'll Fight by Daughtry

High Above The Ground by Daughtry

Undefeated by Daughtry

Losing My Mind by Daughtry

When We Were Young by The Killers

White Blank Page by Mumford & Sons

Home by Nickelback

The Betrayal - Act III by Nickelback

What Are You Waiting For? by Nickelback

Break Me Shake Me by Savage Garden

Desperado by Rihanna

The Sound of Silence by Disturbed

Down With The Sickness by Disturbed

River by Bishop Briggs

Coming Undone by Korn

Pain by Three Days Grace

State of My Head by Shinedown

Running Away by Midnight Hour

Fire Away by Chris Stapleton

Your Betrayal by Bullet For My Valentine

You Want a Battle? (Here's A War) by Bullet For My Valentine

Love On The Brain by Rihanna

Stay by Rihanna, Mikky Ekko

Love The Way You Lie by Rihanna, Eminem

But We Lost It by Pink

I Am Here by Pink

Wild Hearts Can't Be Broken by Pink

You Get My Love by Pink

Try by Pink

Take My Heart by Birdy

Wings by Birdy

Light Me Up by Birdy

Strange Birds by Birdy

Standing In The Way of The Light by Birdy

When She Says Baby by Jason Aldean

Boy by Lee Brice

Turnin' Me On by Blake Shelton

The Wave by Blake Shelton

I Don't Dance by Lee Brice

Red by Taylor Swift

Thunder In The Rain by Kane Brown

21 Guns by Green Day

Never Be The Same by Camila Cabello

Way Down We Go by Kaleo

You Are The Reason by Calum Scott, Leona Lewis

ABOUT THE AUTHOR

Dreamer.

Coffee Lover.

Gypsy at heart.

USA Today Bestselling author who writes about alpha men & the women they love.

When I'm not creating with words you will find me planning my next getaway, visiting somewhere new in the world, having a long conversation over coffee and cake with a friend, creating with paper or curled up with a good book and chocolate.

I've been writing since I was twelve. Weaving words together has always been a form of therapy for me especially during my harder times. These days I'm proud that my words help others just as much as they help me.

www.ninalevinebooks.com